DIGGING
FOR HEAVEN

Visit us at www.boldstrokesbooks.com

DIGGING FOR HEAVEN

by

Jenna Jarvis

2023

ISBN 13: 978-1-63679-453-2

THIS TRADE PAPERBACK ORIGINAL IS PUBLISHED BY
BOLD STROKES BOOKS, INC.
P.O. BOX 249
VALLEY FALLS, NY 12185

FIRST EDITION: JULY 2023

CREDITS
EDITOR: BARBARA ANN WRIGHT
PRODUCTION DESIGN: STACIA SEAMAN
COVER DESIGN BY INKSPIRAL DESIGN

Acknowledgments

I feel so lucky that there are more people in my life I would like to thank for helping this book become possible than I have space to write about here. But I'll have a go because you all deserve to have your praises sung from rooftops everywhere.

First, to my family, thank you for encouraging me through everything. To my brother, Mark, who had to suffer through listening to all the earliest origins of so many stories and who helped develop a house style with me in the soap operas we staged for ourselves with Barbies and Playmobil figures. It was my dad who first made me fall in love with storytelling and who still painstakingly reads through everything I write to comb out the mistakes. Together with my mum, who has always pushed me towards what I was good at and wanted to be doing and for specifically being responsible for making this book more than just a concept, I owe the world.

As a kid, having interest and belief come back to you in response to the writing you put in front of anyone who will read it really does build you up. My wider family and honorary family have always been wonderful for that. To the writing group leaders and English teachers who provided environments to practice self-editing and writing something even when you're not sure yet if you have something to say. And to anyone who ever lent me their favourite book or sat me down to the pulpiest movie they knew, you all helped change my life by introducing me to the stories I wanted to tell. And to countless TV writers who just wouldn't go gay enough with it, thank you for helping me realise what I wanted more of. Then to everyone who ever left a kind word online on a fanfiction I put out there, kudos.

To Bronwyn and Caro, who pushed me on early chapter edits and did their best to remind me that grammar exists; to Lucie, Eilidh, Tasha, Mike and Jess, thank you for being there telling me to go for it and listening to me complain on so many days that were hard. And to everyone else who's been there for me, you absolutely know who you are, especially to anyone who's ever had to work or study or live with me and my general distractedness and the pen that's perpetually falling out of my hair. To anyone who's ever casually introduced me as a writer before I would call myself that.

Thank you to Katie and Jos and Mairi, who read through those very rough early drafts. Your words meant more than I could tell you, and I'm supposed to be good with those. Mairi especially, you defend my life and change it every day just by being a part of it. Litz wishes she had half your competence. And to Ismay, who has been with me one way or another through my entire life always making it better, and without whom I'm certain this book would not have been looked at twice, you're my angel and I don't deserve you. Thank you for the TikTok.

I couldn't have dreamed of such a welcome into the Bold Strokes fold, both from other authors and from everyone involved at every length of the process who helped transform my very long, messy submission into a real book. To Sandy and Ruth, you've always been so kind and fast in your responses to my often silly questions and so dedicated in the process of making this into a real book, along with Cindy, who really does facilitate that. To Barbara for being the saint who hyped me up while line editing lines that regularly didn't make sense and who had to find new ways of suggesting I cut my extra words. And exclamations! Thank you for (mostly) helping me break that habit! I couldn't imagine being paired with a better editor, someone who has absolutely improved the way I write and whose own books I've become such a fan of.

To my beautiful dogs Beaker and then Zoot, you were both as patient as you were able to be. I'm sorry I have no sense of time management and that you were both walked later than you should have been on multiple occasions because of this book.

And especially and eternally I'm so grateful for Cal. You've turned me into a big gooey simp who believes in love. Thank you for reading this even when that's not your bag, baby, for remembering details from it better than I do, and for being every pillar holding up our household. I'm so sorry this will happen again.

to my mum, my hero forever

CHAPTER ONE

However foreign the place she might be visiting, there was always something familiar about markets, Litz decided as she moved farther into the narrow bustling streets of Malya's inner-city walls. Viewing Jeenobi's capital from the cramped and dusty streets that clutched the edges of the blue palace walls made it seem like a place unable to decide where, or what, it was. The people didn't look proud of the streets they walked, either. If they looked up, it was suspicion, not welcome, that lingered in their eyes.

And that's not just your paranoia? A familiar voice prodded in her head.

She rolled her eyes and pulled her head shawl a little tighter around her face. *No, that's what some would call a soldier's instincts. I look too foreign. I'm a head taller than most of the men here.*

Surely, that's helping soothe your soldier's paranoia.

I thought you were supposed to be asleep.

I thought you were supposed to be exploring, her dragon, Loren, observed. Somewhere, Litz could feel the cut of a sharp internal smile at her expense. *You've barely made it out of the palace walls.*

Did you see the maze they surround that place with? Litz bit back. *It took me almost an hour to make it out of there.*

Which had only been after a friendly guard had taken pity on her, she admitted to herself, hoping that Loren wasn't able to catch that. As Loren's rider for fifteen years—over half her life—Litz had gotten a lot of practice in keeping her mind disciplined.

Congratulations on your soldier's instincts. You got lost in a garden. But Loren had gotten equally adept at digging around in it. Dragons tended to struggle with the concept of privacy.

"Fresh fish, fresh fish caught today!"

"A bargain *just* for today, *just* for you—"

"…should take this necklace to ward off the sand terrors, for your pretty neck…"

Litz smiled politely and kept walking, proud that she could understand most of what she was hearing. Though the Aelshian and Jeenobian languages shared a common linguistic root and were largely interchangeable, the dialects and accents sounded so unfamiliar that walking through a noisy place made it hard to distinguish individual words. As her mother had once explained it, most Jeenobian accents sounded "like someone speaking with their mouth full."

Since most of Litz's experience in listening to Jeenobian words and voices was on battlefields, it made it difficult not to flinch when the market sellers shouted too close to her ears. Only a short year ago, the thought of walking through the main streets of a Jeenobian town for any reason other than a reconnaissance mission would have seemed ridiculous. But here she was, flown over as an ambassador—

Well. Technically, you are spying.

Yes, but only in the palace, where they expect that of me. Out here I'm just…nosing.

Ah. I didn't realise there was a technical term for it. But you took your earrings off. I'm afraid that means that you're more than nosing.

Litz tried to ignore Loren's commentary as she walked out into a wider street. She might not actively be trying to spy on anyone, but that didn't mean she needed to go around *announcing* the fact that she was Aelshian. Though many of the market carts and stalls here were larger, manned by multiple sellers, she felt as if she barely had space to breathe. This was undoubtedly a city built with the expectation that only humans would ever live here, and a lot fewer than were currently crammed within the walls for what seemed to be market day wherever she wandered. And the farther Litz walked from the palace, the less maintained the housing and walls became. It was as if the blue walls of the palace were at the centre of the colour and wealth and life of the city. She supposed it was largely the same at home in Verassez, but without outer walls trapping the people in, it seemed less clear, less upsetting. Even the poorest sections of Verassez looked like they were supposed to be there, the buildings famously adapting to the natural landmarks of the forest around them. Here, different styles of architecture balanced on top of each other, as though the street had been designed by a child with a colourful set of toy bricks or a drunk gambler aimlessly balancing his dice atop each other.

Continuing through the market, Litz spared a glance for each stall she passed, mostly seeing the familiar and expected, but one cart made her stop in her tracks, causing several people to bump into her. There was no tolerance for slow walkers here.

What do you see?

Something I'm glad you can't.

Someone's selling dragon parts, aren't they?

Litz remained silent and kept staring. The alliance with Jeenobi had required the kingdom to change several laws, demanding a culture shift from its infamously dragon-hating people. A demand that Litz knew they had not entirely met; she'd seen the way they'd looked at Loren when they'd arrived. This was worse: a common, unregulated market stall with claws, scales, teeth, horns, and even some pickled eyeballs in jars, each as large as a family cooking pot, and Litz was surprised that the weight of the one precariously placed at the edge of the table had not already toppled it.

It turned Litz's stomach.

Don't do anything stupid, please.

I could shut them down.

You could, but even as an ambassador, you're outnumbered and far from the palace. You know this could create a diplomatic incident where I inevitably rescue you.

Litz knew. But it was still nice to dream about flipping tables and interrogating the seller for the names of his suppliers. He was laughing with a customer now, his mouth wide, but his eyes flickered to the other man's purse with ghoulish intent; she doubted he would be expecting any attack. It was strange. She'd heard so many stories of Jeenobian insistence on trading, but here in Malya, they seemed to hold the same interest in coins as any merchant she'd ever known back home.

Since when have you advocated for caution?

Since my human started fantasizing about flipping over tables in a crowded market. And you know this sort of thing bothers me less. Humans have never mastered pragmatism like we have.

Litz took a deep breath and looked around, steadying herself, reminding herself where she was. *I know that. I'm overreacting out of an emotional—*

So take your hand away from the knife at your belt.

Litz blinked and uncurled her fist from where it rested around the hilt of the bone knife sheathed at her belt.

Diplomacy, remember? The reason you're here?

We both know that's not why I'm here.

True, but there's no need to advertise that. That's what diplomacy's all about, or so I hear.

Forcing herself not to look back, Litz kept walking, but she kept one hand hovering near her knife. She'd only brought something small, and unlike the rest of the untouched pieces in her father's collection, its ebony hilt was worn soft with age and use. She would have felt naked walking out here completely unarmed. Open air-bars were heavily curtailed in Aelshia, but here, they blended with indoor shops and outdoor stalls like a strange co-dependent little ecosystem. Drunks stumbled outside and were faced immediately with a vendor trying to sell them food. It all *functioned*, with a chaos only a little greasier and dustier than any forest market she'd ever walked through.

But nowhere back home would ever be selling dragon parts in jars.

Gods, she *was* still trying to keep an open mind. She'd known she was visiting a different culture, that they'd do things differently here, but it still felt as though she saw not just signs of difference everywhere but of evil, something she should have been doing something about instead of walking past.

Trying not to cough as spiced smoke engulfed her eyes, Litz spotted the food stall responsible as she neared the end of the street and slowed to hover around the edges of the crowd it attracted, as it had been pushed out wide into the alley by the circumference of the metal pan. Behind it, a woman with arms almost as thick as Litz's thighs stirred the contents as the man beside her pushed a much smaller spoon toward people's faces, beckoning them closer to have a taste of a stew that was as brightly orange as the dust beneath his feet. No one seemed to have heard of a queuing system and pressed closer as the urge took them.

It was a good thing the smell of the food worked as its own selling point, since the seller was forced to raise his voice comically high to be heard above the sound of the man handling the meat stall next to him, who had a speaking trumpet to project into the crowd.

Some of his goods were already dead and strung up, while others were kept leashed or caged beside it. Litz's eyes rested on a rather bored-looking animal that seemed to be something like a large goat with additional horns. Every now and again, it would swish its tail uselessly at the flies around it.

I think they have meat here that we don't have at home. I know the wildlife north of here—

Different kinds of meat? Litz could almost see the way Loren's chest would be puffing out as she considered this. *I suppose I should sample the local delicacies while we're abroad. You should bring me something back.*

Litz snorted but moved in closer. *Why, of course, your highness.*

Wake me up when you get back. Restrain yourself from flipping any tables, please.

Ignoring this, Litz pushed toward the meat stall. The goat creatures seemed to be a popular purchase. Trying to concentrate on the prices, Litz began to listen to the people around her.

"...heard they lined up three human sacrifices for the dragon that arrived yesterday."

"Three?"

The seller nodded gravely. "You ever seen a dragon eat? They don't eat all the bits. They *pick.* Beast like that needs more than one thing to eat at a time."

Litz resisted the urge to wake Loren up again to share this surprising piece of discourse and settled for making a face that she hoped her shawl succeeded in hiding. The most they'd been met with when they'd arrived were a few terrified musicians and a brief greeting from the king.

"...shoulda just given up that new queen of ours if it needed feeding so bad."

Her fantasies were getting a lot more violent than flipping tables now, but Litz was fighting to keep her temper from showing on her face. It didn't help that she knew her cousin would only find it amusing to know that she was considering defending her honour.

"I thought you liked the new queen."

"I like the way she *looks.*"

Litz was so preoccupied with keeping herself from surging forward and attacking the speaker that she didn't notice the people behind her clearing the way for the rickshaw bike hurtling by until she managed to lose her footing. Which might have been fine if the person behind her hadn't decided they were suddenly desperate to sample the stew and knocked into her side, sending her tumbling to the ground.

Great. She bitterly examined her scuffed hands. She'd not only succeeded in drawing the attention of the opinionated customers but had also further acquainted herself with that red dust she already hated so much.

"Need a hand there?"

Litz wanted to scowl. She'd heard enough of the grating Malyan accent for one day, but with one look at the owner of the proffered hand, she felt her face soften despite herself. "Thank you," she said and let the small woman pull her to her feet.

Unlike Litz's closely trimmed hair, this woman, who had to be of a similar age, wore her hair long in rigid locs that fell down her back and framed her face like royal drapes. Her features seemed almost too large for her petitely sculpted face, which made her eyes even harder to look away from.

She was beautiful.

Litz quickly berated herself for being pathetic because Loren wasn't awake to do it for her.

The woman's head tilted slightly, reminding Litz of a bird. "You're not from around here, are you?"

Feeling her throat close, Litz shook her head. Maybe she was already biased, but that voice, pitched comfortingly low, felt much easier to listen to than any she'd heard that day. It was still distinctly Jeenobian but less regional to Malya. There was also a cheerful lilt to her tone that made the accent hard to pin down, as if she was someone who'd spent a lot of time travelling and less time trying to fit in with others.

The woman clicked her fingers and flashed a bright smile. "Thought not. You'll wanna watch out for those bikes. They know everyone here'll jump outta their way, so I don't think they ever learn how to stop. Not even for a face as pretty as yours."

Litz choked a laugh even as the woman moved closer. "I'll try to keep that in mind."

"Do," her rescuer said, fingers playing with the fabric on Litz's sleeve. The light material was too expensive for a place like this, Litz realised as she took in the navy linen kaftan of the other woman.

Who Litz still felt powerless to do anything but stare at. She was intelligent. She knew she could be witty, charming even, if she strained herself. And yet…

Thankfully, before she could say something that wouldn't have been intelligent, witty, or charming, the seller addressed the woman, who was still staring at her, with a word Litz hadn't heard before. It sounded like "Good-luck-bringer," although Litz was sure the meaning had to be more nuanced than that.

"Please, you honour me. Take one of my chickens."

The woman let go of Litz's sleeve slowly, smiling apologetically. "Thank you," she said, "but I'd rather take one of your rupricaprins for my friend here."

The seller took a moment before nodding earnestly. "Of course, *of course.*"

"Can I take one also?" asked the self-proclaimed expert on how dragons ate.

Litz couldn't understand much of what the seller yelled back, but he seemed to be explaining what exactly he'd be happy for the man to take free of charge.

"I saw you looking at them," the Good Luck Bringer mumbled into Litz's ear.

"Thank you." Litz felt as confused as she was flattered. This woman in the worn garb of a merchant's mercenary seemed to garner more respect than the people's own king. All around them, it was clear that it wasn't just one meat purveyor who had noticed and recognised her presence; a small circle of space was carved out around them now, and the people nearby all whispered, their eyes clouded with awe.

The woman shook her head with another dazzling smile. "I'm about to leave town. But someone should enjoy this charity while it's going. And I'd hate for any visitor to leave my city with an unfavourable impression," she added as the animal's leash was placed into Litz's hand.

There was something interesting about the way she referred to the city as her own, Litz thought as she allowed herself to be led through the gap people were clearing for them. It suggested not ownership, exactly, but more of a deep familiarity, even guardianship.

"Are you planning on staying long in Malya?" she asked Litz as they started walking together, ignoring the stares which followed them relentlessly.

So much for Litz's secret walk around the town. She'd come out here to *avoid* being the centre of attention. "Only a few days," she said honestly. "I'm here visiting family."

"Mmm," the woman said, slipping her hand smoothly around Litz's fingers to lead her down a quieter street, where the buildings stretched even taller above them. "I guess the war would have made that difficult before, heh?"

Litz smiled, trying to concentrate on the conversation and not the way the woman was rubbing little circles into her skin. She hadn't dreamed that the Jeenobian people would be this forward. Though it could just be this particular woman. Litz didn't exactly have a broad spectrum of comparison to work with.

And maybe this particular woman was leading her around as part of a scheme to steal her money or clothes. Perhaps that was why everyone at the market had seemed so in awe of her: they were simply afraid.

Though Litz was confident of her ability to hold her own in any fights that the back alleys of Malya could throw at her, she really wasn't supposed to be getting into any in the first place. "The war ending made a lot of things easier," she agreed, pulling her hand back with some regret.

"Kella!"

Litz blinked and looked toward the end of the alley at the boy blocking it. He looked to be in his late teens and currently a little ridiculous as he planted his long legs wide apart, with both his hands resting on his hips.

Kella, the Good Luck Bringer, gave a small sigh and smiled apologetically at Litz before looking at the speaker. "Brother dearest."

Litz's eyes darted between the two. They did indeed look related. They shared those abnormally large eyes.

"Findan sent me looking for you. You're late."

"We said midday. And it's…" She squinted up at the bright sky. "Y'know. Sun's still in the middle. Ish."

The boy flattened his mouth and marched forward to grab her wrist. "C'mon."

But Kella was quicker and pulled her arm back to stay with Litz. "Sorry about this. Duty calls. Big hunting trip's a go."

Ah. Out of town and the meat seller had known her. Being a successful hunter might not have explained the regard of the crowd, but then again, crowds were strange beasts. Though Litz was sorry to lose Kella's company, she was pleased to have had the mystery of her solved.

"But…" Kella cut herself with another grin. "You need someone to show you the town while you're here? Ask around for me. Say you're looking for Kirasdaughter, and people are gonna know who you mean."

Before giving Litz a chance to reply, Kella leaned up on her toes and pulled Litz down for a kiss.

No, *no one* was this forward in Aelshia, Litz thought, torn somewhere between panic and excitement as she let the kiss happen, ignoring the groans of Kella's brother as she felt those soft lips close over her own, those teeth sneaking out to tug at her lower lip even as Kella pulled away.

"Bye," Litz managed as Kella winked and started walking away, following her brother, who was still berating her for her lateness.

"...know you always try finding something to fuck or fuck *with* before a fight, but this is cutting it way too fine even for you. Findan is going to—"

"She was clearly lost. I was trying to be *helpful*."

"And no one's called you Kirasdaughter for *years*."

Litz stared after them as they rounded the corner and disappeared. They hadn't tried to mug her. But she wasn't sure she could call them "helpful" either. While she hadn't felt lost before, she definitely did now.

"I don't suppose you know how to get to the palace from here?" she asked Loren's soon-to-be dinner.

The animal, something between a small bongo and a large goat, seemed unimpressed and remained silent.

CHAPTER TWO

Ker was lucky to have grown up around many heroes, and he knew that. So on the rare occasions that he was forced into admitting aloud that he admired his sister above all the rest of them, that meant something. Kella was brave, she put everyone before herself, and she never stopped trying to make other people smile.

Sadly, that had never stopped her from being a fucking idiot.

"Okay?" Zebenn asked as Ker walked back over to join them where they stood by the bottom of the rocky cliff face, casting long shadows over the red dust and surveying the crowd behind him with trepidation. As good-natured an expression as Zebenn might be wearing, Ker could tell that they were not happy to have been kept standing waiting around for this.

"So…tell us true. Was she out late last night?"

Ker shrugged and spared a scowl for the sun that had slid down the sky much lower than it should have. Had they started making their necessary preparations earlier in the day—it had taken hours to erect Evlo's stupid rickety podium—they might have avoided attention from the inevitable crowd. Rumour was a magic of its own, as his mami had always said, and the news had not taken long to reach the people of Drenya that Kira Mabaki's daughter was about to avenge their town's recent tragedy.

Much as Ker knew Kella loved working a crowd, she wasn't going to welcome audience participation. Having hundreds of angry spectators only ever increased the stakes of what they did.

"No later than usual," he said, getting a grip on the knife at his belt. It would mean nothing against a dragon—he knew that better than anyone—but it felt better to be holding something in his hands.

As though sensing his thought process, Findan smiled up at him indulgently. She might not be as short as Kella, but the height difference between them bothered Ker more whenever he took notice of it. Bending his neck to take advice from Findan remained disconcerting in a way that it wasn't with Kella or his da. At least Zebenn was still taller than them all.

They were only a few miles from Malya, but staring at the expanse of desert that greeted the eye beyond the rock face the cave was burrowed into made it feel like a hundred. Ker was biased, having spent his entire life in or around Malya, but the city didn't feel like anywhere else. It had a larger-than-life vibrancy to it, making everything beyond its eastern walls feel lacking somehow. In some ways, having the crowd with them was comforting; they carried noise to fend off the natural quiet of the desert.

He didn't have any reason to worry, he reminded himself firmly as he walked into the shade cast by the jagged mountain crags hiding the mouth of the cave. He'd done this, or something like it, probably a hundred times before.

Not that he should get cocky. Rall had gone on more hunts than any of them, and it hadn't been enough to save him. And since the safety of the rest of Ker's team depended on how well he did his job, he needed to be especially careful. Before anyone else could start the business of actually killing anything, he needed to check that the dragon was still where they expected it to be, and he needed to set the trip rope.

Pausing, he spotted Kella as he glanced back over the crowd. Usually, people were normal enough about meeting her in person, but when she was getting to do exactly what she was famous for, what they loved her for, they acted like the Earth Mother herself was walking among them.

Ker knew better than anyone that Kella wasn't a patient person— her bizarre behaviour in the marketplace had proven that—but she was here. Vengeance and closure meant a lot of things to different people, and however much of a show-person she might be, Kella never took that lightly. Malya might be relatively safe behind its famous walls, but out here, it was hard to find anyone who didn't have a reason to feel better for seeing a dragon dead.

She caught Ker looking and shrugged, asking with her eyes why he wasn't getting on with it yet. Shaking his head and smiling, he turned his back on Kella and her crowd and started to edge his way inside the cave while tightly gripping the rope to keep it from trailing and making noise.

They didn't always get so lucky when they ran this sort of siege tactic on a dragon. The beasts had decent hearing, but their sense of smell was incredible. Ker had feared that the noise and smell of the people outside would have woken it by now, spurring it into emerging and wreaking havoc before they were ready. Much as Evlo wasn't exactly Ker's favourite person, the foreign archer was very good at what he did. He'd been watching this cave all day and said nothing had come in or out of it yet, so Ker had no doubt there was at least one dragon in there. But they needed to be sure.

One of the strangest things he found about dragons was their lack of scent. Their caves or wherever they were using as a lair tended to have an odour clinging to them, but that was only from the leftovers of whatever they had eaten, not the creatures themselves. There were no real clues other than the sight of one to know if it was still in there.

As the cave became darker, Ker spotted the hoard and finally, the dragon itself, its eyes still closed. He had always wanted to know why dragons hoarded gold. It wasn't as though they ever tried to spend it. This far out of the city, not even humans were interested in using money to get them anywhere.

This hoard was one of the most impressive he had ever seen. Yesterday, the dragon had raided Drenya, a town hardly known for its wealth. That meant that this dragon had to be old. And judging by the way it was shifting on its pile, it was waking up.

Those horns, spiralled like a saiga deer's and each easily as tall as he was, rose toward the cave ceiling. Ker couldn't breathe. It didn't matter how many dragons he'd stood in front of. It wasn't something he could ever become nonchalant about. The sea might be filled with monsters capable of sending fully armed Doshni vessels to their doom, but there wasn't anything on land or air that grew bigger than a dragon. He could probably stick his full arm up one of its flaring nostrils if he dared.

But it wasn't just about their size.

As always, Ker was grateful that dragons blinked instead of alternating between grotesque licking and endless staring like geckos, but he wished this one would hurry up and prove it.

Until, just like that, it looked away.

And Ker didn't need a voice in his head to know that it was accepting his presence there, that it didn't see him as a threat. Releasing his breath, Ker felt a familiar squirming mix of guilt and wrongness before he forced himself to continue.

Until he noticed the babies and stopped.

Hatchlings. Not babies. Hatchlings.

Already, he knew that if either of the two fluff balls decided to stand on their four legs, they would dwarf him. He had never seen any so young before, but he had a feeling they could already incinerate him to fine powder if they chose to, no matter how soft their scales looked.

But, godsdamn it, they were cute.

Hello, you move?

Ker swallowed and could do nothing but stare at the closest hatchling, that he could see now was blue, that was cocking its head like a bird as it regarded him, twitching. Its sibling had already laid its head on the ground, as bored by Ker as their mother was.

Ker wanted to think he'd imagined the voice. He was alone and stuck in a cave with beings of incredible magical power, beings which rightly terrified him. His mind had to be using that terror to confuse and lie to him.

Dragons didn't speak. So he had to be imagining things and not feeling meanings press against his mind like the grubby fingers of a child. Because they weren't even really words; these were statements burned without language into his brain.

In his *brain*. It was happening again.

Scared?

Ker shook his head, too frightened to speak. *No,* he thought, and wondered if that was enough. *I'm going soon, I just need to finish something first. Is that okay?*

The young dragon held his gaze a few minutes before blinking, settling back down with its sibling.

As Ker tied up the rope across the cave mouth, he tried not to allow guilt to overwhelm him. It might incriminate him, and besides, he was doing this to help Kella. He shouldn't need to feel guilty. Kella was going to defeat this dragon mother because it was dangerous...and because it would make all those people gathered out there feel better.

The adult dragon, definitely awake now, continued to ignore him. It was a murderous beast, Ker reminded himself, but he was less convinced than usual.

Besides a basic lack of athletic talent, this was why he never took point on any hunts. This was why he helped lay traps that dragons in their colour blindness found difficult to spot. He didn't have a killer instinct, and even if his mother had lived and he'd never had any strange experiences with dragons, that would probably still be the same.

He emerged from the cave ten minutes later, just in time to see

Kella throwing her hair scarf into the crowd, which Findan would hate, and touch her hand to the sand. This part had nothing to do with the crowd's needs and everything to do with her own. Kella had never said as much, but Ker saw the look in her eyes; she was letting their mother know she might be joining her in the Earth Mother's kingdom soon. As always, any flash of vulnerability from Kella had the dual effect of being both bolstering and disarming for Ker. At least now, he didn't feel that setting up the trip rope under the frighteningly trusting gaze of that mother dragon had been the wrong decision.

Besides, the rope was mostly there for show.

"You'll want to hit behind the front right leg," he told Zebenn as he returned to stand beside them.

Findan glanced back at the cave, her dark eyes narrowing. "Is it awake yet?"

"Just."

Zebenn beamed with pride, their eyes wide. Ker knew from the twitching of their arms that they wanted to pull him in for a bone-crushing hug and was grateful for their restraint when all they did was say, "Some Mabaki nerves you have up that spine, Kerali. Well done!"

Findan held his gaze a little more carefully but still gave him a slight smile, which counted the same as a grin from anyone else. "Evlo's all set up, and I think your sister's almost finished fooling around."

"That doesn't sound like her," Ker put in, getting a laugh from Findan as he followed her to an overhang above the cave mouth. It was a steep enough hill that it took them a few minutes to make it up to the top, and the comforting sound of the gravel crunching under his feet and the feel of the sun of his face almost allowed him to forget that he still hadn't told them about the hatchlings. They were an unknown quantity in the fight, and he'd given his team no warning, and he certainly hadn't told them that one had spoken. They'd think he was crazy.

Findan might actually believe it. She was always warning them to never underestimate the things they hunted, but that would be worse too. She'd ask questions to find out if it was anything like an Aelshian dragon, who were said to enthral their riders with demonic powers. She might even ask him to try to make them speak again.

Kella might believe him too, but it would frighten her. The last thing Ker wanted was to rattle her before a fight.

"What did it do?" Ker asked when they made it to the top. Below them, Kella stood a few metres ahead of the crowd and was swishing her sword about, still showing off.

Findan didn't look up. "Does it matter?"

Ker shrugged. "You know I like knowing."

Again, Findan rewarded him with one of her small smiles. He was pretty sure that Kella was her favourite, but it still felt good to know he could draw those smiles from her so often.

"Burnt down a farmhouse on its way back from snatching some livestock. Little boys caught in the blaze. Both of them under ten." She tilted her head in the direction of the crowd. "Their big brothers are out there now." She frowned. "And getting far too close. We'll have to be careful it doesn't get too far out of the cave mouth."

"It's a big one, Findan."

"We knew that going in." She looked over at him as she dangled her legs off the overhang, making her seem bizarrely childish for a woman well into middle-age. They'd be in trouble if it decided to fire up at them, but hopefully, it wasn't about to do that. Hopefully, they'd be able to keep it from doing that. Ker had a sack packed with burn salve if not.

"And like I said, you're ready for this. Just watch your expression this time. There're a lot of people down there, and we want them watching Kella and Zebenn, not you looking suspiciously constipated up here."

"I don't…" Ker caught himself as he edged a little nearer the drop. "Really?"

"It's not your best look."

Sometimes, he wondered if, had his mother lived to know him as an adult, she would have had a similar relationship to him as her old hunting partner did. If she would have been teasing even as she was stern.

He wished he knew whether the magic use was something she would have approved of. It made his da uneasy, and he didn't even know how much their hunts had started relying on it as they became confident about taking larger and more unpredictable targets. His family was originally from the more superstitious hill country to the north of Malya, and his da had told them many stories when they were young about the story the world wanted to tell. Magic, he would say, disrupted that story in a way that was unnatural, and that was what was so frightening about dragons. Their very existence was an affront to nature and its narrative.

But Findan wasn't some evil witch who'd forced Ker into this. Learning to use his knack for magic was something he'd begged for.

With his friends and sister constantly risking their lives, he'd needed to offer them more than book smarts. Besides, he could only manage a little Control magic; he didn't do any Creating. And much as using magic to unnaturally affect the natural push and pull of the world made him feel ashamed, it was nothing on the feeling left by that hatchling down there nudging him with its mind. Worse was the knowledge that he hadn't pushed it away.

And then, he hadn't even told anyone they were in there.

"You ready?" Findan asked, her hands raised to interact with the air. It wasn't strictly necessary to shape the magic with the hands, but when trying to aim, it was tough to convince the brain of that.

They were maybe a hundred feet above the ground, directly above the chasm through which the dragon should soon emerge if all went well. If things continued to go well, it would get far enough out of its cave to become vulnerable but not far enough to get to the people behind Kella or to escape. The crowd was rapidly becoming impatient. There was the inevitable shouting and heckling, while others had started to sing songs about slaying dragons and about standing up to the Aelshian empire.

That grated at Ker. The war was over, and he found the lingering nostalgia for it grotesque. Jeenobi dragons almost definitely had nothing to do with the Aelshian army; people blaming the war on every dragon around was like blaming it on the camels and elephants the Aelshian army had also used.

But it was all too easy to understand. If a dragon destroyed a home and the people survived, that tended to be what they remembered, not why or if anyone had sent it there.

A flash of sunlight hitting polished gold caught Ker's eye, and he smiled. Kella had decided to move on to the main event at last. Her helmet had been liberated from another dragon's hoard a long time ago, by Jevlyn, their then prince, now king. It had been one of their last hunts together, and he'd presented it to Kella with such a playful flourish, Ker had wondered if they had quietly started spending nights together again, which never went well for anyone. Happily, that hadn't been the case, and if there was one good thing about Jev's new position, it was that Ker could be certain it remained that way. Jev and Kella had always made for a formidable team as friends and a headache for everyone else on their rare attempts to be something more. Though Kella could be sentimental about a lot of things, Ker knew the only reason she carried this particular helmet around was because it yielded the best results in attracting her quarry. Now she had it pressed over her thick locs as she shouted so loudly, the sound reached to the top of the blue rock where Findan and Ker perched.

"She shouldn't have thrown her scarf," Findan said, voice low as she shook her head at the sight beneath them.

He wanted to smile, even if only out of nervousness. "She'll be fine. She's always fine, remember?"

❖

Kella always loved this part the most. It didn't matter that her body wanted to shake itself apart from fear; it didn't matter that her heart was lodged squarely in her throat. What mattered was that she was strong enough to beat that fear and force herself to remain still. Having spectators helped. It was easier to remember not to run when hundreds of people would judge her for it.

It didn't matter if her mother had ever been as fearless as the songs claimed. The people would always remember her like that. It was what they were there for now: to watch another fearless, dragon-slaying vigilante give them a show. Fearlessness might be out of reach for Kella, but a show? That was something she could manage.

She looked toward the gaping cave mouth that was easily large enough for Malya's East Gate to fit inside. More than large enough for a dragon to make its home. Though she often thought of them as lizards, soaking up the afternoon heat didn't seem all that important to them.

At the top, she could just make out Findan and Ker, perched and ready for the uglier part of the job. Satisfied that they finally looked ready to go, Kella glanced behind her. The crowd had grown again, and parts of it had started singing. The festival atmosphere of these events was always contagious, even for those who were there for justice, for vengeance.

Almost everyone from the town last targeted by this beast was out today, even the children. Kella waved at the few who'd made it to the front. Wide eyes stared up at her in awe, and she grinned, approving. It might not be the safest way to spend an afternoon, but it felt important that children grew up knowing that even dragons could be held to account.

"Might wanna step back a few paces, people," she called as she started tying up her hair to tuck into the helmet, a compromise to Findan. It might not be covered, but it was out of the way.

Clenching a fist around the hilt of her bone sword and letting the crowd's encouragement carry her, Kella strode to the darkness of the cave mouth, bag in hand. She planted herself, her hands on her hips, and scanned for the rope strung somewhere ahead of her. It was a good thing that she couldn't spot it, she reminded herself. That meant the dragon wouldn't either. In the same way, she knew it was also good that she couldn't see Zebenn anymore.

Knowing they were safe was far more important than Kella feeling alone for a few sorry minutes. "C'mon, birdy," she muttered as she shifted closer. "Come and get me." She pulled the gold helmet out of its sack and hoped it was glinting attractively in the sun as she pushed the warm metal over her head. Evlo had a Plan B involving fiery arrows if this wasn't enough to tempt it outside, but she hoped she wouldn't have to wait that long. Ker would have let them know if it was too deep inside to notice her.

It took less time than she'd expected before she heard the heavy breathing of something at least ten times larger than her, larger than that if Findan's estimates were correct. It was an old beast, which would make its wingspan wide and its feather crown thick but its reflexes slow. As she gripped her sword a little tighter, Kella caught her first glimpse of those huge, scaley red nostrils breathing smoke into the clear hot day and thought, yep. Findan had been right about the size.

Dragon eyes were as varied as the colours of their scales. This one had yellow eyes that emerged moments after the nose, along with the blue feathers crowning its head. Goose bumps crept over Kella's skin as she slashed her sword through the air and tilted her head, trying to make the gold catch the light. If it decided to send any flame her way now, the helmet would melt and encase her skull.

"I know you want what I've got, monster."

Even after a lifetime of practice in hunting these beasts, it still took her by surprise when its long neck dipped low to get out of the cave, and it charged. For a moment, Kella wanted to drop her sword and run in the other direction, but when it reached the trip rope, she remembered herself. She couldn't miss her cue.

Luckily, the thunderous sound of the dragon roaring in rage as it hit the wire was unmissable. As it came crashing down over its own feet, Kella jumped solidly to her left to avoid any flame and waited for Evlo to take the shot he had become famous for. The Ghost Archer was what they'd started calling him, both for his pale skin and for the accurate shots he was able to make without ever being seen.

She didn't have to wait long. Even from his hastily constructed perch back behind the crowd, Evlo was still able to send an arrow hurtling right into the dragon's slowly opening mouth, where it lodged in the back of its throat.

Normally, such a shot would have been impossible, but thanks to Findan and Ker *pulling* it back and holding it in place, the dragon hadn't been able to avoid the attack. Luckily, the crowd didn't know or care about any of that, and as the beast screeched brokenly in pain, they roared in victory. It wasn't, of course, enough to kill it, but it was damaging enough for Kella to make her own play.

Dragon slaying was all about teamwork, really.

Not allowing herself any more time to hesitate and wonder whether Evlo's arrow had really broken the skin, Kella nimbly clambered up the injured dragon's snout, thankful that this one didn't seem quick enough to throw her off yet. In fact, she doubted it had even noticed her, but the crowd had. Somewhere behind her, and not far enough behind, she could hear them gasping.

Keeping her legs planted wide to maintain her balance, feet wedged up between the dragon's two horns, Kella spotted Zebenn running toward its unprotected flank, an ax brandished triumphantly above their head, and she knew that this had to be the moment.

Its wings were still too trapped inside the cave to fully stretch, thanks to the constraints of the magic keeping it from manoeuvring them, though it was doing its best to rail against both the physical and unseen forces holding it. If Kella waited much longer, the cave might collapse around her from its efforts. She could almost admire that kind of stubbornness, that inability to give in.

Almost.

"Just. Fucking. Die," she muttered as she plunged her sword into the dragon's right eye and was so deafened by the beast's pained cry that she almost lost her balance.

Blood or eye-fluid—something Ker would know the name for— spurted out, and she tried to ignore the feeling of it. All her focus was on keeping a strong grip around one of the beast's horns and watching Zebenn chop fiercely at its side. They hadn't hit far enough into its rigid scales to reach flesh yet, but they were getting close.

Kella could tell that the dragon's efforts were weakening, but she could also feel the tell-tale increase in temperature on its head. She knew better than to trust that it would die quietly.

"It's gonna light up," she yelled as she threw herself down on the top of its neck and tried with all the strength left in her aching limbs to keep it from turning back to where Zebenn was still hacking away. The magic that kept it from standing apparently wasn't enough to stop its head or its mouth from releasing a torrent of red flame into the sky.

Though the heat of the scales blistered her skin, Kella clung on tight. She couldn't let it win, couldn't let it hurt any more of the people she loved.

The dragon's working eye started to droop, gravity tugging its neck harder than any of Findan's tricks…and bringing Kella down with it. Certain that the beast was dead, she rolled down the front of its snout and took a bow as soon as her feet hit the ground.

"Thanks…" She heaved in a ragged breath and mustered a smile. "For coming, folks. You've been a *wonderful* audience."

She didn't do what she did for applause. But when she'd risked her life only to get covered in blisters and dragon fluid for her trouble, being met by the cheering and clapping from an adoring crowd sure didn't *hurt*. And even if any good preaching sollon would condemn her for thinking like that, let them walk a mile in her sandals, heh?

Someone she vaguely recognised as the Elder of Drenya stepped forward, and Kella inclined her head slightly. It was smart to keep on good terms with the people running the towns. A few polite words might mean they'd be set for bed and board on this side of the kingdom for a long time, which, as Findan was always reminding her, was worth far more than her pride.

"Thank you," the elder said, clasping Kella's hand between her wrinkled fingers. She reminded Kella of a woman whom Ballian, her stepfather, had once sent her to in the hope that she would learn her letters. They hadn't gotten along. "You have done far more to help us than our king would."

Kella did her best to nod good-naturedly but felt painfully awkward. Pleasing a faceless crowd? Sure, that was fun. Making a sincere impression on just one authority figure was a different task and not one Kella ever felt as ready for. "Well, it won't harm anyone again. And its treasure belongs to you now. And your people, of course."

She watched the old woman's face split into a wide, gap-toothed grin that only betrayed a little greed. Kella didn't regret it. With the law against them now, her team needed the kingdom's people on their side more than ever, and none of them did this for the money.

And it wasn't like they were about to leave *all* the treasure behind. They were heroes, not martyrs.

"That gold isn't yours to give away, Mabaki."

Kella regarded the soldier stepping toward her from the crowd with great annoyance, but she smiled. This was the kind of conversation she was on steadier ground with. "That right, Leedro? Tell me, what makes any of this the king's?" She shrugged, still smiling. "This beast that *we* just put down was stealing from his people. Doesn't he care?"

She took small satisfaction in the way the soldier started to shift his feet anxiously as the crowd loudly agreed with her, but his glance back at the troop of guards moving through the crowd knocked her confidence down. Wary now, she let her eyes flick between the guards and their captain as the people nearest to her looked to her with concern. No one was looking at the elder. They were waiting on Kella. This was still her show.

"What, were you just running a bit too late to help out?"

One of the younger guards seemed to be doing his best to look anywhere but in her direction, and she grinned at him and at the old woman standing behind him who was inching closer with malice in her eyes that would put any dragon to shame. These people had just watched a dragon die; they felt invincible.

Kella might be swept up in some of that high, but she'd watched enough dragon slayers meet their end to know where feeling invincible would get her. If anything happened to someone because they were trying to defend her, she'd be to blame.

Which she might be okay with. She *had* just wrestled a full-grown dragon for them.

"It's illegal to hunt dragons now, you know that," Leedro said more quietly. "We've got to take you in this time."

"Maybe it was dead when I got here."

"Don't go making this worse. You know we all just saw you."

"Oh, so you *were* here and decided not to help." She snorted and moved so that her nose was almost pressing at his chin. "I just took out a dragon. You really think an underfunded king's troop has a chance against me? Besides," she added, talking mostly to the crowd now, "that *thing*," she said, tone sharpening as she pointed at the dragon's corpse, "wasn't just stealing livestock. It wasn't just a financial nuisance. It was a killer. You're telling me that our king values its life more than he does the lives of those kids?"

To his credit, Sergeant Leedro managed to ignore the angry rumblings from the crowd and only sighed heavily. When he unsheathed his weapon, Kella took a few slow steps back. Standing her ground didn't mean she needed to be a complete idiot. Behind them, the sun was lowering fast in the sky, and Leedro's drawn blade cast a long shadow toward her over the dust. "Just doing my job, Kella," he said as he continued to hold her gaze.

She grinned, willing away her exhaustion as she raised her own sword. "And I was just trying to do mine."

"Kel!"

She shut her eyes briefly as she registered Ker's voice. He was supposed to have run with the others already, not give her something to protect, to fear losing. She wasn't *that* talented a fighter, and Ker rarely even carried a weapon.

"Kel, I don't think they're bluffing this time," he said as he moved to stand at her side.

While looking at him standing defenceless beside her, Kella felt a rush of pride, though she still had room for annoyance with Leedro, who'd finally taken a step back. Her little brother, now almost twenty, might stand a good two heads taller than her, but he was one of the least intimidating people she knew and possessed about as much killer instinct as his father, which was not saying much.

Ballian. Right. He was not going to deal gracefully with his only son getting arrested.

"I don't care if he thinks he's bluffing or not," she announced, not taking her eyes off Leedro. "I'm not going anywhere, and neither are you. Ker had *nothing* to do with this," she clarified.

"Oh yeah? Who assembled the trip rope, then?"

She knew it was Ker's stubbornness to protect her and not any boyish pride talking, but *gods* she really wanted to hit him now. "Me," she growled.

"Don't worry," Leedro said, giving a nod to his guards to surround them. "We'll be taking you both in, along with anyone else we find back there. And try fighting your way out of this one," he added as his guards drew closer, "and you'll be wanted for worse than dragon slaying."

Kella widened her eyes in mock confusion. "There's a worse crime than dragon slaying now?" she asked, watching Ker carry out the head count she'd already checked multiple times. Twenty-five guards sent to take them in. With Ker and maybe the crowd's help, she might be able to carve her way through. But while some people looked ready for a fight, any potential riot would also involve small children and people with limited or no mobility, who'd chosen to be there anyway, people who would suffer the most if the guards had angrier reinforcements due to join them.

And she and Ker would be on their own. Alone and forced to run to a likely empty village or else trek back through the desert to the city with no water and no supplies.

And surely, Jev wouldn't actually let anything happen to them.

"Fine," she grumbled, sheathing her sword and handing the belt over. "I'll go easy on you this time."

Beside her, Ker sighed in audible relief. She watched a lot of the faces closest to her in the crowd doing the same. If she said it was fine, they were more than happy to take her at her word and leave any heroics to the professionals.

As they were led away from the cave, the crowd, and somewhere, their friends, Kella continued to glare at Ker for his betrayal.

"Jev won't let us see jail for this," he said, seemingly ignoring her stare.

She snorted, her anger with him already fading. "Yeah. He's not *that* much of a hypocrite. He wouldn't get away with it."

Ker shook his head, reminding Kella again how short he kept his hair now. She still hadn't decided whether she liked the change. It definitely made him look older; the sharp edges to his face were more obvious now. The dimples were still there but no longer his most striking feature. "I mean, he *could*. Pretty sure the point of kings is that they get to do whatever they want."

Kella shook her head. "But he won't," she said, forcing confidence into her voice, hoping to make the guards feel nervous and Ker feel better. The performance wasn't over yet because it never was. And the smile Ker flashed as he was jostled forward was more rewarding than the cheers of any crowd, more frightening than the roar of any dragon.

It meant that he was somehow under the impression that she had a plan to get them out of this.

CHAPTER THREE

Litz had been in Jeenobi for two days, and already, she was tired of the sunshine. It wasn't that she wasn't used to heat. Her own land became even warmer in its summer months, but at least at home, the air always had that comforting quality that she'd heard the people of court in their fine heavy clothes describe as "sticky" and "close." Litz preferred a stickiness that promised life and rain to this punishing desert dryness.

Technically speaking, the desert was the border between the countries, with both kingdoms claiming it as their own. But even as a soldier who'd fought to defend the Aelshian right to cross the desert without repercussion, Litz couldn't think of it as anything but Jeenobian. Looking out her window at home had painted a colourful but limited picture. There was only so far that you could see in a jungle. Looking out from her tower room she'd been granted in Jeenobi was… intimidating. A dusty city, clinging to the palace rock like it could protect it from both the sea and desert it was wedged between. The sky was empty, the sun's stern gaze uninterrupted. It was all too much, too open. She wondered that the view didn't send the guards on their famous city walls mad.

"I think it makes the people harsher too," she theorised to Loren as she wiped a cloth over the dragon's green scales. They were finally gleaming, even in the low light of the stable that Litz suspected had been constructed for Loren only hours before their arrival. The camel smell was authentic enough, but Litz doubted the place had always been so large. "They just seem much more *urgent* about everything. Less kind."

You're just upset that the woman in the marketplace had to leave so quickly yesterday.

Litz glared but let the remark pass without comment. Loren was, as always, in her mind. There was no point in denying that it was frustrating to be robbed of time with the one person who'd tried to talk to her, really talk to her, since her arrival. Having arrived without a guard for the sake of speed, she was alone here. She'd barely had a chance to say much to her cousin yet, and most of the guards here stared at her with a hatred they didn't bother concealing. She could accept that. Even if they hadn't fought in any of the battles of the last hundred years, they would have heard the stories and known the part that any dragonrider would have played. It was something that set her apart even from other soldiers at home. Down on the ground, it was kill or be killed. There were different, larger choices she helped make in the air.

"No. It's everyone. Even the king can barely stand entertaining me. I'll be glad to leave."

Perhaps they simply treat you as a foreigner, not as a veteran, the dragon reminded her, nudging her mind with some amusement. *Or perhaps that's all you want to see. You don't exactly spend a lot of time with your own people, either.*

Litz put down the cloth in frustration but felt a smile twitching at her lips, betraying her. "No, I'm not imagining this," she stubbornly went on. "Even their accent is harsher to pronounce. Trying to imitate it leaves my throat aching. Their local mayors are called gharifs. *Gharifs.* I don't think I can even say that without coughing."

The dragon raised her front foot, regarding the dull shine of her claws. *All your human languages and accents sound harsh to me. Why any of you expend such effort on anything so mundane as* chatting *is beyond me. You're worse than little birds.*

Litz hit her with the cleaning rag, feigning more annoyance than she felt as she crossed her arms loosely over her chest. "Whose side are you on here? Remember, they *kill* dragons here? Sometimes for *sport*?"

Loren bared her interlocked teeth in a snarl Litz knew indicated satisfaction. *They wouldn't have tried to kill me.*

"Because that would start a diplomatic incident and possibly another war."

No, because I would kill them before they could dare try.

Reluctantly, Litz allowed Loren to coax a smile from her. At times, her arrogance could be aggravating, but here, hundreds of miles from anything familiar, it was a comfort that *someone* sharing her mind was feeling confident.

"The king himself means to question the dragon killers they

apprehended yesterday," Litz said, shaking her head as she picked up her cleaning rag again. She rather liked this chore, and the time she'd recently been forced to spend in her home palace had taken it from her. As it was for most things, there were always servants to handle that in her stead. Not that Loren ever minded. She was always happy to have new people to intimidate and impress. "I don't think Eisha likes that."

Why? Because her new mate lowers his station by taking on this menial task? Now that their conversation was switching into gossip about someone Loren had an interest in, her head tilted up in a way it hadn't for the brief talk of war and the death of her own kind.

"I don't think so. I think it's because he used to know them personally." Litz gripped the cloth a little tighter as she pushed it over the green scales, only to find that, somehow, there was sand on the cloth. "If the rumours are true, he used to hunt with them. Hunt *dragons* before he became king."

Even half listening, Loren seemed to pick up on the anger in her tone. *You don't like him.*

"Isn't that reason enough?"

I suppose.

"If even half of what I've heard of the man is true, I can barely stand the thought of our alliance with him, but to have Eisha *sold* to him, like bargained goods…"

You told me she wanted to come here.

"She did because she's Eisha, and she thinks it's her duty. But I'm not sure she's happy staying."

Litz sighed. She'd always found people, unlike dragons, more baffling than she had the ability or interest to comprehend. But though she might not have always found her cousin easy to understand, there had always been a closeness between them. As the only two royal children growing up of an age in a small court, this closeness had at first been inevitable but had grown to be the closest human friendship Litz had.

As it became clear that Litz would best serve her king as an officer and representative of the crown in both diplomatic and hostile interactions, she began teaching Eisha self-defence. And from an unusually young age, she'd been able to show Eisha what she'd learned of dragons from her time with Loren, who'd already chosen Litz as a rider, as a human mind and body she wished to work alongside.

For her part, Loren was fond of Eisha. They shared a dragonish fondness for the trivial and bright details of life. And though Litz knew that Eisha's artist's eye for colour and its uses would never be hers, thanks to Eisha's relentless tutoring, she now could dress and decorate herself to a standard worthy of the court. Eisha's help had also been more valuable than the palace tutors in honing her very necessary skills in language.

But nothing could outweigh the service Litz knew her cousin had done for her in making it clear at court that Litz was a woman who preferred other women and would therefore make an unsuitable partner in any political match requiring her to bear a man's child. The word of the girl who was second-in-line to the throne was whispered so deftly among her ladies, and her servants, that even Litz's mother finally listened.

"She saved me from being trapped in a marriage I wouldn't have wanted," Litz murmured. "What kind of friend or kinswoman am I if I cannot release her from the same?"

You're not sure yet that she's unhappy.

"No, not yet, at least," Litz admitted. "But her parents sent her with so few people after the marriage that she must be lonely."

Don't worry, Loren said in a way Litz was sure was intended to sound comforting. *If she is truly unhappy here, I shall burn this sandcastle to the ground and take all three of us home.*

"You would start a war."

You mean restart *a war. It's not as though there's much of a successful peace to speak of yet, is there?*

"A half year of trading instead of killing is worth a lot to some."

Yes, but you prefer the fight, and you are my concern. For now, Eisha is yours. Find her and settle your mind. Hiding down here with me is not what you travelled all this way for. Loren yawned wide and toothily, and for a moment, it looked as though she'd leaned so far back into her feathered neck that her horns would pierce her green spine. *And then we can go home.*

Litz smiled and stood, wiping the dust off her light armour with only some weariness. "I'll see what I can do."

Do. And see what you can find me to eat that's better than that mangy goat creature yesterday. It was chewy and old, and in any case, I—

"Prefer them cooked now." Litz's smile widened as she fondly patted Loren's flank. "Like I said, I'll see what I can do."

❖

With some assistance from one of Eisha's personal guards, Litz found her cousin sitting quietly in the drawing room of the suite she shared with her new king. It was a little grander than Eisha's suite at home, but Aelshians were well-known for being humble in living, if not in demeanour. Litz wondered again if Jeenobians favoured more colourful decoration to make up for the lack of it outside. But cultural differences aside, Eisha was a queen now, not just the second-in-line to a throne occupied by a healthy ruler, and the brightly coloured marble pillars and silk curtains of the high-class Malyan style seemed to suit her well.

Their old tutor would have been proud of the collected poise of the then princess, now queen, as she sat reading on the ornately decorated stone bench wearing the scarf-laden fashions of her new home, although not covering her hair, as was common daywear for Jeenobi. It was a colourful look, and Eisha wore it well, but she could probably manage that with nothing more than river reeds and half an hour's time.

That was Eisha.

"Is this seat reserved?"

Eisha looked up, and her mouth twitched into a smile that didn't quite reach her dark eyes as she patted at the space beside her. "Join me, Litz. I could do with some company."

"Your husband is with the prisoners now?" Litz asked as she sat, feeling a thousand times less graceful in her light silk armour, which she usually felt the most comfortable in, than her cousin seemed.

Eisha snorted just softly enough for it to still be deemed ladylike and neatly tucked a rogue curl behind her ear. "Can't you hear him? He's only seeing the one."

Litz listened and began to discern words and a voice she recognized behind the thick Malyan accent. Which was odd. She hadn't noticed such a regional accent to the king's voice before.

"…and if you thought there was a real danger, why didn't you just come to me?" That was definitely King Jevlyn's voice, so softly spoken at dinner the night before and now raised in pained anger. Even stranger, the voice replying to him sounded familiar.

"What, so you could run and ask it to apologise to those families trying to mourn their dead kids? No, that's not how we do things, Jev, and you godsdamn know that."

There was the sound of one of the speakers shoving their weight into the other. Though none of the king's guards outside the room seemed to be reacting with appropriate concern, Litz suspected that the attacker was the angry woman.

"It sounds more like a family squabble than the interrogation of a criminal," Litz noted quietly, having judged already that the king didn't seem to be aware that they were listening.

Eisha's painted lips pursed into a tight, pretty bud. "Not family. Try former lovers."

Litz gawked. "Lovers? So the rumours—"

"Aren't rumours here but common knowledge? He even has a folk song or two to his name. The people all loved their dragon-slaying king-to-be." Her voice was laced with bitterness, and that broke Litz a little. At home, Eisha had always been smiling, an essential component to her easy dominance of court, but now, she spoke like she couldn't remember the last time she had.

"Eisha—"

"His mother died, and he decided that letting the dragons live was an easy price to pay for a lasting peace treaty on all his borders. I do not think for a moment he believes that dragons are anything more than animals."

As Eisha spoke, the king started shouting, fighting to have his voice prevail as the loudest. "…basically admitted it already, and I know that wasn't just you out there, Kel."

"You don't think I could take one down alone?"

"I think you wouldn't use a trap. That would be Findan's work, or Sky's Teeth, maybe it was Ker. But it's not your style."

"Glad to hear you've got it all figured out, Your Majesty. So what're you gonna do with us? You know you would've been standing out there beside us if this had been a whole six fucking months ago."

Litz caught the moment Eisha winced slightly as they listened to the still naggingly familiar woman's voice scream out the truth of the king's dragon-hunting past. Litz hated her for putting that dulled expression on Eisha's face almost as much as she hated the dragon killing.

"But this isn't six months ago," the king said eventually. "I don't think we need to keep fighting with the dragons in our land, and we definitely don't need another war with Aelshia because of them."

"You'll just let them control you instead through that gift-wrapped princess they sent you? Is that really better?"

As Litz's hand curled into a fist, she felt Eisha's hand flatten over it.

"Shut your mouth, Kel, you have no idea—"

"Oh, okay, so you can arrest me, but talking shit about the better half is off-limits, got it."

"My wife doesn't control me, but our countries did reach something that adults refer to as a *compromise*—"

"Which translates to little kids getting burnt to cinders so you can have an easier homelife, right?"

As they listened to the king growl out a response, Eisha sighed. "He's stuck," she said dully. Her hand still blanketed Litz's tightening fist. "*I'm* stuck."

"What do you mean?"

Eisha shook her head. "This is the first time they've *caught* anyone killing or trying to kill a dragon since hunting became outlawed and not just a form of...of *veneration*." Eisha looked more anxious than Litz had seen her since they were girls "There are no guidelines for how to proceed from here."

Litz's eye caught a large mural on the wall across from them. In it, a lone crowned figure stood against a dragon whose mouth was open, ready to breathe flame. "Does Jeenobi still have the death penalty?"

Eisha nodded. "It's rarely used, and I don't know if it applies here, but, yes."

Litz felt bizarrely relieved that "Kel" was unlikely to be condemned to death for her crimes. Which was odd. Litz had killed plenty on battlefields, and this woman was a proud murderer, yet something about listening to her for this long was making Litz feel as though she knew her. Even if Litz had nothing to do with the sentencing, to know that this might be the dragon killer's last conversation with someone she cared about felt strangely uncomfortable.

"Alive, she could garner the entire kingdom's sympathies. Few accept the new laws, and fewer still accept *me*. But dead—" Eisha looked at her embroidered slippers as though it was their fault she was now on the verge of tears. "Any chance of happiness we might have had in this match will die with her, I know it. And his people will hate him."

Litz blinked in some surprise. "You really think you might be happy here with him? With a man who once found sport in hunting dragons?"

Eisha smiled faintly and pulled her hand away from Litz to clasp it in her own. "Maybe? I'm not…" Her fingers tangled through each other like she was trying to knit some invisible yarn. "I'm not *practiced* at this. I don't know how or *if* we're going to work, but I think we seem to enjoy each other, whenever we have a moment to. And there isn't love there, not yet, but I think there might be a, a *possibility* of it." She looked up sharply at Litz. "Please don't think less of me, Litz."

"For wanting happiness with the person you're married to?" Litz smiled. "How could I?" For the first time since arriving in Jeenobi, she noticed that Eisha had changed her right earring. Now the sigil of her husband's crown was delicately etched into that woodwork, and Litz found herself hoping that the Jeenobian king recognised this subtle gesture of deference made on his behalf. She hoped desperately, for her cousin's sake, that he would grow to deserve it.

"Yes. But if he has this girl he once loved killed to set an example, to *please* me and the peace treaty I represent…he'll never be able to look at me as a person anymore."

Litz nodded slowly. "It would be best for everyone if this woman just wasn't here any longer. Hmm."

"*Exactly.*"

"But that's not really an option," Litz felt the need to say, alarmed by the sudden excitement on Eisha's face. Eisha, whose whole body had stiffened like a hound with a scent.

"Litz, you could do this for me."

"Do what?"

"Make her not here and demand her extradition!"

Litz drew away from her frenzied expression. "Can I do that?"

"Right now? Honestly, I think Jevlyn would love you for giving him such a simple solution. And the treaty *does* state that anyone caught still trying to attack dragons should be punished in a manner adhering with our own laws. How better than *by* our own laws? It's the ultimate deterrent for the Jeenobians who see us as this terrifying dark forest land."

"Really?"

"This way, we wouldn't have to make a martyr out of her."

Litz was far from convinced. She might be new to peacetime diplomacy, but she was sure that just demanding the life of a citizen, especially one the ruler seemed to care about, wasn't exactly playing things safe. But that look of relief slipping over Eisha's face stopped her from airing her concerns. If not for Eisha, it could have been Litz banished to a strange land and trapped in a marriage she could only hope would grow into fondness. She could not leave Eisha now without helping in any way she could. Not on a personal level or a professional one.

Her king had given Litz an order before she'd left: to make sure that her daughter was safe, was happy. It had concerned Litz to be called to see her aunt alone, and to have that be the mission she was tasked with. "I'm proud of this peace I've brokered," King Narin had told Litz. "But if my daughter's happiness is the cost of that, perhaps it isn't worth the price."

And perhaps that was all the official encouragement Litz required. "Should I just go in?" Litz hated the lack of protocol enforced in this kingdom. Much as the stifling Aelshian court rules had aggravated her, now she missed their structure, their help in knowing the correct course of action.

Eisha continued to toy with the invisible yarn she held. "That *might* be the best way to get this started, you're right. Just go in with your stony diplomat face on, and tell him you won't stand for this."

"I don't think I *have* a stony diplomat face."

"And d'you really think your mother would be okay with this, after everything, to see the two of you stuffed with peaches?" she heard from the other room.

"Well, I never got to find out what she wanted, did I? She's dead."

"And do you really want to join her underneath so soon?" The king laughed, and for the first time, he sounded cruel. "That's what you've been trying to be this whole time, isn't it? Another dead hero just like your mother. For fuck's sake, Kel."

"They're not going to stop anytime soon, are they?" Litz said wearily to Eisha, who sighed.

"I think it'll have to be an interruption or nothing."

"Right." Litz stood, a little reluctantly, glancing with some amusement at the few guards lining the room who didn't seem to find the raging argument on the other side of the door particularly disturbing or interesting. She hadn't been here long. Perhaps this was a regular occurrence. "I don't need to announce myself, do I?"

Eisha shrugged, looking the happiest Litz had seen her since her arrival. "I would just walk in."

"Maybe knock? Do people knock here?"

As Eisha nodded, the guard at the wall behind her holding tight to his ceremonial spear nodded along with her. The sun of justice emblazoned on his uniform creased with the brief movement in a way that gave the sun a smile.

"Okay."

She was a dragonrider, a royal ambassador, a captain of the Aelshian guard, and niece by blood to the king of Aelshia. She would remember all that as she kept her back straight to look this new king boldly in the eye as she made her request, no, *demand.* She had the power to make royal demands here, if not at home.

She knocked on the door, and the argument finally stilled.

"Who is that?" the king asked, still not opening the door. "If this is Leedro again—"

Still alarmed by the informality of the speech, Litz stiffened and tried to hold her frame still as the door opened. "It's not," she said. She could see the king standing there in a robe, which looked like it might be the only thing he was wearing. "Your Majesty—" she tried to start, even as his eyes slid past her to see his wife still demurely sitting on her bench.

"Eisha," he said, deflating, but Litz was fast losing her patience and nerve, so she simply walked past him into the room.

As she'd suspected, his prisoner was unrestrained. Despite apparently spending a night in the king's cells, she looked beautiful, and knowing her crimes as she did, Litz wished that it wasn't her second thought about the woman.

Her first thought was that she'd been right: the voice had been familiar.

It was all too clear now why the Malyan marketplace had treated Litz's rescuer like royalty. This was her rescuer, who'd been dragged away from Litz only because her brother had needed her for a "hunt."

No dragon had needed to die the day Litz had arrived, not if she'd used a shred of observational sense.

"I met you yesterday. Who are you, really? What are you doing here?" the woman haughtily demanded, as if Litz was the criminal facing judgement.

The king rewarded her with dagger-filled eyes as he closed the door again before finally ignoring his prisoner and addressing Litz. "Ambassador Woskenna, I do apologise. This woman was caught killing an unknown red dragon out by the desert fringes yesterday. Her name is Kella Mabaki, sometimes called Kirasdaughter. She claims sole responsibility for the crime."

"One woman bringing down a dragon?" Litz didn't believe it for a moment, although as her eyebrows rose, she could admit to herself that she felt something like respect. This woman was much shorter than she'd expected anyone calling themselves a dragon slayer to be, even if they weren't working alone.

"One *me* bringing down a dragon. Totally different story, moonshine." She turned to her king with something like bemusement. "You shoulda mentioned the dragonrider they sent was hot."

King Jevlyn narrowed his dark eyes, but otherwise ignored Mabaki's comment. Litz attempted to do the same, hoping her face hadn't somehow betrayed her embarrassment along with her disgust. Maybe Loren was right, and she really did need to find a "mate," if even a complimentary glance from a killer was enough to make her feel—

What's going on? she felt Loren asking. *Your heart rate's increased rapidly. Are you in danger?*

Politics is going on.

Nope.

There's a pretty girl, Litz admitted, trying not to audibly sigh in front of the dragon-hating Jeenobians. The dragon-murdering Jeenobians. *And she's a maniac.*

Ah, Loren put in smugly, *your type*, before withdrawing from her mind once more.

"Mabaki's brother Keral was also apprehended at the scene, but no others were found," the king was saying. "Since the Mabakis famously hunt in a group, this is unexpected."

"Knowing how familiar you are with their group, I'll take your word for it, Your Highness," Litz managed with what she hoped was a regal sniff. This conversation was flustering her, and she felt like she needed to gain back some traction of her own.

The dragon killer laughed and actually elbowed the king in his ribs. "She's done her homework on you, Jev."

Litz tried smiling in a way that suggested she "had sources" beyond her cousin and marketplace gossipers.

The king didn't smile. He'd obviously had much more practice at this kind of diplomacy than Litz ever had. "As you say, I am certain that Mabaki did not work alone—"

"I mean, c'mon, when have you *ever* called me by my last name?"

"*However*, she seems willing to take the fall. We plan on extending our search—"

"I'm *telling* you, I took that thing down on my own."

Litz couldn't help stiffening at the callous description of the dragon this woman had killed. "They weren't a 'thing.'"

"Oh, I'm sorry, Ambassador," Mabaki said brightly as she turned her attention to Litz once more. "I forgot we had a dragonrider in the room. Doesn't that make you, what, its pet?"

As Mabaki tried to sidle toward her and Litz's hand rushed to the sword at her belt, the king put a hand out, preventing Mabaki from moving any farther. More interestingly, she let him. "That's enough, Kella," he growled.

"Or what? You'll have me arrested?" She looked him up and down, taking in the full length of his robes. "You'll have me killed?"

His eyes skated over Litz before he turned back to Mabaki and lowered his voice. "The last thing I want to do is put you down in the sword chamber, but..."

Litz had no idea what a sword chamber was supposed to be, but she didn't think it sounded amusing. Apparently disagreeing, Mabaki started laughing, her chin jutting out as she squared up to her king. "Oh, I *know* you don't wanna have to kill me. You'd hate everyone to know how much of a fucking hypocrite you really are, Jev. But you throw me in there, and I'll jump right back out again, just you *try me*."

"And what if I throw Ker down there with you?"

Mabaki's eyebrows, which Litz noticed with frustration were incredibly well-sculpted, furrowed. "You wouldn't."

"I am the king."

"He's a kid, you know he can't fight for shit, and he had *nothing* to do with this."

"And you are continuing to threaten this peace we've reached. That *I* reached. A peace stopping other kids getting hurt in a war that's got nothing to do with them."

"With due respect, Your Highness," Litz interjected, "I think my king would prefer to see any dragon killers you convict punished under our own laws, and I think she'd want to see that for herself."

Litz wasn't sure of any such thing—she rarely understood her aunt's political positions—but it did sound good.

"I'm sorry, Captain, but what are you saying?"

"I'm saying I would see this woman extradited, to be brought to Aelshia with me when I leave."

Mabaki gawked at them both, but the king's face betrayed nothing. "That would change the treaty," he pointed out slowly. "I agreed to abide by the traditions of your kingdom regarding dragons, not to cede all responsibility of punishment for those who break them. Whatever her crimes, Mabaki has not ceased to be my subject."

Or his friend, Litz thought. "Forgive me, Your Highness, but considering your wife and her own values, you should be aware of what cultural significance dragons hold for my people. The fact that this murder took place mere hours away from where Loren and I were being housed that day is deeply disturbing to me, and I'm sure my king will feel the same way."

"You and who?" Mabaki's voice sounded hoarse as she started speaking again. "Didn't expect your 'culturally significant' friend to have such a dirt common name."

"*Enough.*" The king groaned, putting his arm out in front of Mabaki again despite the fact she hadn't attempted to move this time. His expression reminded Litz of older dragonriders who had become adept at disciplining their expressions while conversing privately with their dragons.

"Ambassador," he said slowly, "I would be very interested in discussing this further. Would you care to reconvene with me in an hour back in the entrance suite?"

Finally, some attempt at civility. "That sounds fine," Litz told him, doing her best to ignore the gawking expression Mabaki was now wearing. Litz couldn't help feeling that both she and the king were very lucky that Mabaki was disarmed, despite her gormless expression. She could believe now, a little, that this woman had brought down a dragon alone, though she had once watched a whole army attempt the same and fail.

"Kella, you will be punished for your crimes. I will determine who will deliver that punishment. Your brother," he continued, ignoring her mouth open in indignation, "will be released. I accept that he was not meaningfully involved in the attack, and I believe that your punishment will be a successful enough deterrent to others."

He turned back to Litz, a fire burning in his dark eyes as he continued to ignore Mabaki. "Assuming our discussion goes well, you will assure King Narin of my commitment to our peace treaty and take this prisoner as a gesture of that commitment. But that will render her no less my citizen. Whatever your justices decide as her fate I will support, but I would not have her harmed in her journey to them. Despite your position, I expect you to protect her as you would yourself."

Litz nodded. "Of course."

Mabaki was regarding him with a dead look in her eyes. "And if that dragon eats me somewhere over the desert? Will you be punishing *it* in the same way?"

Litz rolled her eyes. "Even someone completely unschooled can't seriously think that dragons eat—"

But the king cut her off again. "For now, you will be returned to your cell, Kella, where you will remain until—"

"Until I'm dragged off into the sunset for you to never worry your kingly head over again, I get it," she muttered. "But you're not gonna stop needing people like me around, and you know it. What were you gonna do if that beast had kept on killing?"

"Perhaps that should be where our new alliance runs two ways," the king said quietly, looking at Litz more intently.

"Dragons don't kill without reason," Litz said tightly.

Behind the king, Mabaki laughed but still didn't smile. "Oh, honey. You're not as smart as you look."

CHAPTER FOUR

It was getting dark by the time Ker made it out of the castle maze and back into the walled city. His city. Right. Although Malya and her mud-brick towers had been his home all his life, every time Ker came back to it, it was smaller and less familiar to him all at once.

He never carried enough money on him when he came home, either. Outside the capital, people rarely had a use for currency, and he tended to forget that promises of trade would be unlikely to mean anything back in the big city.

But there was still one place he could always count on to feel like home.

There weren't many street torches to light the way through the dusty, winding alleys, but he could have found his way back to his father's shop blindfolded. And since he was determined to think about Kella as little as possible, the only thing he was really worrying about was how much stress the news of his children being dragged to the palace in chains would have caused his father. Not that this was his father's first experience waiting for news.

From the moment the already famous darling of the kingdom, Kira Mabaki, Ker and Kella's mother, had strolled into Ballian Pulfer's shop with her partner Findan by her side and her four-year-old daughter's hand clasped firmly in her own, he'd been forced to start waiting.

"I knew that I'd have to meet her again, to make her laugh this time instead of just asking how much she wanted for the salt-arrows," was usually how he told the story. "But I had no idea when she might ever come back to Malya at all, never mind my little shop. There were dozens of shops where the shopkeeper could offer more than gibbering. And that little girl," he'd always add, usually with a light poke at Kella's ribs. "I wanted to know what would happen to her, what with always being on the road with hungry dragons after her."

This had always been Kella's cue to say, "I wasn't *scared.*"

"I could see that you weren't! I thought to myself, Earth below, that's one brave little girl. I sure would like to get to know her."

"And Mami came back the very next day," Ker would say. Almost as soon as he could talk, he could recite the whole story by heart.

"She did. That little girl came running back to me, asking, no, *demanding*, to know if I was any good at doctoring because a wyrm had tried to rip her mami's leg off, and her Auntie Findan wasn't there to help them."

He'd said once, only to Ker, that it was the day he'd realised he'd wanted to be able to make his shop a home for Kella.

"And Mami?"

His da had shaken his head. "I knew that she would always *appreciate* that me and my home in the city were there when she wanted my company or needed shelter for her child, but I never presumed I could tame her. I never would have wanted to. But…" Ker's father had smiled, stopping what he'd been doing to put a hand roughly on Ker's shoulder, using him for support to stand without his cane. "When she told me she was pregnant, I was overjoyed, both at the thought of you, and selfishly, I liked the idea that she'd never really be able to leave me for long." Then he'd sighed, long and low, and Ker hadn't known what to say.

It was past the regular selling hours when Ker made it home, but he smiled to see that the lights were still on in the shop. "Da," he called as he walked inside the unlocked shop, overwhelmed by the familiarity of the smell of cloves that always clung to the lopsided wooden shelves and the neatly heaped piles in the back of the store where his da kept his large collection of scrolls and books that were only sometimes for sale. It seemed to depend on his father's moods and what he thought of whoever was trying to buy them.

The storefront was neatly organised into sections, with the herbs and spices alphabetised and even colour coded in some places. The dragon materials were absent. Though his father still kept them, he could no longer openly sell them under the new laws. This amused Ker greatly; he could think of no one more ill-suited to subterfuge.

"Da?" he tried again, frowning now as he almost knocked into the large stack of cinnamon logs by the corner. He was getting too big for this place.

"Ker?" His voice was hoarse, from crying, Ker suspected, and moments later was unhappily validated in his suspicions as he turned into the back alcove of books. There his da sat on his little stool, a bottle of salki at his feet, tears still clinging to his moustache even as he rubbed furiously at his eyes with the back of his hand, which made the sleeping snake draped around his shoulders twitch unhappily. On his lap was the book he'd commissioned of Kira Mabaki's great deeds, as told in the popular songs.

Ker disliked the book. None of the hundreds of times he'd traced his finger over the illustrations did they look enough like his mother.

The tome fell off his da's lap with a dull thud as he stood to deposit his now thoroughly disgruntled mouser onto the pile of books beside him before throwing his meaty arms around Ker. The python, which Kella had named Fin-Dani for her disapproving expressions, curled in on herself. "Thank all the bloody gods above and below, you've made it home to me."

Ker gently pulled his da in close, allowing himself to be comforted by the musty smell of his apron.

But the questions started the moment his da pulled away, his broad face—flushed from the small bottle he'd consumed—now beaming. "Where's your sister? I knew the king would not dare keep her. When she makes it home also, tell your friends I…I shall throw a party. Celebrating the dragon slayers of Malya because *damn* the law. A party is the least of what you all deserve."

Ker raised his hands to grip his da's arms. "Da, she wasn't let go."

The speed with which his da's whole face fell would have seemed comical in almost any other circumstance. "Not let go? But the king…"

Ker took a deep breath, trying to find something to say that could ease the disappointment echoing his own. The moment Jev had started striding through the echoing corridor toward Ker's cell, Ker had known something was wrong. He hadn't seen Kella since their capture, and he'd known from previous experience that even with connections, nothing in Malya's jail worked that quickly.

"Is it my king or my friend addressing me now?" he'd asked coolly after being told he was free to go, feeling he knew the answer already.

"Does it have to be one or the other?" Jev had asked, tossing Ker's bag into the cell before moving forward, his hands clasped loosely together. Ker had never seen Jev in his royal garb and was still adjusting to how well the bright rich colours of the clothes suited him. Ker had always imagined Jev in his light armour, even in his councils or during formal parties.

"You tell me," Ker had managed eventually, still eyeing him warily. "Where's Kella?"

Jev had briefly closed his eyes as though he'd had enough of dealing with Ker and his dusty cell. By the time he'd opened them again, sighing, Ker's heart rate had increased dangerously.

"What?" he'd asked, getting to his feet and up out of the probably lice-infested bed. As he did so, it became obvious that though Jev still had the broader shoulders and chest, indicating the warrior life he'd always led, Ker now had about an inch or so of height on him.

Ha.

"She's being sent away, Ker," the king had said, his voice worryingly kind.

"The king is still trying to help," Ker explained to his da now, keeping his own anger momentarily in check. "She's being extradited."

"To Aelshia?" The shocked, slumped expression animated into something like panic. "You know, I'm the first to warn not to believe everything you read, but, Ker, they used to cut out prisoners' *hearts* as offerings to their dragon-lords. If they have Kella…"

They'll kill her. He'd said as much to Jev before pausing, expecting him to argue, and felt at a loss when Jev had continued to look at his feet. "They're dragon worshippers, you know that, and you know that she's not about to repent anytime soon."

"Would you have had me kill her in her hometown?" Jev had asked, looking up, his voice somehow even softer. "She hasn't made this easy on me."

"Da, the king is giving us a chance," Ker said now. "They're sending her through the desert with a large escort and only one dragon. They'll be slow-moving, and if I can just get to Findan and the others now—"

"It could take them weeks to make the desert crossing." His da nodded, his chin tightening with new resolve. "I can help you with that, at least. That pale archer boy of yours was here not two hours ago, wanting to know if the two of you had been released yet. He said they'll be spending the night in the Storm's Eye Inn, outside the Northern Gate."

Ker tried to smile. "I know it. Now let me just grab some supplies from you and—"

His da gripped his shoulders again. "Ker," he started before biting his lip. "When you get her back, would you consider just coming home?"

Ker let his shoulders fall. "Da…"

His da looked at his feet, his lower lip quivering with a mixture of shame and stubbornness. "You're getting old for it now, but Fran still says she would take you as an apprentice in the doctoring. You know half the tools of her craft better than any already, and then, if you wanted, you could help keep the shop, could have it after I was gone."

Carefully, Ker slid his da's hands off his shoulders and clasped them. "But you know she can't."

Tears ran unashamedly down his da's cheeks as he smiled. "I know."

"And you know I can't leave her out there on her own. She *will* end up getting herself killed without me."

"Oh, I know that too. Fearless as her mother and twice as bull-headed."

"And you know I…I still need to know…to know *more*."

His da let go of Ker's hands with another small smile. "Yes, that too. But you know there's always things you can learn here." He gestured widely to the books that surrounded him, although not wide enough to topple any of them over.

Ker sagged. "Da, you know I love the books. But I've read them all at least twice, and there are some things I want to know that I don't think will ever be in any books."

A ghost of the beaming smile his da had greeted him with returned, showing off his stained yellow teeth from the root tea he so loved. "Not until you find them out and write them all down for me, heh?"

❖

Somewhere along the walk to the inn, Ker realised he'd never actually walked the strange twisting road down to the northern outskirts of the city alone before. It made him feel like he was missing a limb or a second consciousness.

This area of town was farthest from the palace and so was mostly ignored by the town planners. There would never be any state processions or foreign dignitary visits here. Most of the buildings had started up as a shanty town, clinging to the city like a limpet on the rocks found on the kingdom's western shores, the same shores that sent the wind howling down the streets to hit at Ker's back.

His mother had liked the sea. She'd never actually told him so, but one of the few times he had ever seen her look close to peaceful had been on the beach at Kaiven, her sword at her feet. It had been after her defeat of the legendary Kraken that had been attacking fishing boats there. She'd closed those eyes that the bards had written so many songs about, and the wind had blown up through the stiff locs of her hair. And for once, she hadn't rushed to move somewhere else.

As he turned off the main street, Ker wondered whether Kella was the same and would be calmer near the water. It could make being forced across the desert for weeks that much worse. He almost pitied the people charged with escorting her.

"My new moon child," their mother had always called Kella, mostly every time Kella wasn't able to sleep or was insisting that she was old enough to start fighting with the team.

Ker's father had always thought basing anything on what the moon looked like at the time of one's birth was superstitious absurdity, and although he was usually inclined to agree, Ker often wondered. His mother would say that his tendency to mull over his decisions long before making them was what made him such a half-moon child, always on the edge and rarely making up his mind, that his strong opinions were doled out only with caution.

Which wasn't true of everything, of course. Ker had plenty of opinions about the Storm's Eye Inn, and few of them were positive. Findan had started using it lately because she knew something about the owner that ensured his discretion when they visited.

Since the ancient, well-manned city walls were still the best defence the kingdom had against dragons, it made for an odd mix of desert merchants and lawbreakers of several persuasions who chose to live outside of that protection. Ker was uncomfortable admitting that what they did made them as much criminals as anyone else seeking sanctuary in the inn.

He'd growled at Jev outside his cell, clenching his fists. "But this still isn't enough. Not from you, not for her. She's a hero." He'd scanned the outfit of the man he'd once thought of as his own hero. "And you're just a hypocrite."

"Careful, Ker," Jev had said again in that aggravatingly mild tone. "You're supposed to be the smart one. You broke the law. I'm supposed to uphold it. You spat in my face first."

Trying to squash his doubts about the place down tight inside himself, Ker moved through the crowded tavern, scanning through the room for familiar faces.

"Heard they're gonna *parade* someone out through the streets tonight..."

Thanks to the unmistakable ability Evlo's voice had for grating at Ker's nerves, he managed to hear him across the room long before he saw anyone.

He liked that Evlo was as amazingly quick with a bow as he'd advertised himself to be, but that was about all Ker could honestly say he liked about the man he still couldn't help thinking of as a boy. Evlo had to be at least a couple of years older than him, but that hadn't been easy to determine. They had different time measurements where he came from, and wherever that was, Evlo was completely closed off about it. Ker knew almost nothing of his past before he'd joined them a year ago. Zebenn thought something *tragic* had caused him to leave home. Ker suspected that this was only a useful smoke screen to allow Evlo to seem mysterious in front of Kella.

"Hey," Ker said as he walked toward them. Above the clamour of the noisy pub, no one seemed to hear him. "Hey."

Zebenn finally noticed as Ker reached the table. They rose and enveloped him in a crushing hug, smiling their cynical little smile that betrayed more emotion than usual.

Ker was suitably flattered. "Hey, you're wearing the new dress Kella found you," he managed eventually as the very literal "muscles" of the group released him.

"Suits me, heh? But hey, you're *alive*. Nice to see, kid."

"It is that," Findan agreed from her seat. "Where's Kella?"

"Gods, she's the damn parade, ain't she?" Zebenn said, looking stricken.

"I think so."

"Sky Demons, Keral, you sound grim," Evlo told him, twirling his knife into the table. He was wearing one of his silken red shirts that he seemed to think made him look like a dashing Doshni pirate by the way he was lounging in his seat. Ker thought it mostly made him look skinny. "We'll get her back. And remember, we still killed a big one the other day and got away with it. We should be celebrating."

"A big one and the two little ones," Zebenn put in.

Ker took a step toward the table. "We didn't 'get away' with anything. Two of us were in jail yesterday, one of us still *is*." He swallowed, his brain catching up to his mouth. "Two more?"

"Well, we hid in the cave, see, but it turned out, there were hatchlings in there too. They were right at the back. You must have missed them."

Ker's throat dried out. "They give you any trouble?"

"Nah, course not. Handled them both easily enough and managed to take a few feathers there. Thought your da might appreciate 'em." Zebenn smiled, completely unaware of the effect of their words.

Ker could have done something. Either helped save the hatchlings who had reached out to him or helped his teammates who had been forced to face them unprepared. He hadn't done anything useful. He didn't even know whether to be angrier with them or himself or the dragons for speaking, for complicating things.

Half-moon child indeed.

"He might have another day," Ker said tightly.

"Hey, man, no one asked you to walk right into those chains," Evlo said, but Ker was ignoring him now.

"That was because we were left out on our own with no one rushing forward to defend us," he muttered, finally cracking under the pressure of all that anger he'd kept bottled inside for days. "And no one who was safe up in their little sniper tower could be *bothered*—"

"Enough, Ker." Findan's eyes were flint, enough to warn him into taking a seat. "Evlo couldn't have taken that shot. If he'd stayed where he was when he saw them coming, he would have been the first they'd taken. He was standing on an exposed platform, you know this. We didn't 'rush forward' because we assumed Jevlyn would be merciful, all things considered. Isn't that what you were doing?"

He scowled even as Zebenn put a hand on his shoulder, calmingly rubbing those large fingers in circles over his shirt. He didn't want to be soothed by the familiarity of having his family around him again; he wanted to stay angry.

Except that he'd spent so long trying not to let his frustration and anger bubble over in front of them for fear of humiliating both himself and Kella that it had now become almost impossible to maintain it. After losing his mother, he had spent every day so full of hurt and rage that his skin felt too small for him. Words had never felt like enough to express that to anyone who'd asked how he was doing. He'd spent much of that time in tears, tears of frustration, mostly, but that wasn't how everyone remembered it. Evlo might be new, but Ker was aware that Findan, Zebenn, and even Kella regularly looked at him with worry that he was too *sensitive*.

"Tell us what happened to your sister," Findan commanded, her fingers lightly skimming the rim of her coffee cup.

Ker told her everything as well as he was able to. Much as Findan might be currently annoying him, it never would've occurred to him to do otherwise. When Kella was only small, she had often informed his father that she didn't need a da. She already had a Findan. Their mother and Findan had been partners and friends for a long time before Kella was born, and Ker knew that she'd been as deeply affected as everyone by her death. Findan had always been there as a teacher, a leader, a friend, the person who always knew what to do. Ker needed one of those now.

"You say they're moving her tonight?"

"As far as I can tell."

"S'what I heard," Evlo agreed unnecessarily.

"I know we'll have to move fast, but—"

Findan cut him off with a raised hand. "Moving her to Aelshia," she murmured. "I travelled there once. It's a strange land." She shook her head, making her long earrings jangle. She inhaled deeply before locking eyes with Ker, and finally, his spirits rose because now, they were creating a plan, now they could get moving.

"Ker, I don't think we can go after her."

It took him several moments to register what she was saying. "What about no one gets left behind, heh?" he asked eventually, mouth dry as he looked around the table, checking he wasn't going mad, that they'd heard it too.

"And what about the rest of them?" Jev had asked mildly outside Ker's cell. "I'd thought Findan would be better than letting you both take her fall."

"It's not like that," Ker had snarled.

Now Zebenn looked paralysed with shock, their bearded face locked in an O. Evlo was gripping the handle of his knife a little tighter and looking boyishly uncertain. Findan put her head in her hands. For the first time in his life, Ker thought she looked old.

"Findan," he started again, speaking as slowly as he would to a child. "Jev's giving us this heads-up. And we're talking about *Kella*, who didn't just get left behind, she gave herself up for us. Don't we owe her—"

"We owe this kingdom something too. And I know your sister believes in that."

"She also believes that her family has her back."

"Ker, don't you think this hurts me?" Findan lifted her head only to look away from him. Both hands gripped her cup now. "I've loved Kella like my own her whole life. But I love this team, small as it might currently be. And what we do is too important to too many people to risk taking that all away from them."

Ker laughed. "But this is nothing. What about the two-headed Wyrm of Larin? We're talking about one troop of guards and—"

"And a dragon. With a dragonrider. You can't understand what a difference that makes, but I can assure you, Ker, that would make this like no other fight we've ever gone into. And we'd be rushing into this unprepared and without the numbers we need. Not to mention," she continued as he tried again to speak over her, "that they're heading into the desert. They're going in with supplies, equipment to deal with the weather. We'd be lucky if we even managed to reach them, never mind be in any state to fight when we did."

"We win tough battles all the time," he said stubbornly. "You're always saying—"

"What I'm always saying, as you well know, is that when something looks to be a tough battle, you have to be stronger, and when you can't be, you outsmart them." She looked at him, her gaze softer than he was used to seeing it. "How would you suggest outsmarting the desert, Ker?"

He planted his feet and concentrated on not letting his lip tremble. Kella might not be here to see it, but he wasn't about to let her down by falling back into being the group cry-baby. "So you won't help me," he managed.

Zebenn took hold of his wrist. "Ker, your sister's a brave gal. If she sees a way out, she'll take it. Us being there probably wouldn't help her all that much."

He shook his way out of their grasp. "And you?" he snarled across the table at Evlo. It was strangely unnerving to see him look so solemn. Ker had seen him look less serious at a funeral. Someone had dropped the peach they'd been about to place into Rall's dead mouth, and Evlo had burst out laughing.

For a moment, Ker thought that Evlo was about to get to his feet when Findan put a hand over his and looked up sympathetically at Ker. Pityingly, almost. "Ker, I would go home. See your father. Tell him—"

"Tell him you're happy to let her die. Got it," Ker managed without raising his voice before he marched out into the cool of the night air, ignoring Zebenn calling after him.

He couldn't stop. They were moving Kella tonight. She might already be gone. He breathed in deeply, trying to force his body at least to calm. If he just had two minutes to think. Because Findan was right about one thing. He wasn't going to solve this problem with brawn, certainly not now. He was well-trained, but that didn't make him a gifted fighter, and even if he had been, he was on his own. And there was nothing he could do with magic, not alone, not against so many. Not with so many watching. If he saved Kella only to get her accused of witchcraft, that would be pretty pointless.

He thought about the effort it had taken, with Findan by his side, just to hold back that one dragon from the cave, and how he'd been so proud to help that much, and he remembered how entirely exhausted he'd felt after it. He remembered the preparation that always had to go into making sure no potential audience would ever see behind that curtain and notice what they were doing. Because there'd be no seeming like heroes after that.

There was probably some clever way he'd be able to use magic sparingly and still get Kella away from the crowd, the dragon, and the guards surrounding her. Surely, it wouldn't take much. Kella would take any opportunity he was able to give her, and she thrived under pressure. But even thinking through scenarios, physically removed from the situation, terrified him for all the ways it could go wrong and might get another person in his family killed. Much as Kella was in danger, at least she was still *alive*.

He needed a team behind him. His da, maybe, if the others wouldn't talk to him. Which would force him to risk his living, his life, for a plan that probably wouldn't work and might still get Kella killed.

I thought you were supposed to be the smart one?

There wasn't much point in being the smart one if he was out of ideas the one time it mattered. As he slumped against the back wall of the inn, he ran through Findan's objections again. She had to be wrong about something.

A dragon. With a dragonrider. You can't imagine what a difference that makes.

Or maybe he should be focusing on what she was right about. He berated himself as an idea started formulating in his head. Because it was stupid, foolhardy. And again, *stupid*. But since Kella wasn't there with him, maybe he was compensating.

❖

There wasn't much of a crowd lining the merchant's road out to the East Gate when Kella was wheeled out of Malya in a cage, and she wasn't fond of what there was. She could have dealt with jeering or people throwing things, and she'd have appreciated some cheering; this was worse.

These people were *singing*, singing like they were at a funeral. And in the dark, she couldn't even look to see if anyone she loved was out there.

She knew all the songs people liked to sing in taverns about her mother, all of them, but she wasn't a singer, and it had never felt right to join in. Even when they'd started talking about Ker being a bard someday, she'd never heard him sing them, either, and certainly not this one.

It was about how Kira Mabaki had died.

Really, it was a saga about all the heroic deeds she'd ever accomplished, which never included anything as mundane as raising two children. About how it had all led up to her tragic doom in a surprise attack from a murderous dragon as she'd bravely prevented it coming near her youngest child and how he'd been left to witness her body burn down to singed bones and ash.

"The only way for that slayer to die," the crowd chorused, *"was out in glory and flame, glory and flame; the way she lived, the way she lived."*

As the song tailed off and people started forgetting the words, the tune kept on going. Someone had started humming that horrible catchy chorus that had stuck in Kella's head on a number of hunts, and then it caught, spreading around the crowd like dragon fire, and the tune lined her route out of the city.

They were saying good-bye. They were telling her that she was going out well, that she'd had a good run. To them, she was already dead. She wanted to rage and scream at them for writing her off so easily. Didn't they know how hard she would fight to get back to them? Couldn't they see she was still alive?

But then came the beating of those impossibly large wings stretching out over the city somewhere above her cage, and she remembered how brave, how defiant her people were being, even in this small gesture. She was being led out like a criminal with the menacing authority of a dragon literally hanging over them, letting them know who was in charge, and still, they kept humming a song about someone who had spent her life killing dragons. Telling Kella in their own way that they thought she was a hero. That they would remember her.

That thought made Kella want to cry, and she was suddenly glad for the darkness shrouding her face.

She understood Jev's betrayal. Left here, she clearly had the power to start a lot of problems. And though spending weeks being dragged through the desert in a cage barely large enough to stand in by two of the slowest camels she'd ever seen in her life didn't sound like something she'd ever willingly sign up for, it did give her plenty more opportunities for escape or rescue than flying on the dragon would have done.

She clung to the idea that this was why he'd insisted on her being escorted by his own guard. And because he knew how badly it would piss the dragon lady off. Kella had been stuck in a cell, so unfortunately, she hadn't heard the fight she knew had happened. The ambassador certainly wasn't anywhere near as good at this wordplay business as Jev was. He'd probably destroyed her as she'd squawked about trust and the treaty.

Well. Squawked was unfair. Ambassador Woskenna might be a demon's pet, but she had a nice enough voice.

Part of Kella also hoped that Jev had put these conditions on her extradition because he remembered all her drunken confessions in the middle of the night when he was still her best friend, the prince who'd liked to run around and fight monsters. The kind of nights where they'd thought they could die the next day, and she'd talked about how much the beasts they hunted really scared her, and that her worst fear wasn't even dying like her mami had, but being picked up in a dragon's jaws or feet and flown off somewhere, forcing her to lie limp as everything she'd ever known became distant specks.

She hoped he'd remembered that. She hoped that after everything, he'd still wanted to spare her the last indignity of being flown to her death, unable to do anything but cry and fall apart in terror.

Things could be worse. At least she was on land. At least Ker wasn't in there with her.

The guards might have been paying a depressing lack of attention to her, but that did mean she had the chance to check that the bone dagger she'd stowed inside her hair was still safely hidden. There were benefits to being able to quickly do her hair up in the courtly nest style. She might never attend a royal ball, but it made an excellent hiding place, as did a pocket on her sandal, which currently hid a very useful herb that she'd taken from the shop last time she'd been home.

Remembering these small blessings gave her the energy to perk up and start waving and smiling to the last of the faceless crowd, letting them know they didn't need to promise to remember her; she wouldn't be leaving them for long. Dragon or no dragon, she was not going to stay caged.

But it would be nice if she didn't have to get out alone.

Since getting married, Jev had started using the suite of rooms which had once belonged to his mother. It hadn't exactly been a choice. In the strange and chaotic weeks leading up to his wedding, someone had informed him that this would be where he and his new bride would be staying, and Jev hadn't seen any point in arguing, even if he did prefer his old quarters that were now almost a ten-minute walk away. Which was laughable. Once, he'd been content with sandy tents, and now he complained that his stone castle was too big.

There were three bedrooms off the main living space, though there was only one master bedroom. Jev suspected that one was intended to be a room for their first child, as it had been for him growing up. But seeing as they had not shared the master bedroom even once yet, it seemed unlikely that children would become a part of their lives any time soon.

So they had taken a small bedroom each, and the door to the master bedroom had remained closed. If he hadn't been completely confident in the servants waiting on the room, he had no doubt that the whole city would know of that. But the city would hardly be thinking on it today. Today, they had one focus, though it still concerned his inadequacies as their king.

The good thing about this suite was that the main room had a view of the whole city. The maze ended, and there was the Merchant's Road just behind it, running from the West to the East Gate and out into the desert for some twenty miles. The lights of the crowd escorting Kella from the city were unmistakable. When Jev joined Eisha out on their balcony, she didn't look round at him but continued to stare at the city, her eyes lit bright by the fires below.

"It's a hero's funeral, isn't it?" she said when he stood next to her, now staring as her cousin's winged beast flew high above the city. Jev's city. A huge potential danger was flying over his city, and he was doing nothing to stop it. The catapults of the famous wall-clinger defence line were still.

When he'd been a boy, when these had been his mother's rooms and a war had still raged, his mother the king had stood and pointed at the walls. She'd explained what each of the stations was for and who was in charge of them. Jev couldn't do the same for Eisha now. He didn't know all those answers, though he tried his best to keep himself informed.

"Sort of," Jev said, a lump forming in his throat as he stared up at the dragon and narrowly stopped himself from reaching for his sword hilt. This dragon, and the woman riding it, wasn't supposed to be an enemy. In any case, he wore no sword, it was too far away to attack, and he'd just betrayed the only team he would have trusted to help bring it down.

Not exactly betrayed, Jev reminded himself quickly. They *had* broken his laws. But if Kella lived through this, she would never forgive him, and that was hard to accept.

It felt much more like, in trying to be a good king, he was betraying himself. But Kella would have been merciless if he'd ever tried to say something that pathetic out loud, so he buried it. He certainly hadn't had the courage to say anything to her face. A furious Kella, apoplectic with rage, that he could deal with. But if he found her finally allowing herself to be genuinely upset, Jev wasn't sure duty would be enough to keep him on the course he'd chosen for himself. Much as Jeenobi now enjoyed singing songs about their great doomed romance, Kella had become something far more important to him than a lover; she was a real friend, one who had never been intimidated by his position and who knew something about family expectation. It had been a relief as they'd grown to realise that romance wasn't something either of them expected or wanted from each other.

Though it had been bad enough facing Ker, Jev had thought about going to see Kella after officially agreeing to Litz's terms but hadn't been able to face someone else putting him in his place so quickly. Having spent little time alone with Litz since her arrival, it had been mildly disconcerting to see just how much she resembled Eisha. It was like a taller, more hardened version of his wife had been hashing out terms on her behalf. She'd agreed to talk to the relevant authorities back in Aelshia about assisting Jeenobi with its dragon problem, but since she'd implied those would be dragon authorities, Jev was not hopeful about how those talks would go.

The country's greatest living dragon slayer taken away in chains and Jev still had no real solution. What could he do about a dragon except put it down?

"They're not angry with her. They're angry with you." There was no inflection in Eisha's voice, which Jev now knew from months of experience meant that she was in a particularly guarded mood.

He shook his head. "Only a little. These are city people. She's a hero to them but not a protector against any imminent threat."

Eisha nodded stiffly. "I see," she said. Her neck was lovely and long, Jev noticed again before stopping himself from further observations. It was useless to remember that he found his wife attractive, or rather, it was useless to find a woman attractive who had shown little sign of finding the same of him. They had enjoyed some "moments" since their marriage, moments of succeeding in making each other laugh, of suffering through meetings of state in shared solidarity, and once, he had emerged from a bath and caught her staring at him, but for all he knew, she was like Ker, and not interested *that way* in anyone.

Discreet adoption would, of course, always be an option. To the knowledge of only a few, it had been one his mother had taken.

Kella was one of the few.

But knowing he hadn't simply been born to his role but had been chosen for it had always worn on Jev. He would prefer not to inflict that same burden on his children.

"You know, she won't just let your...friend get away."

"Hmm?"

"Litz. She's a good soldier, and she's honourable to her bones. She told you she will bring her prisoner safely to Aelshia, so she will." Eisha turned from looking at the dragon to glance meaningfully at him. "Just in case you were wondering."

He nodded. "It's good to know. Excuse me," he added and started to walk away, leaving her out there alone. That did give him a small twinge of guilt, but he couldn't make himself turn back. His own feelings were crushing enough without trying to bear hers too.

CHAPTER FIVE

If they must go with her, can they not just deliver her at their own slow pace?

Litz scowled and tightened the strap on the wide hat that was largely keeping the sun off her. Slow as they were flying, the desert winds kept almost succeeding in taking it from her. *I gave my word to the king I would see his prisoner into my country safely, Loren. Besides, my king may not even allow them into the country without escort.*

Your king would also expect you back and at her beck and call by the time you said you would be, not weeks later, with a small troop of Jeenobi soldiers trailing behind you as they guard a prisoner your king will want nothing to do with. And you don't even like her, so do what you will.

I love and respect my aunt—

Don't give me that. I am in your mind. You may care for her more than you do her groomed successor, but you certainly don't like her much. You barely even know her. So say the word, and I will help you depose them. I suspect about half the Circle would follow our lead.

You are in a bad mood.

I have been circling this motley band of useless dragon-haters the entire time we've been flying, just to allow them to keep pace with us. Of course I'm in a bad mood.

Litz gently patted on Loren's neck below her green plumage, the only part of Loren's warm, gleaming scales she could reach from her position on her large leather saddle. *Remember, we're doing this to help Eisha.*

I remember. But she should have helped herself first and avoided picking an unworthy mate from an unkind land.

Yesterday, you berated me for being predisposed against it. And I thought you liked the desert.

I like the heat. The scenery is dull enough to drive anyone mad. No wonder there seem to be so many bizarre dragons in this land.

What do you mean?

The humans here have no respect or love for us. You think that would happen if any dragon here was in their right mind? Loren snorted, and a puff of smoke blew back onto Litz's face. *It's strange here. I don't like it.* Loren glanced at the ground, and Litz felt amusement sputter through their mental link. *And there's something else you shouldn't like.*

What's going on down there? Litz asked, looking and making out nothing but dots until Loren sent her an image. Dragons saw in fewer colours than humans, but their sight was much sharper. The image was of the prisoner, who was laughing and looked to be very much not in her cage.

This was only the first afternoon.

Litz sighed. "Take us down."

❖

It was exactly the sort of idiot move that Findan had spent Kella's entire life warning her against making. Or Findan would have said that, if she had to, she definitely shouldn't make it on the first opportunity. So Kella had waited until the second opportunity, and about an hour after they'd started moving again, she'd asked her closest guard to let her leave her cage to relieve herself. After several attempts to ignore her, and one more attempt to scold her for not going before they left that morning, she was given an escort and taken about twenty metres away from the main group, who had all been forced to stop for her.

But the important point was that the dragon and its rider were maybe miles up in the air and unaware of all this for now.

When the guards walking her over had, to Kella's surprise, actually turned their backs to allow her some privacy, she almost felt bad for hitting them both over the head and kicking in their knees before starting to run, the little bone knife she'd slipped out of her hair now grasped tightly in hand, allowing her locs to bounce hard against her back.

She guessed she could have saved the knife in case she'd needed an honourable opportunity for suicide. But fuck that. If she was bound for the Earth Mother's judgement before her time, something was going to have to force her down there.

Only seconds passed before the guards she'd hit called for their comrades' attention, but luckily, the strength of the desert winds meant that not many heard them. Those who did stood ready as they saw her running toward them, clearly not expecting her to actually run *at* them.

Spending her life fighting beasts she should by all logic have lost against tended to make her bold in her attacks. When every move she could make was a bad one, it was always better to make it before she lost her nerve or before her opponent could make an eerie judgement of what she was about to do.

Kella had already decided which camel was both close enough and laden with enough water to be worth moving for. She knew from experience just how long she could do without food, but she wasn't about to go racing across the desert without any water. She wasn't *that* much of an idiot.

The camel's rider had been foolish enough to dismount, and Kella tackled him to the ground before anyone else had the chance to reach her. In moments, she had him pinned, her little vegetable peeling knife pressed against his throat. "No one move," she ordered, "or this guy gets it in the jugular." She'd never actually killed a person, and she was only vaguely sure that the jugular was somewhere on the neck, but she apparently sounded convincing enough for the hands that had been grasping at her to fall away.

"Now, if you'll just stay like that for a moment, folks," she said, speaking slowly to let her heart rate calm again as she leant back to reach her prisoner's belt, "and let me just…" She slid out the guard's sword and ignored him as he started struggling again, keeping her knees tightly pinning his arms to the ground while compressing her thighs around his chest. "Take this off your hands, I'll be away."

It was a nice sword; the metal was light and well-balanced, she thought as she pinned her hair back up with her little knife. Clearly, Jev was starting to make some long-needed changes to his guards' equipment, if not their training. "Now, if everybody just lets me nicely get back to my feet, I won't have to hurt anyone."

"I'm not letting you do anything nicely," the man underneath her spat, his face getting increasingly flushed.

Kella flashed him a smile. "Like I said, if you'd just let me stand up, *nicely*, I'll do that without breaking either of your arms, okay?" She glanced back at the guards circling her. "Remember whose team we're all on really, heh?" She quirked her lips up farther. "When demons descend from the sky, all the people can do is stand steadfast together on Earth," she said in her best preaching sollon voice.

No one smiled.

"Fine, not nice," she muttered and leapt off her prisoner without warning, tucking her sword hand to the left and rolling through the guards keeping her from her camel and her freedom. It was amazing how often surprise kept even seasoned soldiers from acting. When she managed to stand, it was her against all of them, the still unconcerned camel at her back.

"I'm okay with the fun way too." She huffed, plastering on a wide grin. After all, she'd been dying to stretch her legs, and she had absolutely nothing left to lose in the world.

Litz knew that Loren's entrance, descending heavily in a cloud of smoke with her wings outstretched, must have seemed impressive for guards who were unused to dragons. It was only knowing Loren as well as she did that made Litz aware of how lacklustre the performance really was. Considering the circumstances, Litz would have preferred making it clear that their authority wasn't worth challenging with something a little more memorable.

"Thanks for the energy," she muttered as she swung down the rope attached to Loren's saddle and jumped to the ground.

If you need anything else, you know I'm here, but I imagine you can deal with one little human on your own, however badly her fellow countrymen seem to be faring.

For a moment, Litz couldn't help but watch and admire the joy that this crazed, dangerous woman seemed to be taking from the endless fight she'd started, in which none of the participants looked to be trying to seriously injure each other. It was a bizarre sight. Ten of the guards that King Jevlyn had assured Litz were some of his best were all being beaten back by one small woman with her back against a wagonful of provisions, one small woman who was ducking, thrusting wildly with her sword, and at one point, biting her attackers to maintain her position. And if the presence of Loren bothered her at all, she didn't show it.

Litz gritted her teeth and started marching. "I'll be fine."

Two guards were on the ground, either physically unable to get to their feet or faking it well. Litz walked past them and planted herself at the edge of the fight, barking, "Enough," in her best officer voice.

When they all fell quiet and began to back away from Mabaki, Litz nodded stiffly and glanced at them all. "Sergeant Adani?"

"Ma'am." The voice came from the man standing closest to the prisoner, and it sounded out of breath. Mabaki blinked at them all with what looked like amusement.

"If you would lead your people away now, I would be grateful. I'll escort the prisoner back to her cell myself."

Mabaki's eyebrows shot right up toward her hairline. "You will?"

"Yes," Litz said, unsheathing her sword. "I will."

"Ma'am—"

"If you all return to your stations now, I will not ask how this situation arose."

One by one, the king's guard began to back away from Mabaki, the camel at her back seeming completely unfazed by the events it had been witness to. Only one man lingered. "That's my sword," he said, pointing toward Mabaki, who laughed.

"Oh? I'll be sure to return it to you," Litz said as her last subtle reminder of his cue to leave. The man's scowl deepened, but he did back away, leaving Litz to face Mabaki alone.

She wasn't worried.

"Hey, nice hat. You gonna do what all of them couldn't, Princess?" Mabaki asked. The way she spoke made her sound like she was singing. A cover, Litz suspected, for how much she was still trying to get her breath back. "They told me that's what you are. I wonder why Jev didn't lead with that?"

"Assumedly, your king did not consider it the most notable thing about me," Litz said calmly, taking her hat off and wondering if she even needed her sword for this; Mabaki did look exhausted, and despite her crimes, Litz had no interest in harming her.

But she was also still standing after an attack from ten of her king's guard, so Litz wasn't about to abandon precautions altogether. "Come with me now, and I won't have to hurt you," Litz said, keeping her voice calm as she began pacing closer.

Mabaki swung her sword as casually as she might a toy, shooting Litz that wide smile that had so quickly caught her off guard in the market. "Honey, I ain't gonna let you. Now, if you just let me mount my steed back here, I'll be out of your hair, and I won't have to hurt *you*. Or your steed."

Insulting but amusing.

Litz sighed. "And now you've insulted Loren." That usually did enough on its own to intimidate, whether or not she was telling the truth.

But Mabaki only widened her eyes and not from fear. "It really is in your mind? That's disgusting."

It annoyed Litz that such a comment had the power to sting. What would a dragon killer know of the honour of being chosen as a dragon's companion? She held herself back from delivering the lecture she wanted to and settled for narrowing her eyes. "You know that even attempting escape from here is foolish. You're vastly outnumbered, and even if you did survive us all, Loren is faster than any camel. We're miles from any settlement, and you have no one to help you." At her last words, Litz could have sworn that a fleeting moment of vulnerability passed over Mabaki's face, but in an instant, her expression hardened, forced once more into a grin.

"Thought you were smart enough to have marked me for a fool already, Princess."

"Oh, I have," Litz said, stepping forward without warning. When Mabaki lurched to meet her thrust, Litz tripped her up by the ankles, leaving her off-balance and easy to knock to the ground with a blow to the chest. Litz didn't have to look up to know their travel companions were watching, which suited her fine. She wanted them to see.

Mabaki continued to struggle, hissing like a cat in pain as Litz leant down to pull her arms roughly behind her back, forcing her to drop the sword as she was dragged back to her feet. Her face was now slightly bloodied from the rocky ground and covered completely in dust.

"Right, now. Back to the cell."

Mabaki looked up with the deepest disdain before spitting at her. She missed.

Litz only began to haul her back toward her cage.

"Royalty," Mabaki said, panting slightly, "shouldn't be fighting like that."

"Like I said," Litz murmured, allowing herself a slight smile, "my status is not the most notable thing about me. And what of your king?"

Mabaki snorted as she let herself be bundled back into her cell. "He only fought monsters." Then she shrugged and smiled slightly as she leaned back on her cell bars as though to indicate that her unsuccessful escape attempt had been worth a try.

CHAPTER SIX

Kella had known from the start of her escape attempt that it wasn't going to work. Sort of. But she still couldn't help feeling a tearing sense of panic and loss as Ambassador Woskenna walked away from her because then the rest of them turned their backs on her and started moving again. Like nothing had happened.

The whole thing was probably less about seizing an opportunity and a lot more about needing one last effort to prove that she was still dancing, still a force to be reckoned with, still alive. Even with that horrible song still jammed in her head like a coin in a street crack.

The only way for that slayer to die…

Gods, she really wasn't ready to die yet.

And now, she'd probably blown her only chance at getting away. The Royal Dragon Bitch looking down on her with those sharp, judging eyes had been right: another few days and there'd be no point in running, nowhere she could reach before dying from dehydration. She might get away, but no one she cared about would ever find out.

Since they'd left Malya, Kella had given a lot of thought to the people she was leaving behind and whether it added up to a meaningful sum for a woman her age. She'd definitely taken a respectable, or maybe not so respectable, number and variety of lovers, but none of them now felt like people she could count as hers. There were many she still held some fondness for, or even shared a closeness with, but she'd never cared about any of them in the way that most people seemed to be searching for.

She didn't even really have anyone she could call a friend outside of her close hunting group. Was that out of a practical focus on work or because there was something lacking in her?

That was an uncomfortable thought. She'd always measured herself by what she did, and now she couldn't do anything.

She did her best. After recapture, Kella whistled her way through the rest of the day, folk tunes, drinking songs, anything but that godsforsaken funeral dirge, and only occasionally stopped to complain of hunger whenever the guards' silence became uncomfortable. She'd certainly made no friends among them, another pillock's move, as Ker's voice in her head constantly berated her. She did her best to ignore that voice, even if it was almost comforting, imagining he was there with her. She wouldn't be as nervous, as afraid, if he'd been there with her to do enough worrying for them both, if she had to pretend that she thought they'd find a way out.

But then again, she'd have made any deal Jev asked for if it meant Ker wouldn't have to be there with her.

After a while, she stopped whistling and gave up on staring at the minimal scenery they passed. No longer able to pretend that everything was still going according to some kind of hidden plan, she just did her best to ignore the niggling voice in her ear.

A literal voice arrived to torment her after the guard change. Because of course, the guy she'd humiliated needed to keep her updated on his feelings.

"Dude. It's still not my fault you're bad at your job. So would you just…leave it?" she said after around ten minutes of ranting and sly comments that were probably meant to sound threatening. Her eyes closed to better pretend she was alone, Kella felt the cell lurch to a stop before he could answer. Maybe she'd finally lucked out, and it was dinnertime. Maybe now, her escort would have to go away and leave her alone for a few minutes.

"You just wait. You think you're some kind of hero." He sneered, hands lingering on the bars of her cage. "But all those famous friends of yours, where are they now? No one's coming to save you, moonbeam. But I'll be with you the whole way to that demon kingdom, and let me tell you, I am gonna get bored."

Lazily, Kella opened one eye and regarded his face, which was shining from the heat and still scuffed from where she'd pushed it into the ground. "You finished yet?" she asked. "Because let me tell you, I'm *already* bored."

The man's large eyes darted around the camp setting up around them, and he eventually said, in what he seemed to think was a whisper, "Well, maybe I'll just join you in there later and see if I can't do something about that."

Kella regarded his mean, narrowing eyes. If he really was stupid enough to let his guard down and open the cage, this could be her second chance of escape. If she played this smart.

Think of the long game, and make your sacrifices now, as Findan would tell her.

She made an attempt at fluttering her eyelashes, ignoring the grains of sand falling from them as she did so. "Do what?" she asked, pitching her voice higher than normal as she began to move her head toward the guard's hand, giving one of his fingers a little kiss. It was ridiculous, and it got sand in her mouth, but it threw him off-balance enough to let her take his whole finger in her mouth. For a moment, she allowed him to push two fingers into the back of her throat, a look of satisfaction twitching on his own lips and his pupils blown wide.

"That's it, girlie."

Kella did her best to smile coyly with her eyes as she bit down until she could taste blood. She'd always wanted to try this; she'd heard it was easier than biting a root vegetable. If she stopped thinking about it, it certainly wasn't harder. Distantly, she heard him scream, felt his other hand slap helplessly at her face.

Before she hit bone, she pulled away and wiped her mouth roughly with the back of her hand. "Oh honey, you just taste so good."

He snarled with an animal's rage as he clutched his bleeding hand. "You're paying for this, bitch."

She raised an eyebrow, laughing now. "What, are you gonna come in here and show me who's boss, just like last time?"

"Oh, I'm gonna fucking—"

"Corporal Bligen. Do not finish that sentence. Leave now to find a member of your troop with medical training. By your actions, I'm assuming you're not one of them."

Bligen seemed to wrestle with himself as he processed Ambassador Woskenna's words.

"With respect…" he started, still not turning to look behind him at Woskenna, who was carrying two bowls of food.

"With respect, *Corporal*, it's my sworn duty to both our nations to deliver this woman safely into my kingdom. You don't currently appear to be an asset in aiding me in that, and I feel sure your king would agree. I relieve you of all future guard duties at her cage."

Now he turned just as Ambassador Woskenna was almost beside him. "Ma'am, my squad leader—"

"Will defer to me as he's been ordered to."

"Ma'am—"

Something in her gaze sparked enough self-preservation in Bligen to prevent him from continuing. Kella watched their stare-off with great amusement because it was one that Woskenna, the tourist who'd been so easily flustered back in the marketplace, was clearly winning.

She was taller than most women Kella had ever met, but everyone said that Aelshians were freakishly tall, standing at around six feet, maybe more. It was a soldier's body, all muscle, with no room for softness, with a square jaw and high cheekbones that made Kella want to drool, and a long nose that made her look still more severe. Despite the green Aelshian uniform hanging loosely off her frame, the way she stood made it appear that everything she was wearing fit too tightly.

If there'd been no dragon hunt and Kella had left herself enough time to ask Ambassador Woskenna her first name and had never heard about her titles, she would have relished the chance to take her apart, to find out what she looked like smiling.

When Bligen yielded and left them, Woskenna didn't smile as she walked toward Kella's cage, but there was satisfaction in the way she held her mouth. "Here," she said to Kella, passing the small bowl of ugali through the bars.

Kella took it and tried to catch her eye as she smiled. "Can't complain about the service here, at least."

"Mm." Woskenna moved back to sit on the ground with her own bowl.

"You really are planning on keeping close," Kella noted as Woskenna continued to show no interest in anything beyond the tasteless food.

"I wasn't lying," she said, giving Kella only the most perfunctory glance. "You have the power to start a war, or more specifically, your death does. And although I believe the soldiers here are all well-meaning, you've raised tensions. And Loren does not like the way some of them look at you."

"Ah, so you came over because your dragon told you to and not just because I'm such a great kisser."

This got no response.

"And really? We're talking human nature here, and you're relying on what the dragon's gut instinct tells you?"

Woskenna snorted quietly. "You don't know much about dragons, do you?"

"I'm really good at killing 'em, so I figure I've got the basics covered."

That at least got under Woskenna's skin. She didn't exactly lose her composure, but the way her surprisingly delicate fingers closed into a tight fist made it clear that Kella was getting to her. "You're not dealing with Corporal Bligen anymore. I'm not going to be riled," she said with a mildness Kella was sure was feigned.

"What, am I too beneath you for that, Princess?"

Woskenna returned to concentrating only on her meal but eventually said, "They say guarding prisons damages the minds of those who work there. What of those who kill for a living?"

"Wouldn't know. Not a killer. I stop monsters. I don't hurt people."

"Funny. I could have sworn the corporal was bleeding when he left. Are you telling me he did that to himself?"

"I don't hurt people who aren't trying to hurt me. And c'mon. You've met the guy. Tell me he didn't deserve all that and more."

Woskenna held her eye strangely for a moment, and Kella was sure she was being sized up before Woskenna nodded and looked away.

"Was that you making your mind up about me? What did you figure out?" When this got no response, Kella pouted. "You know, you totally owe me. I got you a free rupricaprin. So you should just…let me out already."

This effort got not even the slightest acknowledgement, so, defeated, Kella slumped and watched Woskenna eat her food as she continued to ignore her own, a sudden terror distracting her from the hunger which had consumed her for hours. What if Woskenna never spoke again, what if *no one* on this godsforsaken desert trek ever spoke to her again? And what if Kella stopped being brave and annoying enough to fill the silences and let them go quiet, let herself go quiet, so that by the time she reached Aelshia…

"What's going to happen to me?" she asked, surprised that she'd let herself say the words aloud.

Woskenna finally looked up again, and Kella tried to harden her jaw. This wasn't weakness, it wasn't fear, she just wanted to know.

"In Aelshia. What punishment do you have for people like me?"

Kella thought a flicker of pity softened Woskenna's eyes. She wasn't sure she could stand that, but then Woskenna spoke, and it was even worse because her tone was apologetic. "We don't have people like you in Aelshia. I'm sorry, but I have no idea what fate will be decided for you, only that, with our most severe crimes, enslavement is generally attempted before a death penalty is decreed."

"No one like me, heh?" Kella laughed, trying to push some bravado back into her tone. She'd never even considered life as a slave, and now that she was, she couldn't think of anything worse. If her mother was watching her from somewhere below, her mother who had valued freedom above all else, she would feel so much shame.

"People don't make a habit of trying to kill dragons where I come from."

"Honey, I don't try, I succeed," Kella said as she threw a lump of ugali in the air and unsuccessfully tried to catch it in her mouth. "What, are they too afraid?"

"Too respectful," Woskenna answered with a shrug. "They would gain nothing from it." She narrowed her eyes at Kella. "What did you do it for? I hear dragons in your land hoard gold since you mine such a great deal of it."

"I didn't do it for gold," Kella said, incredulous. "I mean, hey, I didn't *not* think about gold, but that was never the reason."

"Then what was?"

Kella stared for a moment. Woskenna seemed intelligent enough. Was she honestly this stupid? "The reason I kill dragons is to stop them killing people."

"But dragons don't—"

"I know they don't always do it on purpose. Sometimes, it's just because they're big and powerful, and they're not all that philosophical. Why would they care about whether they hurt us or not?"

"That doesn't sound like any dragons I know," Woskenna said quietly, picking up her food. "They might be big and powerful, but they have nothing to gain from being aggressive. We're not threats to them."

Kella laughed. "I guess it could be that your dragons are different, like with the gold thing. But I killed that dragon last week because it killed two kids. Maybe it didn't mean to, but that didn't make them any less dead. You know what burning flesh smells like?"

Woskenna was quiet for a moment, blankly assessing before eventually saying, "Yes."

Kella stared, trying to do some sizing up of her own, and she could see no regret from those eyes that probably had a dragon staring out of them. Eyes that the fading sunset had rendered a lovely shade of gold. Kella shook her head in disgust. "Might as well send back that corporal," she said, leaning back against the bars with her food still in her hands. "At least he wasn't a smart cunt."

"You mean, you had a better chance of escaping on his watch."

"That too."

"I wasn't lying," Woskenna said, still looking at her. "Your safety on this trip is my priority. I won't have it jeopardized."

"Yeah? Well maybe I'd *prefer*—"

"What you'd prefer isn't my concern," Woskenna snapped. "Now, eat your food and…shut up."

It was pathetic, but Kella wanted to cry more than ever now. She'd spent a lifetime learning how to deal with injury, grief, and having her family's tragedy become a national legend, but she'd never really had to deal in her adult life with being told what to do or with being ignored.

And she had a bad feeling that Woskenna wouldn't hesitate in either ordering her around or ignoring her.

I don't think she's lying, Loren's opinion came through as Mabaki asked if Litz knew what burning flesh smelt like.

What? She must be lying.

I don't think she thinks she is. Her thoughts don't flicker in panic.

Litz looked again at the challenge burning in Mabaki's eyes. She did look righteous, with her nostrils flaring, and her chin proudly raised. She wore her confinement like the most steadfast of martyrs.

It was infuriating.

And the worst part, Litz thought as she sat and pulled out a scroll on Jeenobian battle tactics from her bag, was that Mabaki didn't seem *evil*, not like Litz wanted her to be. And for being wrong with the best intentions, Mabaki might end up dead or broken and enslaved, which Litz could imagine would be as terrible a fate as death to Mabaki who enjoyed having the freedom to flirt audaciously with strangers in marketplaces.

You care about what happens to her, Loren pointed out in an uncharacteristically gentle nudge at her mind.

I…she clearly has so much potential, and it's been wasted *on something so evil.*

Litz felt the weight of Loren's consideration and heard Loren sighing out a puff of smoke from her position across camp, terrifying several of the Jeenobian guards in the process. *Evil requires choice, is that not the popular philosophy? And in this girl's mind, she was doing something good. And maybe in some ways she was.*

She killed—

I know what she's done. But you watched how she treated her guard. She didn't react until she considered him a threat.

But dragons—

I don't know much about dragons here. The thought was so small and almost ashamed, Litz wasn't sure that she'd understood her correctly.

What?

I told you. I don't…I don't like it here, Loren admitted in something more like her regular tone. *There is an uneasy feel to the land, and I know nothing about its dragons except that they are hunted.*

An uneasy feel?

I have crossed over the territories of several of my kind on our journey, Loren said slowly, *and not one of them has taken any kind of interest in me, in us.*

But—

"You getting schooled by your big scaly mistress in how to deal with me?" Mabaki's voice pulled Litz lurching back into the physical now. "Or does she trust you to talk to people on your own?"

Litz snorted and tried to ignore Mabaki. She had a feeling that she wouldn't like that. Her suspicions were confirmed when only a moment later, Mabaki started chattering again.

"Y'know, I've got a friend who visited your country before. She thought everything was pretty weird, maybe not as weird as the stories we tell about it back home but definitely all kinds of fucked-up. And the way she talked about the dragonriders…" Mabaki shook her head and finally raised a spoonful of food to her mouth. "Like, dude, I was really not expecting you to be anything like this good-looking or even *normal*-looking. I thought you'd have scales or, like, glowing eyes or something."

Litz tilted her head slightly, reluctantly amused. "You didn't expect me to look human?"

"I mean, there *is* a dragon in your head, right? And they're, like, toxic with magic."

"Toxic isn't necessarily a good term for it."

You need to stop squirming whenever you hear someone mention magic, Loren chided her.

I'm not built for deception.

You don't need to tell me.

"What, is your dragon overlord enjoying my expectations?"

Litz looked up sharply. "No, that was…something else. But you're good at noticing."

Mabaki shrugged. "You've got a pretty easy to read face, princess."

Told you.

"What are your earrings all about?"

Litz blinked. "My earrings?"

"Yeah. What are they for?"

"It's an old custom," Litz said slowly, a little suspicious. "It shows who we are. The right is the side listening to duty, and so it shows which family you belong to, although this can change with marriage or for a higher duty."

"And yours is…"

"The sigil of my house, now with a dragon."

"'Higher duty,' huh?"

"Mm. The design of the left earring we pick on our coming of age. It shows who we consider ourselves to be. It's…become something of a joke. That someone boring picks their own name for their left ear."

Mabaki made a face, apparently considering this. "I like that. So what do you have? Are you boring?"

"A torch and a book," Litz said, fiddling with the etching on her earring as she did so, remembering her day of choosing.

"That doesn't sound like a good combination."

Her mother hadn't thought so either. "Maybe not." After pausing only for a moment, Litz leaned in to look at Mabaki. "Tell me, do you feel shame in betraying your king?"

"Where did that come from? But, no, he betrayed me first. I've got nothing to feel ashamed of."

Litz nodded to herself, thinking about her frequently mixed feelings on her own monarch. "Is it true you and King Jevlyn were sexually involved?"

Mabaki blinked. "Jealous? Seriously, what's with the grilling?"

Litz said nothing and waited, having already learnt in the short time she had spent with Mabaki that she didn't tolerate silences patiently.

"I mean, *yeah.* Any gossip in the godsdamn kingdom could have told you that. But he wasn't King Jevlyn then," she added. "He was just the palace nerd that hero-worshipped my mami."

"But he was kind? He was good to you?"

Mabaki looked at her and smiled. "She's your cousin, right? Queen Eisha?"

Litz nodded. "I worry for her."

For an instant, something about Mabaki's face softened. "I get it. For what it's worth, Jev would never intentionally hurt a woman. Hell, he couldn't even talk to one properly, other than me, until he was, like, twenty. And he *had* to sometimes for official reasons, which was always hilarious. And I think he likes her," she said, turning her gaze back to her bowl of food before putting it down again and hugging her knees a little closer. "The people like her too, mostly. Not that anyone likes the rest of you guys, no offense, but she's young, and she's pretty, and they can tell that Jev likes her, which still counts for something."

"Do you still love him?" Litz hadn't meant to ask the question. It was far too personal, too prying, completely inappropriate, and besides, knowing the answer would serve no real purpose.

Mabaki laughed. "I don't know if me and Jev have *ever* been 'in love,' so even if you weren't dragging me off to your foreign jail or whatever, I still wouldn't be posing any competition for your cousin. And yes," she added, putting both thumbs up and pointing at Litz. "Still single. But, yeah. Even if he is a two-faced little harpy, I'd still be there to have his back if he ever needed me." She seemed to catch herself from getting too close to meaningful emotion and frowned. "Y'know, if I wasn't being carted off for execution or whatever."

Litz smiled slightly, having mostly recovered from those two fingers pointed at her. "Hmm. I'm sure he appreciates that."

"He's got a bad way of showing it," Mabaki said, starting to pick at her food again and following this by gagging slightly. "Sky's teeth, they really kept to the provisions budget."

"I was told it would taste better hot."

"Thanks for passing the message on."

"I'm sorry if the service here isn't to your taste."

Mabaki glared at this, but there was an appealing glint of laughter nestled in those dark eyes, and Litz couldn't help thinking…

Remember what she's bound for, Loren put in gruffly but not unkindly.

I remember.

"Hey, you got any dice?" Mabaki asked her.

"You are still my prisoner, remember?"

"Yeah, and I might be good, but I'm also not gonna escape with a set of dice. And what else do guards even do when they're guarding?"

"We're not going to play dice."

"I doubt you'll get any of the rest of that lot to play with you. And forgive me for making assumptions, Princess, but I'm guessing dragons don't have much of an ability to hold dice, even if they are special Aelshian ones."

I could if I wanted to.

Litz ignored Loren and glared half-heartedly at Mabaki, hating that she continued to be right. But how much more would the guard troop hate her if they saw her socialising with the prisoner?

Do you care so much about what others think of you?

Sighing, Litz gave in and pulled out her pair of eight-sided dice. "I only have it in Aelshian Eights."

Against the bars, Mabaki nodded with some approval. "We can work with that. What game do the sailors gamble with over in Aelshia?"

"You must know we're an inland nation. Our 'sailors' are very different, I hear."

Mabaki waved a hand dismissively. "Okay, then, what game do all you rich people play? Or hey, you're a soldier, what do you play whenever you're too drunk to remember your own name, and you just want to spend all the money you don't have?"

"I assure you, I have never been in that mood in my life."

"Are you sure you soldiered?"

Chapter Seven

Ker knew the mountain paths which stretched up from Malya's northern outskirts toward the Nayona border fairly well. He must have helped undergo hundreds of hunts up there, chasing dozens of different dangerous creatures. He knew which of the gnarled trees and bushes lining the narrow path had berries which were safe to eat; he knew how far the river was from the path; he knew to stay well clear of the cliffside area which sheltered dozens of gryphon nests.

But following Zebenn's sure steps in the daylight was a very different thing to navigating the small rocky path carved out by generations of travellers and merchants all alone in the dark. And there was often something rustling the bushes, too big to be a bird, too light-footed for a harpy, too small for a gryphon.

He estimated that he'd climbed up several miles into the mountains when he gave in for his second night alone and found a place to rest, somewhere sheltered and far enough off the path to avoid any curious eyes but not so far that he would struggle to find his way back to it. He'd given himself almost no time to pack anything, so in some ways, having only a blanket made finding a place to camp for a night easier. Which didn't mean he didn't regret making more of an effort to find a tent.

He should have thought ahead about a lot of things, things he was usually good at remembering or remembering for Kella, who would have been the one to march out of Malya with no plan. He'd left without even attempting to say good-bye to his da, even knowing how much danger he was intending to put himself in.

Maybe this was how Kella lived her *entire life*.

Without much more than the stale bread in his pack to think of for a nightly meal, Ker got settled quickly, leaning up against a rock he'd judged to be a good shelter and probably not infested with anything. At least, now that he'd wandered up this high and so far from any paths, he shouldn't need to worry about humans trying to attack him as he slept. Only wild animals—please, Earth Mother, not baboons—venomous insects, and maybe even dragons.

Hells, he had to hope there were dragons up here, or else instead of a *bad* plan to save Kella, he'd have absolutely *no* plan.

But despite that fear, considering that this was the longest stretch of time Ker had ever really spent on his own, he felt like he was handling himself well. It was satisfying, if tiring, to be climbing up these familiar hills. Zebenn always said that you got nothing from no effort, and even if his plan was likely going to fail, with Ker finding himself lost or dead or all of the above, he was sure he was moving in the right direction. He tried to congratulate himself for that, out loud because the silence had started to get to him, as he pulled his extra cloak tighter around him.

When he woke again, the stars were still glinting high above him, and he wasn't shivering but only because his entire body was frozen. This wasn't like the sleep paralysis he'd seen overtake Kella before; this was something different, Ker reasoned, desperately trying to think instead of panic. This was something being done *to* him. Instinctively trying to force his vocal chords into screaming, he found that the only sound he was capable of making was a pitiful whining noise. Maybe thinking was no more comfort than panicking.

"What are *you*?" a low croaking voice asked him.

Unable to answer, Ker forced out something like a growl.

"Right. Got it," the voice said. Ker felt the muscles in his face relax again as he processed that a little man had just jumped onto his chest. Or not a man. It was more like a toad that had been stretched out and taught to walk on its hind legs, but parts of it gleamed like a dragon.

"You're a gremlin," Ker said.

The gremlin narrowed its unblinking little eyes and latched its hands to its hips. "Pfft. We didn't ask you what *we* are. We asked what *you* are," it said, poking at Ker's chest sharply with a toe.

"I'm a human," Ker growled. "Now, would you let me up? I'm not about to hurt you."

"A human couldn't understand what we are saying. We weren't spawned yesterday, so speak straight to us."

Ker felt something drop low to his stomach. He'd never heard any stories about gremlins talking, but considering the weirdness of the last few days, he'd been prepared to accept it. No one really knew much about gremlins, and he'd never seen one up close. They'd been dying out as a species, making the stories around them gradually more mythic in tone.

"That's all the answers I've got for you," Ker said eventually. "Now, let me up. I'm a Mabaki. You threaten me and someone's going to come after you."

The moment Ker used his family name, the creature's eyes flared red. "Such a name that almost warrants its own species type," it said, its voice even lower, and Ker started to feel more afraid than he'd thought he could possibly be of a creature four inches tall. He heard the hatred in its voice and remembered, too late, how utterly at its mercy he was. "And what is a dragon killer doing wandering so far from its clan?"

Good question. "I'm seeking a dragon," he said, and the creature laughed at him, a strange croak that Ker knew was intended to be mocking.

"Want to kill one all on your own? Oh, child. Your little quest goes no further. Dragons may not be what they once were, but a *gradachh* would rather suffer endlessly than willingly aid their tormenters." As it spoke, the gremlin increased the pressure of its taloned feet, and a toe dug into Ker's chest deep enough to draw blood.

A horrible little gremlin, that was what Kella had used to call him when she was mad at him. Mostly if he ever stole her things because that was the one thing everyone could agree on about gremlins: they liked to thieve. But as far as Ker knew, Kella had never seen a gremlin.

"No, no I'm not trying to *kill* a dragon. I'm just trying to *find* one."

"And why would *you* want to *find* a dragon?" The gremlin squinted closer to his face. If he'd been able to move, he would have squirmed away. Up close, the creature looked even more bizarre, and those bright eyes just kept staring and staring, like it, or *they*, could see and understand him right to his core. Like they were watching all his worst moments and deciding what to make of them.

"Are you trying to crawl back to your maker?"

Vomit rose up in his throat, which Ker fought down to snarl. "I don't *have* a maker." He paused. He was doing this for Kella. "Though if I did, he's dead."

The gremlin nodded as if this was unsurprising. "None of us choose what makes us," they said in a tone that suggested they were quoting something. "Only *how* it makes us."

Ker attempted to shrug before being forcibly reminded of his paralysis. "So do you choose to let me up? How long can you even hold this for?"

"Oh, days if need be," the gremlin said too quickly.

"Liar."

"How *dare* you—"

"Look, let me up, and I swear, I won't hurt you," Ker promised, feeling odd to not have his hands free to express himself. "And, and if you do know where the dragons up here are hiding, I'd really like your help."

The gremlin snorted. "And if we did, why would we?"

Ker gave a meaningful glance up and down the small form still standing on top of him. "Your scales don't gleam like they should."

"It's *night.*"

"I'm willing to bet you could use a dragon to help you with that."

The gremlin scowled. If the little Ker knew of them was correct, and between Findan's stories and his da's books, he suspected it was, gremlins survived by eating the dried skin on the dragon's back, keeping them a more powerful people than they otherwise would have been. It was a little like a magical version of the oxpecker and hippo relationship. Gremlins needed dragons, and this gremlin didn't seem to have one.

"We doubt you'll be able to find a talking one anymore," the gremlin muttered. "They've all turned into savage beasts now. Horrible things."

"I didn't know they were ever anything else."

"Then why look for one? You must be crazier than...than a *dragon.*"

Ker pressed his lips together tightly. "That's me. Now, will you help me or not?"

"Hmm." The gremlin leapt off Ker's body in one quick movement and stretched out its hands.

His mobility returned. "Thank you," he said, politely ignoring the gremlin's twitching stare from a safe distance as he got to his feet. "Would you mind keeping watch while I sleep? You don't need much, right?"

The gremlin squinted at him suspiciously. "You'd trust us with that?"

Ker shrugged. "You haven't killed me already. It'll probably be less dangerous than no one being here at all."

The gremlin continued to glare at him but edged a little closer. "You're a strange one, cub of Mabaki."

"Actually, Ker's fine."

"Hmm. They call us Sallvayn. Sleep now, and when the light comes up again, we will talk."

Ker smiled and nodded. He wasn't exactly as comfortable as he claimed to be, sleeping in front of this unknown creature, but he needed the rest. It didn't take him long after lying down to drift off again, dreaming of nothing.

CHAPTER EIGHT

Most of Kella's dreams became the same old nightmare in the end. She could be dreaming about Doshni pirates or Ballian's sugar puffs, and by the end, everything would end up on fire again.

She wondered if it was better or worse that she'd never actually seen how it happened. Unlike Ker, she was never going to wake from a perfect repeat of the day their mother had been incinerated, but Kella had a decent imagination, especially when she was unconscious. In her dream, the green dragon—though the dragon that had killed her mother had been golden—swooped toward her mother, who had her arms stretched wide to shield her son, who in this dream was appearing as his present-day self. Their mother's sword was outstretched toward the beast approaching them, and it glinted in the sunlight.

Kella had loved that sword. Growing up, not being strong enough to pick it up had never stopped her from trying to wield it. When she'd commissioned her own sword, she'd thought of creating a replica. It wouldn't have been difficult to recall every detail for the smith.

But the way it had melted and melded into Kella's mami's arm would now always mar her memory of it, so she'd used dragon bone instead. A little flashy, maybe, but it had felt fitting.

And in the dream, although Kella hadn't been there, she watched it all, powerless to do anything to stop it happening all over again. Her mami was reduced to a screaming voice engulfed by flames until there was nothing left of her. She'd heard people claim that Kira Mabaki had shown no weaknesses, no fear, even at the end. Kella remembered enough about that day to know they were wrong.

Ker stood, covered in blood and soot, trembling but unharmed. She'd had to walk over to him, over the remains of their mother, ignoring Findan's screams, and hold him. To tell him that he had to keep this a secret. He'd been choking on the smoke, eyes wide and filling with tears. And just when she'd began worrying he would never breathe again, he'd started to wail. But in the dream, Ker lunged at her, fire burning in his eyes and claws stretching from his hands, and she had to *wake up* because this was all *wrong*, but it was also far, far too close to being true and—

Her eyes opened, but the feeling of trapped helpless terror refused to leave her, and her attempts to calm her breathing weren't working. It wasn't working; she couldn't *breathe*. It was too dark to see anything, but she knew she couldn't breathe and that she was trapped, and she was never going to get away and she couldn't...

"Mabaki!"

That was her mother's name, her name, a dragon killer name, but her mother had been killed *by* a dragon, and she'd soon be dead *because* of one, because that was how her life was apparently doomed to fucking go. She'd be leaving Ker all alone, Ker who—

"*Kella.*"

That was *her* name. The hands were reaching through the bars to clutch her wrist belonged to someone who cared enough to know her name and who... Kella blinked, feeling her heart rate calm. She rolled over, finally able to force her body into movement and focused on Woskenna, who was still holding her wrist. "I didn't know you knew my first name, Princess."

"You expect me not to remember the name of the person whose life I'm in charge of? You do have a low opinion of me."

"What's your name?"

"You heard my—"

"I mean *your* name. What is it?"

There was a long pause. "It's Litz."

The pressure on Kella's wrist softened to almost a stroke before Litz pulled her hand gently back through the bars. But in the low light of the fire's embers, Kella was able to focus on her face, and she narrowed her eyes because her gaoler was looking uncharacteristically nervous. "What are you doing out of your tent?"

"I couldn't sleep. And then I heard you."

"And what did you use on me?"

"What?" But Litz was twitching like she rarely had, even while lying to Kella through multiple games of dice.

"You magicked me. You Pushed the fear down."

"That's ridiculous," Litz said, her voice pitched a little higher.

"Yeah, well, thanks. It's the only thing that's ever been able to snap me out of a dream like that." Findan had used the technique on her a couple of times. But Kella trusted Findan. She wasn't a witch; she just hunted them sometimes and had picked up enough tricks over the years. She'd always made it clear the knowledge wasn't something she was proud of possessing, even as she'd taught Ker how to use it.

And now here was Princess Litz, Aelshian ambassador, with it. Did dragon riding breed moral corruption, or had she just had too much spare time and too many spare books as a kid?

Litz bit her lip. "What did you dream about?"

"My early life trauma, obviously."

"I didn't mean to ask something so personal."

Kella squinted to make out her expression. "Well. My personal's always been pretty public. You seriously haven't heard what happened to my mother?"

"I…" Litz seemed to catch herself. "From what I heard, she made a career of killing dragons, as you have. So I would assume that one fought back at the cost of her life."

Kella swallowed. She wanted to say something to prove her anger, but the dream had left her too exhausted to muster much emotion. "Yeah, that's about right. 'Cept she didn't attack first. It attacked her because she found it hurting my brother."

"*Hurting* him?" Kella couldn't make out much of Litz's face in the dark, but she suspected it was scrunched up in disbelief. "Why would a dragon try to hurt a child?"

Something of her earlier ambassador tone had crept back in, and Kella couldn't help but make her responding sneer even more childish, knowing Litz couldn't see her face either. "Why did one have to leave my stepfather walking with a limp his whole life? Why did one try to burn down the memory hall of Kanceeni?" She held up a hand and shrugged. "And how come an Aelshian princess—somewhere I'm pretty sure that's even tighter on their magic laws than we are—is using magic just to help a criminal sleep better?"

"You weren't breathing," Litz said quietly, "and you're imagining things."

"Like fuck am I imagining things. Now I've got an idea," Kella added, seized by sudden inventiveness. "Let me go, and I won't tell anyone about who you are or what you can do."

Laughter bounced softly off the cage bars. "I don't think so."

"If there's something my people hate worse than dragons, it's witches. A dragon witch…they'd kill you straight out. You'd never make it to your dragon."

"I think you're forgetting to factor in said dragon."

Kella pressed her face a little closer to the bars. "Rumour can be a dangerous thing."

"And Loren is *always* a dangerous thing. I gave my word and bond I would deliver you safely to my king. I won't release you over a childish threat, I will not let you torture yourself in your sleep, and I will not allow others to harm you."

"They really would turn on you," Kella insisted. "Dragon or not, they'd forget all about me and turn on you, and I don't know how that would go."

"Well, I do. Loren is all the protection we could need. Do you think you'll be able to sleep without my assistance now?"

Oh, Kella had so many bad jokes sitting on the tip of her tongue, but she just didn't have the energy. "I mean, the dream's probably gonna come back. But just pass me a bottle of the ourzen I know they have out there, and I probably won't notice."

Litz didn't move. "How old were you when it happened?"

"When the dragon set my mother on fire? I was fifteen. But Ker was only ten. And he saw the whole thing."

"And you weren't there to save them."

"No. I got there too late. Are you trying to psychosoothe me?"

"What?"

"Y'know. Get me talking through all my *issues* and my *experiences* and have me forgive myself?"

"I've never heard of that. I was simply curious as to why this memory particularly haunts you and not, say, the memory of anything you killed yourself."

"If you mean the dragon killings, you're not going to get me to regret any of those."

Litz sighed, and Kella judged she was starting to move away. "Exactly. It's strange what incites guilt and nightmares when in your waking life, you seem so unfeeling."

"Believe me, I feel a whole lot. It's just usually anger." Immediately after saying it, Kella felt embarrassment clutch at her for the whining tone of her delivery.

"At least that makes some sense. Your life has become an irrational coping method, a vengeance mission."

"Glad to hear I'm all figured out, Princess. But what about you? What motivated your magic-using? Is it true what they say, are you feeding your dragon?"

Litz seemed caught off guard. "*Feeding* her?"

"Y'know. They say if you use magic, it feeds the demons. And everyone says Aelshian dragons are basically the same thing. Are you all witches?" Much as she was enjoying annoying her, Kella genuinely was curious.

"*No.* It has nothing to do with... In any case, you're alive. You should sleep."

"Your concern is touching," Kella said sweetly as she listened to Litz walk away. "Did you use magic to beat me?"

"*No.*"

"See, now I can't trust you."

"You're...you're teasing."

She shouldn't be, Kella knew. This was the enemy, and Kella knew her weakness now. She should be working out how to exploit it for all she was worth. But Litz was just so *awkward* about everything. And maybe it was less that Kella didn't have the energy and more that she didn't have the heart.

Yet. She might feel differently in the morning.

That was reckless, and foolish, and—

Litz pushed her way back into the tent, thanking the gods that as an officer, she had one to herself. *I'm fine. She's not going to say anything.*

You don't know that. She might. You know next to nothing about her, and she knows enough about you to see you destroyed.

Litz shook her head and lay back down in her covers. *You wouldn't let that happen.*

Not here. You know that even without me, those guards are barely a threat to you. But when you bring her home, and she stands before your king for questioning?

Even knowing how useless it was to try to pretend, Litz swallowed and tried to hide her fear. She had been stupid, but she'd be damned if she admitted that. *So, what, I should kill her to ensure her silence?* Despite herself, Litz looked at the tent exit that tempted her as it had before. She hadn't been able to sleep and had meant to go to Loren, but the pained sounds coming from inside Mabaki's cage had left her unable to turn away.

She felt Loren sigh with her whole body. *I know you can't, shouldn't, and won't. But allow me my right to worry and feel frustration with your actions. She was never in any real danger, and you know it.*

It was Litz's turn to sigh. *I know. But I couldn't just—*

You have before. You've watched soldiers, friends, die rather than revealing yourself.

But I've saved others when I had the chance. And there was no one around this time.

No one except her. A dragon killer and your prisoner, and you revealed yourself to calm her down.

Shut up, please.

What was that?

Litz sank down in her covers and closed her eyes. *Just, please. I could use some sleep. And I'd like to know you have my back.*

You know I always do. But I'm struggling to remember which way you're facing.

Litz resisted the urge to get up and walk across the camp to give Loren a real hug. *We'll be home soon. And besides. People won't take a Jeenobi criminal's word over mine.*

You would think so. But I've given up on expecting humans to be predictable.

"So. You want to catch a dragon, force it into letting you ride it out into the desert, where you hope to locate your sister and rescue her. Is that everything?"

Ker ignored Sallvayn as he tore into the last of the hardened bread he'd brought with him. If he was lucky, he'd soon find something better able to sustain him as they travelled. Gods, he should have packed more food.

"That's it? The whole entirety of this plan, hidden details and all, nothing held back from us?"

"Yup." He didn't need to look up to know that Sallvayn was goggling at him.

"That is the *thinnest* idea we've heard in fifty years."

"Thanks for the feedback."

"No, seriously." Talons curving into the dirt, Sallvayn paced in a circle, crossing their arms.

"It's still the best plan I've got."

Sallvayn put their hands on their hips, a gesture Ker had noticed was a habitual one. "You don't force a dragon into something, into *anything*."

Ker prodded his fire one more time and went back to cooking the vegetables he'd peeled. "I've had a lifetime of pushing dragons into doing what they don't want to do."

"You mean dying? That's very different than getting something to *live* a certain way."

Ker poked at his food. "If you've got any suggestions, I'd love to hear some, Sall."

"That is not our name," Sallvayn said before huffing out a long sigh. "We'll start with the obvious," they said as they wrinkled up their face at the smell of Ker's cooking. "You have something no one else of your kind has much of anymore, and that might be of interest to the dragons you'd like to 'control.'"

"That's never worked out well for me before."

"Have you ever attempted something like this before?"

Ker frowned at his food. "Not exactly. So what? You think I should just walk over and look 'interesting'? You think that'll be enough to get a dragon to do what I want?"

Sallvayn snorted. "No. But it might be enough to encourage one into speaking with you."

"Dragons don't talk," Ker said, less confident than he should have been and remembering the baby dragon with an unwelcome lurch in his stomach. "They say in Aelshia, their riders can speak with them, but—"

Sallvayn shook their head. "We don't know anything about any human sand lines, but we know this land is cursed, that the dragons here are sick and have been for a long time."

Looking at Sallvayn's small face, Ker saw that they seemed almost closed off and uncertain, almost as if there was information they didn't want him to know. "You're saying there're dragons out there that aren't monsters?"

"We're saying that it might be time for you to be more open-minded about the creatures you seek help from," Sallvayn snapped.

Ker finished off the last of his bread with a distaste he tried to keep hidden. "Okay, open-mindeness. Where do I start with that?"

Sallvayn scratched their head. "We hear things."

"Okay."

"Things like the dragons north from here got away from this area for a good reason, and they were able to think well enough to do that. We're guessing you supposed as much, which is why you're up here."

Ker nodded, curling his fingers a little tighter around the stick, feeling his hand burn as he wondered if Kella was getting enough food wherever they had her. "We never had to hunt up here. We never heard of anyone getting hurt, so there was never a good reason to. But Findan figured there were some up here since she knew there'd been sightings. I wondered if the dragons were just different up here. Was I right?"

Sallvayn held his stare. "Partly. The farther you get away from the centre of your country, from the big city, the more likely you are to find the dragons who kept hold of their own minds. Or maybe, most of them realised that being anywhere near humanity was not sensible, *not* that that's always protected them against people like you."

"You really think any of them might talk to me?"

"We think if we can find the right sort, they probably won't attack you on sight. They'll sense the dragon in you, like we did, and if we're right, we'll see how things go."

Ker looked at his food, trying to pretend the information didn't bother him.

"Don't tell us you hadn't worked as much out for yourself."

"I...suspected," Ker forced out through a hoarse throat.

"We should hope you wouldn't have camped up here at all if you hadn't."

Ker bit his lip. "I was hoping I was wrong."

There was almost sympathy in Sallvayn's voice when they next spoke. "Was it a rabid that left its mark on you?"

"A rabid?"

"The ones without any reason."

He remembered the smell of his mother's hair as she'd burned in front of him. "Yes."

Sallvayn eyed him carefully for a few moments. "That doesn't seem to have affected you."

He tried not to scowl. What had Sallvayn expected him to be like?

"Do you think they did it on purpose? Changed you?"

"I don't know and I don't care," he lied, rolling his blanket back into his sack and standing. "C'mon, we should get going."

"You promise you're not going to try killing anything?"

He sighed. "I promise."

"Because it sounds like you have a whole assortment of issues."

"Just take me to them?"

"Okay, okay. Bossy." Sallvayn sneered. Then they started staring up at Ker's shoulder.

"What?"

"Could we perch up there?" Sallvayn looked almost embarrassed, and Ker got the impression that if Sallvayn were more bird than amphibian, they would have been ruffling their feathers. "It's…we don't have big hard feet, and walking for a long time, we may only slow you down."

Ker made a face. "Fine." He bent slightly and held out a hand, only to find that Sallvayn had jumped a surprising height and was already weighing his shoulder down.

They tugged slightly at his ear. "Right. Onward!"

For Kella, Ker reminded himself, his jaw firmly clenched down. And if, *when*, he got her back, he hoped he'd find her grateful and not laughing at him.

Or worse, afraid of him.

CHAPTER NINE

When Litz climbed on Loren's back that morning, Kella Mabaki still appeared to be asleep in her cage. Litz thought about walking over and asking whether she'd slept well. But if she really was sleeping, then asking such a question would defeat its own point while also making Litz look pathetic. Someone else would bring Mabaki her breakfast, would listen to or ignore her sarcastic comments.

But Litz wondered what Mabaki looked like in those first moments of waking up. She wondered if she would, for once, look caught off guard.

You're developing a fixation.

I wouldn't call it that.

As someone who understands the workings of your mind through the dubious virtue of being constantly connected to it, I'm struggling to provide a more accurate description. You think of little else but this woman who kills dragons. And now you're avoiding her.

Litz breathed out slowly, the sound of which was lost on the wind. *I want to be able to work her out. I know she's not a bad person, not entirely, and yet she's committed such unforgivable crimes.*

That could be said of many of your kind. This is what comes of trying to stamp morality on people.

The better dragon way of doing things would be?

Loren gave a mental shrug. *Someone acts, you react. The world keeps going.*

Hmm. We do have a tendency to complicate things.

It's as I am always saying. Humans are the strangest creatures.

Stranger that you ally yourselves to us.

Hmm.

Litz had to smile to hear Loren send her any non-word, especially one that she'd undoubtedly picked up from Litz. It made her sound very human.

I've been wondering about that, Loren admitted eventually.

About what?

About why none of the dragons here form any connections to the humans. Why they allow themselves to be hunted like animals.

So you believe what Mabaki was saying?

Loren huffed, and for a moment, Litz felt Loren's whole body go warm. *Not exactly. But I do think that there's much here that doesn't add up, and I can't...*

Litz frowned when she did not continue. *What?*

I can't believe the Circle didn't know. But I know that they would have warned us if they did.

But you believe it anyway?

Loren remained silent.

C'mon. You always have something to say.

Not right now.

Litz curled her fingers a little tighter around the straps and stayed quiet, feeling oddly disconnected by this rare awkward silence. This strange mission and the long, scorching journey still stretching ahead was succeeding in raising tensions between them. The last time she could even remember them feeling so disconnected was when Litz's uncle had started tutoring her in magic. Loren hadn't liked that. And she still pressured Litz to somehow purge the knowledge from her brain rather than live with something she would only be vilified for if anyone ever found out about it.

And now someone had.

Eisha didn't know. Litz's parents didn't know. None of the good friends or lovers who had fought beside her had ever known. But the dragon killer she was sworn to deliver to justice? Now *she* knew.

And Litz knew that she should be frightened of the risk, as Loren was. But all she'd felt when Mabaki had stared at her the night before, her tone more curious than denouncing, had been something like relief. Even if it was by an enemy, and it left her so very vulnerable, it was nice to be seen.

See? Fixated.

Litz rolled her eyes, smiling again before glancing at the figures still walking slower than Loren liked, their dark clothes stark against the bright sand. They'd be crossing the dunes soon. Litz wondered how the odd metal cage they'd locked Kella in would fare on that terrain.

They might have to leave it behind and force her to walk. It wasn't as though there was anywhere for her to escape to. Not that Litz would put it past her to try. *What do you think the king will do with her?*

Deal with her. Pass her to the judges.

No, I mean, really.

You should be able to best anticipate your aunt's actions.

Ha.

Loren paused for a moment, chewing on this. *The sensible thing for her to do would be to eliminate the threat*, she said eventually. *But she may decide to take risks.*

Risks?

She and the Circle have been eyeing each other unhappily for over a decade now. The balance of authority is shaky there. Eisha's young husband certainly wouldn't have understood how that balance works. They barely do themselves.

So?

The king seeks new ways to control the Circle every day. Now we deliver to her an expert in killing dragons.

Litz bit her lip, feeling the warm wind chapping it. She'd become a soldier to get away from the family scheming. *Surely, even she would not be that...*

Ruthless? I don't think she would even need to see it so bluntly. She wouldn't need to think of deploying her as a weapon, only holding her as a...resource. And you know how she loves her libraries.

A slight chill ran through her Litz. Her aunt was one of the longest serving rulers in Aelshian history. That meant that she was good at her job, well-liked by her people, and cruel when a situation demanded it. And she'd never known quite what to make of Litz. *If that's really what she plans, I don't think I'm comfortable bringing Mabaki to Aelshia.*

Would you prefer that she killed her?

Litz sighed before catching herself and laughing wearily. *I almost miss the war. I liked knowing who the enemy was.*

❖

After a day of travelling up the mountains, the roughness of Sallvayn's skin had begun to chafe at Ker's shoulder, even through his shirt.

Usually, he enjoyed travelling up around here. The wildlife seemed more interesting, there was shade everywhere, and the worst of the winds were blocked out by the mountains. The memories the scenery reminded him of as he kept near the path and occasionally passed merchants and other travellers coming down from Nayona were nostalgic too. There were the rocks he and Kella had once raced up; there he and Findan had once sat for her to teach him the names of the stars; there the place he'd once been attacked by a hungry chimera, ending their hunt for it quicker than any of them had expected. Zebenn had noticed him being dragged away with just enough time to sound the alarm and run back to rescue him. Kella had mostly been bitterly disappointed that she'd missed the chance to see it.

But after a few hours, he stopped trying to reminisce. Thinking of their now-broken group was painful, and Sallvayn was starting to lead him higher, farther away from anything he recognized. "So," Ker said, when he started noticing the sun slipping in the sky and decided he was bored after a day of mostly silence with intermittent small talk. "Your pronouns." He didn't turn his head, but already, he could feel the way Sallvayn was glaring at him. "What do you, y'know, prefer? Y'know, to be called?"

"What pronouns? Ah, we're a they. That's how gremlins think of themselves."

"But it's not like you don't have a...sex."

Sallvayn scoffed. "That would be private information."

"Well, sure," Ker allowed. "I mean, I have a friend, Zebenn. They don't feel like a man or a woman, so we don't talk about them like that."

"Ah. Then in that case, we suppose most gremlins feel that way," Sallvayn explained as Ker took a step up a large rock, looking up the hill to where rocks seemed to assemble before them like steps.

"But the way you keep saying we?"

"Oh. That's because we're a plural. We don't have only one personality. That would be a ridiculously small-minded thing to believe."

Ker tried to work this around his apparently small mind. "You have multiple personalities? And all gremlins do? Do all your personalities have other names?"

"*No*. We only acknowledge that no one body can be the same person to all people, not all the time. Humans are simpler creatures," Sallvayn continued casually, "but even you must see that. It would be stifling to remain the same person all the time."

Ker tried processing this before giving up and smiling passively.

He was hungry, he was tired, he was getting concerned about how much water he had left, and he was especially worried that Kella had already gotten herself killed, but in an odd way, he was actually having a good day. The company might not be ideal, but it was interesting, and best of all, for once, he didn't feel like he had to hide anything of himself.

Even around his family, even when he knew there could be no chance of saying or doing anything strange that might betray him, he always had to keep his emotions from running away from him, especially if they were skewing toward anger. Talking about his mother or the dragons they hunted, those were all topics of conversation almost constantly brought up, and they remained topics that made him flinch, made him go quiet. But eventually, he'd gotten better at tuning things out and copying the brave face Kella plastered on whenever something upset her.

Up here, with only a gremlin who claimed to "sense the dragon in him" for company, it didn't feel as though there was any point in worrying about how he appeared or managing his reactions. He could *relax.*

"What about you?"

"What?"

"You. You're a *man*, yes?"

"Yes, yes, I am," Ker said, resisting the urge to laugh. He supposed it was as fair a question as his own had been, but mostly, he found it amusing to be referred to as a man. Maybe because he'd never gone through any rites of passage; he'd always been his father's son, Kella's little brother, Findan's pupil, and the youngest of the group. And none of that had ever changed, nor was it ever likely to. He wasn't ever going to put himself up for that apprenticeship, and his father knew it.

"Does that mean you have a preference for women in mating?"

"Y'know, not all humans are like that," Ker said, feeling uncomfortable.

"Really?"

"I don't actually." He frowned. He'd barely even talked to Kella about this. Why was he telling a gremlin he barely even knew? "I don't think I want to 'mate' with anyone." He forced himself to keep walking as though he didn't care what Sallvayn's reaction would be.

"Not anyone?" Sallvayn said eventually.

"I don't think so. I like people. I just don't enjoy the thought of…"

"Ah. We see. We know gremlins like that."

"Really?"

"Oh yes. We just always assumed that humans were more obsessive over that sort of thing."

"Believe me, most of them definitely are." As they reached the top of the hill they'd been steadily climbing, Ker stopped, realising their trail dwindled off into a jagged cliff edge. When he looked over it, he could see no sign of a river down there. His sense of direction was worse than he'd thought. The farther they climbed, the more signs of vegetation there were, but they still hadn't seen any fresh water. "Where now?" he asked.

"We think, up the hill from here," Sallvayn said, turning Ker's head in his rough little hand to force him to face left, to where there seemed to be full-grown trees.

"Okay. Up," Ker said with a nod as he tried to adjust his pack, the weight of which was beginning to frustrate him. But Sallvayn's hiss stopped him before he could move forward. "What?"

"Listen."

Ker concentrated but could hear nothing out of the ordinary. "I don't…"

The unmistakable sound of a dragon roaring cut him off. It sounded loud, as though it was right beside them, but Ker knew firsthand how far that noise could travel. It was coming from a mile away, maybe two.

"That one isn't up," Ker said, a grin splitting his face.

❖

Growing up, when Litz had the luxury of sparring at home, she would often fight next to water or even in it, usually on a boulder half-submerged in the river by her parent's house. When the stakes became falling backward off the rock into water on a hot day, they didn't evaporate, but they certainly became less intense. She would emerge soaking wet, and her father would be staring at her to say, "Again."

Nothing else before Loren had made her feel so alive, so focused on. He wouldn't have knocked her in if he didn't believe she could pull herself out again. Ever since, the idea of training in the heat without water to be doused in after or during the fight had become unbearable. Their forest home had been dark too. Far easier to save herself from the distraction of her opponent's weapon being caught in the light.

Sparring on a desert evening avoided sparring in the hot sun, with only the campfires providing light, but falling on cooling sand was not the same as into water. So Litz did not intend to fall.

It was the third night but second evening of their journey, and she had been invited to share food with one of the younger guards she hadn't spoken to much, and that had led to this request for a sparring match. Though the attempt to include her was surprising, it was nice. As Kella had pointed out, the guards had all kept their distance so far. She was a dragonrider, and the reminder was looming over them if they ever succeeded in forgetting that detail.

But this girl—and it was difficult not to think of her as such, though she couldn't be many years younger than Litz—was an oddity for being friendly, smiling, and apparently genuine, the opposite of every Jeenobian Litz had so far met except Mabaki. There was a soft roundness to her body that reminded her of Eisha, and she held her weapon loosely, like a toy. Had there been any sign of guile, Litz would have wondered if it was part of an act to get Litz to drop her guard.

"I'm sorry. I am remiss in my command. I have already forgotten your name," Litz admitted as she drew her sword, trying not to allow much apology to seep into her voice. Her old sergeant would have bullied her mercilessly for still being a polite princess under the soldier's armour. They were starting to get attention from the other guards too. There wasn't much entertainment around, and Litz was still an oddity.

"It's okay," the girl said, smiling. Litz's sergeant definitely wouldn't have approved of her, either. She was guilty of Not Taking Shit Seriously Around a Commanding Officer. "I guess I'm only a little under your command, so that makes it okay. Corporal Anra Maello, ma'am."

"It is good to meet you properly. 'Captain' usually suffices for me." Litz curled her lips in on themselves, considering. Her sergeant wasn't here, and she was out in the middle of the desert. Which, he would say, was only more reason to maintain discipline amongst her troops. "But Litz is fine while we're not moving."

Maello smiled shyly and inclined her head. That was all the warning given before she lunged, sword grasped confidently in her right hand. "That tends to be when the action starts with our prisoner, though, heh?"

Litz narrowed her eyes and took a step out of the way. If she was in a real battle, Loren would be able to skim the mind of anyone who was truly a threat and warn of their approach, but Litz did not need that here. "She's famous where you come from, isn't she?"

Maello nodded a little as she brought her sword up to block Litz's. "All the Mabakis are, really, or—" She took a breath as she dodged, nearly tripped by Litz's footwork. "Her mother was, anyway," Maello continued, her balance somewhat recovered. "She was the last *really great*—" Her mouth clamped down like a bullfrog with too much mucus gluing its jaw together, and she stopped moving, seemingly expecting a blow she would now deserve. "I'm sorry," she said as soon as she seemed brave enough to open her mouth again.

Merciless, Litz moved in again. She wanted to snap something back in a very un-commanding-officer tone, or maybe in a very commanding officer tone and a royal one. Because Maello wasn't sorry she'd thought it; she was just sorry that she'd said it within earshot of Litz. To kill a dragon was still a game for heroes to her, whatever the law said.

"It's okay," Litz said as their steel clashed once more. Loren snorted at the lie. She always did that, zoned in on her conversations only when she could feel Litz react in a way she found amusing.

"I'm out of practice in speaking to officers," Maello admitted. To avoid Litz's last blow, she had fallen to the ground but had rolled and was back on her feet fast. "I've had nothing to do but guard the walls for weeks now. That's partly why I signed on to this mission."

Litz decided to change the subject out of pity. Around them, her troop had gathered a little closer, ringing them more tightly. For now, they were still holding off on cheering for anyone. "Is it true they used to keep witches up there?"

Maello blinked before laughing nervously but not nervous in a way that made Litz think she was lying. More like she wasn't sure how to react to Litz's witlessness. "No witches that I've ever seen, ma'am." Her next blow was almost enough to send Litz skidding back a little in the sand. It had been a while since she had fought in the dark.

"I've just heard so many stories," Litz said, parrying again, "of Malya's mysterious witch defender."

"Oh, me too." For a moment, Litz thought Maello was going to forget they were fighting and stand like they were gossiping friends meeting by chance in a marketplace. But through her jabbering, she kept her feet moving and her eyes on Litz's blade. "My cousin Alvonn swears he saw a burst of lightning come out of this man standing on the wall, and that's how no dragon ever made it through the defences."

Litz moved in again with fury.

"Back when being sent up there wasn't—" Maello was knocked off her feet again before she could finish, and this time, Litz held her blade to her throat.

"A job for rookies?" Litz asked, starting to feel petty.

Maello stiffened, confirming Litz's suspicions; the king had sent his best? Oh, of *course* he had, just as Litz's king had sent her best diplomat. But to her credit, Maello continued to smile and graciously accepted the hand up that Litz offered. "Yeah, I guess you could say that. I'm pretty new at this still." Maello smiled and brushed the sand off her uniform. "Thank you for the practice. I still need it, as you can tell."

Litz clapped her shoulder. She was still a little uncomfortable playing commander to a group of enemy strangers, but at least now she might have broken in that sandal a little. "Everyone does."

The rest of the party dispersed. It was becoming too dark to see all their faces, but Litz hoped this had helped prove that her victory against Mabaki had not been a fluke. There were more of them keeping close than before when she and Maello sat next to the fire again.

"Do you have any war stories?" Maello was keeping that smile up, but Litz was cautious to continue. Everyone had lost someone to this war. And even if she was a rookie, Maello no doubt had a clear idea of how every major battle had gone down.

"Hmm," Litz started as she took the first bite of her abandoned food. It seemed a little better than the night before, but it was still disturbingly not solid. Whoever had fed Kella had probably gotten an earful, though she had seemed quieter today, and there'd been no new escape attempts. Litz wondered why that almost disappointed her. "I'm not sure I was at any battles you might have heard of. Loren's an experienced dragon. She's not necessarily suited to fighting when she could be used for strategy."

"Strategy?" Maello said, laughter edging its way shakily into her voice.

Litz resisted the urge to pull back and walk away. "Yes, strategy."

Nodding politely, Maello allowed her to continue, though it was difficult to continue talking when her audience clearly thought what she was saying was crazy.

"We primarily patrolled the Nayona border, and there were a few scraps out there. As you'll know, the area was hotly contested throughout the war."

Are you teaching a class? Loren put in dryly.

"My brother was at the Saltplains Fort."

Litz kept her face carefully still. "You come from a military family."

It seemed to have been the right response. Maello sat up a little straighter with some pride.

"I heard about Saltplains, but I was rarely stationed so far west. And I never came as far as Malya. This week was my first visit."

"How did you find my city?" Maello asked, her smile returned.

Litz bit down on the smile that threatened to split her own face. That was almost exactly what Kella had asked her back in the market. "Surprisingly…welcoming."

Kella ate her food without a fuss. When that uncomfortably felt like giving up, she glared at her surroundings, hoping her gaze alone could break her out of her cage. And meanwhile, Captain Litz was over there ignoring her and smiling at some other Jeenobian girl's jokes.

"You guys are talking to the dragonrider?" Kella noted sullenly and started a little when the guard beside her flicked his ear to show that he was listening. Maybe he was feeling just as bored and left out as she was.

"Nah. That's just Maello. She's friendly like that."

Kella made a face, mimicking the grizzled guard, who actually wore an eyepatch, which Kella could admit was cool. "Well, it's a bad idea," she said when she finished making faces and was left with that aggravating silence. "Especially sparring with her. You can't trust what she'll do."

"The dragon slayer doesn't trust the dragonrider. How shocking," he said.

"No. I mean the dragon riding's creepy, but man, didn't you hear?"

"Hear what?"

"She's a witch. I thought everyone knew."

Kella watched him digest this with a coldness she wasn't used to. "How would you…"

"Know that?" She snorted and smirked to herself in the darkness of her cage. "Our new king talks in his sleep." If she was going down, she was dragging everyone who'd ever relied on her good-natured discretion down with her. And if she had to elaborate a little to do it? She was still the one in a cage, right?

"If the king was still lowering himself to sleep with you—"

"You're damn right he lowered himself. He was lowering himself right between—"

"...then he wouldn't be sending you out to Aelshia, now, would he?"

Kella barked out a laugh so violent, it had tears prickling at her eyes. She wondered if she seemed like she'd gone mad. Maybe she had. It probably wasn't something someone noticed happening. "Dude," she said, once she'd started to recover. "Believe me, this is all politics. It's gonna go right over the heads of you and me. But no way am I staying in this box much longer."

He was silent for a while, giving Kella a chance to attempt a few bites of food. As she swallowed, she considered how terrible she wanted to be. She could tell everyone that the last king had adopted Jev, as she'd sworn she never would, but spilling that specific secret wouldn't get her anywhere right now. And it would make her feel bad.

"What kind of witch?"

"What?"

"The dragonrider. You say she's a witch. What kind?"

Kella frowned. She'd never practiced any magic herself; the idea repelled her on a basic level, and as much as she and Findan had always been close, they'd never been able to fit easily into a master and student relationship. Findan's unwavering sternness would have Kella playing the clown whenever she didn't understand her lessons the first time, which would aggravate Findan into becoming sharper with her, and around and around they would send each other. Magic, by all accounts, was something difficult and in many cases, impossible to learn, so it was never something Kella had been interested in attempting. But she understood it enough to know that there were no "types" of witches. There were simply magic-users who had more skills. This had, of course, never stopped people coming up with nonsense superstitions about witches of the night or the sea or the sand.

But it wouldn't help her to reveal herself as knowing an above average amount about witches. "Aelshians don't like witches either," she said, keeping her voice low and careful, as though divulging all of her royal secrets slowly. "So when they let one be trained, they make sure it's *worth* it. I haven't seen her in action but..." She whistled.

"Between her and the dragon, if they decide to snap"—she snapped her fingers, and the guard flinched—"*ooh*, then we are all in trouble. Most witches direct their power through their hands, right? But this one," she said, hurrying her speech as she got lost in her own tale, "this one can light fires from her *eyes*. But there's a price for that kind of power." She went quiet, waiting to hear if she had her audience.

"Oh yeah?"

She grinned. She wasn't sure *why* she was doing this or even where she was going with her tale. Was she hoping this rumour would break her captors into factions, leaving her more wriggle room to escape? Was it pure spitefulness and a desperation to feel she had power that stretched beyond her cage? Or was she really just pathetic enough to be missing an appreciative audience already?

And did her motives matter if her methods were working? "They say witch blood doesn't even look red."

"Oh?" the guard asked, sounding considerably recovered. "What colour is it?"

She shrugged and started picking at her nails. "Well, if the dragonrider starts bleeding, you let me know."

❖

As he stretched out next to Sallvayn the first day, Ker blamed carrying Sallvayn around all day for the ache of his legs after their fruitless hunt around the mountains. He was supposed to be tougher than this. A day and a half's worth of directionless mountain hiking had exhausted him. But in fairness, he allowed as he leant on the rockface and stared at the stars that felt closer now, they weren't small mountains.

The pass to the land of Nayona from Malya was the simplest and kindest route through the mountains, and even that notoriously required a guide. The erratic, off-the-path route he and Sallvayn had taken to chase after the ever-moving dragon noises had been more wearing. With no well-worn path to follow and little shade, Ker's spirits had dropped through the day, along with his food supplies. He was trying hard not to think about that now.

Sallvayn seemed restless, but Ker was only able to guess that from their wandering eyes and from spending a whole day studying them. Gremlins didn't seem to exhibit the same clear markers of boredom as a human or bird or dog would.

"Do you know any songs?" Ker asked eventually, not tired enough to sleep and running out of things to think about that didn't involve his worried father or abandoned sister.

Sallvayn frowned but sat up a little straighter. "No. We do make music, but I am not one of those with that talent. Are you?"

Ker smiled at the fire. "I can sing okay."

That had always been his role in any journey away from home. Findan would make a plan, Zebenn would usually make the fire, Kella would cook, and Evlo, lately, would sharpen the weapons. And Ker would sing for them. Sometimes, the others would join in, and occasionally, they even volunteered to teach him new songs. Most of the old sagas he knew by heart were thanks to Findan. Zebenn knew hundreds of obscure farming songs meant to cheer up a weary crowd of workers. Recently, Evlo had taught him a strange sad song in his native tongue. Afterward, he'd explained that it was about choosing someone to grow old with but having that person die young. He had seemed very awkward when he'd brought it up and had been quiet for the rest of that night.

Sallvayn sniffed. "You should be singing. Since you brought it up, and there is nothing to eat."

Ker had almost forgotten about the lack of food. "Okay," he said before regretting it. His voice sounded very quiet, with the darkening night feeling gaping and empty. Songs usually helped with that. But what song made sense to sing to a gremlin at the end of a frustrating, lonely day journeying toward something he was terrified of?

Still thinking of the song Evlo had taught him, Ker hummed experimentally, trying to see if he could remember how the first notes should sound. There was more to it than the three verses he could remember, and he knew that his voice was tired and dehydrated, but the haunting little tune was an odd comfort as he stared at the moon, making Her his audience.

If the sollons were right, the moon and the earth had once been lovers, and all the people on the earth were their children. Ker wondered if that was true, if they missed each other. When he was finished singing, Sallvayn was staring with eyes wider than Ker had noticed on them yet.

"What?" Ker asked, feeling increasingly uncomfortable.

"That was not in your normal words, was it?"

"Uh, no. I don't really know what it means. I learnt it from a friend. He's from overseas."

"Ah. We forget that humans have so many of these languages." Sallvayn smiled slightly. "It was the strangest thing to listen to. We know that it was a sad song about a lost love, but we understood no specifics."

Ker leaned forward, resting his elbows on his knees. "Is this about what you were saying before? About me…" He swallowed. "About me being 'dragon enough' to understand you?"

"A little. You did not think we were addressing you in your own tongue, surely?"

Ker screwed up his face. He *thought* he was listening to Sallvayn speak Jeenobian, but now he was concentrating on the words he thought he'd just heard, and they weren't ones he recognised.

Sallvayn smiled toothily. "That's right. You're hearing us, and we're mostly hearing you. And we are physically speaking in a way that gremlins would understand. But from the dragons, we learnt much about conveying meaning." They trailed off and looked at the ground, seeming very human. Ker had learnt quickly that bringing dragons into the conversation tended to have this effect.

"What makes gremlins prefer dragons to humans?"

"More style."

"Heh." Ker tried to settle his blanket over himself, but he couldn't get comfortable and still didn't want to be alone with his own thoughts. Gods, on a normal hunt, that would be all he'd be craving, and he'd never get it, not even in the night, not with Evlo's snoring and Kella waking herself up every few hours, gasping desperately for breath. Sometimes, Findan wouldn't even sleep at all.

"Sall, when you said that you don't make music?"

"Yes, we did say that."

"Surely you do *sometimes*."

CHAPTER TEN

Kella didn't hate all her guards. She wanted to dislike the girl who'd fought with Litz the night before and made her laugh, but it was difficult. Corporal Maello had been walking by Kella's cage all morning, acting friendly, chatty, even, and didn't appear to be holding Kella's escape attempt of the previous day against her. She was insufferably harmless, and although she was likely the same age as Kella, she seemed to be something of a fan.

"I was actually there when you brought down the harpy swarm that was wrecking Malya, oh, three years ago?"

"I mean, I didn't exactly do it alone."

"Oh, it's the prince we remember that night." Maello smirked. Kella recognized that smile from years of watching people talk about Jev. Something about a royal title really rotted people's brains. "But I saw you. And seeing you up on that roof, surrounded on all sides and no one coming to help you, it made me want to join the army in the first place."

"Heh, that's cool. Wanna break me outta here?"

Maello laughed, and Kella had to admit that it was a nice laugh. Great big smile too. Made her eyes light up.

And Kella needed to get out of this metal box before she went completely stir-crazy and started getting attached to all her captors.

"Tell you what? I'll bring over your lunch when we stop, how about that?"

Kella raised her hands, palms stretched wide, and tensed her shoulders. "That's literally your job right now."

"Sure. But most of my colleagues probably wouldn't do it." At Kella's scowl, Maello's face softened as she continued to keep pace with the wheeled cage. "I don't think anyone here would actually hurt you. But you didn't exactly make yourself popular yesterday."

"Yeah." Kella went back to picking at one of the large scabs on her arms, pushing her sleeve back a little farther. "No one will hurt me till I get where I'm going."

Maello nodded noncommittally and looked away. "What do you think Aelshia will be like?"

Kella had been doing her best not to think about that at all. "You've never been?"

She shook her head. "The war was over by the time I'd passed training. I never needed to. My father fought out there, though. Not, like, in Aelshia itself, but on the southern border. Said he could never forget all the people cooked to death in their own armour by the enemy's dragons."

"You don't," Kella agreed quietly.

"I'm sorry. I know your mother—"

"Yeah, well. Long time ago and all that." When Maello continued to say nothing, apparently embarrassed, Kella sighed. "I've heard a lot of strange things about Aelshia. They might sacrifice me to their dragon overlords."

Maello glanced up with a mixture of fear and amusement at the dragon flying high above their heads. "She doesn't seem like a sacrificing type. Although, one of the guys did try to tell me she's a witch. But Aelshians don't like witches either, do they?"

Kella bit her lip to keep from grinning. "I wouldn't be surprised," she said, flicking a scab fleck out of her cage. "Anyway, it's probably not gonna be her personally doing the sacrificing, is it?"

"The dragon doesn't act like ours, either. They must have it really well-trained or something."

"Or something," Kella agreed. It made her uneasy watching how well-behaved the dragon had been throughout their travels. It had dutifully circled above, keeping a slow pace for the group, and had not made so much as a warning snap at anyone. It had been a lot less trouble than about half the camels they had if the curses of the soldiers were anything to go by.

It made Kella more uncomfortable than if it had just acted like a dragon because this made her wonder if it really was the dragon pulling the strings. She knew firsthand just how cunning they could be. It was a low sort of cunning, like a hyena's, but there was definitely an intelligence in all the dragons Kella had seen before. They needed to be smart; without that, they would just be wild predators and not the sun demons they really were. And there was that eerie mind-skimming ability they had, letting them predict what you were going to do before you did it.

"They look almost pretty when they're not attacking people," Maello remarked, hand shielding her face as she walked with her eyes tilted to the sky.

"Yeah. Just remember that conditional," Kella said grimly. "Loads of killers can be attractive. There's nothing mutually exclusive to it. Just look at you."

Her cheeks darkened as she looked back at Kella with alarm. "What?"

"You're a soldier, right? I'm sure you must have had to kill people before, and I bet you're good at it too."

"I…"

Kella repressed her smirk as she watched Maello struggle with her words. It made her feel a little less caged to know that she could still fluster people outside it. It had been downright fun teasing Litz. Not that there'd been much of a reaction on that front yet, not since Litz had revealed herself. That hadn't been teasing at all. Whatever Litz tried to claim, she'd put herself at risk—her life, her reputation, everything, probably—just because she didn't like the thought of her prisoner having nightmares.

It was bizarre. And maybe a little flattering too.

"Wait," Maello was saying, getting her colleague holding the reins for the camels pulling the cage wagon to bring it to a stop. She had seemingly finished being flustered and started being a serious soldier again.

"What's up? Why are we stopping?" As she looked out to her right, Kella could see sand rising with the wind, not enough to be a full-on storm but enough to be an annoyance to those people up front. She put the pieces together when the screaming started. "Shit."

"Stay here," Maello ordered as Kella curled her fingers around her cage bars.

"Literally cannot move, and hey, come back, I can help," she shouted, rattling the bars.

"Not our fault you got yourself locked up, is it, girl?"

Kella sighed heavily at the sight of Bligen, her previous paramour-cum-attacker, returned.

"C'mon. Your guys were pillocks thinking you could cross the whole desert without smarter precautions. But this is my job. Get me outta here quick, and I'll help you clean up your mess."

Bligen moved closer to her cage and grinned with horrible slowness, like he really thought he had all the time in the world. "Maybe I'll be lucky enough to clean up the mess the sand terrors leave of you."

She stared at him incredulously. "Do you have any self-preservation?"

He started to reach through the bars. "Touching as your concern is," he said, but before he could finish, he was rapidly pulled back, and his entire body was slammed to the ground.

Corporal Bligen wasn't having a lucky week, Kella noted as she leaned over and forced herself to watch the thickening sand in the air form into the shape of a tall woman. As he cursed loudly beneath the creature's foot, she grinned and pressed down hard. The sand from the ground rose into the air and seeped into all his orifices, his eyes, his ears, his nose, and as he started to scream, his mouth. As the sand inflated his body until he stopped moving, the creature winked at Kella before dissipating.

Slowly, she let go of the breath she'd been holding. Strange. Usually, sand terrors enjoyed making more of a meal of their victims, really cooking up the fear and emotion for as long as they were able, gaining all the knowledge of the lives and stories their dish had to offer. Apparently, this one hadn't thought Bligen much of a meal. But meal or not, cunt or not, he hadn't deserved an end like that. No one did.

Pulling her headscarf down and tying it roughly around her head to cover her nose and ears, Kella watched the rest of the sand terrors feed and promised herself she wouldn't become one of their victims. But this was the first time she'd ever seen so many in one place. This was a swarm.

And she was still locked up with no one coming to rescue her.

Awesome.

"Let me help," she yelled, her voice muffled through the fabric. No one turned to look. They were all ignoring her because they were too busy dying. She hoped Corporal Maello wasn't one of them. She'd been nice. "Oh *gods*. Water, you fucking idiots, they don't like water." She slumped on the cage floor that had become no more comfortable with overuse. She was going to die before Litz even had a chance to deliver her to her king. She was going to die without ever getting to see her family or friends again. Worst of all, she was going to die without being able to do anything to stop it.

When more sand blew at her face as the wind changed direction, she thought the sand terrors were coming for her next and braced herself for the worst. Until she realised it was the air being swept forward by the dragon's landing.

It had to be the first time she had ever been relieved to see a dragon. Or more accurately, she was relieved to see the woman swinging off its back, sword already outstretched. Maybe she would listen. Gods, maybe she even had an idea about how to fight these things, unlike the rest of the King's Idiots. It was getting unusual to see sand terrors at all these days, never mind so many. But on a long-haul desert crossing like this, someone should have at least considered the possibility.

Kella watched with academic curiosity as the sand terrors swarmed, unformed, over the scaled body of the dragon as if uncertain who held the natural advantage. Dragon scales were near-impervious, but trying to hurt sand terrors was like attempting to fight sand itself. It wasn't gonna work, not even for a dragon on the attack. Its flame did manage to hit one of them though, and the glass the impact formed shattered when it hit the ground, narrowly missing some of the soldiers.

It was odd. With more interesting prey to torment, the terrors left the camels alone, but for some reason, they still targeted the dragon.

Litz was watching too, but although she seemed horrified, she didn't linger. She pulled up her hood and covered her face with both hands, and at her dragon's roar, she ran into the battleground the camp had become. From twelve soldiers, only about five seemed like they could still be saved, and they were huddled in one tightly shielded ball. It wouldn't protect them for long against any concentrated effort, but they were probably safe for another few minutes. When Litz strode through the camp and started shouting, none of them showed any sign they heard.

"Over here," Kella growled out, rattling her bars again until Litz started paying attention. Despite herself, Kella's hopes rose a little as Litz jogged toward her cage. They could still survive this.

Her hands were wrenched from the bars as she was dragged away and pushed to the cell floor. When she looked up, it was her mother standing over her, mouth widening in a smile that didn't belong on her mother's face, not even when it was made of sand. Kella rolled her eyes. "Seriously? You're starting with the mami issues? Is that really the best you've got?"

Kira Mabaki disintegrated into a cloud of sand, and for a moment, Kella thought it was giving up on trying to scare her and was gonna skip straight to destroying her, but the sand began to reform as another familiar face. At the sight of her newly finished torment, Kella sighed. "I'm not afraid of my own brother, idiot. C'mon, up your game."

The sand copy of Ker shrugged and pressed his foot on her chest as if to ask, *Really?* His form began to change a little more. Although it was still recognizably him, he was growing horns from his forehead, his eyes were lengthening around his head, and scales crept over his body. Before Kella had the chance to think of some retort, the demonic figure of her brother was stabbed through the chest and dissipated.

Litz looked curiously, head tilted, at where the Ker-thing had been. "Is that what you thought I was going to look like?"

"You're late to the party." Kella grunted, ignoring Litz even as she let herself be pulled to her feet.

"Sincere apologies," Litz said dryly before hauling Kella out the door. "Don't look at me like that." She sighed as Kella raised her eyebrows suspiciously at the hand still curled around her arm. "I assume you know how to tackle these monsters if you're half as good as they say you are."

"Hey, I'm *twice* as good as people—"

"...and I know that although you want to escape, you don't want to die, and you don't want to let these people die when you could save them. Now, how do we spot them before they appear?"

Kella glanced around. "You usually hear them before they show up. And can't you just magic them away?"

Litz let go of her arm. "Don't be ridiculous. I'm not about to reveal myself, and it would use up resources I probably don't have. How would you fight them normally?"

Sighing, Kella slipped Litz's sword from her grip, stabbing through the creature that had been forming behind her. Allowing herself a smirk at Litz's shock, Kella tried to think. "Okay, first, we look for water," she said, keeping a grip on the sword. It had a nice weight to it.

"We're in the middle of the desert."

"Normally I'd tell you that you to start digging." Kella stretched, fighting the urge to sing at the feeling. "Since we're not gonna get the time to do this properly anyway, I guess we go for Plan B. Meaning, we want a different liquid. Something sticky."

Litz blinked with a confusion that would have been cute under normal circumstances.

"Human remains, putting it bluntly. Blood. That's the key ingredient to the best plan we've got."

Litz's face contorted in horror, and Kella braced herself to hear a,

"How could you?" or maybe a, "That's awful," but Litz only nodded. Despite herself, Kella was impressed. "And the water supplies we've got won't do?"

Kella shook her head and bent to pick up Bligen's sword, seeing as he'd no longer need it. "We shouldn't waste it, and blood will work better anyway. Hopefully. I've got a *different* sort of plan. But I think it'll work."

"Okay. What's the best way to keep them away and the group alive until you're ready?" Litz asked, eyes darting around, even with Kella still clutching her sword. There were no threats, no pleas, just an assurance that, for now, they were working toward the same goal.

"Keep your face covered as much as you can. Use a little of your water to make a circle around you and the others. They don't like crossing wet sand. Oh, and when they're corporeal, anything which would hurt a normal person should make them fuck off for a few minutes. And watch my back," Kella added, only a little reluctantly. "I'm good, but I'll be—"

Litz's knife came out of nowhere and stabbed at something behind Kella's shoulder. She heard the hiss of sand at her back and gulped, forcing herself to be cool enough to not turn around.

"Concentrating."

Litz gave her the ghost of a smirk before narrowing her eyes in real concentration and snatching her sword back to hurry over to the remaining guards. Maello stood from the overturned cart she'd been hiding behind and followed, and Kella had to mentally fortify herself to keep from doing the same.

Today, she had the messy witchy job to deal with, not the heroic action stuff. Because someone had to do it, and the actual witch wasn't stepping up.

❖

What was bothering Litz the most was that she hadn't expected to *lead* the soldiers she was travelling with. Had she known, she'd have ensured they were all capable of working as a cohesive unit. She would have drilled them on their weaknesses, their strengths, and most importantly, found out how willing they'd be to follow her orders, despite her being a foreigner and a dragonrider. Though she might not have established trust, she'd have trusted them to act as expected. But now, they were all trapped in what was more chaotic than a battle situation, and bar her short sparring match with Maello, Litz had next to no expectations of what she was working with.

"Everyone to me," she shouted and held her arms out, waiting, as no one moved.

"That'll make us quicker to pick off," Sergeant Adani shouted back at her. She hadn't realised he was still alive. "And why let the prisoner out of her cage?"

"Because," Litz said through her teeth as she started encircling them with a thin line of water, "she's the closest to an expert we have on these things, and her life is being threatened along with ours." As she closed the circle, water splashing from the sand to hit her ankles, Litz thrust her sword through the chest of yet another sand beast who had just materialised. This one had looked like Eisha, and she'd have been lying to say that didn't unnerve her.

But she couldn't let it because somehow, she had to trick both herself and the Jeenobians currently under her command that the thought of being buried alive from the inside out by blistering sand didn't bring her close to panic.

But she'd been in the middle of battles that looked futile. There was nothing necessarily futile about this situation, if she trusted Mabaki. And apparently, she did. If nothing else, she had faith that the dragon killer would keep killing.

As Litz kept one eye darting for more threats and the other on Mabaki, the remains of the guard gradually drew toward her. The sand seemed to be taking its time before making another strike. Litz wasn't sure if that was a positive sign or a worrying one. She didn't know enough about these demonic creatures, and that frightened her. She liked knowing what she was up against. But these things were creatures of myth to her. Rarely did she hear of anyone encountering them and coming back alive.

But Mabaki had said they would go away if you "killed" them as you would a human. And as a soldier, Litz was good at killing people. "Right. If everyone stabs at them as they would a normal enemy, the sand should temporarily disappear," she said, partly to remind herself. She got a few scattered nods in response. "And if everyone stays inside this circle, we should be safe."

"We have this at the word of the criminal we're escorting? The criminal who's already convinced you to let her out?" Adani asked.

Litz tried not to let herself think about how much smoother things might have been if he had died in that first wave of the attack.

"How do we know she didn't summon those things to kill us while she makes her escape?"

Litz found it hard to take her eyes from Kella going about the strange, blood-soaked work of cutting into her dead countrymen, but she was also listening to the pained, angry bellows of her dragon and could barely register the soldiers still talking. If the demons' tricks were all about feeding on fear, maybe this was part of the plan. Give them space to worry, to argue, to *wait*. "A Mabaki wouldn't do that," she said, hoping she'd found the right words for these Jeenobians who were technically still within their country's bounds but a long way from home.

"What she's doing looks a lot less like hero-ing and a lot more like witchcraft to me."

Litz wanted to roll her eyes but forced herself to keep concentrating on the empty space in front of her. What Kella was doing looked nothing like real witchcraft, though Litz understood why it was frightening the soldiers. Mabaki seemed to be trying to coat herself and the sword she'd picked up in the liquid parts of the dead, but the look in her eyes unsettled Litz more than the gore. She'd seen eyes like that before on battlefields, people who killed and believed in why they killed and were ready to kill again. Eyes that didn't see the dead around them unless it suited them.

It made Litz worry about what she'd released from its cage.

Now that her scarf had floated away in the sandstorm the terrors had caused, Kella had become blood-drenched to her scalp, the locs of her hair brightly stained. Catching Litz staring, she grinned before looking wildly around her. "You gonna come get me already?" Kella shouted with a grin as she bent and started covering her skin in sand.

As if the mocking really had worked, sand hissed on the air, making them all a little jumpier as it threatened to reform. And Litz was so busy watching the one shaped like the king forming behind Kella that she didn't even notice the one behind her little group until someone yelled.

"Just pretend they're a normal attacker," Litz ordered as she listened to another of the soldiers she was supposed to be leading, *protecting*, be destroyed from the inside. They must have moved outside the circle.

Or Mabaki might have been lying about that. Or wrong. Litz didn't know this woman, and she certainly didn't understand her undisclosed plan. When the blood was inside the bodies of the victims, it hadn't created any resistance for the sand demons. How was it supposed to help them now?

It didn't seem like any witchcraft Litz had ever seen, but there Kella was, dodging and lashing at the creature that looked exactly like her king, and she sounded like she was chanting. It was like a cheap imitation of what people believed witchcraft to be. Maybe when Mabaki had claimed she knew how to save them all, she'd been lying so she could get out of her cage and die on her feet. It was an insane thought, but insane hardly seemed out of character.

How are things?

Litz had to catch her breath. It took a lot to make Loren this exhausted. *Bad, I think.*

I hate these things more than monkeys and sky demons combined. Get yourself out of this, and we're never crossing the desert again.

Litz smiled briefly and tried to send some feeling of comfort through the bond. She did believe they'd get out of this alive because they always did. She just hadn't worked out how yet. Or how many people they were going to be able to keep safe.

I'm going to try flying up. I don't think these things can go far from land or their swarm. Call if you need me.

Even knowing Loren couldn't see her, Litz nodded and tried to keep her face calm as they all listened to Loren give a roar and begin flying into the air.

"Captain—"

"Stand firm and keep your mouth closed," Litz snapped, her eyes drawn to another of the sand demons, still unformed, swarming toward Kella's back. The escape attempt had proved she was good at fighting more than one opponent but not when they were coming at her from different directions. And the sand creature still crept closer, and Kella still hadn't moved, hadn't seemed to notice.

I have to do something. She's the only one able to do anything.

Join the fray if you must, but if you're thinking of revealing yourself—

"Mabaki," Litz shouted as she blocked Loren from her mind, but the roar of sand surrounding her little group of survivors was muffling her words. And probably covering and shifting the wet sand.

And all Litz wanted was to be bigger and stronger than the threats she was looking at. She wanted to be able to protect, and there wasn't any time to move, to think.

So she Acted.

Chapter Eleven

Something in the air and the ground shook for a moment, and the now familiar hiss of sand behind Kella let her know that something had either just appeared or dissipated. When she turned and saw nothing, she recognized her chance and stabbed the terror wearing Jev's face right through the heart and dropped to the ground, rolling her wet, sticky body over the sand. She stood as Findan had taught her a long time ago and addressed the sand still whispering, unformed in the air. "We will depart this place and leave this food alone. There is better elsewhere, and we are full."

It was a complex language for creatures with such undeveloped senses of themselves. But their lack of individuality was their downfall: standing covered in the sand which made them, smelling of the blood they'd just feasted on, she didn't appear as anything other than their own. And they made decisions unanimously, usually.

Though Kella held her breath for a few moments, none of them rematerialized. "Hey," she said, breathing out. "S...and that's everything." For effect, she shook her hair, letting a shower of sand briefly surround her and stretched her fingers toward the bright sky.

The soldiers stared at her, eyes glazed with confusion, and then at the empty space where Litz had been standing. She didn't look like one of the victims, so the fact that she was sprawled on her side had to be battle exhaustion. To Kella's relief, the dragon had returned to the ground and seemed to have passed out too. One less worry to factor in.

"C'mon, no applause?" Kella asked, taking a step toward the crowd of five left standing around Litz's unconscious body. "She okay or what?" As she moved closer, the soldiers all stepped back. She supposed she'd take fear and awe over them stuffing her back in her cage, but this was getting a little creepy. "I promise, they're not coming back," she assured them, looking Adani in the eye before bending to feel for Litz's pulse. When she confirmed it was still pumping healthily, Kella allowed herself a grin before looking back up at the soldiers. "Now that I've saved the day, there any chance you'll lend me one of those camels now?"

Maello watched the others' reactions and shrugged, clearly exhausted. Adani sighed out a ragged breath as he regarded the carnage the sand terrors had managed to wreak on his troops in what couldn't have been longer than twenty minutes. "We'll return to Malya," he said quietly, almost as if he wasn't aware he was speaking aloud. "If we kill the witch and her dragon now, they won't be able to follow us. With any luck, the sands will cover them, and no one will have to know how this happened."

Kella's jaw dropped, even as the five remaining soldiers seemed to find this a reasonable-sounding suggestion. "Do you want to start a war?"

He glanced at her, seeming surprised she was still there. "They're no danger now, but travelling with a dragon was bad enough. I'm not going anywhere under the command of a witch. And if we don't do something now, they could catch us, pick off what's left of us." Behind him, the five all nodded.

"Are you fucking with me here?"

He ignored her comment and continued to talk at her. "We'll return you to the king. He'll be more merciful without a dragon breathing down his neck. If you kill the dragon now, we'll finish the witch."

She didn't have time to wonder about what "the witch" had done to reveal herself, but she was curious; whatever it was it seemed to have taken it out of her. "Dragons, you know I'm all over that," she said slowly, trying to bite down her annoyance. Now that they were removed from society, they were okay with breaking the law, heh? "But people, I don't kill people. That's never been my job."

"Well, it is ours," Adani reminded her, not unkindly. "And I don't plan on drawing this out, lass."

Trying to force her lip not to tremble, she held his gaze. Half an hour ago, Litz had held Kella's life in her hands. Now their situations had been flipped, and Litz wasn't even awake to speak for herself. And maybe they'd all be less ready to jump to murder if Kella hadn't told them about Litz's magic use. Findan would tell her to get Jev's troops to Malya and slip away after they made it back. She'd be home, there'd be one less dragon in the world, and her legend would have grown.

Sent off in chains only to return as the saviour of her captors. Ballian would advise the same, but he'd be kinder in how he spoke to her. He'd remind her that nothing she did while she was under duress was her fault and that the most important thing was always that she made it home at the end of every fight.

Ker might tell her to play it smart. Her mami? She had always been a hero, and that had killed her. But none of her family were there to tell her what to do, to watch as she made her choice. She was completely alone. And covered in sandy blood, which wasn't going to be easy to get off in the middle of the desert. "But she saved you."

"*You* saved us," Maello said quietly.

"Yeah, but she could have just flown off and left us to die, c'mon."

"It doesn't matter why. It's about what she is," Adani said firmly. "You did save us. And though it would be simpler to leave you here with her, I'm not going to do that if I don't have to."

Slowly, Kella straightened until she stood once more at Adani's eye level. "Five minutes ago, you were cowering. Your people would have all died if it had been up to you."

"And we still might if it's an angry witch who wakes up in a moment. I'm sure I don't need to tell you they can cause as much trouble as a dragon or more, if they've a mind to it."

"And if we get back and I tell the king how this really happened?" Kella raised her eyebrows. "You're not gonna let me walk back into Malya knowing I might. Though, I'm betting you'll keep me around to deal with the dragon and anything else you need rescuing from, heh?"

"Now—"

Kella shook her head and took a step over Litz's limp body. Gratifyingly, Adani inched away from her. "Now what? You're all gonna gang up on me after I saved your asses? Because guess what, I ain't letting you kill a person. Especially not just because you're afraid of what you think she can do." Meaningfully, she swung her sword, gripping with two hands to keep it steady. It felt good to finally say the words aloud. Because it just wasn't in her. She was supposed to be the hero. She couldn't let, *help*, them kill someone, not when they couldn't fight back, not like this.

It wasn't fair like this.

"Leave me a camel with food and water, and I'll give you five minutes to get out of here."

One of the younger guards whose face was hidden behind his fellow soldiers dared to laugh.

"Oh, I'm sorry, do you not remember yesterday when you had twice as much backup, and you couldn't beat me?"

"Yes, but we wouldn't be playing friendly this time. We don't need to keep you alive."

Kella licked her lower lip and grinned, knowing it must look a sight with her face still gleaming crimson. "Just try me," she said, looking around them, knowing that if they attacked right now, she'd be dead and Litz with her.

At least a sand terror hadn't got her. Instead of gruesome, this was just going to be sad. Killed by the people she'd just saved over someone who, if they ever woke up, was probably still going to try to shove her back in a cage.

This wasn't how she was supposed to go out. She was supposed to go out…

…in glory and flame?

"C'mon, hurry up, or I'll call back the terrors," she added, probably too late to be believable. "I banished them. I can bring 'em back just as fast."

"Last chance, girl," Adani said, bringing forward his sword.

Grinning, Kella thrust forward. It was clumsy; she was tired, and she knew she wasn't going to win this one.

A roar from behind her distracted them all, making Kella freeze. The dragon. How had they all forgotten the dragon already? The thing about full-grown dragons was that while they didn't normally make a lot of noise, when they decided to, the sound could rattle right through the bones.

The young soldier who'd come closest to pulling his sword seemed to have pissed himself. She didn't blame him. Even at the sound of a dragon yawning, people started to cry, and this dragon was *angry*.

"Better go," Kella said quietly, forcing herself not to turn and check how close the beast was.

The soldiers exchanged fervent looks and began backing away as one. Kella smiled wearily as she watched them grab their supplies. To her surprise, they left behind both camels still attached to the cage, more than she'd originally asked for.

With any luck, the dragon would wait until the soldiers had left before eating Kella, and she could keep her pride. "Yeah, that's right, you run," she shouted after them, sword hand trembling as the dragon roared again.

Steeling herself, she slowly turned to face it. "Hey," she said, swallowing, dropping her sword. It still wasn't attacking. "Look. I'm not gonna try to hurt you. I just wanna see how your girl's doing. That sound okay?"

The dragon was a lot closer than she'd judged it to be, and the sight of those nostrils flaring made it hard to stand her ground, so she started to slowly crouch, hands outstretched, facing the dragon. She felt humiliated, but she didn't change her mind. As Jev had pointed out in what felt like a whole other lifetime, taking down a dragon alone, even a weakened one, wasn't something even she was reckless enough to attempt. Unless she had to.

When she put a hand to Litz's cheek, both eyes still on the dragon, she heard Litz whimper in her sleep. She didn't think Litz was planning on waking up any time soon. "She do this often?"

The dragon gave a low rumble, as though it really was listening and responding to what she was saying. Which was probably something she should consider. Litz had talked about it like it was smarter, and so had Findan, come to think of it, on the occasions she had mentioned her visit to Aelshia. And the old stories spoke about dragons being able to not just skim minds but to enter them, control them.

Much as that freaked Kella out, she didn't want to believe she was alone with a monster, either. "You understand what I'm saying, don't you?"

The dragon did not change its ready-to-pounce stance, but there was something about the way it was tilting its head that made it look almost like it was mocking her.

"I'm going mad," Kella said to herself. "I'm going to die alone in the middle of the desert doubting my own sanity."

You're not going mad, you're learning, although I can understand why the two might seem interchangeable to you.

Kella gasped and scrabbled her fingers through her bloodied hair, her other hand clutching her chest, trying to reconcile herself with what she'd just heard, what she'd *felt*. Because she hadn't actually heard anything, but she knew someone had just *meant* the words at her, really hard. She felt sick and wondered briefly if maybe everyone thought dragons couldn't talk because their minds were too tough to ever let them in.

Maybe this weakness was a family thing.

I find this repulsive, believe me, the dragon said because it had to be the dragon. There was no one else there, and it was still staring her down, creepy and unblinking with its huge fucking eyes. *But I know that for whatever reason, you want her to get better. So do I. Make it happen.*

A slight grunt followed the words, and for a moment all Kella was capable of was staring. She felt as though her whole world could be crashing down around her, like the day her mami died. But her mami, she would have told Kella to deal with the job in front of her before she freaked out about anything else.

And the job right now was to look after Litz. She could examine the reasons she'd made it her job later, the most urgent reason being that this dragon would probably kill her if she didn't show that she could be useful. "What did she do to take this much out of her?"

The dragon snorted, making Kella flinch. *She was worried for you, so she destroyed three of the creatures, I think. To keep them from killing the soldiers and killing you.*

Kella swallowed and nodded, looking properly at Litz's face for the first time. She'd thought it would be something like that. "Can't you help her? Through your…" Kella made a face and tapped above her ear.

The last thing she did before using her strength was block me out. She knew I would have tried to stop her. The dragon appeared to finally decide that Kella was of no immediate threat and slumped to the ground. *I can give her shade, though,* the dragon added and stretched a wing above them.

Kella couldn't help it. She looked up, and there it was.

Yes, I am vulnerable around the join of my wing. But make no mistake, it would be the last bad decision you ever made. The show the dragon made of baring her teeth kept Kella quiet as she shuffled farther under the shade the wing provided.

Water. Even if they were both healthy, they would need water after fighting in this heat. And the soldiers had left them a considerable amount, being too busy fleeing for their lives to think about preserving them.

Right. She could manage that, she thought, forcing herself to her feet without meeting the dragon's gaze. The mind-talking thing she could just about let slide, partly because it was weird enough to pretend she'd imagined it. She just wished she could pretend away the intelligence in those eyes.

Chapter Twelve

K ella knew that Ballian had been hoping Ker would train as a healer for some time, and she understood why. If he continued hunting, healing would be an invaluable skill for both him and his team, and it could be very lucrative knowledge in knowing what to stock for the shop if he remained there. But most of all, Ker had a wonderful manner with people who were ill or vulnerable. He'd perfected this wonderfully measured, firm yet reassuring tone from years of having to deal with Kella when she was drinking. She could only imagine that Ker helping at a sickbed would be a great comfort.

She did not have one of those tones. "Hope I get some real fucking appreciation whenever you wake up," she muttered to Litz's sleeping form as she dug a knife she'd liberated from one of the corpses back into the dirt. She had to speak to Litz as if she was awake. She didn't like remembering that her captor was asleep and vulnerable.

The thing was, Kella hadn't saved many people throughout her career. Oh, she'd pushed onlookers out of the way a handful of times or helped with evacuations, but usually, as with the dragon she'd been arrested for killing, her team heard of some kind of disaster that had already happened, and that put them on the trail of a specific beast. Kella was far more likely to be the instrument of vengeance rather than rescue. She certainly didn't hang around to find out how those she helped managed afterward. Someone else would have the job of playing caretaker. She didn't watch them sleep and worry about them waking up.

The dragon was sleeping now too, or at least Kella hoped she was, but she'd still managed to keep her wing outstretched to shelter them. Since the dragon had been ignoring her after their initial conversation, Kella had grown brave enough to stand and tend to the bodies. She didn't want any of their things going to waste if it was something they could use, and she definitely didn't want to find herself surrounded by curious scavengers or insects. Or move on while being tailed by spirits angry at their ill-treatment.

Despite the fact that she'd removed most of the excess blood from her body, at the expense of her skin, now rubbed raw from sand, Kella still had insects circling her. It wasn't lifting her mood. It was the sound of wings that drew her from the dragon's protective shade. Though she still didn't trust it enough to keep her back turned, it wasn't what she was looking at, but at something smaller, more feathered, and far more aggravating.

In hindsight, Kella should have expected harpies. They loved creeping around where dragons had been, like opportunistic little fish following a big shark. But harpies weren't complete carnivores. They seemed interested in whatever was easily available. She'd rarely seen them around noisy town centres, but on the outskirts, they constantly stole fish from boats, maize from carts, chickens from pens, and bins from street corners. As Maello had reminded her, Kella had once fought a handful of them determined to fly off with a whole food cart, causing chaos one market day.

They didn't really hunt in packs, but still, it was rare seeing one alone, especially one so young. Its grey feathers were still fluffy where they reached its neck and the part of its anatomy Kella had never been able to stand looking at.

"Two-faced bitch of a harpy," Kella remembered hearing her mami say under her breath about Findan after one of their biannual blazing rows. She'd called Jev the same the other day. Because that was the thing about harpies. Like some kind of insect faking a predator's eye on its wing, harpies had a wide, high casque on top of their heads, overhanging their large parrot beak, and it looked like a crude mask of a human face. They didn't all look the same. Some had their human mouths open or the eyes narrowed. But it wasn't just the head that completed the grotesque effect; harpies also had spindly little black arms which dangled from their feathered torso. As far as Kella knew, these were functionally useless, but they completed, at a glance, the effect of a human child with wings.

This one's chosen prize was one of the guards Kella had seen around but had never caught the name of. The harpy bent with that huge beak that could crack coconuts and bit off the corpse's nose.

"Hey," Kella yelled, stepping forward heavily. Sometimes, that was enough. They were only scavengers, after all.

But apparently, this one was bold and stupid as well as young. "Hey," it croaked. Which was the other thing about them being metre-high parrots. They were mimics.

Kella really, really hated them. She took another step forward over the bloody sand, sword out as the harpy returned to its awful pecking. The sand terrors hadn't left much of the man's eyeballs behind, but what there was wouldn't be there long. "Any help here?" she yelled over her shoulder. *I'm asking a dragon for help,* she registered dully through her heat-addled brain, keeping her eyes fixed on the harpy's false face and not its bloody beak.

"Any help here?" the harpy called back before taking a bite of cheek and gulping it down its exposed throat.

Kella was glad she did not know the dead man's name, gladder still she did not know how he would have acted had he lived through the terror attack.

The dragon's response was no shrill attempt at mimicking human speech but more measured. *Why should I care what takes the battlefield scraps?*

Because they were people. They're not scraps. With that, Kella charged with a roar, reaching for the small knife once again holding up her hair, and flung it at the harpy. She missed the chest, but the knife lodged deeply in the harpy's wing so that when she jumped at it, the creature was unable to fly off. They landed together. Kella was not usually one for depending on her fists, but having dropped her sword, she hit the beast until its false face fell off and hit the ground with a thud.

She kept hitting until her knuckles bled, and the creature lay limp beneath her. She took a long breath in and asked the empty air, "Do you eat harpy?" There was a long pause, and she wondered if the dragon had lost interest in her.

Maybe later.

She smiled toothily at the sun. It was good to fight for an audience again. Even if that audience was a dragon. Right.

Is it harder for you to kill creatures that look human?

Groaning at the creak in her knees, Kella stood and looked at her fallen foe. It didn't look human anymore. "No," she said, not turning. After brushing the sand off her knuckles, she reflexively gave her wounds a lick. She had never considered herself spiritually minded, but she couldn't have left the bodies she'd cut apart and stripped of their possessions to rot slowly in the sun. So she spent a few long, hard hours hauling them into graves carved into the hard dirt, dug shallow in the heat, murmuring over each one, "To the Earth you return, to the Earth you return, to the Earth you…"

To reach the Earth Mother, they had to be facing down, and to remind them not to speak on their long journey, they needed to be buried with a peach in their mouth. Kella didn't have any peaches, and she wasn't sure she would have wanted to waste them on the dead if she had, so instead, they were gagged with balled strips of clothing, even Corporal Bligen. He was dead now, so what happened to him next would have nothing to do with Kella.

Though the task gave her something to do other than thinking about running, she couldn't stop her mind wandering in the direction of her mami. There'd been nothing left of her to bury, in the right way or otherwise. But surely, the Earth Mother would not be so unkind as to ban her from their realm, and Kira Mabaki wouldn't have given up easily. Sure, it might have been harder to get wherever it was she needed to go, but she'd have gotten there.

She hoped the dragon wasn't listening to these thoughts.

She was well aware that one of the more popular myths that had sprung since her mother's death was that she hadn't really died at all but had simply disappeared to return home. The people who believed that thought of Kira Mabaki as the Earth Mother incarnate to teach the value of hope, fortitude, and hard work to her children above. Kella had never been sure what this scenario made her and Ker.

She's still not waking, the dragon observed as Kella returned to the shade of the wing and laid the back of her hand on Litz's forehead. Shuddering at the feeling of those words being seared into her brain, Kella looked at Litz's sleeping form, attempting to ignore the dragon shifting above them. *She'll need water.*

"Yeah, well. Tricky to get that to her when she won't wake up. You watched me splash water in her face, but that didn't exactly work out, either."

Do something. There was desperation tinging that voice's calm authority.

"You really care, don't you? About her."

Obviously.

There were a lot of good reasons Kella had never considered dragons caring for humans. She'd assumed the relationship between dragons and dragonriders was somehow all about control. She'd just never made up her mind about who was really holding the reins. She ran her fingers carefully over Litz's hair. Ballian used to do that sometimes for her when she was sick, but it was different when the woman had less hair than Ker. "We could tell stories. Try to make you feel better. Do dragons tell stories?"

Not like humans do. You wouldn't even understand my explanation of them.

Kella made a face and was relieved the dragon wasn't directly looking at her.

I can see you.

Returning to stabbing at the sand, Kella pouted. "Okay, I get it, I get it, you're the big bad dragon in charge. Me small human, causing no trouble."

Damn right.

Despite her best efforts, Kella's snarl quickly became a smile.

Litz never thought much about her uncle Denone when she was awake, but he turned up in her dreams frequently. In some ways, that suited him better; when she did think of him, he was always changing, never solid, never seeming real even when he'd been right there in front of her, showing her how something worked.

"Sometimes, to concentrate, you may want to focus so completely, you stop hearing your dragon, stop hearing your world. It will help the magic flow easier," he was saying again, arms spread wide, gesturing at a world Litz's unconscious mind had not filled in the details for. "But be careful. Doing this on too little strength could render you…asleep?" As it always had, his voice hesitated over words his Irehnonian accent struggled with pronouncing. "And after being asleep like that, my dear, it could be very difficult to wake again."

Litz nodded at him, smiling. She was vaguely aware that she should be listening better to what he was trying to tell her, but it was difficult to summon any urgency here. She felt completely calm, completely herself, for once not needing to struggle to allow her own thoughts to be heard over the strength of Loren's. She had nowhere to be, she just needed to…she just…

She was doing something. No, she *had* been doing something. There'd been a battle.

Litz didn't often dream of battle. Loren was right; that time in her life had largely been a happy one, whatever that said about her. But some things were impossible to remember fondly, even if flying out on Loren in the early morning into an empty sky was exhilarating no matter the context. And obliterating a threat to her troops was satisfying. If she thought much about it, it was better than winning a battle. It was removing the need for one.

Mabaki had asked if she was familiar with the smell of human flesh, and she was; of course she was. It never left her mind, much as she usually did her best to retreat into Loren's during the events causing it. This time, the dream was showing her she had been in the air, but she was also somehow on the ground, one of those coating the enemy tents in alcohol. She was up close to watch the surprise on faces she couldn't have seen before. They had expected the fort they were approaching to be abandoned. They hadn't known it was still in a dragon's sights and therefore, still held. And now defended.

Loren angled her wings down, catching the air and riding it into what remained of the camp. Burning was not a quick way to die. And with the shifting logic of dreams, Litz was again on Loren's back, swooping far lower than they had in reality to personally eviscerate those lucky enough to begin fleeing, those who had survived being burned in their sleep. They hadn't bothered tormenting the remainders of the enemy company. After all, regrouping seemed impossible, but they did now. If they had working eyes left to see it, a dragon's unstoppable fury and power would be the last thing they saw.

My brother was at the Saltplains fort, Maello had said, and now here she was, not a relative with her face, just Maello. Litz watched her pull herself from the ashen, bloody ground to stand straight in time for her face to change and become Kella. She was still unarmed, her clothes singed, but she stood with her hands on her hips, like she believed her small body was enough to prevent even a dragon from touching her.

Stop! Litz begged, reaching to Loren on instinct, no longer sure who she was afraid for. When Loren reached back, pulled her into the present, Litz opened her eyes with a gasp.

Welcome back, idiot.

Loren?

You nearly died. Apparently, I can never let you out of my sight in a battle situation ever again.

When something took a grip on Litz's arm, one of the only parts of her not aching, she swerved to look, tensed for another attack.

"Hey, *hey*. Chill, dragon witch. Danger's long gone."

Litz narrowed her eyes to focus better on what she was seeing. "Mabaki?"

"Gods, you'd think we'd have made it onto a first-name basis by now. Yeah, it's me, your dedicated nursemaid. Here, drink this," she said, pushing a container into her hands.

It's safe, Loren assured her, but Litz was already downing the contents.

"How long have I been out?" she managed eventually, feeling drool roll off her bottom lip.

"We were attacked in the morning, right? The sun's starting to set now, so…"

"Are the rest dead?"

Kella laughed, but she still looked tense, like she might spring back at any moment. She kept her hand gentle on Litz's arm, though. "Might be. They ran off home after some persuasion from me and your big friend."

Mostly from your big friend.

"Not much gratitude from Jeenobian soldiers, then."

"After they saw *how* you saved them? Oh honey, you'd be digging for heaven there."

"I meant for you," Litz said, trying to sit up a little straighter and finding her head was still scrambled, her vision blurred. The magic was like a muscle, Sandrez had always said, and she'd barely exercised it in months before lifting all these metaphorical weights. "What do you mean by that, anyway?"

"Heh?"

"Digging for heaven. I've not heard that before."

"Oh. It's a figure of speech like, uh," Mabaki scrunched up her face completely, which seemed to be a common reaction to her thinking her way through a problem. "Like it's sweet that you're trying or hoping, but it's probably never going to get you anywhere."

"Is it related to your Alpick Mines?"

"You've heard of those? Yeah, that's where the phrase comes from. My uncle, my stepfather's brother, he's actually one of the miners."

"Really? They're still running?"

"Well, sure." Kella grinned wearily and leaned back, taking her hand away at last. "Still enough idiots wanting to believe they can just mine their way down to the Earth Mother, so the mines still run. It's like a holy quest to them still. Less of them than there used to be, though."

You were right. The Jeenobians are *stranger than ordinary humans.*

Litz smiled but ignored this. "You didn't go with them."

"The miners?"

"The soldiers."

"I mean, yeah. Sitting right here, so…"

Litz was still feeling a little wobbly, and Kella really did have a very pretty smile. Her officer training was supposed to prepare her for any eventuality so that no matter the situation, she could at least look like she was in control. But she wasn't sure there was much of a precedent for this.

No way to do it wrong, then.

I don't know what to do, Litz admitted to herself and Loren.

I know. Neither do I.

And there Kella was, looking at her with a strange, grim fondness. Litz definitely didn't know what to do with that.

"You're talking to each other again." Kella shuddered. "I don't know how you do it all that time. It feels like you've got a ghost walking through you."

I had to connect to her while you were out. Neither of us treasured the experience.

You were able *to connect with her?*

A mental shrug came through from Loren. *I took what I could get. She was less unpleasant than that river town politician you made me speak with last year.* Loren's shudder at the memory echoed back through Litz, forcing her to smile.

She gave Kella a closer look again. She didn't seem noticeably changed as a person. "Now you've felt Loren's mind on yours, do you still think her an evil beast?"

Kella shrugged and leant back, letting her hands provide support. "Not sure," she said, eyes darting to Loren. "I'm not regretting my whole life's work, if that's what you're asking."

There was a slight defensive waver to her speech that made Litz unsure how much she was telling the truth. Whatever she might be feeling, she didn't look certain about it.

"I suppose we'd better start making up something like a shelter for tonight," Kella said as she got to her feet, hands assuming their familiar position on her hips as she scanned the camp like a meerkat. "They took the tents with them. I checked already."

Litz followed her gaze. "You buried the bodies."

Kella wouldn't look at her. "Course. Wasn't just gonna leave 'em lying out like that, was I?"

Litz might have. She'd seen many battlefields in her not-so-long career as a soldier, and a person didn't come out of that without quickly gaining pragmatism in how they thought about death and the dead. At least while they were still standing in the field. But she nodded and looked at the dunes awaiting them. They seemed to stretch above Loren as though to be purposefully intimidating, advertising that they were as cruel as the terrors and less likely to be reasoned with. "Loren should provide most of the shelter we'll need, but check if there's any food around. We'll start flying in the morning."

Kella raised her eyebrows. "Uh, no. *We* are not going to be flying anywhere. Ever."

"I am grateful to you for saving me," Litz said slowly, hand shifting to hover above the knife at her hip and feeling Loren tense behind her, "but we have to get somewhere, and I gave my word that the somewhere would be Aelshia. I'm sorry, but I'm not just going to—"

Kella tossed her head back, making the beads strung into her hair jangle. "Ugh. Okay, so I get that a little heroism wasn't about to dislodge that law-and-order stick you've been ramming up your ass your whole life. You still wanna try doing your duty and take me in? Fine. Have a go. But I'm not *flying* anywhere."

Litz blinked sand out of her lashes, deciding to ignore the comment about the stick. "You suggest we continue walking through the dunes?"

Kella folded her arms. "I'm not suggesting anything. I'm telling you that I am never going to be flying anywhere on a thing like that." She nodded at Loren, eyes narrowed. "No offense."

"You're still outnumbered here. If I—"

Kella barked out a laugh. "Just basking in the gratitude now. Look, I'm just saying that if I think you're going to try to fly me somewhere, I promise I'm gonna find a way to kill myself first." Her smile was bright, and her eyes were burning. "You know I can be resourceful."

Litz held Kella's gaze as she got shakily to her feet. "I can't believe you. You can't admit that the crimes you were imprisoned for might have made you wrong about something, and you refuse to conquer your fear—"

"Hey!" Kella growled, her arms firmly folded now. "I don't hear you regretting all your past sins."

"*My*—"

"Yeah. The magic I don't know much about, but the soldiering..."

That mocking smile curled into a sneer. "Don't stand there expecting me to be begging your forgiveness when we both know that you must have killed more people than I've even *seen* dragons. And those were my people you were killing. So don't try acting the precious moonbeam now, *Captain*."

Strange that such rage from a prisoner came as a surprise, but it did shock Litz to hear all that venom dripping off Kella's tongue, so much that she almost didn't notice Loren growling to her defence.

"Oh, give it a rest. Let her fight her own battles," Kella spat at Loren, leaning toward her with no hesitation. "Or if you've been listening, maybe you do want to make this your fight. In which case, I mean, come at me," she added with a smirk as she drew a small knife and twirled it in her right hand. "Maybe you wanna know if you're the one dragon tough enough to survive me."

Litz was about to grab her wrist to shake the knife out of her hand and the feral grin off her face when Loren touched at her mind. *Your 'prisoner' is baiting me. She did say she wants to die.*

"Okay, awesome. Just talk about me while I'm standing right here, that's cool. No worries, guys." She blinked and stared harder at Loren. "Wait, are you still in my mind?"

No.

It was very difficult for dragons to stretch their mind to more than one person at once, and the fact that Loren was projecting herself, tiring herself, for such a petty reason, made it difficult for Litz not to laugh.

"Oh, you think this is funny?" Kella yelled, rounding on Litz again. "Guess I know where all the creepy mind control stories come from now." She spat on the ground like that finished the conversation.

Litz sighed and started moving toward her. "I never—"

"No. I get it, I'm still someone's prisoner. That doesn't mean you're making me anyone's slave." And still sneering, Kella sat on the ground, crossing her legs. "This prisoner's staying grounded."

Litz sighed heavily, still uncertain how to proceed. "We'll make camp, cook up something to eat," she said slowly. "Will you promise to stay with me without a fight while Loren hunts?"

No.

You must. I know you've eaten nothing since we left, and the farther we go into the dunes, the less food there will be.

Actually, I ate a harpy earlier.

A harpy?

Your dragon-killing pet found me lunch. Not much eating on those things, though. But that won't need to be a problem if I'm flying over the dunes in days.

Please. I think we need this space for now.

"Why would you trust me at my word?"

"Is it important?" Litz asked wearily, rubbing at her temples. "I'd like to hear you promise. Can you give me that?"

Kella stared, looking distrustful and more than a little confused. "Fine," she said dully after hesitating a moment. "But only because I feel sorry for you. You're too floppy to fight anything right now."

"Oh, believe me, my ability to fight has not been impaired."

Kella snorted and turned away. "Sure."

If I do leave the two of you alone, are you going to hurt her?

No promises.

Hmph. Be careful. That one has madness in her eyes, and you are tired.

I want to talk to her, and I don't think she'll talk with you here.

Loren turned her large head slowly and looked Kella, who had her chin raised and her eyes narrowed. *Fine. But I won't be far. Call for me. No more blocking yourself off.*

I can promise that.

"Fine," Kella said as Loren very slowly started to turn away and flew off. "How well can you cook, Princess?"

❖

Kella, to the surprise of almost everyone who thought they knew her, enjoyed cooking. It was about the only skill that Ballian had ever tried to impart that had stuck in more than a rudimentary sense. She was uncomfortable with sums, and attempts at writing frustrated her, but she could still make something tasty out of the meanest of raw materials.

One of her earliest memories of living with her stepfather had been when he'd started to understand that she would reliably sit still only when she was waiting for food and forced her to watch him prepare it. The delicious smells, so alien after her early life on the road, would hold her there, and eventually, it became something she loved taking part in. Not just because she could see how happy it made Ballian but because it was nice to have something to share that was only theirs.

Whenever her mami went away and Kella had been unable to think of anything but her coming home safe, Ballian would take her small hand in his large one and lead her to the shelf of cookbooks and methodically choose a recipe which would take them all day to get through. Almost twenty years later, it was still something she used to calm her nerves, to stop herself from thinking too far ahead.

For the first time since she'd been put in Jev's dungeons, she let herself wonder about Ballian's reaction to any of this, and she wondered how Ker had broken the news. She'd been trying not to think of Ballian most of all. Everyone else had the power to do something about the situation Kella was stuck in, but he wasn't a warrior. He was a shopkeeper and amateur scholar with only one good leg, who still started crying whenever anyone brought up her mami in front of him. This could break him.

"Are you crying?"

"I'm chopping onions. Of course I'm crying."

"Would you like me to help you with—"

"No, back off." Kella sighed and rubbed her eyes that were only slightly damp. She wasn't crying. "Sorry," she added before catching herself. "Wait, I saved your life today, you're still dragging me off to a probable death, and I'm cooking you dinner. You get no apology." When she looked up, she found that she'd drawn out something close to a smile from Litz.

"I'll admit, I expected you to be more difficult. But you did offer."

"I don't trust your cooking. You're royalty, *and* you're a soldier. I've never heard of either of those cooking for themselves." Not as difficult as expected? Kella wasn't sure whether to be ashamed or proud of that. True, she was fighting hard to keep her anger hidden, and she'd always been a passable enough liar. But currently, all she had left in her was rage, simmering so shallow beneath her skin that surely, it would burn Litz if she decided to touch her. She was amazed it wasn't visible.

Most of that anger was still directed at Jev. He'd turned on her as she'd never been capable of doing to him. He'd sent her away, passed judgement on her for doing something he'd once admired her ability for. And though she was fighting it, she was angry with her family too. She hadn't planned on the feeling, but there it was. Evlo hadn't even been with them that long, and she knew she wouldn't have thought twice about coming after him in a flipped situation. There should have been some sign of them by now if any of them had been trying to reach her at all.

And of course, she was furious with Litz. For keeping her in a cage and only letting her out when she might be useful, like a muzzled dog; for coming to Jeenobi with her dragon and the uneasy questions of what made it so different in the first place; for giving Jev a choice he could live with; for daring on top of everything to be someone worth saving. The fucking gall of the woman.

But mostly, if Kella was mad with anyone, it was herself. She could have quit hero-ing for two seconds and just let them kill Litz. It wouldn't have been hard. Carrying a sword around was a strain on the wrists, no matter what name she had following her own. Setting it down was always a relief.

And she hadn't.

"I can cook adequately."

Kella snorted and concentrated on getting all her onions in the pot. "Let me guess, you make a mean stew." When she got no answer, she smirked.

"They were really going to kill me, weren't they?"

"That's what they said."

"I know, but..." Litz sighed. "I'm sorry. It's just, it's odd. It's something people just hate so much. It scares me, trying to understand that."

Kella shrugged. Again, she wanted to be mean, to poke at that ignorance, that naivete. But again, she found it hard to reach for any cruel words. "People hear all sorts of stories about entire kingdoms in the north ruled by witches," she found herself saying, her voice steady. "That scares them. Not everyone grew up wanting to be a magic-user."

"I didn't."

"Mm?"

"I grew up wanting to be a librarian."

Kella laughed and walked over to grab the cured meat she'd found in one of the dead soldier's leather sacks. "Huh. Your book earring? Yeah, well, I wanted to be a pirate. But turns out, I get seasick in a rowboat, so that was another heaven dig."

Litz smiled, clutching her cup of water tightly, and in the increasing darkness of the evening, her teeth flashed dazzlingly bright. "I imagine your king might have had something to say about that."

"Oh, he tried to give me a good long lecture on civil responsibilities when I told him about that. But soldier's a long way off librarian. What happened there?"

"I still like books."

"You'd get on great with my stepfather if you could both get past the dragon thing."

"Yeah?"

"He really loves reading. Got that bug in my brother too. I think the shop's just a cover to have somewhere to keep the books."

"Your brother's your half brother?"

"Yes," Kella said, tone sharpening slightly. Gods, why was she even having this conversation? Because she was lonely, homesick, pathetic over a pretty face, and the talking dragon had rattled her whole reality, she supplied for herself and scowled. "Not that it matters."

"Sorry, I didn't mean to—"

"Nah. S'fine. So you're an only child?"

"Is it so obvious?"

"*Oh* yeah."

Litz snorted. "I am. But Eisha and I grew up like sisters. Neither of us was close in age or, well, close at all with her older sister, so we were the royal children together."

"The crown princess a bit of bitch, then?"

"She's been training under her mother to be our country's next leader before she could walk. She's a lot more than 'a bit' of anything."

Kella grinned. "Ah, royalty. But her little sister's all right?"

Litz met her eyes with a knowing smile. "You're hoping this marriage will work out for them as much as I am, despite everything. You still care about him."

"Of course I do. He might have literally thrown me to the fucking dragons here, but he's still grieving and doing it badly."

Litz nodded. "His mother's death came unexpectedly, I understand."

"Yeah. It hit Jev hard. She was amazing, the old king. She always thought I was a bad influence, but I think she kinda liked me for it," Kella said with a smile. "And, like, one minute she was there, alive, *fine*, and the next, he was the king and arranging her funeral. And it wasn't just her he had to deal with. There was also—" Kella stopped herself. There was making conversation, and then there was Talking.

"There was also?"

"Guy in our team. Rall. He was maybe forty? He got his legs ripped off and bled out in the sand a few weeks after the king snuffed it. And course, Jev wasn't fighting with us. He was up at the palace playing the dignitary." Kella hoped Litz assumed it was a dragon. It could have been a dragon. Gryphons were usually easier for a smaller group to take down; it would have made more sense for it to have been a dragon. But life didn't always make a lot of sense.

"Do you blame him for it?"

Kella scoffed. Of course she did, almost as much as she still blamed herself for not being faster, not being smarter, for not being the one it had gotten instead. "What'd be the point in that?" she said instead. "He had someplace he needed to be, all of us knew that. But he blamed himself. And I just knew that he was gonna do something stupid. Like either training up the whole army to do our job for us or what he actually did and—"

"Banning it. Restricting you."

"Yeah."

Litz said nothing for a few moments and only watched as Kella deposited the chopped meat in the pot and started stirring it in. "I think they might be a good match."

"What, the onions and—"

"Your king, my cousin." She smiled with only a little hesitation. "It sounds as though they'd both do whatever it takes to get what they want, but lucky for everyone else, that's not usually a bad thing."

Kella smiled tightly into her pot. "That what makes a good couple, heh? Similar mindsets?" Looking up, she was gratified to see that her words had succeeded in flustering Litz.

"I suppose I wouldn't really know."

Kella could still see the weakness there, the hesitance, and her impulse was to pounce on it, to tear this woman who still claimed control over her body to shreds, to bring up the marketplace. But for some stupid reason, she only shrugged. "Me neither, I guess. My mami and stepda made each other happy. But I think they made each other miserable almost as much."

Litz looked as though she wanted to say something to that but caught herself and only shifted to lean on her knees. "What're you making?"

"Not decided yet."

"That doesn't sound very—"

"Did I ask for a kitchen helper?"

Litz pouted moodily, looking about six years old. Then, for some reason, she looked up, bending her neck back and said, "Sky is blue."

"*What.*"

"Do you not know this game?"

"You want to play a game? Maybe I should just take my chances running off on that camel."

"I would still stop you," Litz put in casually. "Or Loren would catch you. Or you would run off the wrong way and die of thirst."

"Not if—"

"C'mon, it's fun, I promise. I say, 'sky is blue,' and you say something like, 'Blue is ocean,' and then I'd say, 'Ocean is vast,' and you could say—"

"Vast is my boredom."

Litz beamed, teeth glinting. "See, you get it. You really don't have this game in Jeenobi?"

"We like playing games that are actually fun."

"Like that game the other night?"

"Mm-hmm. Classic."

"That was a stupid game."

"You're only saying that because you loh-ost," Kella sang, not looking up from her pot. If she concentrated on the cooking, she could almost pretend that Litz was a new onetime hunter out with them. That the rest of her crew was away for now, but they'd be back. She wanted so badly to pretend something was still normal, just for a minute.

"I only lost because you *cheated*."

"A soldier who fights fair? Now *that's* stupid."

"No, that's sporting."

"That's even stupider."

"That's not a word."

"Oh *gods*, shut *up*."

❖

Litz enjoyed her meal more than any she'd had since leaving Aelshia, a feeling that lasted even once she worked out that that the name Kella had given it roughly translated as, "Cuisine Who Cares What You Call It."

Actually, she'd wanted to smile at that but had resisted the urge.

The fact was, despite Litz's attempts to ignore it, Kella was *likeable*. She'd saved Litz's life now, which, if anything, should be the factor most affecting Litz's loyalties, but she was a soldier. People saved and ended lives constantly, so although she was grateful, it wasn't a novel experience, and therefore, still easy enough to set aside.

But Kella's charm was far harder to ignore. She believed she might be put to death at the end of their journey, and she spent their time alone together telling jokes, cooking, and helping Litz set up a rough sort of stand-in tent with a few blankets and sacks left behind. She didn't make any kind of fuss but looked at Litz in a way that set her so off-balance, she was certain Kella was doing it on purpose.

"Can she still hear you from here?"

Litz looked up from their small campfire she hadn't realised she was staring at. "What?"

"Your dragon. Can she hear you talking at her from here?"

"My dragon has a name, you know."

"I remember." Kella kicked with one foot, nudging the legs Litz was keeping drawn tight to her chest. "C'mon. Tell me if she'd know if I tried to kill you and run off right now."

Litz tried to squash the uneasiness squirming in her chest at the grin Kella flashed her. "Something about the fact that you risked death to protect me takes something out of that threat," she lied.

"Liar. You have no idea what I'm gonna do next because *I* haven't even figured out what I'm gonna do next."

"I believe that. But to answer your question, yes, if I tried to contact Loren now, she would hear me, but it's more difficult for us to hear what each other's thoughts are if we're not trying."

"Right. She can't do that with me, right?"

Litz blinked, then had to squint a little to make out Kella's expression. "What do you mean?"

"Your giant fire-breathing lizard. She couldn't just push into my mind like that again, could she? Not from wherever she is now."

She couldn't help herself. Litz shifted forward and had to smile. "You're really worried about that?"

Kella stared like she'd grown a second head. "Well, yeah, it's creepy, and I don't understand it. But I guess I'm trying to understand it. What's the point of you if your dragon can take over just anyone's brain for a chat?"

What Kella was asking was common knowledge for even the smallest Aelshian child, but for some reason, Litz still hesitated in explaining it. Perhaps it was the memory of how Kella had been so boastful before about knowing everything she needed to do the job she did. Telling her any more about dragons would feel like a betrayal, although Litz wasn't certain who she thought it was against. She couldn't imagine Loren would care. "You understand that dragons aren't group creatures, pack animals like we are. Like, how eye contact with a dog is fine, but a cat will take it as a challenge."

"Really?" Kella nodded, apparently bouncing this new information through her mind. "I guess that's why cats never like me."

"Just because dragons can talk to anyone doesn't mean they like talking in the same way we would."

Kella frowned. "All right. Like how some people smoke because it calms them down, and some people do it because it makes them look cool."

"Yes. Communication for humans is necessary to stop us from going mad. We don't usually need to say something every time we do, but we do it anyway because we take some enjoyment from it. Dragons sometimes might but not as often. Most 'conversations' they have with other dragons can be expressed entirely through body language. Sharing their mind is something they'll do only occasionally with someone they like and trust absolutely. No offence, but Loren would probably never have tried to speak to you if…"

"If she wasn't so worried about you."

"Exactly. She can chat to me like it's nothing. But that's because of what we are to each other. That's partly why she has me in the first place. I can do the talking."

"You're her spokesperson."

"Yes. You know what dragons call us?"

"What, humans?"

"Yes. They call us the storytellers."

Kella snorted. "So they're not big on story time, either. Go figure."

"No, or at least, not in the way we would understand them. But they do have something they can share. It's called the Echoes."

Kella cocked her head to one side, the lines of her face lit up by the fire between them, and waited with a surprising patience for Litz to continue.

"They don't need to use words. But if they're trying to explain something important that's happened to them, like something historical or that's really emotional to talk about, they can open themselves up completely and let you feel an echo of what they felt. And once they've felt it from someone else, they can pass on a perfect copy."

"That sounds intense."

"Oh, it can be."

Kella shifted her weight forward to peer at Litz closer in the dimming light. "Is dragon riding something you had to do because you're royalty?"

Litz smiled and stared into the distance behind Kella. In the darkness, the dunes stretched out like endless folds of sequinned cloth. "Far from it. They almost didn't let me because of the royalty thing. It helped that I wasn't in direct line for anything. And because Loren insisted so strongly," she added.

"Huh. What was the big deal? Little I know of royalty, I would have thought they'd like the idea of a little extra power in the family."

"No. The way our political balance continues back home depends on a separation between dragons and the royal family."

Kella scrunched her face up tight. "Lotta power in one place, I guess."

"Exactly. Usually, the dragon gets the ultimate choice in who they'd prefer as a human companion, but in this case, there was a clash of interests." Litz shrugged, remembering. It had been a strange time at home for her. She had never been so interesting to either of her parents. Her father hadn't stopped telling her how proud he was of her. Her mother hadn't stopped crying.

I caught something.

Litz blinked at the shock of feeling Loren's presence in her mind. *That took a while. I hope it was worth it.*

Shockingly, food supplies are scarce out here, but I did manage to find one of those strange hopping creatures.

You mean a kangaroo.

Yes. That. I don't like those things. It tried to kick me on the nose.

By your tone, I'm assuming it also succeeded.

For a moment there was no response to this.

Cheek.

Ah, so it did kick you. Finish your food and make it back to us?

That might take some time. If I can't make it back until morning... I'll be fine, of course. I'm always fine.

That's possibly the least reassuring thing you have ever said to me.

Litz smiled fondly. *Take your time. I'll see you in the morning.*

"She on her way back?"

"Not yet." Litz smiled, trying—poorly, she suspected—to mask her awkwardness. "You really are good at noticing when I speak to her."

"Not exactly difficult to work out. You go all spaced out, like you just took a nostril-full of *ronja.*"

"I don't know what that is."

"I'm thinking you get the idea, Princess."

"I suppose I must look very strange."

"Oh yeah."

Litz supposed people didn't normally spend much time watching her facial expressions. Or if they did, they never would have mentioned it. Which might, now she thought on it, be a little sad.

Kella looked at the sky and then to their makeshift tent. "Getting pretty dark. Guess we should try to sleep."

Litz allowed herself a smile. "You're welcome to sleep. I'll watch."

"Thought we were over you not trusting me."

"Maybe not to hurt me. But you're unpredictable and, no offense, more than a little foolish."

"*Hey.*"

"I wouldn't be shocked if you tried making a run for it tonight. To save us both the hassle of having to deal with that, I'll stay awake."

Kella narrowed her eyes before crossing her legs and arms. "If you're staying up, so am I."

She'd never considered herself dramatic, but something about conversations with Kella made Litz frequently want to let out a long breath for no better reason than effect. "Why?"

Kella shrugged. It was getting harder to make out her expressions in the dimming light, but Litz suspected she was pouting. "Like you said, I'm unpredictable. Maybe I want to stay awake and annoy you."

Litz had a feeling that this meant Kella didn't know why either. "Self-destructive, foolish—"

"Well, since you still might be marching me to my death and I'm acting pretty fucking chill about it, sure, I'll take self-destructive." The light from the fire made her teeth, bared wide in a grin, shine yellow.

And Litz couldn't really believe that she had ever been "chill" about allowing something to happen to her in her life. So, yes. Acting chill. And it was an act that made Litz angry for reasons she wasn't sure she wanted to examine too closely. "Do you want to play dice again?" she asked dully. She had a feeling this might be a long night.

The grin stayed. If anything, growing wider. "No. We're all alone by a campfire. There's only one proper thing we can do."

Litz felt her face heat in a way that had nothing to do with the fire, unsure of what Kella was going to say next.

"Tell stories."

"What?"

"Your dragons don't call us that for nothing, right? It's dark. We're stuck in the middle of a desert that's already tried to kill us today. You wanted to be a librarian, right? Tell me a story."

"I was always more of a nonfiction reader," Litz told her, letting out a slow breath.

"Really? You never wanted to be something different than you are?"

"No?"

Kella snorted. "Fine. I'll tell one. But I think you'd hate most of my good ones, so you're gonna have to bear with me through some *old*, old ones." Litz nodded, but Kella seemed no longer able to see this because a moment later, she asked, a hint of irritation or nervousness— or something unfamiliar—in her voice, "Are you listening?"

"Of course. That's why I didn't say anything."

Apparently satisfied with this, Kella began to speak. She was what Litz's mother would have called an "animated speaker," except that she would have said it with a sniff to her voice. Litz wouldn't. The way her hands moved as she spoke made it seem like she was caressing the firelight like a living creature. "When still the world was new and still its people were learning to make it their own, the Sun looked down on them once again. When he saw how his sister the Moon's children suffered under the tyranny of his own creations, the dragons, he offered a compromise. He recognised that his actions had upset her, and he wished to make amends.

"He sent to the Earth a sword that he claimed was capable of killing any living thing, including a dragon. For years, humans fought over the sword, yet on the rare occasions they turned it toward a dragon, they failed before even getting the chance to approach.

"It took many decades, but eventually, a human was clever enough to understand that the sword alone would be useless. He learnt to devise a trap for a beast with the help of some friends, and for the first time, the sword struck true, and a dragon was slain. The stories tell that the death of a dragon in what is now the city of Malya flooded the area with blood and melted gold. That year, the best fish and the best harvest were recorded, and the cures to many ailments were discovered. And that's why the Aelshian forest is so monstrously huge. Because so many dragons live and die there."

Litz wrinkled her nose. "No, it's not."

"Fuck off, it's a story. Let me tell it. Anyway, the slayers were the first ones called Graebneaschtin, and they made their leader the first king."

"Good Luck Bringer? That's what they called you in the market."

Kella groaned in hesitance or possibly embarrassment. "It's less now about bringing luck and more about the gods making you lucky. It's a way of saying you think someone's doing great things. Not necessarily that they're a great person, but that they're, y'know, having an impact."

Litz nodded. "At home, we say the gods choose where you go when you die. That if you've done something notable, they'll care enough to fight each other over whether it was good or bad. I suppose a good luck bringer would always be certain of notice."

"*Anyway*," Kella continued sternly, "the Moon thanked her brother, though she asked what would become of her children with only one talisman in the whole world to protect them. The Sun admitted that the sword had never been anything special. It had only ever been a tool to teach her humans of their own dangerous potential. We had it in us all along, hurrah."

CHAPTER THIRTEEN

The first time Ker had seen a dragon up close, he'd been seven years old. He'd glimpsed them from afar many times, flying miles above Malya or more often, fighting with his mother while he watched from a safe distance, his da holding him and pretending that the comfort of the embrace was only for Ker's sake. But this had been different. Kella had been part of this hunt, and the idea of not watching, terrified for her life in a way he hadn't felt he needed to be for his mother, was unthinkable.

So when Kella had run back to him, crowing her victory, Ker hadn't been far away. "I killed a dragon!"

"You helped kill a dragon," Zebenn had corrected her, ruffling her hair before turning to Ker. "How you doing down there, little one, you enjoy the show?"

"It's…it's dead now? It's not gonna hurt anyone now?" he had asked, slipping his hand out of his da's finally relaxed grip.

Zebenn's smile had widened. "It's dead, honey. You wanna come and see?"

The first dragon Ker had ever seen up close had been dead. And even then, before anything about him could be called strange, he'd thought it had looked beautiful.

"Ain't he a little young to be looking at something like this, Kira?" Rall had asked, face covered in blood and his arms folded across his chest.

The corpse had sighed out a smoking breath, and Ker had wondered if he was a bit too young to see this after all. But then his mami had come over to put a hand on his shoulder, and he'd heard the small smile she gave without needing to look up. "He's seen us gut fish and chickens at home before. And you're never too young to know that there's no evil too big to be brought down."

It had been a lie, Ker thought to himself now as he looked ahead to the trail of smoke rising into the sky from the trees, but he still thought that it was one of the good lies.

"See. Told you we were close."

"You told me that yesterday morning," Ker reminded without much venom.

Sallvayn folded their arms and leant against Ker's right ear. "We were. But you don't move very fast."

"I've literally been carrying you everywhere."

"Only because if you didn't, we'd forget to keep as slow as you, and then we'd lose you." Sallvayn finished making their point by sniffing loudly.

Ker sighed but kept his eyes on that smoke. There was a particular scent attached to dragon smoke that wasn't entirely unpleasant but did unfailingly conjure an image of meat being turned over a flame. It was wafting all through the trees, unnaturally darkening the air and forcing Ker to pause for a moment before continuing down the rocky slope toward the cover of the trees. He couldn't afford to lose more time. Not even thinking about what he was supposed to do once he found a dragon.

Especially because he was certain that if he thought about that at any length, he would start panicking. Which wasn't a practical response.

"You smell nervous."

"You're telling me you can actually *smell* fear?"

"It's probably healthy," Sallvayn went on, ignoring Ker as he took them down the hillside. "We would be concerned if you weren't frightened. They might kill us on sight. We can't be certain these dragons will be even capable of conversation."

"Thanks. You're being so comforting."

"Really? We were trying to frighten you into taking this seriously."

"Oh, I don't think I need any more frightening."

They were finally at the base of the hill in front of a thick wall of trees and bushes clustering around the valley's stream. And something in there was making the unmistakable sound of a dragon sighing as it moved.

"All right, we're getting off here," Sallvayn announced, climbing down Ker's arm like a monkey from a vine and letting themselves drop to the ground.

Ker raised his eyebrows, trying not to show how nervous he was. "You're leaving me here?"

"Oh, not now. No, we just want to make sure we can run away faster than you should we need to."

"You know, I can run fast."

Sallvayn reached up and carefully patted Ker on the leg in a way that was probably meant to be reassuring. "We think you'll do your best."

Shaking his head, Ker pretended this wasn't unnerving and stared down the trees facing him. Kella, he was doing this for Kella. As long as he remembered that he'd be fine. "How do we do this?"

"What was your original idea before you found us?"

Ker swallowed. "Find a dragon. And. Y'know. Jump on its back, have a long piece of vine or, or rope or something with me that I could loop around its neck like reins—"

"That is a terrible idea."

Ker's shoulders slumped. "I wasn't exactly in a great place for thinking up any better ideas."

Sallvayn groaned and slapped a little clawed hand to their forehead. "Okay. Here is a better plan. You walk in there slowly. You don't put your head up for any of them, you don't meet their eyes. If they want to speak to you, you'll know, you'll feel it in here," Sallvayn said, tapping at the side of their head.

"And if they don't wanna talk?"

"Then it would be too late for you to do anything apart from show us how fast you can run."

"Awesome. And why can't I raise my eyes?"

"Because you've come seeking their help. Didn't your parents ever teach you some respect?"

Ker only had one parent left. If something happened to him, his da would hopefully just think he had disappeared and hadn't died in the same way as Ker's mother had. And probably Kella, if Ker couldn't get to her.

That thought alone was almost enough to have him running home, brimming with apologies for their family's recklessness, but he had to keep remembering that Kella needed him. There was still a chance they could both get through this. And he knew that, despite his da's scholarly image and bad leg, if he'd known what Ker was planning, he'd probably be up there with him. People often made the mistake of thinking that Kella and Ker did what they did without their father's enthusiastic support.

"Are you ready?"

Ker tried to smile, doing his best to channel his sister's charm. His sister, who would always choose to look dragons in the eye. Who wouldn't be here for any reason other than killing them. "Sure. Course I am."

"If this goes well, you invite us with you, yes?"

"Yeah, course."

Ker had a feeling it was going to be a big if.

"We would like to offer a hope that you do not get burnt to cinders."

At least if he did, there wouldn't be anyone around. He'd never been able to get the smell of his mother burning out of his brain. If gremlins could smell fear, maybe that smell would be ten times worse to Sallvayn, if they were close enough. "Thank you," Ker managed eventually. "And, uh. Thank you for bringing me here," he said, starting to walk away before turning back one last time to see that Sallvayn had already hidden.

Swallowing, Ker walked into the trees, trying desperately to convince himself that he wasn't scared. Already, he could see the hide of a large red dragon some way ahead. Dealing with dragons, that was familiar, and to some extent, that was even safe. He would never go in without a plan, without knowing what he was doing. Without backup. Now he was looking at those gleaming scales growing even closer and racking his brain to figure out what his contingency plan was supposed to be, and he was coming up with nothing.

You're supposed to be the smart one. But he wasn't. He was just the stupid kid of the operation. An operation that had abandoned him, leaving him with one last stupid plan and no backup plan if it went wrong. He didn't even really have a plan, just a stupid, stupid hope that the parts of him he'd always avoided thinking about were interesting enough for a bunch of dragons, *dragons*, not to kill him on sight.

As he reached the edge of the trees, he stopped to catch his breath. It looked as though there were three of them lying over the stream to cool themselves down. One was yellow, one was red, and the last was an unusual dark purple colour Ker hadn't seen before. And they looked no different to the man-killing dragons he'd grown up fighting all his life. Were the non-rabid ones supposed to look different?

He breathed in deeply and focused on the large spider resting above where his hand was leaning on the tree. It seemed to be staring at him as though to ask what he was doing there.

For Kella, for Kella, for Kella, he was doing this for Kella, she needed him.

He took a step. It felt loud.

The yellow dragon raised its head and turned to look at him on the fourth step.

"Fuck," Ker breathed, feeling unable to move. Those eyes were so very big. Then he remembered that he wasn't supposed to be looking at the dragon's eyes at all and rapidly bowed his head, forcing himself to stare at his sandals. And what could be the harm in taking another step? Ker thought, almost hysterically as he took three more steps, his heart hammering his ribcage.

There was a mild grumbling noise, louder than a lion's roar, as one, or maybe all, of them started to move to their feet. Getting a better look at this annoying little insect boy with maybe a smidge of dragon in him. Sallvayn said he would just feel it if they wanted to talk. But what if he didn't notice? What if he had to look at them and—

He was maybe a metre to the left from the flames that shot toward him, and it was enough to have his neck jolting back up. He didn't even turn to see which dragon was after him. He was already scrambling away, running back toward the trees.

"Fuck, fuck, fuck, *fuck*," he muttered as he ran. The dragons, luckily, seemed reluctant to destroy their source of shade and weren't bothering to give chase. That didn't mean he felt sure enough to stop running yet.

Was that one flying above him now, ready to wait for him back on the hill? And where had Sallvayn got to? Why had he started trusting a gremlin to bring him safely to meet a bunch of dragons?

Back the way he'd came felt too obvious. Instead, he started running farther up the valley, still under the safety of the trees. And he had to be fast, but he also had to not trip over his feet or run himself into a spiderweb. When he noticed the cave nestled into a curve the river had carved into the mountain, he took a moment to register that what he was about to do was a Stupid Idea before rushing out of the trees and up toward the cave anyway. There might be an area at the back that would be difficult for any dragon to reach. Maybe.

There might be one in there waiting on him.

He ran in anyway, still hearing the roars of angry dragons shaking the trees behind him and managing not to trip over the stony floor of the dark cave. But he only made it a few steps in when a voice in his head sapped him of his urgency to move.

What...be...you?

Though he had stopped moving, Ker didn't feel brave enough to answer yet.

What be *you?* it asked again, not exactly with words, but it didn't stop him from understanding what they meant. And something up ahead of him rumbled, the sound echoing through the cave, and he swallowed. It was impossible to guess at size when it was this dark, when he was this frightened. But he was sure that whatever was in front of him was *big*.

Somehow, he managed to croak out, "Ker. I'm Ker. And I be pretty fucking freaked out right now."

The large silhouette in front of him that he had been praying might somehow be a rock formation began to shift and move closer so that a gigantic pair of gleaming yellow eyes were able to fix on him.

Dragon eyes.

Ker. I am...Ellonya. Why are you here?

"I was looking for a dragon," he said slowly, fighting the urge to laugh aloud. He wasn't sure why he was still speaking out loud. He was pretty sure the contents of his head were laid bare to the creature staring down at him.

Which was terrifying on an entirely different level.

Well, you have found one.

❖

Kella was shockingly unconcerned to wake up to find a dragon staring at her. In fact, much more rattling was the realisation that she must have fallen asleep sometime in the night.

She was happy she'd woken up first. That was something. Because there was Captain Litz, curled up between the huge paws of her dragon, one of them propping her up as a large scaled pillow. It shone with drool. Altogether, it didn't look a very comfortable position, but that hadn't stopped Litz from spreading her whole body out, satisfied as a starfish.

The fact that she looked so obviously relaxed was helping Kella fight the nagging impulse to attempt to rescue her from her own dragon. "She always this graceful a sleeper?" Kella asked the dragon as she rubbed sandy sleep from her eyes and tried in vain to work the crick out of her neck. Since she'd fallen asleep anyway, she probably should have just slept in the makeshift tent.

The dragon did not even blink.

"What? It's not life-or-death anymore, so you won't speak to me?"

Now the dragon blinked and slumped its head to one side, giving Kella a full once-over.

"Y'know, I could have run last night. Or made a fuss. But I didn't. I even made the fucking dinner. But it's cool, I murdered a bunch of your kind or whatever." She splayed out her hands, only a little frustrated. She was talking to a dragon. "Which is…actually, fair enough."

I don't hate you. I just don't like what you're doing to her.

The feeling of that mind nudging at her own was becoming familiar, but it was still shocking enough to leave her feeling she was unable to say anything but, "What?"

I know her as well as anyone can know anything. Meaning I know that she does not deserve the hurt you will put her through.

"Hey, it was her decision to have me extradited or whatever."

The dragon blinked very slowly, and Kella got the feeling she was failing to impress. *Yes. You've been hurt too. But you are not my concern.*

"And neither are any of the dragons I've killed, huh?"

Though I understand the evolutionary advantages to humanity's excessive empathy, no. I will not claim that the deaths of those I have not even seen before bothers me personally. It concerns me on an intellectual level, but I will not cry human crocodile tears for them.

Kella scrunched up her face and regarded the dragon with a scowl. Then, she nodded, shrugged. "Okay. I can get behind that. You're not a faker."

The dragon continued to stare but as though she had just made a decision, nudged her front right foot slightly to the side, stirring Litz abruptly into consciousness.

Kella couldn't help herself. "You've, uh. You got a…"

"What?" Litz asked, bleary eyes focusing slowly on Kella's hand held at her lip. Then, she furiously wiped at the spot, embarrassment seeming to cause her arms to stick to her sides in military style, much to Kella's amusement. "Oh."

"I don't *think* last night's leftovers are going to kill us if we try them for breakfast," Kella said, generously ignoring how flustered Litz remained. "But I am now wondering about how we should clean the pot."

Groaning, Litz put a hand across her stomach and slowly got to her feet. "Not killing us sounds like a good selling point to me."

"Awesome." Kella scrambled to stand. She was used to being the short one, but for some reason, it bothered her that Litz had such a height advantage on her. She wouldn't cede any more of that, even when she knew she had two concealed weapons on her person now in addition to the sword Litz knew about.

Though she did have a slight worry that the dragon knew about both of those. Shuddering only a little, and avoiding the disconcerting amber glow of the dragon's eyes, Kella moved to start a fire. "How long do you reckon it'll take us to cross the whole thing?" she asked a few moments later as she crouched by her new fire and stared across the dunes awaiting them. Not looking back because there wouldn't be anyone running up behind them to rescue her. There was no use looking back.

Litz shrugged, turning to follow Kella's gaze. "I'm not sure exactly."

"You're not *sure*?"

Litz frowned. "No. I've only ever crossed this desert by flying with Loren, and even that took us a couple of days. I hear stories of travellers taking a year."

"A year?"

"But most manage in weeks or a couple of months. Much depends on weather and other circumstances."

Kella jabbed a finger into the sand. "I mean, why did we even bother going to war? We're too fucking far away from each other."

Litz smiled, reminding Kella that she was a soldier. "Not when we use the others' territories. *We* are being polite. In any case, the desert was only really used for unsuccessful sneak attacks," Litz went on in a voice that sounded better suited to reading a shopping list than describing a war she'd personally fought in.

"Someone tried to tell me once that that's what sand terrors are," Kella said, still regarding Litz thoughtfully. "Soldiers who never made it to the fight but still want to kill their enemies, only they don't remember who that's supposed to be anymore. Soldiers who never got buried right." She shrugged when she noticed she'd gotten Litz's attention. "I mean, it's not true. They're more like diluted demons, I think."

"Diluted demons?"

"See, they don't steal souls completely. They just pick at them, right?"

Apparently having nothing to say to that, Litz went back to looking at the dunes they'd yet to conquer, a hand above her eyes to shield them from the glare. "Gods, I can't stand this sun."

"It's not like this at home?"

A smile. "No. It's not like this at all."

"Is it true what they say about the dark creepy jungle?"

"What? No. It is a forestland. But Verassez, my home capital, it's beautiful. We have a lot of infrastructure, thank you, but most of the larger buildings are shaped different to yours. As pyramids so the trees have room to grow out as they grow up. It's like we tried to work with the forest, not demolish it. And there's space for the dragons but mostly by the river. The river's so wide—"

"Wait, dragons swim?"

"Of course. Ah. You only really have seawater, and dragons hate salt."

"Knew that one. But, huh. Then they're not that closely related to sea serpents. Jev was right after all."

"I'm not so sure—"

"I think I owe him six gnottis." Kella smiled and leant toward her fire. "Heh. He's not getting that outta me now."

"Oh no, I'm sure the king will come chasing you down for that," Litz said, causing Kella to blink rapidly in surprise. Sarcasm wasn't something that suited Litz; she seemed to have sincerity tied into her very essence, and Kella wasn't sure what had possessed her to try it.

But it still succeeded in making her laugh.

Maybe today wouldn't end up all that bad. Or maybe it would at least be better than the day before.

So you came here for your sister.

"Yes," Ker said. It was becoming a little easier to breathe now.

But she does not like dragons.

"Not really."

Why?

Ker swallowed, taking in the full width of the creature's neck. If another hero type decided to wander by and try to save him by chopping through it, the weight of its fall would easily crush Ker flat. She was a young dragon, Ellonya, something he'd rarely seen. Though her wings were slight, the rest of her was fully grown. Maybe she wouldn't easily crush him, but there'd be a lot of broken bones. "There's a few reasons."

Thankfully, Ellonya—and *fuck*, dragons really could talk—didn't question this. *And if she is dead? What then is your plan?*

Ker had always thought he was pretty good at understanding animals. He liked cats, his da usually kept several around the shop, not to mention his snake, and he'd always gotten on well with the street dogs in Malya. He knew when they were interested in him and when they wanted him to leave them alone. Staring back at Ellonya, he couldn't understand any of her body language, what this stillness and concentration meant. But he had a feeling that he wasn't being led into a wrong answer. "I don't know," he said honestly.

Ellonya snorted, and that seemed a human response. *And why did you think this plan would be helped by me?*

This isn't about you specifically, Ker wanted to point out but held back. "A dragon to catch up with another dragon. That makes sense, right? I don't, or I didn't, exactly have a lot of options available to me."

No. That's not true.

"Excuse me?" Ker said and felt the urge to clap both hands over his mouth. He was talking to a dragon, a dragon he needed help from. He wasn't even supposed to be looking her in the eye, and he'd been staring straight at her since he'd got in.

Ellonya moved her head to one side, and Ker got the distinct impression that she was being patient with him. *You are resourceful. And you wasted time you might have used to find your sister in finding me. No, this was always something you wanted to do. You have finally been freed enough to do it.*

"Freed?"

Finally, you are alone. Finally, you can be honest.

Ker breathed in slowly and looked back up at Ellonya's eyes, trying not to think of how he'd felt the day before, travelling with Sallvayn, hiding nothing of himself. "I'm here to save my sister. But if you need me to bare my soul before I can do that, then fine."

Nothing of what he could see of Ellonya seemed to move or outwardly change, but Ker knew that she was smiling. He just wasn't sure yet if it was the sort of smile he should be happy about.

❖

It was strange, Litz thought as she smiled over at Kella. She had seemed so at ease with Loren while stationary on the ground, and yet she was so obviously unnerved by her flying high above them now.

"You're like a little brocket deer," Litz said to her after they'd been travelling for a few hours. She'd found it simplest to navigate a path of least resistance through the dunes, with the merchant's trail they'd been following having faded away. They were riding camels, and Litz was thankful there was nothing for Kella to run into on the empty dunes for the amount of time she spent staring into the sky.

"Like a what?"

Litz smiled at finally getting her attention. "A twitchy little forest animal. It's always alert for predators, so it never gets to relax."

"Hey," Kella put in moodily, leaning back to create the effect that both she and the camel were swaggering. "Could get called a lot of things but twitchy is not one."

"Don't act so twitchy, and I won't call you it."

This earned a scowl, but Litz had started differentiating between Kella's theatrical expressions and her genuine ones, so she didn't react. "I don't think that it's, that *she's*, a predator. I'm not an idiot," Kella said as though Litz was forcing the words out of her one by one.

"I didn't call you one."

"But you gotta get that if I ever forget she's there, and I see a dragon out of the corner of my eye trying to circle us…" Kella let out a long breath, and Litz saw her knuckles lighten with the effort she was putting into clutching her camel's reins. "It's just fucking creepy, all right?"

"It's a good thing she doesn't circle as fast as she used to, I guess," Litz said, sending a fond smile skyward. "She's getting older."

"How old is 'getting older'?"

"She'll be reaching her two-fifty soon."

"Like, she'll be a hundred or two hundred and fifty?"

"Two hundred and fifty."

"Fuck."

Litz had to laugh. Her camel groaned as she asked, "How long did you think dragons lived?"

"I guess I didn't think on it much? I knew they could live a lot longer than people, but yeah. *Fuck.*"

"Fuck indeed. Most of the dragons making up the Circle are well over three hundred years old."

"Okay, so ignoring 'fuck indeed,' though I really think we should come back to that, what's the Circle?"

Litz regarded Kella's open face, which seemed to reveal nothing. "You're chattier today."

"Sure." Kella shrugged, dislodging some of her scarf from her head. "You've kidnapped me, whatever. I'll probably never see home again. I wanna hear about where I'm going. I've heard it includes a scary dark forest, war atrocities, dragon worshippers, and tigers, which I hear are basically lions except they have stripes. Or spots. Something. Please confirm, and tell me about this mysterious Circle."

"It's not all that mysterious," Litz said, trying not to think of her recent conversation with Loren. If the Jeenobi dragons were somehow different, there was no earthly way that the Circle would not be aware of it. That was an uneasy thought. "First, tigers—it's stripes, by the way—are actually *very* different. They can swim. And second, this is not kidnap. This is a lawful—"

"Yeah, yeah, yeah, I know that bit. What's the Circle?"

"They're the high council of Aelshia's dragons, involving several dragon representatives for less-developed neighbouring lands."

"Any Jeenobi dragons there?"

"No."

"Huh."

"I think that's mostly due to the war," Litz said, recovering quickly.

"Heh. So dragons aren't quick on the diplomacy front."

"They're not really big on the need to socialize with their own kind at all. But the Circle represents their intention to be included in our king's decision-making so that dragon issues are not forgotten, either in war or in city expansions." Litz shrugged. "Honestly, that feels like most of what they argue over."

"They argue a lot?"

"Sometimes. It is government," Litz said, feeling uneasy as she remembered Loren's concerns about Kella being used as the king's political pawn. She wasn't sure if that meant she should try to keep her ignorant or educate her on the politically nuanced situation she might be walking into.

"When did that start? This alliance you guys have with the head dragons?"

"The stories say it was part of our winning the region. They had little interest in the humans of the forest until we were warring, and a common enemy emerged for us."

"Which was?"

"Well, the forest clans."

Kella smiled tightly. "Okay, I'm rusty on my ancient history. But from what I'm hearing, for all your moralising about my country's evil, you colonised a bunch of people, just like you tried to do to us, so you could get a hold of the ports, and you guys teamed up with dragons to win." She whistled, looking ahead. "Sounds like cheating to me."

"Most of the clans-people were magic-users back then. We wouldn't have stood a chance without—"

"Sure, because this is all in the past."

"Yes, it is. It has little relevance to today," Litz insisted, trying not to think about it too much. The truth was, the story had always bothered her. It had sounded like cheating. And the clans who hadn't assimilated with modern Aelshian society still scorned the Empire as being toxic and oppressive. On bad days, Litz was inclined to agree with them.

"I mean, with you guys and the dragons still in power, I'm guessing your clans wouldn't see it that way."

Litz ignored this but thought back to her uncle, who had expressed similar sentiments on more than a few occasions. Seeing as he was an outsider to Aelshian culture, he frequently saw things in a different way to most people Litz knew.

Whether Kella respected that Litz wasn't exactly ready to talk or she was disgusted from talking to her at all, for almost half an hour, they travelled in silence. This ended when Kella pointed at something in the sand ahead of them and gasped, her face alight as a child at a festival. "Look."

"I'm not sure—"

But Kella was already off her camel and racing toward what she'd pointed at, skidding to a stop. "I don't fucking believe it."

"I'm sorry, what are you looking at?"

"Come see for yourself," Kella told her, not looking up.

Sighing, Litz dismounted and walked stiffly over to her. "It's a… footprint?" she guessed. That seemed to be the only thing the mark in the sand could possibly be, but she still felt stupid for suggesting it. It seemed large enough for a lion who had wandered very, very far from its territory, but there was something bizarre about it. The toes looked wrong. And the tracks didn't match up. The back footprints looked nothing like the front. They were much smaller, a little like the forest deer she had earlier named. "It doesn't look like the same animal," she said eventually.

Kella nodded fervently. "Exactly. And you see that drag behind it?"

There was a line behind the footprints, like the strange animal had a long heavy tail or a snake in hot pursuit. "What are we looking at?" Litz asked eventually, dumbfounded.

"Chimera. A real live chimera passed this way, and it couldn't have been long ago." When Kella looked up, those wide eyes were shining. "We need to chase it. Please."

"No," Litz said. "I need to get you to Aelshia, not waste any more time running around after monsters in the desert."

"*Please?* The tracks are fresh, and it won't exactly be hard to spot out here." Kella flung her arms wide in a circle around them. "C'mon."

Litz sighed long and heavily.

What? Loren asked.

We might have to change course. Just a little.

If you're happy with it, it makes no difference to me. We're already moving slowly.

Litz sighed again before shrugging in defeat. Kella wasn't about to change her mind, and this didn't seem a good reason for a fight. There would be fights, Litz had no doubt, and she wasn't sure how many she would have the energy to win without having to get Loren involved. "Fine."

"Yay!" The childlike impression persisted, Litz observed as Kella leapt back into her saddle, practically vibrating with anticipation. This was the warrior Litz had watched the day before, the one covered in blood, who had looked around her with a similar exhilaration.

Litz also remembered the woman she had met in the Malyan market who had stolen a kiss and run off on a very different chase.

"C'mon, we're losing time," Kella whined.

Despite wanting to find something smart to say, Litz could only smile and get herself into her own saddle. There was no one else around, and who was to say this wasn't how Litz wanted to spend her time?

CHAPTER FOURTEEN

It was shortly after Ellonya had unceremoniously left to hunt that Sallvayn found Ker, and though he had been pleased to see them, he'd been less pleased that Sallvayn's first words to him again were, "You're still alive?"

"'Fraid so."

Sallvayn squinted up at him suspiciously. "Anybody ever tell you how abnormally lucky you are?"

Ker remembered Rall running over to him and Kella where they were motionless, standing in vigil over the ashes their mother had become, and the way his face had crumpled, his eyes streaming as he'd reached out and placed a hand on Ker's scrawny shoulder. "Fuck, kid, you're so lucky to be alive."

He and Kella had very deliberately not looked at one another, Ker knowing and Kella suspecting that luck had little to do with any of it. "Nope," he said, making Sallvayn frown.

"Great. So what happened?"

"Well, those dragons didn't like the look of me."

"Yeah, saw that part."

"And then I ran in here."

"Uh-huh, guessed that."

"Would you let me finish? I ran into a dragon in here, and she started talking to me."

"Does she seem friendly?" Sallvayn asked, glaring eagerly at Ker, who sat at the cave mouth to feel more at eye level with them. He was no longer worried about the other dragons; they seemed to be sleeping or maybe had wandered off. He couldn't make out any smoke rising from the trees anymore.

"I'm not sure," he admitted, fiddling with a small, shiny brass clock Ellonya had hoarded. It was a meagre hoard for a dragon with an established cave. The clock was one of the more impressive pieces. "She's…it's not like talking to most people or even to you. She's really different."

"Dragons are."

"I mean, I get that, but like she seemed really, *really* different. Like she didn't seem sure of her own name."

Sallvayn frowned and sat beside him. "That is odd."

"Right? Even dogs know their names."

"Hmm. Still. Even a half-infected beast may be better than none, for both of our purposes."

"I still don't get what you mean by infected, so sure," Ker said moodily as he stared at the tree line horizon the sun would soon be setting over. Another day of Kella out there on her own. And whatever any dragon said about it, that was what mattered most to him, even if the one saying it *was* able to see into his head.

Beside him, Sallvayn sighed. "It makes us sad that you cannot understand, that you have never met a real dragon, whole and healthy. You only know of the creatures who attacked you today."

Ker shrugged. "I've heard some old stories, but…"

"You might have met one before and never known it. Dragons are picky about who they talk to. And obviously, you've met a talker before."

Ker refused to look at them. "Tell me what you meant about infection, and I'll try telling you what I think happened to me," he said eventually.

There was something about the rattling way gremlins sighed or the way this one did. It sounded as though they were judging him for wrongdoings he hadn't even thought of attempting yet. "We barely remember, we told you. We heard some blaming the gods, that this was a curse on the arrogance of dragons." They looked at their toes, stretching them out. "But that's not true. All we know is that one day, the dragons here were the most magnificent, the wisest, and the next, they started to lose the ability to communicate. They pushed away their humans, they stopped communicating with non-infected dragons, they became senselessly violent." They shook their head. "They became like beasts. Without reason. And the gremlins began to die out. And without dragons to stop them, humans began to kill each other."

"We're not right now. Well. More than usual."

"Is that so? We imagine that whatever did this to the dragons won't like that much."

Ker snorted. "Ominous."

"Was it? Good. A little pessimism doesn't normally do harm."

Ker smirked and paused to soak up the quiet of the late afternoon. He could hear birds, but for some blessed reason, the cicadas were quiet. Maybe the bugs were wary of dragons as they weren't of humans.

Though he didn't turn to look at them, he was aware that Sallvayn continued to look at him, waiting. Now he'd been asked to, he did want to talk about it. He still couldn't imagine anything worse. It was like preparing to stick his fingers down his throat. "I was a kid," he said eventually. "And I wasn't a very special kid as kids go, I don't think. They'd only just started letting me be around for my mami's hunts. And they told me to wait by these rocks while they moved on and set a trap for a dragon they'd been tracking awhile. I think it had sent almost half a village up in flames, and nothing had been done about it yet, so there they were."

"Being heroes," Sallvayn said, and there was no inflection behind that word.

"Yeah," Ker croaked, feeling a lump the size of a peach clogging his throat. "Anyway, I was alone. And the dragon found me."

"You said before it was a rabid. But it wasn't completely, was it?"

"No. It spoke to me. Or, or it tried. It said that it liked the look of me. I felt it say that in my head, and I wasn't frightened, not really. I just…it looked so beautiful. And I knew from its thoughts touching mine that it wasn't planning on eating me, that it thought I looked interesting and alone. Alone like he was alone."

Sallvayn hummed. "Some humans, their minds can be more attractive to certain types of dragons. It's like any kind of attraction. It can't always be put into words. It just is."

"Yeah. Some weird…" Ker shook his head. "Something happened. My mother, she saw, and she thought it was hurting me, and maybe it was, and she ran back to save me. She tried to fight it off, but it flew back and rounded on her, and she told me to get down, get behind her. But she should have gotten behind me. It was just her it was trying to hurt, just her I even think it could have hurt, and I knew that because he was in my head the whole time. So I let her die." He had never actually said it aloud before. Now that he had, he tensed, waiting for the world to implode in on him.

Kella loved him, he knew that. And that had always meant the whole world to him since he'd always known that she suspected what he'd done, what he was, and if that had affected her feelings toward him, it had only made them fiercer. Almost as if she was loving him out of spite.

"I let her die." It was easier to say it now. It was getting more natural to remember to breathe. It had been almost a minute, and no one had appeared to throw rocks at him; no bolt of lightning had been aimed down his way by the Sky; the Earth hadn't shaken in disapproval. He'd said aloud what he'd spent half his life pretending away, and the birds were still singing. The world was taking no more notice of him than usual.

A small scaly hand curled around his knee. It wasn't exactly a comfort, and he got the sense it wasn't really meant to be. But it was encouraging.

"I let her die, and I'll never get to apologise to her for that. Because she's dead. Can't get forgiveness from a dead person."

"That would be difficult. But it was yourself you robbed of a mother." Ker tried hard not to flinch. "Do you think you can forgive yourself? For being a child who listened to their elder?"

He swallowed and looked at the sky, ignoring how his eyes stung. "Heh. Maybe. If I save Kella now."

"That is what you're trying to do."

"By getting the help of a *dragon*." Ker flopped his arms uselessly up, gesturing at the now dragon-less sky. "This is an insane plan."

"We told you this already."

"Yeah, but I knew I had to try. Now I've tried. I'm not dead. And I'm not sure why or what I'm supposed to do now." That was the part that got to him the most, really. He was supposed to be the smart one, the one who came up with the plans, and he'd had one plan, and he'd gotten to the end of it, and he still wasn't any closer to saving Kella.

"What did the dragon do when you found her?"

Ker licked at the inside of his mouth, trying to will away the dryness. He should make a run for the water if the other dragons really were gone for now. "She asked me why I was there. I told her I was trying to help my sister, that she was being taken across the desert. And she asked me about that. Then she made some comments about 'binding' or promises or something and kinda implied I should wait here for her, and she flew off." He shook his head. "I just...I know what we want from her, that makes sense. But what does she want?"

Sallvayn stared at the horizon, their hand slipping away from Ker's knee. "We might know. But it will be interesting learning how much she understands what she wants if she barely knows her own name."

"You're gonna tell me what you know before she gets back, though, right? C'mon, we're a team, y'gotta keep me in the loop where you can."

"We don't 'gotta' do anything." Sallvayn sniffed. They paused. "But we will. What do you know of dragonriders?"

❖

"Okay, I think we've done enough wandering in circles," Litz announced as she slowed her camel.

"I'm telling you, we're getting close."

"I can't believe that."

"So close I can smell it."

"And I *don't* believe that."

Kella rolled her eyes from the tracks they'd been following for hours and sat still, staring at the skyline that now included a large rock formation. She suspected it might be hiding an oasis, part of why she was determined to catch up with this creature. This was well-trodden ground now, and though rocky shelter might be attractive, she didn't think it warranted this much foot traffic, and she knew that Narani traders always spoke of the ways they had of charting the few sources of open water the desert had left to offer. She wasn't saying anything about that because the last thing she wanted to do was make a promise she couldn't deliver on. She would consider killing to have an actual bath, to wash all the blood and sand off her body. "I'm almost certain it went through there. If I were a chimera, that's the sort of shade I'd want to chill in."

"Oh, so now you're only almost certain. A second ago, you could smell it."

Kella sighed loudly enough for the noise to carry over the wind. "Can you drop the pedantic soldier routine already? You wouldn't have followed me out here if you didn't at least want a look at this thing."

"Maybe I'm reevaluating my priorities based on how capable my guide is proving."

Kella snorted. "Your guide is doing *awesome* under the extreme stress of being held captive. It's ruining my skin, you know."

"I thought that was from you scratching off the blood you left on your face."

Kella raised a hand to flick self-consciously at her cheek. "Yes, but if I hadn't been dragged out here, I wouldn't have had to smear any on in the first place."

As Litz said nothing, Kella returned to staring at the trail. It had been Zebenn who had taught her how to track. Rall had been a discharged soldier first and foremost. Findan the academic, with the most experience of dragons, and a longer and more mysterious career in magic-use. But Zebenn had, in an old life, been a farmer and for the sake of protecting their goats, a hunter. All of them had their sad stories for being there, and Zebenn was no different. But they also had an unquenchable fascination with the creatures they hunted.

But they hadn't followed Kella's cage tracks into the desert sand.

"Kella." Litz rushed her camel forward. "Loren saw something up ahead."

She lifted her eyes. "In the rocks?"

"Yes."

"Awesome, let's go. I told you."

"I feel like you say too many things to be able to use that as an effective retort."

"Gods, can you shut up? And can you actually quiet down? I don't wanna spook the thing."

All dutiful soldier, Litz shut her mouth and nodded, confidently urging her camel on while keeping one hand hovering over the hilt of the sword belted at her side. Kella did not mimic her in this, but her camel strode forward into the welcome shade with a confidence she wasn't sure she possessed anymore.

She'd never faced a chimera before. Ker had, and Kella had been forever jealous of his experience. He had got to see one up close, and he hadn't even able to give a satisfying description of it. "Okay," she murmured, keeping her voice as low as she was able, "let's walk from here."

Litz nodded, and they slid to the ground to tie their camels to an emaciated bush, which felt unnecessary since neither beast looked interested in moving anywhere. But they left them, and Kella paced ahead, hearing Litz follow closely behind. "I hear that seeing a chimera is a terrible omen," Litz whispered, her lips almost achingly near Kella's neck.

Kella snorted but kept her head vigilantly facing forward. "Sure. But only if you piss it off."

They walked for around five minutes before hearing something that sounded like a very wide yawn.

"Me too, pal," Kella whispered with a grin before inclining her head to show Litz which way they were walking next. They passed another corridor of rock face before catching a glimpse of colour and ducking down.

"That's it?" Litz mouthed.

"Think so." After strategically evaluating their situation for about half a second, Kella decided to raise her head above the rock and see what they'd been chasing. And then she felt her face melt. "Stand up," she ordered Litz, tugging at her sleeve.

Suspiciously, Litz did so before letting out a small gasp. "It's… it's sleeping."

"She's beautiful," Kella said because she was. There was the head of a young lioness, looking as blissful in sleep as any napping house cat. Its tail, a large snake, maybe a python, was curled up, also sleeping. She wondered if the two heads always did that together. The creature's stomach was scaled like a dragon's; its hindquarters were like those of a large mountain goat. On its back was a mound around the size and shape of a camel's hump. Some said chimeras could grow a third head there or even small dragon wings. Kella wondered which shape that hump would eventually end up as.

She hoped it would be wings. Without daring to move any closer, she felt like it deserved to fly.

"It'll be vulnerable while its sleeping. But is there anything I should be aware of before we attack?"

Kella blinked. "Attack?"

"You brought us here to hunt this creature, did you not?"

"Why would I do that? Look at that angel. It's never hurt a thing in its life."

Litz was staring as though Kella was the bizarre and rare creature they'd managed to track down.

"It's a baby," Kella insisted.

"It's definitely not that young."

"A *baby*." Kella frowned. Ugh, *soldiers*. "I'm not that kind of hero type. I'm not going to kill what wouldn't try to kill me."

For a moment, Litz looked lost before recovering. "Then why are we here?"

"Why? Look at it. Don't you feel better about this whole shit of a journey now you've seen her? I mean, how many people can say they've seen a chimera and not be lying? We're lucky." Kella bit her lip and went back to staring at the oblivious creature. "Nobody can even agree on where they come from, you know."

"No?"

"Not yet. I think my brother'll work it out one day." Kella beamed and kept staring at the creature. It was beautiful, mostly because it made no sense. The mind looked at it and kept failing to wrap itself around what it was seeing. "He's going to write a lot of books. His da's always saying that's what happens when you read enough of them, and he's definitely read his share."

"Did you get to see him before you left? Your brother?"

"Before you dragged me from my home in a cage? No." She was a little worried about that. They'd never been split up like this before, and she wasn't sure how well Ker was going to deal with it. Probably better than she would've.

"Thank you."

"What, for being—"

"For showing her to me," Litz said, but something about the fond way she said it and the directness of her stare made Kella feel like she was really saying, "Thank you for showing yourself to me."

Kella couldn't meet that stare for long, so she swallowed and turned back to the chimera, sighing. "I want one."

"Well, you can't have one."

"But I *want* one."

"And what on the good earth would you do with one?"

"Love it? Have it tear off the faces of my enemies?"

They were slowly, by unspoken agreement, beginning to back away from the chimera's resting place, and as they finally grew capable of looking away from it, something green poked above the edge of the rocks.

"Hey, Princess."

"What am I looking at now?"

Kella pointed at the inviting green shapes ahead. "Me being right."

For a brief moment, Litz smiled in relief before crinkling her nose critically. "How is this any proof of you being right about something?"

"Because I…it's an oasis." Which wasn't an expectation she'd gotten around to saying aloud. "I led us here," Kella insisted, but as she kicked at the stones by her feet, she was smiling.

❖

Ker had grown up with the niggling feeling that he wasn't a very capable communicator. Meeting new people had always been a struggle for him, but that had never bothered him much. Because whenever he failed to charm or make himself understood, Kella would be right there beside him to step in and take charge, to finish or translate his sentences where necessary. Little scared her, and speaking her mind had certainly never made the short list of things that did. But Kella wasn't here, and though he doubted talking to a dragon would frighten her, he couldn't see it as something she'd attempt. He was on his own to plead his case.

Ellonya hadn't been openly hostile since her return with food. She'd offered some to Ker, though she'd seemed surprised at his desire to cook it. She was definitely young, Ker was sure about that part. He had never seen a grown dragon with feathers that still looked this fluffy and almost dishevelled. Her long sinuous body dwarfed her young wings into looking stubby when she wasn't using them, which made the idea of her flying anywhere seem ridiculous. But Ker had seen her use them just fine, which meant that she shouldn't have a problem in getting him to Kella.

"Do you think she's ever going to talk about what I asked from her?" Ker muttered, glaring as he watched Ellonya slowly close her eyes.

"We don't think dragons are easily rushed."

Ker ground his teeth. "We can't just sit here saying nothing to her while my sister might be dead already."

"Dragons are not easily rushed because they are not used to the concept that something might try to rush them. They are more solitary than humans and consider no other species their equal."

"They still sound like dicks, even if they're not trying to kill us, great."

Ellonya's eyelids almost flickered at that, but she didn't sit up.

"Not an untrue statement. But the same could be said of many species. The dragons' decline hurt our people, but humans have been steadily hunting us to extinction."

Looking uneasily at them, Ker grimaced. "Yeah. Humans suck. Are you saying, what, you'd like to get some balance back?"

Sallvayn nodded. "Dragons and humans are alike in the danger they pose to other species and in their egos. It is important that one has the other. For our people also. We depend on dragons for the preservation of our abilities, our beautiful appearances."

Diplomatically ignoring the beautiful comment, Ker was curious enough to continue to press. "And you need humans because?"

Sallvayn shrugged. "You have your many faults, but as a species, you have a talent for creating, for farming the land, for breeding animals." Sallvayn put all his asymmetrically aligned teeth on show and grinned. "Our people need to have someone to steal from. Of the many stereotypes held against our people, that one is not untrue."

❖

The oasis wasn't large. Someone was clearly cultivating it—the way the palm trees surrounded the water was too deliberate—but it was by no means a busy trade stop. The setting sun shone on the water from a spring that was only a little longer and wider than Loren. Rocks and vegetation obscured the full effect, though, and as Litz rounded around another large boulder after Kella, she became aware that something was already at the water's edge. She heard the low growling before she moved to see anything. And more bizarrely, the bleating.

Kella's chimera had not been alone.

This one had no hump but a fully formed goat's head on its back, and those eyes had all the malice of a small animal whose only recourse in most situations was to charge. The lion head, by comparison, regarded them almost sleepily, using its mane to shake the flies from its bloody maw. He tossed his head, turning away from his drink to face them. Litz stilled and opened her mind, her eyes, to Loren.

I see a rescue is in order.

It would not be unappreciated.

Kella whacked at her arm and shook her head but remained still. "Lift me," she said out of the corner of her mouth.

Litz watched the lion head watch them. "What?"

"With your magic. You can, right? Get me in the air. I'll do the rest."

Whatever her plan was, there were surely easier ways of ending this. But Kella's dark eyes still held her attention despite her focus on the now hissing beast in front of them. Those eyes shouldn't be any more trustworthy or commanding than those of the snake or the goat or the lion, and yet, Litz found herself nodding. *Hold off for now.*

She concentrated on what *pushing* Kella's small body off the ground would take from her without giving too much weight to any specific place. This could break a bone or worse if it went wrong. Her uncle had told her stories of many magic-users breaking backs in the attempt to make each other fly. Kella had a hand on her sword, which gave Litz a flash of inspiration. "Put both hands on your sword but don't unsheathe it."

Kella did so and stood there waiting.

The chimera, still some three metres away from them, did not seem in a hurry. Assumedly, they were pack animals to some extent and likely unused to the presence of humans. Even had it not been hunting alone, it wouldn't have immediately known what to do about them.

"Now," Litz murmured in warning before *pushing* the sword into the air. She watched as Kella hesitated for a moment before contorting her features into a gleeful snarl and letting out a loathsome scream. She thrashed around in the direction of the chimera's heads, and Litz worried he might move in for a bite, but he stepped back, intimidated or at least confused by this floating, screeching, kicking fiend moving slowly through the air toward him. There was a last grunt and a hiss before he backed off completely and ran.

The pool was, for now, theirs.

Slowly, Litz pulled the sword back to the ground. Kella gave a last whoop of victory and let go, falling with her knees braced for impact. This wasn't enough to provide a steady landing, and she quickly lost her balance, falling backward like a tipped turtle. She was still giggling as Litz helped her to her feet.

"I guess chimeras are just big cowardly house cats with more heads," Kella said as she gripped Litz's wrist with both hands.

By the time Loren arrived, Kella had most of her clothes off and was wading into the water. *Not looking at her so deliberately gives you away even more*, Loren informed Litz.

Shut up, Litz shot back as she managed to hold off on looking at the water until the splash of Kella submerging completely forced her eyes.

I mistrust this place, Loren told her.

That's because you're always suspicious when good things happen.

You're mistaken. We just don't always agree on what a 'good thing' is.

Litz sighed and looked at the idyllic pocket of green surrounding them, which was just a little too small for Loren to lie down in for fear of crushing the vegetation. There was more colour, more signs of life here than she'd seen in days. It was like a tiny slice of home, and looking at it had homesickness gnawing uncomfortably at her chest. Gods, she'd been getting tired of seeing dirt and sand wherever she looked.

This desert has tried to hurt us too much already. It's hard to trust it can still give us something good.

Litz focused on her once-caged charge, now floating in the water, eyes closed as she faced the sky with an expression of childish glee spreading over her features. *Sometimes, good things happen.*

Hmm. And the oasis might be one of them. But that girl is not, and you know it.

What?

Making you go and look at monsters with her is not a romantic gesture. Even for your bizarre human standards.

Okay, I am aware that human courtship contains more subtleties than dragons', but please, how could you honestly mistake—

"Talking about me?"

Litz blinked. Kella was emerging from the pool again, the setting sun blazing behind her as she kept both feet in the water. "I was just noting that the chimera today was…unexpectedly lovely," Litz said, biting back a smile as she started walking toward Kella while ignoring Loren's offended huff. Unfortunately, it was harder to ignore the reality of Kella's body now that so much of it was exposed. It wasn't just the curve of her breasts or the jut of her collarbones but the scars. A deep ragged cut stretched from below her right knee and right up her thigh, and Litz now wanted badly to stroke it.

"Yeah," Kella looked down, smiling, and kicked one foot up to splash before she sat on a rock. Mercifully, her smile didn't seem to carry too much awareness about where Litz's thoughts had turned. "They're funny looking things."

"It actually reminded me of a dance we have back home, one we dance at weddings and other celebrations. It's sometimes called the chimera, and I think I understand why now."

"Okay, yeah, you've lost me," Kella admitted as she wriggled along on her rock to make room for Litz to sit beside her.

"It's traditionally called the Quineah, and it's very *odd* to look at from the outside. It's a group dance that involves everyone, with one couple weaving around the group and always coming back to each other." Litz shook her head, smiling now. "The most bizarre version of it I've ever seen was when our king took on another consort, who became my youngest cousin's father, and in the celebration, they had to make the partner dance fit for four different people and—" She almost started to laugh at the memory but caught Kella giving her a look and composed herself.

"You would have to see it for yourself. The point is that it always looks ridiculous from far away, but when you're dancing it, when you're in the middle of everything and up close...it's still confusing, but it's beautiful, and it makes you feel so connected to everything. Yeah."

"Looking at the chimera made you feel like you were dancing?"

"Sort of?"

"Cool." Kella nodded, apparently accepting this with only mild amusement. Then, she frowned slightly, still looking at her feet in the water. "Do dragons dance?"

Litz made a face as the familiar voice at the back of her head put in an indignant *Yes.* "You would call that dancing?" Litz said, startled into speaking aloud.

"Some disagreement there, ladies?"

Litz rolled her eyes. "Loren is reminding me that dragons do have a custom of—"

Dancing.

"Circling one another in the air. It's lovely to watch, but—"

We do most of our movement in the air. Why would our dancing not take place there also?

"Fair," Litz allowed. "She says I shouldn't consider it any different than our dancing, even though it's very different."

Kella seemed to think this through before nodding and saying, "Fair enough."

Unable to help herself, Litz narrowed her eyes. "How are you so okay with all this?"

"With what?"

"With Loren, for a start. Considering that two days ago you were telling me she was an evil monster controlling my every move, and now you're asking if she can dance? Surely, that's a big change in worldview."

Kella kicked her other foot in the air, the splash almost reaching as far as Litz before dipping back in the water. "My stepda has this thing he says a lot," she said slowly. "He says there's the things that you think and the things that you feel. They're both important, but you shouldn't get them mixed up or expect them to keep up with each other." She shrugged, the frown stealing over her face betraying her less than unfazed attitude. "I'd be a pillock to get through all this and still be thinking the same and not be ready to at least try to learn other things. But that doesn't have to mean I feel any different yet. But, hey, maybe I will later." A smile lit up her face so brightly, it seemed to be made of lightning. "I reckon we could manage to catch some fish for dinner before the light goes. And I checked through the packs again this morning, so I know we still have alcohol left of some description. It's all looking suspiciously home-brewed, but I'm willing to take a gamble."

At Kella's wink, Litz shook her head. "Bad idea. Not that it would make my fishing any worse." A thought occurred to her that made her groan. "No. We should catch *more*. Because we can't rely on getting this lucky again. I think some of the trees back there might—" As Litz spoke, Kella seemed to be putting herself through some kind of internal struggle.

"I could...ugh." Kella clenched her hands into angry fists and pushed them into her face as she groaned. She sounded like she was in considerable pain. "Look, I really hate not eating. If we start getting starved, and like, I mean, really, if..." She sighed heavily. "Like dying from starvation out in the fucking desert was not on my list of things I wanted to do with my life, so yeah, if it comes down to it, I guess my thinking's caught up at least that much and..." She groaned loudly again and shook her head, hands falling to her side again in something that looked like defeat. "Look, if we have to, I'll consider riding the godsdamn dragon, okay?"

I'm sure I should count myself lucky to be considered.

Litz smiled slowly. "Yesterday, you said—"

"I know what I said, all right? And I'd still rather do almost anything else. But it's, yeah, I guess it's an almost now."

"I know you still had to note that she was a 'godsdamned' dragon, but I still feel a little—"

"If you tell me that you are any variation on proud of me, believe me, I will actually stab you."

"I believe that you would actually try."

❖

The longer Kella looked at the oasis, the harder it was to remember that she had been forced out here against her will. It reminded her of the gardens the old king used to keep in the upper balconies that she had frequently hopped over to sneak up to Jev's window, like someone had tended to it on purpose to help it look this beautiful.

One look at the dragon, who was warily watching and definitely not napping, was enough to clear up those feelings that she was on some sort of insane break from her problems.

Maybe, a treacherous voice that sounded uncomfortably like Jev's pointed out, she was relaxing into this so easily and not trying to escape because part of her didn't want to go home. Go home to the brother she needed to protect, to watch, to convince that everything would be all right. Go home to the man she wished she could call her father, who was so damn proud of her. To the king who'd betrayed her, to the team who hadn't fought, or hadn't fought hard enough, to get to her, to the people who expected just so fucking much. And a bunch of killer dragons she would be expected to keep killing, regardless of everything she'd seen now.

Litz seemed to think that she was keeping herself together. She was, mostly. She was almost certain that she'd never killed anything that hadn't killed people first. Though, she had mostly just turned up where Findan had told her to.

"Are you all right?" she registered Litz asking.

Focusing on calming her heavy breathing, Kella watched her fingers curl into the cold sand of the small beach, feeling like they didn't belong to her anymore. "I'll be amazing if we keep that alcohol coming. I think it's a sort of homemade ourzen."

She was expecting librarian-like objections but instead heard the thunk of the bottle they'd been sharing being placed at her feet.

"Thanks."

❖

Litz was beginning to wonder if those feelings Kella had referred to had started catching up with her thoughts in a way that might turn ugly, but she allowed the drinking anyway. She'd already decided it wouldn't be sensible to have much. She had initially kept it in case they needed any later, most likely for medicinal purposes but potentially for trade with any of the nomadic clans.

Tactically, it would be a good idea to avoid other people. Litz might be new to diplomacy, but she felt that being found travel-worn and dragging a foreign prisoner across a desert was not the ideal way to represent her country. Since she wasn't so great on her western languages, they might not speak a common language.

But also…maybe she didn't want this illusion they'd been keeping up together to have to end. It was getting harder to remember that Kella was her prisoner and not something more like a comrade, not to give into the feeling that they were, in a strange way, in this together.

Except that Litz had rarely been close with any of the warriors under her command, so comrade didn't exactly work either. Anything more than respect was usually out of reach when the reality of who she was created an immediate distance that was hard to cross. Litz also hadn't wanted to feel the guilt of losing people she cared about, who she could have saved, had she feared revealing herself less.

But she had revealed herself to save Kella.

And now look where we are.

Stop listening, Litz snapped, frowning. *And I saved her to save all of us.*

You did, and you didn't. Over at the other end of the oasis, Loren's eye gleamed in the reflection of the firelight. *Do you think that word of your powers will get back to your king?*

Litz spared a glance at Kella, who seemed to be fascinated by the almost empty bottle clutched in her hand. *I hope not.*

You know the Circle would not like it either. And if the king chose to defend you, it could result in a historic rift between them.

And that kind of civil war would end well for no one. Especially with Mabaki in the mix.

You think of her by her first name. Don't pretend with me.

For a few moments, no one talked either aloud or within Litz's mind, and she simply listened to the crackling fire and Kella's slow turning of the fish they'd caught over it.

Would you do it? Kill her if you felt it would help stave off civil war?

And restart the war with Jeenobi? No. I might not be a good diplomat, but I hope not to reach that low point within my first few months on the job, Litz tried to joke.

I ask because I don't think you'd be able to anymore. Loren gave a sort of groan that made Kella flinch and sit upright. *Aggressive socialization. Very stupid.*

Litz ignored this and kept looking at Kella until she bemusedly offered her the bottle. Litz was about to refuse but reasoned that there really wasn't much left and finished it instead.

Kella was still looking at her strangely, and Litz found herself looking back with new eyes. She'd dismissed Kella's stories concerning monstrous dragons, but that felt wrong now that she had seen Kella's attitude to the chimeras. With that first one, they'd surely had a great advantage over it—it was sleeping and young and alone—but Kella had felt affection toward it, had never intended to harm it. Litz had assumed that she must have steeled herself to be able to kill anything monstrous, anything nonhuman, and from there, her aggression toward dragons had arisen. But she'd expressed less distaste for magic than most Litz had ever known, and she'd let the chimera go. Many things no longer added up.

As Loren had said, why had none of the Jeenobian dragons ever taken a rider? Why hadn't they spoken up for themselves?

Kella made a face and turned away, and Litz smiled, despite her inability to dislodge Kella's story from her head. The way she'd spoken of her mother's death…Litz had seen battle, known grief, but she knew that she had never known horror like Kella had gone through that day. And she'd hesitated when she'd claimed that the dragon had "attacked" her brother. It didn't sound likely to Litz, especially considering that the boy, who Litz had seen briefly for herself, had grown up healthy and strong. But though an attempt at bonding from the dragon was still a bizarre idea, it seemed to make more sense than the former.

How is a bond formed, anyway?

What? There was a squirming amount of discomfort mixed into Loren's feelings now. *You were there. You know.*

But I don't. It was so difficult to admit. Loren was always right. And she was in Litz's head, always. To not trust completely the person who shared that space with her was unthinkable.

So why was Litz wondering if her dragon was lying to her?

You've spent too much time speaking to no one but Jeenobians. Loren huffed, brushing past the point. Litz wanted to let her.

You're avoiding the question. Why? What could you possibly have to hide from me?

It's not a matter of hiding. It's about what's acceptable to speak of.

Polite. I'd thought that was a taboo term for dragons.

Litz looked over at Kella, who was holding herself still as if waiting for Litz to finish her silent conversation. "Disgusting," she'd said when she'd first seen that Litz really did hear Loren's thoughts and feel her feelings. Litz couldn't make out any of that disgust anymore, but there was still a wariness there.

Some things, Loren thought carefully, *are not correct to share with humans, whatever we feel about them.*

But I'm not 'humans,' Litz said, not bothering to hide her irritation now. *This is my brain we're talking about here.* Loren's silence had her shaking her head, frustrated.

"Something you wanna say?"

Litz set the empty bottle down, realising she'd been holding it up as Loren had been speaking. "Yes. I've been wondering. How did you get the sand demons to leave us alone?"

"The sand terrors?" Kella grinned at the charring fish and sat up in a crouch that seemed a less comfortable angle. She really struggled with keeping still. "How d'you think I did it?"

Litz tried to think back, remembering the sight of Kella covered in blood and grinning the same grin she wore now. "I think you used yourself as a kind of weapon against them."

"As a…hey, that sounds pretty awesome," Kella said slowly. "But wrong. Nah, I just asked them to go away."

"You just…"

"Asked them, yeah." Apparently deciding the fish were finished cooking, Kella slowly lifted the stick she'd speared them on above the fire. "They're not the smartest things, but they have language, and I know enough of it to get them to listen to a few simple suggestions."

"It must have looked like witchcraft," Litz said with a small smile.

"Yeah. Heh, I was actually worrying they'd turn on me for that but figured, hey, they've already arrested me, what more could they plan on doing? But then your trick majorly overshadowed mine, and I didn't have to worry anymore." She arranged the fish with some leftover polenja she'd already left in two bowls.

"You think they made it back okay?"

"I'm judging them if they didn't. We weren't *that* far out, and they took most of the supplies." Kella passed her a bowl and shrugged. "They made their choice, and they chose to be dicks. You don't kill someone while they can't fight back, even if you're scared of them."

"But you, you're not scared of me."

Despite still chewing, Kella stuck out her tongue. "Should I be?" she asked, mouth still full. She swallowed loudly before Litz could say anything. "I guess I've never really thought about magic much. Like, it's useful, but so's cleaning up after a sick baby. It's y'know…" She made a shuddering motion, then smiled, looking apologetic. "I've known people who use it. I know people who get really freaked out by it. And I mean, it makes sense. People don't really understand what it is or how much people who use it can do, so if you don't know a person, it's like they've got an invisible knife that they could stab you with whenever they like." She shrugged again and returned her focus to her food.

Litz tried to do the same.

"How come you learned, anyway? Can't imagine you'd be so fucking secretive about it if they taught this in princess school."

"There was no princess school."

Kella raised her eyebrows as she continued to chew aggressively. "Humour me, Princess."

Gripping it a little tighter, Litz looked at her bowl. "I learned because I wanted to learn. Because it seemed like no one could give me a good reason why I shouldn't, and I'd always been taught to learn how to do something if I thought it would be useful. Learn languages, combat skills, embroidery, tree husbandry. It just felt like one more thing like that."

"Except one that you couldn't tell anyone about."

Litz nodded, feeling uncomfortably understood. "Yes. It was… mine. How are you finished already?"

Kella wiped the back of her hand slowly over her mouth. "I was hungry."

"Eating doesn't need to be a race."

"Something might have attacked while we were eating. Good to be ready."

"Out here?"

"I've heard enough of your judgements, so I am going to go get some more alcohol," Kella announced, standing.

Litz groaned. "Don't, we might need that," she said, aware she was whining.

"Calm yourself, Princess, it's not the only bottle left."

"How many did they bring?"

"Again, you're supposed to be a soldier. You're really saying that you're surprised by how much these guys were drinking?" Kella shouted over her shoulder, already pulling another bottle from one of the camel's sacks and showing that there really were two more left after that. And Litz was sure the Jeenobian soldiers hadn't left them with everything.

"Fine. I guess, bring it over," Litz said, giving up on sounding like she was in charge.

When Kella handed her the bottle, she drank from it happily until she noticed the odd texture to the rim. "Ugh. The sand even gets in here, that's horrible."

Kella held out an expectant hand. "Honey, we're still in the middle of the desert. What the fuck were you expecting?"

After obligingly handing back the alcohol, Litz shook her head and looked at the tops of the trees surrounding the small lake. They looked so small, so lonely compared to the ones she was used to. "I just, I hate thinking that all of the desert was probably like this place maybe a thousand years ago. Maybe less."

"Oh yeah?"

"Mm. Whenever the edges of our forest were destroyed, they'd eventually become part of the desert. Not the grasslands. They really just die. We didn't take care of it well enough, so it died."

"Nah, I don't see it."

"What?"

"Well," said Kella, after taking another drink and sitting up a bit straighter. "Then, how d'you explain this?"

"I—"

"If us westerners are the big evil idiots who chopped down our forests, how come there's still places like this? I think the desert and all the stuff around it…it's doing its own thing, y'know? It's got all these weird plants and animals that do okay out here but would get eaten in like, seconds, back in your forests." Kella narrowed her eyes, and Litz thought she caught another glimpse of the anger she was keeping so well buried shine on the surface of them. "Sure, sand's a pain. But I'll bet the dark scary jungle can't be paradise all the time."

Litz forced her lips into a smile. "No. I'm sorry, it should have occurred to me that this might be an element of natural history studies more than a little influenced by current events."

"Don't worry about it. I mean, we think you guys feed your babies' hearts to dragons. Like, the babies you don't want. That you have this little corkscrew tool, and you just pry it out for them like a fancy delicacy."

"I hadn't heard that one yet."

"Mm. I mean you don't, right?"

"*No.*"

"Well, you can't just *assume* these things."

Litz wasn't sure whether she wanted to laugh or press for more details on this disturbing story and to work out in the process whether Kella was messing with her but instead only shook her head and set to finishing her food. It wasn't exactly tasty, but she had no doubt it was better than anything she could have come up with herself.

"Hey, Princess."

"Mm?"

"That dance you were talking about?"

"Yeah?"

"Want to show me what it looks like?"

Aggressive socialization, Loren repeated.

But Litz only snorted and, feeling slightly woozier than expected, got to her feet. "Okay. But you'll need to stand up too."

Limply, Kella raised both arms up expectedly, and with only minimum eye rolling, Litz took both hands and dragged her to her feet.

"We start by holding hands like this."

"Okay."

"But we need to be standing closer together. Okay, yes, that's good." Kella was now standing so close, Litz could see that the bridge of her nose was in exact line with Litz's chin, but only because Kella was balanced on her toes. Though they'd both finally had the chance to wash, the smell of the road still clung to Kella in a way that, strangely, wasn't unpleasant. "Now we spin."

"What? Oh, right," Kella said as Litz led them into twirling over the sand.

"And we both raise our right arm," Litz said, demonstrating. "That the person behind us twirls us with."

"But there's no—"

"Imagine," Litz said firmly, releasing her hand from Kella's to twirl with her invented partner and waited patiently until Kella had done the same. "And now we link hands again."

"Okay."

"And twirl under our own arms like this."

"Fuck, warn a girl next time."

"And then we spin again."

"All right, I'm dizzy now."

"Don't worry, you get used to it. Now we run this way."

"I *said*, warn me."

"I *did*."

"*As* you were dragging me!"

With slight concern, Litz checked Kella's face but saw that she was laughing. "You wanted to see how it was done. And now you tell me that you can't keep up with my people's recreational—"

"Did I say I couldn't keep up?" Kella asked, panting slightly as she let Litz lead her toward the lake. "Did you hear me saying I couldn't keep up?"

"No, I didn't, but you appear to be—"

Litz felt a firm hand at her back as Kella began to lead the dance as she would have much later in the sequence. And then Litz was being dipped, her body bent back toward the sand.

And that wasn't due to happen in any version of the dance.

Especially not with Kella standing over her with something that might have been fear flickering over her face before she leaned down, her lips pressing to Litz's in a way that was as achingly gentle as it was hungry.

And Litz was letting it happen. Again.

And *gods*, she wanted to do more than just let it happen. This was one of those good things, maybe not one she could trust, but Litz still wanted to be able to seize it for herself.

She wanted…

She wanted too much.

Though she knew she'd had less to drink than Kella, her head was still fuzzy from the alcohol and fighting desperately to catch up. But before it had the chance to, Kella was already pulling back, only just holding on enough to not drop Litz in the sand.

Loren was loudly silent.

"I'm guessing that's not in the dance."

"Not in the traditional choreography, no."

"Cool. We're coming up with new things," Kella said, still keeping up that "joking" tone as she gently raised Litz back to her feet. "Originality," she sang.

Obligingly, Litz smiled, feeling, for what must have been the millionth time since she'd left Malya, like she had no idea what the correct thing to do was. She'd always liked knowing what the rules were, even if she didn't always follow them. That way, ignoring it became a choice.

"But, yes, that's the gist," Litz lied as they continued to stare at each other, with Litz suppressing a mad hope that Kella would start attacking her again so she'd feel back on familiar footing.

This is...awkward, Loren said.

The dancing was a bad idea. I should never have agreed to that.

As you say, I understand little of humanity's courtship rituals. But I would say so.

CHAPTER FIFTEEN

Ker hadn't realised he'd fallen asleep until he was woken by something nudging his foot. Zebenn used to kick at his feet to wake him on their mornings on the road, so he woke expecting to see them standing above him. But he slowly processed that what was nudging at him wasn't a foot but something with a completely different weight and shape. And texture. A scaled texture.

"Fuck me," Ker muttered as he squirmed his way into sitting up and almost hit his head on the jutting back wall of the cave while putting as much distance between himself and Ellonya's tail as he was able. "Could you warn a guy?"

That was my warning. You are awake. Now we can begin.

A glance out the cave mouth confirmed Ker's suspicion that it was still the middle of the night. He was about to start complaining until he remembered that Ellonya finally taking notice of him was exactly what he wanted and had been what he'd been attempting to stay awake for before assumedly falling asleep. Forcing himself not to yawn, he cracked his neck and tried to peer past the large glowing dragon eyes fixed on him. Seeing nothing, he sighed and felt around to find the remnants of the fire he'd made before sleeping. The power to create something like fire from nowhere was very different to controlling objects in close proximity, and Ker had never mastered it, had never even wanted to try.

Apparently sensing the direction of his thoughts, Ellonya gently breathed flame on the remaining pile of sticks. Unsure how to process that, Ker focused on not moving. Ellonya gave no indication she'd put any thought into the gesture. More interestingly, in the new light, Ker could now see Sallvayn perched comfortably on Ellonya's back and looking healthy. The smug expression they were wearing was the first thing Ker noticed, but the very close second was the way their skin seemed almost to glow, the way they sat up with new pride. He wouldn't have said that they had looked unhappy or unhealthy before, but now the change was stark. He could even make out colours on their skin, where before there'd only been a dull greenish brown.

Apparently, Ellonya had accepted their offer of mutual improvements. Or maybe that was just something that started happening because of their close proximity. Ker filed that away as something else to ask Sallvayn. "Looking good, Sall," he said sleepily instead of articulating any of those questions.

"Yes," Sallvayn agreed, nodding.

I think we should bond.

"Right now?"

Yes.

"Okay." Ker gulped, trying to focus on what Sallvayn had told him earlier and not the image of the moment his mother's hair had caught fire. "What do you need me to do?"

He could feel Ellonya attempting to form a thought to send his way, but she seemed uncertain, like most of the thoughts she had weren't appropriate.

"You don't know?"

I've never had the reason to know.

He closed his eyes, trying to pretend to himself he was still sleeping. "All right. If this is going to take a long time for us to figure out, why don't we rescue Kella first, then work on the magical connection stuff?"

No. Besides, you cannot trust that I will consider her a priority until after we are bonded.

He slumped, unsurprised. Then, attempting to channel Findan's school teacher manner, he took a deep breath. Kella, he was doing this for Kella. Who might hate him for what he'd done to find her. If he ever actually did find her. "Okay. What do we all know about this bonding business? Sallvayn, you said you knew something last night, yeah?"

Sallvayn drew themselves up a little higher and said, "We have never seen it done, but we have heard of it. It was something most dragons wanted to do at least once or twice within their lifetimes," they continued once they seemed assured of Ellonya's attention. "In the same way they may have intended to sire or bear clutches. The best thing a dragon aspires to have is a mind said to be so wide, so open, that it is hollow, where new ideas can bounce easily and quickly. Connecting meaningfully with a compatible human mind is a widening experience, and one they believed helped them become more powerful, more developed, more mature, to help them become unique from any other dragons they knew."

Ker nodded. This was essentially a repeat, though on the first hearing, he had found it fascinating; now, he was just impatient. But there was a kind of yearning in how Ellonya was looking at Sallvayn, as though she desperately wanted to remember or be capable of understanding what they were saying but couldn't yet. It made pity clutch tight around Ker's heart.

It may help me become less like them and more of what I was meant to be.

He nodded. Infected, Sallvayn had said. And Ker still wasn't sure what they'd meant by that. Or if they knew. "Yes, but how does it happen, and how is it any different than just touching minds?"

Sallvayn screwed up their face. "It's different because it wouldn't just be touching minds anymore. It would be touching souls."

A shudder ran through Ker, like he could feel his future self looking back on this moment with emotions he didn't even have in him weighing heavy on his heart. "Okay," he said. "What makes that different, and how do we do it? Is there like a ceremony or something?"

Ceremony, Ellonya mused. *Maybe, maybe.*

He wanted to push her on what sounded like she was trying to remember something, but he had a feeling she was as frustrated by her memory as he was.

"What do *you* remember?" Sallvayn asked, and after a few beats, Ker registered that the question had been aimed at him.

"Me?"

"You've been bonded to a dragon once before, and you've been vague about it. More than bonded, we think, because it was so sloppily done. So what happened?"

His mother had burned, and the smell of it felt imprinted in Ker's nostrils. It was hard to think about anything that had happened before that, anything that he had seen the creature do that wasn't killing her over and over again. "I—"

But Kella hadn't burned.

Yet. Probably.

He swallowed. "We talked. He thought I was interesting." He had been lonely and afraid. "I know that he wanted to…to connect. To not feel so on his own." He shook his head and narrowly stopped himself from announcing that this was stupid and that there was no way they could possibly piece this together. He'd been a kid, about to experience life-altering trauma. But he knew he'd be lying and that the creatures staring at him, waiting, would tell him that.

"It was like he…he breathed on me, like he was going to breathe fire. But he didn't. It was *like* fire, but it was green, and I wasn't frightened," Ker said, realising it was true as he said the words. When he remembered that moment, the thought of what happened next clouded his feelings, and he was unable to feel anything but a churning sickness in his stomach and guilt and a heart-stopping anxiety. But back in that moment, he knew he hadn't been scared. "It didn't feel like anything. I, I don't know what it was," he added apologetically. "But after it was *pushed* at me, I could feel the dragon pushing everything in his head at me too. And I…I could feel it."

"Feel what?"

"Everything. Every thought this dragon had ever had, every feeling. So much he'd lost, so much he missed that he couldn't even remember well enough to know what it was he was missing. And this rage. At what had reduced him to this and that terror of losing himself completely. That's why he'd been so desperate to latch on to me."

Just like me.

"Yeah." Ker held Ellonya's gaze, unsure how he felt, but Sallvayn seemed jittery. "It's like you and the gremlins but different, right?"

In what way?

"It's. Y'know. Like, a symbiotic relationship thing. They get something, and you get something back. I always guessed that the dragonriders in Aelshia gained status, and the dragons got someone to control, but it's more than that, isn't it?"

Ellonya kept on staring, but Sallvayn seemed to have formed an opinion. "We always heard it described more as a human marriage. Beneficial to both parties but meant to be more of an emotional tie than a practical one."

"So this would be like, what, a marriage of convenience?"

Except, Ellonya put in, processing her thoughts slowly, *I do not know how to make this green fire. I have never even seen it.*

❖

The last thing Kella said to Litz before they both curled up to sleep in their tiny tent—that looked even more sorry for itself than their attempt the night before—was, "By all the gods, stop freaking out about the kiss. I can hear you freaking out."

Ever since their dance, Litz had been acting strange, twitchy and even more awkward than usual. Eventually, they separately wrapped themselves up for bed, and as soon as Litz started breathing heavier, Kella returned to the planning she'd started moments after the aforesaid kiss.

That Kella didn't *regret*. For one thing, she was probably going to die soon, and it had been a good kiss, and for another, it had finally forced her into reevaluating her priorities. The plan had always been to escape. She'd let herself get distracted, let herself feel like she owed something to Litz, who was still planning to deliver Kella back to her country as a prisoner. She'd let herself become weak, get stupid, because she'd been lonely.

Pathetic.

But the problem, as it always had been, was the dragon. The dragon currently keeping watch over them both. Attempting to kill it alone would be idiotic, and Kella wasn't even sure she had the stomach to go through with it anymore. But she'd had a lifetime of dealing with enemies that were bigger, stronger, and more powerful than she was. Surely, *surely*, she could think of something now that Litz's guard had hopefully been dropped.

She was halfway to congratulating herself on that when she remembered that she still wasn't coming up with a plan and that the kiss hadn't been a planned seduction, but a…

Yeah. Nothing really.

Wondering if the dragon was currently trying to browse through her thoughts, Kella sent out an obligatory *fuck off out of my thoughts if you're in there.*

She got no response. And for some reason, that only made her feel lonelier and not relieved. Great, she thought sarcastically. You're alone for a couple of days, and you imprint like a fucking baby bird on whatever happens to be around.

But a plan. She could still make one of those.

❖

"Never? You're sure?"

Ellonya looked so flustered that Ker started to edge back, worrying she might lash out in frustration, but he held her gaze. *There's a lot I don't know. But so far as I can remember, no. I am sure I have never done this, nor seen it done.*

He slumped. He really wished he had his books. Days ago, he'd so confidently told his da he knew them all by heart, and he mostly did, but it still would have been comforting to flip through them again. Though he was sure that none of them had ever mentioned green fire. He would have remembered that. And if it was the key ingredient to the creation of dragonriders, Aelshia would have jealously guarded that knowledge.

"It wasn't really fire," Sallvayn said slowly.

"No."

"And it wasn't some kind of venom some of them grow?"

"I don't think so." Ker sighed. "Look, this sounds daft, but is there a way that dragons can show their soul?"

Sallvayn looked up. "Like a physical echo?"

"Sure," he said, having no idea what that meant.

I don't know how to do that. The words came to Ker's head with a great wave of exhaustion. *I was foolish to hope for anything better,* she thought before she pulled back all her thoughts at once and started to turn away, Sallvayn making confused faces at Ker from her back.

"Wait, we can't give up now," he tried. "Why don't you try asking the other dragons down there?"

There is so little left of them, I would be lucky if they heard me. They never listen. Mostly, I don't think they can.

The weight of her sadness, her anger, her loneliness, and the knowledge that she had lived in this cave for some time, so frustratingly close to other dragons, was almost physically crushing.

I shouldn't have tried, she thought, a heartbreaking dullness reverberating through Ker at the words. *We are dead, we are worth nothing now. We don't even have the echoes left of what we were.*

"But you can't just give up."

Why? She moved her head back to stare at him, and though he wanted to squirm away from that gaze, he forced himself to remain motionless. *Because you need me to help you, because you do not feel this is how your 'story' should go?* The words were sad but somehow not bitter and certainly not unkind. For some reason, that had Ker flinching from them even more.

"No," he said eventually. "Because I think we both need something from this, and you haven't even tried yet."

She was silent for a few moments, and he began to worry that he'd offended her. *I haven't.*

"No. But we could do that now."

We…I wouldn't even know where to start. There is no one left to show me how to be. *No dragon I have found knows any more of what we are or...or what we were than I do.*

　　Gingerly, Ker placed a hand down on Ellonya's tail. "With humans, and we're a lot more sociable than you guys, we're always having to figure everything out on our own." He recognized that frustration leaking in with Ellonya's thoughts and wondered exactly how young she was for a dragon. "Well, most of the important stuff at least." He scratched his nose and shuffled forward as far as he felt safe in the dark. "Look, I think the green fire was like the dragon's soul came out of its body and touched me," he said slowly when Ellonya stayed quiet. "And I think he put out more than he meant to. It never went back to him. I'm not sure if it was supposed to."

　　"It might change you," Sallvayn admitted, moving closer to Ker. "Bonding to two dragons could make you more dragon than most humans are ever capable of becoming. I'm not sure what that might look like."

　　Is she worth this risk?

　　"If she's still alive," Ker said grimly. He still wasn't letting himself consider any other possibility, but he hoped that acknowledging the high odds he faced might succeed in tugging at any heartstrings the dragon might happen to have flapping loose.

　　I will help you, she said. *Even if bonding is impossible, I will help you. Though I would like to try first.*

　　"Thank you," Ker said, shocked. "But why, what made you change your mind?"

　　You make me think. Even if I was not worried about losing the contents of my mind, I think it is good to be around someone who does that for you.

❖

　　Litz had been dreaming about watching Kella try to climb the tree up to the king's palace. It had achieved its fame for being built around one of the biggest trees in the forest, and other than guards, it had no real protection beyond the fact that to gain entrance, you either had to climb the tree or walk in through the front door that was far below the main building.

　　But there Kella was anyway, pulling herself up the thick bark by plunging knives into it while covered in blood and sand, the way she had been when she'd ordered the sand terrors away and grinning the way she had then too.

In the dream, Litz was watching from the ground. She was aware of who she was and that she should be stopping her or raising the alarm, but she was still hesitating when Loren ordered her to wake up.

It was still dark when she dragged herself from the dream and opened her eyes, but the dimming light from the embers of the fire gave her enough light to notice that she was lying in their tiny tent alone.

She ran. Loren growled, sounding pained. *I'm assuming you intend to chase her.*

I guess we'll have to. Can you fly? Litz asked as she got to her feet and wrestled her way out of the half-fallen tent.

Why wouldn't I be able to?

Loren, I've got to assume that she wouldn't have gotten away if you were really *okay.*

Is it a crime now for a dragon to sleep?

Of course not. But I thought we were supposed to take shifts?

Maybe you were drunk, and I didn't trust you to swap with me effectively.

Or maybe you're evading my questions. For a moment, there was nothing making noise except the cicadas in the nearby trees as Litz carefully made her way to Loren. Contrary to popular belief, dragonriders did not gain heightened night vision, but when someone was in her head, it was difficult not to have some awareness of where they were.

She tricked me.

And how did she manage that? C'mon, you know I'm not upset.

No. But you're amused, which is far worse.

"Mostly, I'm glad she hasn't managed to harm you," Litz said as she put a hand on Loren's scales and to her surprise, felt her wince and draw away. "What? *Did* she hurt you?"

Loren gave a short growl of frustration. *No. But she...I heard a noise that sounded like another dragon, so I started moving toward it and didn't notice as she clambered on my back.*

"Did she hurt you?" Litz asked with a little more urgency.

She had vilrose leaves.

Litz processed this for a few moments, understanding now why Loren seemed so evasive. The scent of those flowers was enough to kill a human or send a dragon to sleep. "How?" she settled for asking.

She could have carried them all the way here from Malya. None of those idiots would have known what they were looking for.

"It must be rare stuff all the way out here," Litz said slowly. "I've only ever seen them in the jungle." Not that she usually had the chance or inclination to get close to them. Vilrose plants were a very beautiful, common pink flower throughout Aelshia's forest and only flowered every other year. When they did, humans would walk around with knowing winks and more than a little fear at the thought of dragons getting high.

She pushed them up my nostrils, Loren said with obvious disgust. *And it's not funny*, she insisted as Litz climbed to her seat. *Can we put her back in a cage when we find her this time? Chains, at least.*

"I may have to think about that," Litz admitted grimly as they took off, leaving their last camel staring up at them with mild curiosity.

No more dancing. When we find her, you are going to tie her up and throw her on my back, and we are flying straight home.

I know, I know.

You're still laughing at me.

❖

Kella knew she should be feeling proud of herself. Considering the circumstances, it had been an elegant escape, and sure, they might catch up to her, but she also *might* get herself hidden first. Her plan was to run as far as she thought she could get away with on the camel before doubling back and hiding in the rocks where they'd found the first chimera, next to the oasis.

With any luck, they'd keep following the wrong trail, and she'd be safe to spend a few days making sure she had everything she needed before she headed back west on the camel that, assuming she had a chance of making it that far, might even get her out of this whole misadventure with a profit. Maybe she could try running north and bothering her uncle Colleo out of his labouring sabbatical down the mines. She had lots of options about where to go next. She was free.

But however she planned her next moves, she couldn't escape the feeling that she wasn't escaping; she was *running away*. Running away from a dragon she could have killed but hadn't wanted to. From a version of herself who had been curious to see a country which would want her dead if she ever made it there. Running from the woman she hadn't been able to stop herself from kissing, who'd looked at her like…

Like?

Like someone who was honour bound to bring Kella to justice however she decided to look at her. And Kella owed it to her family to make it home and not be one more tragedy for them, one more body they weren't able to bury. So why was she torturing herself over doing the right thing? She owed Litz nothing. If anything, Litz owed Kella her life and a couple of meals too.

"Think we can start turning back now, buddy," she said, patting at the camel's neck as it started slowing. "I think that's us for tonight." But as she spoke, she had a strange feeling that she was wrong, that Litz wouldn't be so easy to shake off. She had conflicting feelings about the possibility of being found, but she planned to ignore all of them and focus on not letting it happen.

When she looked at the dark horizon stretching in front of her, at the sunlight finally starting to break through, there was nothing to see but sand, fucking sand, and more—

Not sand. There were figures, human figures, moving toward her on what looked to be horses.

"Okay, maybe we don't turn around just yet," she said, nodding as she pushed the camel forward. Hopefully, these people, whoever they were, had heard of Jeenobi's most famous living dragon slayer. "Hey, over here!"

❖

Ker was doing his best not to fall back to sleep, and he was almost succeeding. "Let's try again," he said, yawning widely.

You are tired.

"I know, but hit me again. *Longing.* We're thinking about what you *long* for, and it's useful if that's a joint longing that we're both feeling? Right?"

Gremlins might not sleep as much as humans, but Sallvayn seemed to be peacefully passed out and clutching Ellonya's scales. Of course, it was just as likely that they were simply avoiding the conversation Ker and Ellonya had spent the last few hours circling.

"I'm not sure what it's supposed to mean for dragons exactly, but for me, it's about connecting to something. To someone." *To feel through the dragon how it had felt to burn his mother into ashes.* "To become something more than just myself. To widen my experiences, my personality, my…"

He could remember how it felt as the dragon, burning his mother, but also how much worse it had felt in that moment to experience his dragon's death, which had left a gaping tear in his chest that he'd never managed to heal. In the aftermath, his grief had been threefold: his mother's death, the fact that he'd helped cause it, and the death of what had been, for a few moments, a part of himself. It had almost destroyed him.

The idea of doing this scares you.

He nodded. "Yeah. I haven't been sure how human I am since. And…and it hurt."

To bond?

"No. To lose it."

Ellonya nodded. *To feel good is to risk feeling bad.*

"I guess."

For a longer period of time than I know how to measure, I have felt almost nothing. Maybe what I long for is to feel something.

Making a face, Ker folded his arms. "That's deep."

Deep?

"What you said. It has a lot of meaning."

Thank you? I just meant…what I meant.

Ker nodded, fighting a laugh. "That's cool."

I think I might have an idea of what to do, of something to try. She turned to look at him, and he was sure she was nervous. *I'm not sure this will work, but—*

He sat up a little straighter. "Let's give it a try. That's what we're here for, right?" His voice was pitching higher with every word, but he wasn't sure how to stop that.

It's like projecting my thoughts toward you, I think, but focusing that on what I feel, and—

"Okay, let's go," Ker said, remembering that if Kella was doing anything this foolhardy, she'd be smiling. He might not be capable of mustering a smile, but he could keep his breathing steady.

The fire escaped her mouth like a sigh, an inviting, bright, fluid thing, tentatively moving toward him like a solitary wave. It was so beautiful, and he could only stare. Yes, beautiful, *beautiful like it had been beautiful before.* And it came closer, hovering gently in front of him, reaching for something he wasn't sure he had left for it to take.

He'd given so much before. Everyone had stared at the ash, the place where his mother's body should have been left for them to bury, and no one else had looked at the dragon, at his dragon, whose eyes had still been twitching as he'd choked slowly to death on the throwing star that had flown into his throat in his last moments. Rall and Zebenn had marched over to finish him off...

But Ellonya wasn't down, her eyes weren't twitching; they were staring at him with *hope*, and he felt safe, and that fire had reached his face now. It was warming him gently.

But he had trusted in the comfort and safety of a dragon's inner fire before, and the human with the sword, with the hidden, biting knives, had still come storming in. Protecting him, trying to tear them apart, and he was going to *end* her, and oh gods, Ker had killed his mother.

But he could breathe, he could think, and he could trust because he *had* to for Kella, for Kella who'd never looked at him the same since. He couldn't let her die, couldn't kill her like he'd killed their mother, and *oh gods, she was dead, he was dead, Ker was*—

Alone. Ellonya had gone. And she'd taken the warmth of her green flame with her. The cave was dark again, with only the pathetic embers of the fire giving it any light.

"Okay, okay, *breathe*." It wasn't Kella this time looking at him with a desperate concern he didn't deserve and shaking his shoulders but Sallvayn. Instead of shaking him, they laid their hand patiently against his leg.

Obediently, he slowly let a breath out. "I fucked it."

"She might have killed you. *Then* you'd have 'fucked it.' But lucky for you, she didn't get angry. She just seemed—"

"Disappointed." He choked out a laugh and started wiping his eyes with the back of his hands. Gods, when had he started crying? "She might as well have killed me," he muttered, knowing that he sounded and must look pathetic, with his long legs sprawling on the cave floor like a dropped doll. "She's gone, and it's too late to find another dragon who might still help. And even if I did, what would happen?"

Despondently, he raised his arms and let them both drop back down to his sides again. "Another exciting repeat of whatever that was. I knew I..." His voice caught in his throat as if something in him didn't want to let more words out. "I knew I shouldn't have gone after her alone. I'm not some big hero like the rest of them. If I'd caught up to Kella on my own, I wouldn't have been able to do shit. But I'd thought, I'd thought for a minute that I might actually have something the rest of them didn't. And now, Kella's got no one."

"We misjudged you," Sallvayn said quietly, withdrawing their hand.

Ker really wanted to cry now. But with some effort, he found his voice. "Oh yeah. I almost forgot. I didn't get us a dragon friend like we planned, or at least, I didn't get one who wanted to stick around for me. So I understand if you need to go off without me now too." Gods, he sounded whiny.

"Why do you think we joined you in all this?"

For a moment, he was shocked out of what Kella would have called his "self-indulgent pity session."

"Uh, you wanted to find a dragon."

Sallvayn huffed. "We thought you were interesting. We thought that if anyone had a chance at pulling one of them back from the edge, it was you."

"Yeah? Well, I'm sorry that you were wrong about that. That must be a shitty time for you."

"We weren't wrong."

"You'd call this a success?" Ker snorted, feeling his heart rate rise in something like panic again. "No dragon, one still very broken human—"

"We would call this a first attempt. And you're not broken. You're upset and understandably so. You just tried to redo something that hurt you so badly, you've barely been able to speak of it since. It robbed you of both your mother and your dragon and part of your soul. Of course your soul is still guarded, is still upset. You're scratching at a wound you never stopped to clean. But we thought you were the sort of person who could push past that because you cared about something enough to give you cause to."

Ker breathed in and stubbornly continued to stare at the ground, away from Sallvayn. "She's still gone."

The hand returned. "She wants this as badly as you do. Possibly more. You don't really think she went far, do you?"

❖

Litz suspected they were only a few hours behind Kella, so it wasn't difficult to get a hold of her trail and follow it back through the rocks the way they'd come. She wasn't sure what she was expecting, but Kella had to know she couldn't outrun a dragon, so Litz kept a close eye on the ground.

She could have started walking a separate direction from the camel to throw us off.

She wouldn't last two days. She's not that stupid.

Are you certain? She ran off alone into the desert at night, Loren pointed out moodily.

How awake are you feeling? Really?

Awake enough, Loren assured her with feeling before speeding up.

Wait. There, up ahead.

I see, Loren said. *You think your fugitive ran to them?*

She knows she can't get far alone, and we know how much she enjoys being the centre of attention. Can we get down there?

Loren's only answer was a heavy sigh as she began to slow and angle toward the ground. *They don't seem afraid,* Loren noted of the crowd looking up at them.

Litz frowned. Even in Aelshia, it would be odd to not see hesitancy from those about to be caught near the landing of such an imposing creature. But these people didn't so much as flinch when Loren swooped down next to them. Litz was close enough to see the light from their torches illuminating Kella where she knelt on the sand, her arms neatly tied behind her back.

"Hey," Kella called dully, looking as though she might have waved had she had free use of her hands. The impact of Loren's landing sent a light wall of sand flying at her face and made her choke on whatever it was she would have said next.

Shaking her head now that she knew Kella was unharmed, Litz changed her focus to the crowd surrounding her. They looked to be some of the Narani people, desert nomads whom she knew little about. They were frequently referred to as stargazers, in a manner which certainly sounded derogatory. Most of them were seated on small, lightweight horses, implying that their current base could not be far. Perhaps they had even been using the oasis.

And Litz could be sure from their expressions and Kella's position that she had failed to charm them.

Give her time. You took her two whole days, after all, Loren put in, which Litz chose to ignore as she dismounted, leaping to the ground with a landing that had sand flying back up at her.

There were maybe fifteen of them, all well-armed, and rather bizarrely, out at night with scarcely more than the moonlight to guide them.

It might not be so bizarre for them, Loren reminded her.

True.

"Hello," she tried, exhausting the majority of the Narani vocabulary she had a grip on.

The woman at the front of the troop nodded behind her to a younger man, who dismounted from his horse and stepped forward. "Greeting. Your accent is poor," he said in Litz's language with a more Jeenobian pronunciation.

She nodded stiffly and made the tactical decision to drop her attempts at being a linguist.

Don't knock yourself. You do speak four languages.

Yes, and nobody speaks Narani. I thought the Narani barely even spoke it. "My greetings return to you. My name is Princess Litz, Captain in the Aelshian Royal Guard, Ambassador to Jeenobi and the rider of Loren the Mighty."

Might want to make up a few more titles for yourself there. They don't look impressed.

Shut up. "The woman you hold there is a prisoner of King Jevlyn, who I am holding in custody until her extradition to Aelshia for her crimes. Thank you for re-apprehending her for me." Her father had always told her to assume that everyone was trying to do you a favour; it would make them more likely to feel obliged to.

The woman at the head of the group continued to stare at Litz as she spoke for the man at her side to translate. "We thank you. You flatter us with the gifting of your names. However, we are afraid that this woman is now our captive, and we cannot hand her over without due compensation."

What's a diplomatic way of reminding them that there's a fire-breathing dragon behind me?

Loren snorted. *I don't know of a nice way to say that. I do know of a few subtle demonstrations, though.*

Maybe. "What compensation were you considering?" Litz asked as she risked a glance at Kella, who shook her head, making Litz's forehead crease in concern.

She's trying to distract you.

Maybe. "My party was attacked by sand terrors yesterday. I'm afraid that I have almost nothing to offer. We do have the camel you now hold with you and another not far from here that we would be happy to bring you."

The way Kella's eyebrows rose gave Litz a good idea of her thoughts on this offer. *Two camels? Two? That's all I'm worth?*

"That would be a start," the translator said. "But we happen to have specific compensation in mind."

"And what is that?"

"We wish the return of our ancient landing site that your king has currently banned us from."

Litz breathed out slowly. Real diplomacy, then. "I do not possess the authority to promise anything, and I am not close enough to the people who do. All I could promise is to try upon my return."

One of the only reasons Litz knew anything about these people was because of the recent Narani dispute over land. In the wake of the war, the Aelshian government had tightened their borders and explicitly included the southern region of Ralin in their territory. According to the Narani, it wasn't theirs to include, but since the Narani had no standing army, their grievance hadn't progressed to much.

Litz had been there, and it wasn't much to look at. However, it was where the Narani believed humans had first arrived on Earth following their long journey from the stars. From the little Litz knew, it seemed an odd religion, an odd culture. They believed that humanity had no historical, natural connection to the Earth. Instead, the Narani believed they were only visitors. Her father had told her once that Narani meant "awake" in their language because they felt that they were the only humans who remembered what they needed to know. Whatever that was, they kept it very private.

"We would not have believed you if you'd claimed you did. But we are willing to bargain."

They're still so calm. I don't like it.

They're either very stupid, or they know something we don't. None of their surface feelings are giving anything up. Whatever they're doing they're confident in it.

"Exactly what kind of bargain do you plan on making? I warn you, the prisoner you hold is not so important to my king that she would be willing to lose land over her." Admittedly, Litz wasn't sure the land was worth much. It had long lost most of the strategic value it might once have held and was only fostering bad feeling with the Narani merchants they depended on. But that wouldn't be the diplomatic thing to say.

"No, but we assume you are."

"But you don't have me," Litz said slowly, giving in and glancing in Loren's direction.

"We do not sing songs for killers of dragons, Ambassador, though dragons have scourged our people in the past. Do you know why?"

She wasn't sure which instincts were overriding her logic enough to send her walking slowly over to shield her dragon, but Litz felt it. The smile from the woman in charge was putting her on edge.

"We don't sing songs for dragon slayers because we have no need of them. We are capable of catching them without any need for violence."

I...I can't move.

Rare as her own fear was, feeling Loren's was an even stranger experience, and it almost paralysed Litz along with her. *What?*

Something's binding me. I can't move. Someone's using magic against me.

Litz's gaze flashed over the group holding Kella. One man at the back caught her eye. His eyes kept fluttering closed, his hands tightening and loosening on thin air. It was unlikely he was powerful and well-trained enough to hold a whole dragon still without help, but it was the only explanation. "Release my dragon," she demanded.

The woman in charge did nothing but smile, but it was apparently enough of a communication for her translator to understand. "You will travel with us to Aelshia, Ambassador, and you will explain to your king that when she releases our land, we shall release you and yours."

Litz's mind whirled, considering her options. Kella's help would be useful if she could get her free, but it would be foolish to rely on her. On her own, she would have a good attempt at taking them all. They assumedly wanted her alive, and she could use that against them, but the odds were stacked wildly against her. If she could kill the man holding Loren with his magic, she would no longer need to worry about the rest.

She could attempt to kill him from where she stood, but doing so would reveal her sole advantage and probably cost her more time and effort than she could afford. Especially when she was exhausted and out of practice.

Whatever you plan on doing, I suggest you do it before they finish closing in on you.

Still trying to think her narrowing options through, Litz unsheathed her sword and regarded them all with her haughtiest royal glare, trying to emanate the aura she'd seen so often from her aunt, that unmistakable warning that although they might succeed in touching her, they wouldn't live long enough to regret it.

The dim light was frustrating, but Litz could feel Loren watching her back, which was, if not yet practically helpful, calming her nerves.

As they advanced, Litz thrust her hand out in the direction of the other magic-user and *pulled*. He thudded to the ground, clutching his ribs. But still, he continued to stretch out his hand until she *pushed* his wrist away, satisfied to hear the snap of it breaking even from metres away.

"We had heard that Aelshia disdains magic," the translator said, still frighteningly calm as he watched the magic-user scrabble at the sand, screaming.

"Aelshia might," Litz managed to say as she watched the magic-user finally give up and cradle his hand. "I'm open-minded."

Kella, who Litz now suspected was staying quiet because she had been made unable to speak, flashed a smirk as if they were in this together, as if this was all part of some elaborate scheme they'd devised.

Clutching her sword tighter, Litz asked, *Can you move yet?*

No.

On the ground, the magic-user did not look up from his hand.

What? It was him. It had to be him.

"You are a woman of unexpected talent, Ambassador. However." As the translator spoke, several of the group began to laugh. "You are misplaced in your instincts. This is the magician who triggered what holds your dragon, but he is not necessary in its continuing effect."

More magic-users. This isn't good.

No. It's not. Litz grimly took in her surroundings once more. *If I let loose with the magic and free Kella, we might be able to—*

"You see, he was not our only magic-user."

Very slowly, the entire group now surrounding Litz raised their hands. She could feel it on them now that she was concentrating, that unmistakable aura of people who were used to regularly manipulating the forces of the world.

"It would not be wise for you to move anymore, Ambassador."

It would be very unwise.

Litz risked a glance toward Kella, who looked apologetic, although that might have been wishful thinking on Litz's part. Slowly, she made as though to drop her sword, nodding as she did.

I want to tell you not to, but...

Litz couldn't keep herself from snarling as her sword fell into the sand, and she raised her own hands.

You know that won't help much.

But before Litz had a chance to try her one shot at the leader, her arms were pulled to her sides by some invisible force. The last thing she tried before a hand on the back of her neck drained her remaining energy was to *pull* up the feet of the man coming toward her. It did nothing to help her situation, but it still felt good to watch him hit the sand.

❖

Loren could feel the same strength that was clamping her fire, and much of her physical movement, coming for her mind. As she watched them haul Litz's body onto one of their horses, she roared her frustration. It was a cry she made both aloud and through her mind. Unseemly, maybe, to send her feelings out into the world in such a blast, but it seemed to be the only freedom left to her.

Usually, it was something that could only go a short way. But she was angry. She knew her feelings would go echoing for miles and miles and farther, for any dragons or gremlins or humans attuned to magic. As Loren felt herself grow smaller inside her own mind, she looked at the floored Narani around her with grim satisfaction.

If they were lucky, it would reach Aelshia before anything else could hurt Litz.

❖

The pain, frustration, and sadness Kella felt that dragon blast through her threatened to drown her much smaller body like an unexpected wave. She wanted to weep. She also wanted to throw up and felt a little better about herself only when she saw that some of the Narani had already acted on that same urge.

❖

Litz almost woke up.

❖

Sallvayn had offered to join him, but Ker felt this was a conversation he owed Ellonya to have alone. Reliving his experiences must have been almost as difficult for her as it had been for him. Maybe.

He was grateful for the brightness of the moon as he clambered down the hill he had so frantically dashed up before. He had wanted to bring one of the sticks from his fire with him, but he feared bringing it through the trees toward the river, where Sallvayn had claimed he'd seen Ellonya land.

He'd also feared that the fire would attract any other dragons. Because of course he'd feared that. That was all Ker did: he thought too much and got scared. He knew Kella wasn't the invincible hero she pretended to be—he wasn't a child—but if she ever let worry affect her, it was over the safety of others. Never her own. And she certainly spent no energy worrying over other people's opinions of her. Ker wished he had that kind of bravery. But here he was anyway, and his mother would have told him that was what counted. Or she would have if he hadn't gotten her killed.

When he reached the water's edge, he had a real chance to look around, despite the darkness. It was easier to pay attention when he wasn't afraid he was about to die. The river, maybe ten metres wide, had steep, pebbled beaches on either side. And just downstream slept a dragon. She was farther down than Ker had been told to expect, but he started walking toward her, already attempting to compose the best apology he could cobble together.

What did you even say after something like that?

"Hey, I'm sorry about that panic attack I just had back there. That's a thing that humans do sometimes. You won't have seen much of it before, of course. You've probably been involved in more socialising today than in what sounds like your entire life, and that must have been a big enough dose to put you off it for now. But anyway, I'm up for trying again if you can still look at me. I can't promise it won't end up with the same result, and actually, it almost definitely will. I might not be 'broken,' but I'm not fucking fixed yet either."

When he stood a few paces away, his foot cracked down on a piece of driftwood, and half on purpose, he snapped it. In an instant, the dragon uncurled its head to face Ker with sleepy amber eyes.

Ellonya's eyes were much more yellow than amber.

Gulping, Ker slowly raised his hand in a mechanical wave. "Uh, hey. My name's Ker." He tried not even to breathe after that.

For a moment, the dragon only stared, and Ker had a hope that maybe this one was "a talker" as well and wouldn't try to hurt him. Then the dragon blinked, seemingly jolting itself into wakefulness. It growled.

"Shit," Ker breathed, and ran toward it just in time, narrowly escaping the wall of flame it sent roaring in his direction.

Or, that *they* had sent in his direction, but that was probably the last thing he should be worrying about getting wrong. Not dying seemed a much higher priority. He remembered how much he didn't want to die now. Heart thumping uncomfortably loud in his chest, he leapt over the tail whipping toward his ankles to get nearer the river. He wanted to dive into the shallow water, but he was almost sure that the dragon would be able to boil him alive, and he was very sure that wasn't the way he'd like to go out. So instead, he started running up the beach. He did his best to zigzag, but the beach was rocky, and his stupid long legs had him tripping over his feet.

He grazed his knee and face when he hit the ground. He wanted to scream, from frustration more than fear. If only he'd been faster, if only he hadn't scared off—

There was another dragon roaring in the distance.

Ellonya. He was almost sure it was her and not one of the others come to fight over the piece of meat scrambling over their beach.

Hello, Ker.

Thank the gods *it's you.*

Or just thank me, Ellonya told him, her voice cold but not malicious as she opened her relatively short wingspan to face the purple dragon who'd been coming for Ker.

They had their back turned to him, but he knew that by the tensing of their wings and tail that they were baring their teeth at Ellonya, but she continued to stand strong, proud and unfazed, her orange scales turned a dying fire under the moonlight.

You look amazing, Ker thought at her, not sure if she would hear. He still had no idea how any of this worked, but he was here, giving it a try with no books to turn to, no friends to ask for advice. And he could swear that she looked bolstered as she dipped her head and pitched her shoulders high, her tail twitching and swaying like a cat's.

The purple dragon took a few steps back, prompting Ker to drag himself back into a sitting position, fighting to get away from them. But his panic proved worthless. Just like that, the other dragon shrank lower before they sprang, bounding into the river and flying up into the night. Ellonya watched them depart.

Thanks. You saved my life.

It was in need of saving. She lay on the beach and looked across the river into the darkness of the trees on the far side.

"Are you, like, a big deal around here?" Ker asked as he stood and walked toward her.

The others who shelter around here are wary of me. I know more than they do, and this worries them. Though I don't think they know why.

He walked to the shore and sat. "I'm sorry. That must have been hard." When she continued to stare and say nothing, he asked, "What *do* you know that they don't?"

It's not really what I know. It's what I learn. I don't think they learn from one day to the next one. Not anymore.

He hugged his knees and looked at her as she continued staring at the moonlight on the water. "I'm sorry," he said quietly. "I know you could feel that back there, but that wasn't about you. Not really."

No. That hurt was all yours. But you bearing it alone did not make it any smaller. She paused. *That must have been hard.*

He smiled and edged a little closer to her, feeling the sound of running water soothe his nerves like Findan's magic did for Kella's night terrors. "You do learn." They sat in companionable silence, and Ker thought about what a thing it was to have someone he could do that with. *I think we should try again,* he told her before figuring out that this was what he wanted to say.

Really? She snorted softly. *We don't know each other well. Perhaps that's something this requires.*

He laid a hand on her scaled paw. *I can't think of a better way to get to know someone than by sharing their mind.*

But you fear...

He stiffened.

...losing yourself again. And I wouldn't force you into risking that, not when I have now understood exactly how and why you feel that way.

"It's not what I fear most," he said aloud, sounding hoarse. "Not exactly."

Then what is?

I think I fear being hurt like that again. But it was what came after. Being left alone.

But now you want to save your sister more than you fear losing something.

I do.

I just want to stop being alone. I just want to...to learn more. To have someone to do that with. What? she asked as Ker put his head in his hands, badly hiding his laughter.

"I just...this isn't how I imagined talking to a dragon would go."

Ellonya's mouth twisted up in what Ker suspected could be amusement. *Am I a disappointment?*

Fuck, no. He smiled up at her. *Weren't you listening? I think you're amazing. I think even before…I think I always didn't trust that dragons were what we thought they were. It didn't ever feel like the whole story.*

I'm glad I helped you find your answers.

I'd like to help you find yours if I can.

There was a warm pause, and Ker had the sense that she was trying to reinvent the feeling of gratitude out of sheer unfamiliarity with the concept. *Thank you. I would like that.*

She froze, and a moment later, Ker understood exactly why. He felt barely aware of where he was, who he was, because far more concerning was the oppressive new feeling of an unknown dragon's anguish as she cried out desperately for any kind of help that could hear her. Well, not unknown. Ker now knew as much about her as he did about Ellonya. Perhaps more. In her frenzy, she—*Loren*—laid her whole soul bare, to such a degree that Ker was certain it couldn't have been on purpose. He could feel the love she felt for her rider, her weariness from travel, the mixed feelings she felt about returning home to where she no longer trusted the Circle, whatever that was.

He had found himself on the wrong end of a dragon's thought-blast before. It was why Kella had worked so hard at keeping her actions in a fight so unpredictable, making them hard to influence, for the dragon to see, but he'd never felt something like this. Those had been mindless attacks, stings, really, outbursts of anger. These thoughts, though faint, were clear, and in so much pain.

He saw why. There were humans—magic-users—all around her, ready to take her away, and she was useless; she had let this happen. And it was all so confusing and frustrating because if only Litz had listened to her, if only the girl hadn't run away, if only this desert wasn't so vast, so unjust, so capable of turning every dragon who flew across it mad.

And then the blast of personality from across the dunes clamped shut as suddenly as it had opened to them. Slowly, as Ker tried to process a hope, an idea of who the girl who'd run away might be, he became aware of Ellonya's feelings.

I'm not alone.

Chapter Sixteen

When the man who had bound Kella's voice tripped up, she was finally free to laugh, loud and long. She wasn't entirely sure which part of the situation that she'd gotten them—gotten herself—into was so funny, but the laughter probably had as much to do with the aftereffects of Loren's blast of feeling as it did to anything else.

Even after the feeling had gone, the sound of the dragon roaring in rage and pain was able to stop her laughter before the raised fist of the man beside her was able to. She must have listened to that sound hundreds, thousands of times. Until now, it had never occurred to her that it could draw any empathy from her.

I'm sorry, she thought before she could stop herself. The dragon probably wasn't listening, and Kella would still maintain that no one should be blaming her for running, but it was a reflex. Someone was hurting, and she'd caused it.

Someone else was grabbing at her arm and pulling her up beside them onto a horse. As she kept her face turned to the sky, it occurred to Kella that this would be her first time riding a horse. All their torches had blown out; they were riding with nothing but the moon to guide them.

And the part of Kella that still wanted to see how well piracy would have turned out as a career thought that was pretty badass. Which didn't make anything better but was something to admire. In fact, as they started moving, Kella couldn't stop thinking that the entire situation was like one of those bad-to-worse word games that Ker used to badger her with whenever he wanted to drive her nuts on long journeys.

The good news was that she'd escaped from being forcibly dragged off to Aelshia and maybe executed.

But the bad news was that she'd only managed to run right into more chains.

But the good news was that it should have been easier to escape from witches than a dragon.

But the bad news was that there was no way to know they didn't have dragons of their own. They seemed to know enough to catch one in a way that shouldn't have been possible, even with the practised team they had.

But the good news was that they were probably better at keeping her and Litz fed and alive better than they would have themselves.

But the bad news was that now that they were a "we," Litz had gotten captured. She wouldn't like that. She didn't deserve that.

Oh, shut up.

She'd met some of the Narani before, obviously. She even knew some she would loosely call friends. Being of neither Jeenobi or Aelshian affiliation, they made better merchants and sources of information than most Jeenobians could hope to be. Kella knew the basics of how to speak with them.

She knew that when haggling, you didn't do so alone. They would take you less seriously if they couldn't see visible proof of your allies. They thought humanity came from the stars, and they considered this the dragons' world, and one day, all the humans who knew how to "sing their way home" would get rescued from it. They cared a lot about singing but never did so in public. She knew how to introduce herself, to say good-bye, express her deepest thanks, and tell someone their father had once bred with his own horse, and they were the result. Which was a much catchier phrase than it had any right to be.

She'd never heard anything about them using magic. She had never dreamed that it was so common, so accepted, by *anyone* on the continent, but they *would* keep that quiet in Jeenobi. She'd never heard anything about their land being stolen by the Aelshians, either, and she would have thought they'd have been more open about that.

Kella had always assumed that since they were all nomadic, they wouldn't bother about any particular patches of land. Had Jev ever talked about dealing with any of their clans politically?

Fuck, she needed to *think*.

Findan would have known something more about them. Ker definitely would have, with all his reading.

Okay. Observation. She could manage that. Since they were travelling at night on horseback and not as a full clan with any vulnerable members, they must have come out knowing she and Litz were there. As far as Kella knew, there was no magic which could help them with that, but before tonight, she'd known of no magic that could completely bind a dragon, either.

The Narani had no kings, she was sure about that much. And from what she'd heard, they seemed pretty egalitarian with their process of leadership. They followed whoever seemed like the best decision-maker, and that would change naturally over time. Which would probably make it worth getting on the good side of the woman who'd had her words translated to Litz.

It was hard to see in the dark, but it seemed they'd put Litz in front of a different rider, having already tied her hands. Kella suspected that they were keeping her powers bound as tightly as they were her dragon's fire and wings. Findan had told her it was possible to bind a witch's powers and had said that if Kella understood magic, it would make sense to her. Because Kella wasn't like Ker, Findan didn't have long academic discussions with her. She just pointed her in the direction of her next target.

As the rider she'd been paired with shifted his weight, Kella allowed herself to wonder how Findan might have reacted to her extradition. Findan was family. She loved Kella, *obviously*. But she was also hard to read. And the fact was, if they'd wanted to rescue her, they would have done it a long time before now.

Of course, they might have thought Kella was capable enough to get out of this situation alone. Maybe she shouldn't have worked so hard on the tough slayer act. It might have been nice to be the one getting rescued for once. To be someone worth rescuing.

"Hey, sweet thing," she murmured, patting the horse's flank as they started moving faster. Narani horses were famed for their beauty and swiftness, but Kella had rarely gotten the chance to see one up so close. "You're lovely." She couldn't see, but she hoped they'd brought the camel with them. It might be a regular evil camel, but it had suffered through far too much to end its days abandoned in the desert.

❖

Litz woke up to the feeling of warm metal beneath her cheek and rope binding her wrists at her back. She felt weak, felt the weight of someone keeping something inside her *pushed* down, unable to push back at the world. Seeking comfort, she reached for Loren like a child for a blanket in the night. Then she reached harder. Perhaps Loren was asleep or trying to concentrate on something. But as Litz kept trying, she realised she felt nothing. She might as well be running into a locked door and expecting it to swing open.

Whimpering a little and hating herself for it, Litz forced herself to sit up and blink at the glaring sun. Surely, Loren could not be dead, surely, they wouldn't dare.

"Hey," a voice said beside her as Litz felt a foot on her arm. She hissed at it.

"Hey, you're okay," the voice said, Kella's voice, Litz registered as she remembered to pay dim attention to something other than the crushing fact that she couldn't feel Loren.

"Where is she," Litz heard herself growl.

"Litz—"

"*Where?*"

"Your dragon's safe, she's over there, okay?"

Blearily, Litz focused on where Kella's foot was pointing. Assumedly, her hands were also bound. And there Loren was. Except it was almost hard to see her, to understand that she was there when Litz was feeling nothing to back that fact up. There was no answering voice, no mirrored feeling of relief that meant they were both okay. But when Loren stopped moving her head where it had been bound by ropes to pull her along—like a muzzled dog, like an *animal*—Litz could see that she'd noticed her, but she didn't know it because she couldn't feel it.

"Why can't I feel her?" Litz croaked, knowing she sounded like a child but unable to conjure any appropriate shame.

"Okay, my Narani is super patchy, but I think I overheard one of them saying that the dragon's binding should have finished, like, *setting in* by now. At least, I think. So maybe—"

"They bound all of her." Litz shook her head, unable to take her eyes off Loren. "They've pushed all of her inside herself. Gagged her."

"Well, I don't know if you've noticed yet, Princess," Kella said, giving the bars on their moving cage a nudge, "but we're not exactly a whole lot better off. If you really want to get your observant hat on, you might even notice that this is the same cage I was stuck in the other day, which is probably what they used to track us. Really, if you think about it, this all heavily ironic."

"No. We can still speak. We can still move. Our minds aren't…" Litz pushed past the crack in her voice and shook her head again. "Where did they learn such magic? It's disgusting."

"I mean, people say the Narani are—"

"Shut up," Litz said wearily, and to her surprise, Kella actually went quiet. Litz wanted to follow that order with the question of why Kella had run off, to remind her that everything happening to Loren was all thanks to Kella's selfish—

"I'm sorry," Kella offered.

Litz snorted and reluctantly turned to look at her. "No, you're not."

"No, I'm not." Kella stared back, her expression unprecedentedly measured. "I'm not sorry I ran. But I am sorry you ended up stuck here with me."

Litz shook her head. "Loren won't forgive you for that trick you pulled."

Kella flashed a smile. "Y'gotta admit, it was effective."

"And the kiss, the dancing? Did that go as effectively as you'd hoped?"

Face solemn, Kella leaned back on the bars behind her. "I didn't mean to kiss you."

"If you didn't want to, why did you do it?" Litz asked primly, settling in a bearable sitting position.

"I didn't say I didn't want to, I said I didn't mean to."

"Semantics."

"Same reason I kissed you last time."

"Which was?"

Kella shrugged as much as she seemed able. "It seemed like a good idea. You were there. You were looking pretty and like you might be okay if I went for it, and I thought I was going to die soon."

"Last time—"

"Last time, I was about to go fight a dragon." Another attempt at a shrug. "I always think I'm going to die before getting into a fight. That's why I'm still here."

"Here in this cage for the second time?" Litz asked, raising an eyebrow and trying to ignore the suffocating feeling of absence throbbing through her. "How is it the same cage?"

"Like I said, I think they must have found the last battleground, which was how they knew to track us. They also picked up our camels, if you were wondering. They must have seen this poor old thing and thought it looked like it'd come in handy. Gotta say," she added, bouncing her legs about, "it's a lot, heh, *cosier* with two."

"See, if you'd just had a more effective escape plan, I wouldn't be in here with you. And you could have had all that luxurious legroom you so enjoyed previously."

"My plan was foolproof before these idiots showed up. I had this whole strategy to—"

"You ran right up to them, didn't you?"

"Shouted 'help' and everything."

"Genius." Litz sighed and leant back on the bars. "If you have any more genius plans, let me know. I want in."

Kella narrowed her eyes after glancing around, evidently checking how close their guards were. Insultingly, there weren't any nearby. "And what would be in it for me this time?"

Litz made herself think it over before she said it, but the loneliness battering her skull was making it hard to think at all. "I'd let you go."

Kella blinked. "Just like that? Vows be damned?"

"Vows be damned," Litz said, nodding. "I can't do this, this separation from her. It could send us both mad. Mostly me."

"Really?" Kella cocked her head to one side. "Like, you guys can't cope alone after a bond is made?"

"Not comfortably."

Kella's jaw tightened, her disgust not subtle enough for Litz to miss.

"Also, it would not please my king if this was how I arrived home."

"Sounds like an understatement," Kella said, snorting. "But how do I know you'll actually let me go if I get you out of this?"

"I guess you don't. You've just got my word."

Kella stared for a long time, and Litz had to resist the urge to squirm as she wondered what it was Kella was looking to see. "Guess I don't have a whole lotta options. Escaping with you or staying stuck in a box with you. Which could definitely destroy our grips on sanity."

"I'm sure we can make this a pleasant enough ride if we try."

Kella waggled her eyebrows. "What exactly did you have in mind, Princess?"

Litz managed a small smile despite the loss of Loren still rattling through her. She had to convince herself that Loren was not dead by glancing over every few seconds. She was allowed to keep on breathing.

"Play a game with me," Litz said before cursing herself for opening the conversation to yet another string of innuendos, but to her surprise Kella nodded.

"No hands for dice."

"Too much thinking right now anyway," Litz said tightly.

"All right." There was some concern creeping onto Kella's face now. "I'm just gonna ask you a bunch of questions, and if you feel like it, fire a few back at me."

"Okay," Litz said, looking at Loren again. She looked so proud, like a king forced to stand among commoners. Not letting herself be dragged but walking, slow and stately, and forcing the party to keep to her pace.

"So, uh, when was your first time?"

Litz blinked, wrenching her gaze away from Loren. "First...first time having sex?"

"Yeah."

"What kind of a question is that?"

"The standard first question for this kind of game. What were you expecting, math puzzles? We're stuck in a big metal box, might as well get to know each other. Also, I will kill you if you make this a math game."

Litz shook her head, then sighed. "I guess I'll answer if you will."

"No problem, but I asked you first. Unless you're not into sex? I mean, I know some people like that."

"No, I, I am. Into...yes."

"So?"

"Fine. My roommate back in officer training."

"Your *roommate*. That's beautiful. How old were you?"

Litz quickly applied some mental math. "Twenty-two?"

"You didn't have sex until you were twenty-*two*? Oh, honey."

"Well, how old were you?"

"Sixteen, just. There was an apprentice in my stepfather's shop for a little while. I think I corrupted him horribly. I don't think he minded, though."

"Okay, but sixteen's still a child."

Kella gave an awkward, one-shoulder shrug. "What can I say, I want something done, I get it done. Okay, next question." She pursed her lips and twisted them strangely. "Are the trees in Aelshia as big as everyone says they are?"

"How big does everyone say they are?"

"It's probably camel shit. Especially now I know the whole baby sacrifice thing's a lie. But there's stories about trees five times the height of elephants."

Litz briefly considered how tall she remembered elephants growing. "Oh, our trees can reach much taller than that. The oldest ones, anyway."

Kella goggled. "Does that mean you all live in tree houses?"

"Mostly the very rich or very poor but, yes. We have many other kinds of buildings, though."

"I'd love to see it someday," Kella said with a wistfulness that Litz believed to be genuine before Kella started frowning in suspicion. "Doesn't mean I've changed my mind about you letting me go."

"And when I let you go, are you going to go back to killing dragons?"

The frown spread from Kella's eyebrows and dragged down the rest of her face. "I'm not sure."

"What?"

"I said I'm not sure," Kella said, defensively curling her knees up to shield her torso.

"How can you not be sure? You've spoken to Loren—"

"Okay, sure, I spoke to your dragon, and I'm almost sure I didn't imagine that. But have you ever spoken to one of my dragons?"

"What?"

"Have you spoken to any—"

"Yes, I heard you. Why would that change my thoughts?"

"Because I don't think any of them can speak," Kella said tightly. "You're asking me to believe that every dragon is like Loren. Can't you even give the benefit of the doubt that just maybe, I have some life experience that's a little different to yours?"

Litz said nothing, remembering the chimera, and after a few moments, Kella scowled. "Fine, you wanna be like that, I guess I'll try getting some sleep. Didn't exactly get any last night," she said, shutting her eyes and wriggling down until she fell on the floor in a way that sounded painful. The clothes Litz had first met her in were now looking dusty, bloodstained, and ragged, her beautiful headscarf had long since disappeared.

"Kella?"

"Yeah?"

"I'm sorry."

She received a grunt in response.

Gods, she really hated having to ask for help. "But can you please keep talking?"

Kella opened one eye as Litz attempted to keep her voice, her breathing steady. Asking was one thing, begging was another.

"It's quiet. It's so quiet. Please, can you—"

Opening her other eye, Kella sighed. "You ever hear the one about the dragon, the king, and the Narani horse trying to find an inn to stay at together?"

Shaking her head, Litz managed an unsteady smile. "No."

Kella wrestled back into an upright position, groaning all the way up. "All right. So a king, a Narani horse, and a dragon…"

Unlike his sister, Ker didn't drink much. Most of alcohol's more unpleasant side effects had happily passed him by, but he'd seen them work on Kella. On one memorable occasion, she'd been moments away from a fight before seeming to sober up and too late realising where she was, unclear of how she'd gotten there.

Ker had laughed at her, but now, going through a similar experience, he felt terrible for that. This was terrifying. He wasn't sure he could pinpoint the first thing he registered as he became aware again, but the fact that he was flying was definitely one of the first things.

"Fuck," he breathed, barely able to hear his own voice over the wind. Gulping, he clutched harder at the vine he was gripping that Ellonya was holding in her mouth.

Are you okay? That was Ellonya in his head, Ellonya who he was sitting on, whose wings were scything through the air, keeping them high above the ground, but her voice felt different now. He knew she was speaking to him, but he could also *feel* her speaking to him, and he could feel her confusion at his reaction, could feel the tiredness in her wings from having been flying this long.

Findan had told him that dragons relied on magic for everything they did. Especially flying. A dragon without the influence of magic was like a human unaffected by gravity. They would still exist without it, perhaps, but as unrecognisable creatures.

And now gravity and its pull were very much on Ker's mind. "Oh gods," he said aloud, looking in the direction of the Earth only to make out clouds. They were above the fucking *clouds*.

There was a tapping at his shoulder. Sallvayn, clinging to him, asked, "You okay, boy?"

"No?"

Sallvayn patted at him in a way Ker suspected was intended to be comforting. "Okay."

They managed to scurry over Ellonya's feathers to her ear, and shortly afterward, she started descending.

"This is worse," Ker shouted as he was faced with the clouds they were diving into. He felt strange, like everything was in a state of *happening too much.*

"You're safe, boy," Sallvayn assured him in his ear, somehow back by Ker again. He shook his head violently as the wind rushed against his cheeks. But even as scared as he was, he knew he was safe. He could feel that knowledge from Ellonya without having to pry for it, as surely as he knew that if he delved into his pocket and tossed something out, it would fall to the ground. She wasn't going too fast, she wasn't going to let him fall, and nothing mattered more to her than keeping him safe.

She had wanted so badly to have something matter to her this much, to have an effect on someone in return. As a baby, her mother had fed her, had protected her but hadn't spoken to her, hadn't taught her anything, hadn't been capable. One day, she'd forgotten to come home or perhaps hadn't been able to.

Her name, a gremlin had given her that name. Ellonya wasn't sure what had happened to them. She'd been alone for so long, and it brought tears to Ker's eyes to think of it.

Relax, she was saying to him. *We did it.*

I mean, I can see that. I can feel that, but how? When?

He felt rather than heard her sigh. *Last night. We were hoping you were in your right mind enough, but in any case, we will land.*

And land they did, which was almost as terrifying an experience as waking up in the air. They were still in the mountain range, but they were reaching the tail end of the mountains that separated Nayona from Jeenobi. There was less vegetation here, and the altitude was lower, Ker remembered as he awkwardly slid off Ellonya's back, feeling as stiff as if he'd…what, been there for hours? He probably had.

His legs felt shaky, which made it hard to stand straight. "Okay, what the fuck is going on?" he said slowly, and he believed, reasonably. But Ellonya didn't think so. He could feel how patient she was being with him.

We tried again when we were by the river. I reached out my soul and conveyed some of it to you. Or copied some of it into you? I am still not sure what it was we did, but we succeeded.

"Okay, then what?" He tried scrambling through his mind to figure out the last thing he could remember: talking with Ellonya the night before, trying again, her trying to find that green fire. About him making the effort to be more open-minded or open-hearted or something.

I think you took to it well. Perhaps too well, which would explain this memory loss.

What do you mean, too well?

I don't think you were prepared for the emotional bond forming in you all at once, especially not with the combined weight of your previous bond that has never left your soul. How...tearing for you.

Though Ker could feel her—*his* dragon, for they would be tied together for the rest of their lives—feel a flash of jealousy, stronger than that, he could feel her sadness for him when she spoke of his previous dragon bond.

It's almost as though being filled with so many strong emotions at once was too much for you to consciously deal with. As though you were riding some sort of artificial high. You were full of strength, perhaps drawing on mine for the first time, and you were very determined to start moving.

I did? I was?

Yes. You do not remember anything? Now there was disappointment seeping in behind the curiosity, and Ker felt awful to have caused it. She'd been through enough and didn't deserve that, didn't deserve him, a dragon killer and another dragon's used parts.

No. Stop thinking like that. You brought me hope for the first time in longer than I am capable of remembering. I feel like I am starting to heal somehow. Or grow.

He moved forward, feeling a little unsteady on his now bow-shaped legs as he reached out a hand to Ellonya's muzzle, drawn in by the beauty of her as she gleamed in the sun. And when he put his hands on her, oh. There was a warmth to her hard scales, but he could also, if he concentrated, feel himself, his small fingers sliding down her scales, how appreciated it was making Ellonya feel and how surprised she was with that.

We will continue searching for your sister?

Yes. Ker took his hand away slowly, still staring at it in wonder. "Though I think we'll have to look for more food," he said aloud for

Sallvayn's benefit. It was getting difficult to remember to speak aloud. How much worse would that become by the time he found Kella?

It will be all right. If she loves you, she will accept this in you, will she not?

Ker smiled briefly as he curled his hands up. *Yeah. She'll be okay,* he agreed, almost believing it. *If she hasn't gotten herself killed already.*

❖

"Okay, okay. New question."

"Hit me," Litz said without lifting her head from its position under her hood.

It had been a few hours since they'd succeeded in breaking each other's bindings, and so far, none of the guards seemed to think this worth noticing, which was a little dispiriting. They'd managed to cover their heads and were able to eat the meals thrust through to them with less humiliation, but that was all.

Making a slight humph noise at the lack of enthusiasm she was receiving, Kella leant her head back on the bars. "What do you find most attractive in a person?" She watched as Litz pouted thoughtfully and started to give her lips as much new consideration as her answer.

"Self-awareness."

"Heh?"

"You know, when you're able to recognise—"

"I know what self-awareness is. Tell me why it's attractive."

"It demonstrates a certain amount of intelligence but also proves a sense of humour and an ability to laugh at yourself. It implies a level of compassion based on being aware of what effect your actions will have on others."

"Heh. Okay, I'll give you that."

"Good. I'm quite pleased with that answer. What would you say?"

"Ass? I guess?"

"*Gods.*"

"What? Tell me that's not something you consider."

"All right, I'll admit, it's something I consider."

Kella snorted and looked smugly up at the cage ceiling. Bizarrely, it felt more spacious with two.

Litz rolled her eyes. "Fine. My question. What age were you really when you first killed a dragon?"

"Aw, c'mon, you know this is only gonna upset you."

"I want to know," Litz said simply.

Kella sighed and slumped back against the bars, letting the rattling soothe her. "First time I helped out, I was ten. It was poison, so not a lot of danger involved, but that trick doesn't work much. Dragons don't scavenge as a rule."

Litz nodded, looking uncomfortable but not enough to stop Kella talking.

"First time I really got involved I was older, fourteen maybe. First time I took point, I was seventeen. Though it wasn't really supposed to happen like that. It was supposed to be Rall, but he got thrown off, and the dragon was moving in on Jev, who'd been out there trying to distract it, so I ended up leaping in." She was surprised to find her mouth was as dry as she remembered. Jev had been about to die, and they'd run out of plan, and it had been so much more frightening than she'd expected.

But so much more thrilling. Being alive when she hadn't expected to be was still an unbeatable feeling. "It didn't die quickly. I wasn't very good at it then." Kella shrugged. "I guess I could give you a few answers."

"I see." Litz showed no obvious reaction. "And you were fifteen when your mother died?"

"Well remembered, Princess." Kella rubbed at her eyes, wishing they had better shade or even a chance to stretch their legs. It was hard not to feel like falling asleep when she wasn't able to move. But they had been brought through the heat of the day with more water than they probably would have allowed themselves, and they were working a lot less, so maybe she shouldn't complain.

But Kella enjoyed complaining.

"When was the last time you saw her before…"

"Before she was ashes?"

Litz looked a little uncomfortable, but only a little. She was a soldier, after all. She shrugged almost apologetically. "I'm sorry. Back home, it's polite to ask what the last thing you saw the deceased doing was. It's supposed to give some insight into the nature of your relationship."

"Well, the last time I saw her, nosy, was a few seconds before she was gone." Kella gulped, the dryness in her throat beginning to bother her again. "I saw the dragon with Ker, and I raised the alarm. Only, I didn't really. I just told her because she always knew how to handle everything on her own, and she always protected us better than anyone else could. And she did. Ker was fine." She tried very hard to keep the bitterness out of her tone, but since she wasn't certain she'd succeeded, she finished with a smirk. "What does that tell you, princess?"

"Several things." Kella watched with some concern as Litz's eyes slid to where her dragon was being dragged somewhere behind them with no sign of managing to get free.

"Hey. She's as fine as she's gonna be right now. Quit looking back, you're not a crocodile mami. She's a big dragon that can look out for herself."

Litz ignored this and continued to stare. Irritated, Kella went back to fiddling her hands together. They'd gotten the ropes away but not without an uncomfortable amount of rope burn. "She's seen something she doesn't like."

"What, the desert? The people keeping her trapped out here?"

"No, are we approaching anything?"

Kella leaned her head to one side and squinted into the distance, just north from where the sun was starting to set. And on that horizon… "Yeah, that's a settlement. Looks like we might get some real rest for the night."

"In this cage?"

"We won't be moving, and that'd be something."

"Hmm."

A loud rumble Kella would recognise anywhere rang out into the sky from the direction of the settlement. "That's…that's another dragon up there."

Snorting harmless amounts of smoke, Loren lifted her head up and began to roar back, though the sound seemed slightly nasal. And the difference between the two calls went deeper than that. The first sounded aggressive and almost lost, Kella now realised after years of listening to it. But Loren's sounded to Kella like she had a purpose, with an enough awareness of her situation to be sad about it.

It seemed like the odd poignancy in it should have been able to draw softness or empathy from the one she called to. But after several beats of nothing, the roared reply sounded the same. They called the sound a roar, but it was really more like an eagle's caw, with a thunderous resonance. But this one really did remind Kella of a bird just mindlessly repeating itself.

A few of the Narani, obviously in a stage of slowing, loosening up now they could see home, started to laugh. "*Marruwi*," one close to Loren shouted to her, still chuckling.

Kella frowned. She knew that one well enough from marketplace talk, usually if they thought the price you were naming was too low: No good, no point, that's ridiculous, don't even bother.

"What are they saying?" Litz said in her captain's voice.

"You might not like this," Kella said slowly. Gods, she'd assumed she'd be smug if this moment came, knowing what Litz was about to see. But showing that thing to her now felt like leading a child into a fresh battlefield. It made Kella want to break her way out of their cage for no better reason than to stop them heading in that direction.

Rightly or wrongly, Litz saw these things as important, better than humans. Not beasts. This would hurt her.

"I think," Kella said quietly, "that you're about to meet one of *my* dragons."

CHAPTER SEVENTEEN

Though being on the ground helped, Ker was still shaky even a good half hour after they'd landed. It was like he was coming down from having too much of his da's kofi while also feeling like he was only just starting to sober up again. As he stared out at the sunset from his cliffside view, the scenery sharpened into better focus the longer he stared, the rocky hillsides and cliffs before him revealing more detail, more colour in their jagged plants.

Maybe that was the dragonrider night vision coming into effect. Though he was almost certain that was a myth.

"Did you find any food?" Sallvayn asked, appearing from behind him at his leg.

"Not yet," Ker said, glancing back at Ellonya. "Though I was thinking about going out looking for some before it gets too dark to see anything."

"Hmm. These hills aren't always kind. Would you like us to accompany you?"

Ker smiled. "No offense, Sall, but I'm a lot bigger than you. I think I'll be okay."

"But you're also a lot slower than we are."

"But I've got a dragon at my back now," Ker reminded them as he shrugged and started walking away from the cliffs. He was almost sure he recognised the area now. They were maybe a half mile from the last imperial watchtower set up by the Aelshians before they'd been forced to retreat from these lands, some time before Ker had been born. In the day, it cast welcome shade that followed you for a time as you walked back westward along the hill path beneath.

"That doesn't make you invincible, you know," Sallvayn said but made no attempt to follow. Ker could admit some relief to that. He was grateful that he wouldn't have to face anything ahead all on his own, but he missed his own space, his own thoughts.

Does it bother you so, sharing your mind?

No, Ker answered, *honestly, I thought it would, but, no, not really. I'm just used to being alone, to having time to spend alone. I guess it's a little bizarre not having that.*

Not just bad bizarre, though?

Ker smiled to himself as he navigated down the hill. *No. Not just bad bizarre.*

Good. Her voice felt almost shy. It warmed him from the inside as he pushed past branches and tried to concentrate on his feet. *Because this is good bizarre to me*, she told him, and he could feel the way she was fluttering her wings, billowing them before settling down again. And he knew that she missed the comforts of her hoard, her cave but was thrilled to be out free and travelling.

He could also tell that she wanted to ask whether he would want to leave her after they found Kella but was both too afraid to mention it and also already knew that he wouldn't. *I wouldn't*, Ker assured her anyway. *I'm still not sure how I feel about what happened to me before. And though it still aches, I don't feel so incomplete, I guess.*

I can feel it, she told him. *I can feel how it's worn at you, the pain that you bore alone, barely understanding what it was.*

And I can feel what it's been like for you too, he reminded her. *You've been alone for so long, not sure of your heritage, your family. It must have been terrifying*, he said before having to flinch back from that section of her memories.

It was. Thank you.

He smiled sadly, recognising her thanks for what it was. After being so alone for so long, being so misunderstood, even by herself, being seen was important.

It wasn't as though he had fixed her. Ellonya could still remember little of who she was, where she had come from. But as she'd said before, he was helping her think, helping her feel, helping her remember she was made up of something more than her instincts. That she had things to want and care about beyond her next meal and maybe finding something to hoard. That she always had but had just needed another mind to connect to, someone to remind her what those things were.

Why do dragons hoard gold? he asked abruptly. It had been one of those questions he'd asked incessantly as a child, only to find that no person or book would give him a satisfying answer. *You remember to do it even when you're—*

When we're like the others.

Yes.

I think because we've always done it. But I think we do it because it's what humans do.

He blinked. *You mean, this used to be so that dragons could buy things?*

I think so, yes.

If dragons have always expressed an interest in human affairs, this explains Aelshia better, he mused as something caught his eye. It wasn't food, but it was fire, and that might mean someone cooking.

If you need fire, you know that I could provide a superior one.

He snorted. *I know. Thank you, but I'm interested in what the people lighting the fire might be able to give me.*

But you have nothing to give them.

Nothing physical, no. But I might be able to give them a story, a song. Something that would please them.

And humans accept this as currency? Perhaps dragons should begin hoarding songbirds.

Ker almost laughed aloud. Even with their bond, it was hard to be completely certain, but he was almost sure that Ellonya had just made a joke. *Not all of us will all the time. But my family thought I might apprentice to a bard at one point. I know a lot of good epics, mostly by heart. And I can make up what I can't remember.*

I am intrigued.

I've been told my voice isn't bad either.

It certainly seems effective, Ellonya assured him. *You know many words.*

The closer he came to the fire, the more he started stooping and the quieter he started moving. Dark as the night was becoming, it wasn't yet dark enough to conceal him.

Why do you keep hidden if you plan on introducing yourself?

Because they might not be friendly enough for me to want *to introduce myself to them.*

Ah. But if they are cruel, I could always make them give you the food you need.

Thanks, but I'd prefer you didn't. If word gets out, things could get very interesting back home. Jeenobi doesn't have any dragonriders, remember?

*If you insist. I will only fly over and make them give you the food
if I am also about to kill them.*

No, really—

He stilled as he grew close enough to hear the people speaking.
For a moment, they had sounded like...

"My arm isn't working well enough to clamber up these mountains
tomorrow. I'm gonna need a day's rest."

"Don't be ridiculous, Evlo, it barely spat at you. You'll be fine by
tomorrow. Did you rinse it properly like I told you to?"

"Yes."

That really was Findan telling off Evlo, who, if Ker knew him at
all, would not have rinsed his arm properly at all, whatever it was they
were referring to. They were *here*.

They couldn't have followed him, Ker reminded himself. Couldn't
know Ellonya was here. But something in Ker wanted to make a hasty
retreat back to her to make sure she was as safe and out of their reach
as she could be.

Are they so terrifying?

They're my family, he said, though he was sure she already
understood that much. *And they have an almost one hundred percent
success rate in hunting dragons.*

I see.

*I don't want them to know you're here, and I don't want them to
know I'm here either.*

Then why aren't you moving?

I want to know why they're here, he said eventually, knowing that
she would be aware he was not giving her all his reasons. The pull to
get closer to them, the sharp pang of homesickness in his gut he felt at
the sound of them was so strong that she must have understood exactly
what he wasn't admitting.

"That all went quicker than we thought it might," Zebenn was
saying, breaking the silence they'd fallen into. "We pulled that off okay
with just the three of us."

"Yes, we did," Findan said quietly.

Ker risked moving in closer. He had missed that voice especially
and did not want to miss more of what she was saying.

"Are we going after the twins now?"

Ker stilled, feeling hope pound at his idiot heart. The twins was
what Zebenn had started calling them when he and Kella had shared the
same height and hairstyle. Zebenn had found this adorable, something

they'd loudly and often informed everyone of, and the name had stuck for a long time after it became irrelevant.

They couldn't go looking for him and Kella now. It would only complicate everything for him and could put Ellonya in danger. But he also wanted them to care about him, about both of them, enough to do something stupid.

"Zebenn, we've talked about this," Findan said in the same tone as she would have used while instructing Ker in his rudimentary magic lessons, chastising him for his poor form. She'd taught them better than this.

"It wasn't really a good talk, boss," Evlo said, and Ker could hear without getting a good view that Evlo was lazily leaning on a rock like it was a pile of silk cushions. What universe had he stepped into that Evlo seemed to care more about what happened to him than Findan, the woman who'd helped raise him?

"Evlo—"

"I mean, just think about it. We've got ourselves in the best position to intercept the ends of the desert road without having to go in too deep. Meanwhile, it's been days, and the king did not exactly send his best. If we found them, we'd probably only find half the folk left. I bet that's what Kerali was thinking."

Ker gritted his teeth at the name as he listened harder.

"Probably what you were thinking too, or else why would we take a job all the way out here?"

"That's enough," Findan said, her tone low and dangerous.

Ker fought to remember that he didn't want them following even as his heart sank.

"We're not talking about this anymore."

It did seem like there should be a reason Findan had moved them all so near to where Kella might be. Even though the most likely scenario was that Findan was hoping Kella would make her own escape, and maybe they would be able to assist. He might not always understand just what or how much Findan was feeling, but Ker had a lot of experience in following how she thought. They were all silent for a few moments, and Ker wondered if he should quietly return to his dragon.

"Stop scratching at your arms."

"They're itchy, and in pain."

"C'mon over here and let me see 'em," Zebenn sighed, and Evlo moved over so that he was now facing Ker if he ever decided to move.

"Here. I'm going to put a salve on it and bandage you up. How does that sound?"

"Awful?"

Zebenn gave a ghost of that booming laugh Ker had missed so much and continued to dab at Evlo's arm, who to his credit, bore it stoically. Ker knew just how bad that healing salve could sting. Zebenn moved up Evlo's arm, dabbing at burn scars, and came to what looked to be a jagged, angry scar stretching up from his elbow. "And what's this one here?" they asked quietly.

Evlo melodramatically looked up as though buying himself time to think up a joke. "This one here's a parting gift from my homeland."

"You don't talk much about your home," Zebenn prompted as they gently finished bandaging.

"No, I don't," Evlo agreed, winking. Which was pretty much the extent of what Ker had ever been able to get out of him.

Ker suspected that Findan must have just given him one of her *be polite* stares, which forced him into continuing. "I didn't always get on with everyone there," Evlo explained, looking down. Had Ker been with them, he might have asked if anything had changed since. "They all like dragons, for one."

"Like in Aelshia?"

"No." Evlo laughed bitterly. "No dragon where I'm from would ever let a person ride them."

"Why do people tolerate them? Are they held sacred by the gods?"

"No," Evlo was silent for a moment as he practised stretching his bandaged arm. "The dragons are the gods."

Ker couldn't see from where he was crouching, but he knew that Findan would be nodding. She never brought anyone into the group without feeling sure she knew everything about them that she needed to. But Zebenn, like Ker, was surprised by this new information.

"Shit. You wanna talk about it?"

"No. But look, if there's anyone who doesn't deserve to get caught up in a mess that dragons have made, it's Kella."

"I know," Findan said quietly. "But some things have to happen. Things that give us the will to fight harder."

"No disrespect, but that is some messed-up advice. Excuse me," Evlo said and stood.

At first, Ker thought nothing of this until Evlo started to walk toward him.

Awesome.

"Fuck," Ker said to himself and tried to make himself as flat as possible, feeling ants crawling over his hands. He sent out a fervent prayer to any god that happened to be listening that they weren't biters.

Do I need to come and set someone on fire?

No! Definitely not, and I'll be back in a bit, it's fine.

Ker froze as a foot pressed into the ground by his hand. "Wait. Then follow me," Evlo muttered as if speaking to himself before walking on.

His breathing now slowing, Ker nodded farther into the dirt and the ants. Which were biters because of course they were.

He listened to Evlo's steps disappearing down the hill and counted up to three hundred before pushing slowly into a crouch and stumbling after him. He didn't even consider until he was most of the way down that he could have just run in the opposite direction and gotten away before Evlo had realised. Instead, Ker followed the hills to where they sloped raggedly toward the desert, the greenery clutching at them losing its grip as the rocks merged into sand.

At first, Ker couldn't see him anywhere and wondered how much farther down he had wandered when Evlo stood out from behind the nearest bush and said, "Boo."

"Fuck, man, don't do that."

Evlo snorted. "You can't tell me what to do. You're not even supposed to be here. Why *are* you here?" Before Ker could think of something to say, Evlo was waving a hand dismissively, his skin pale enough to follow thanks to the bright moonlight. "Don't answer that. You've been following us, haven't you?"

Having nothing better to tell him, Ker nodded slowly.

Grinning, Evlo slowly crossed his arms. "I fucking knew it. Knew you wouldn't give up that easy." He shook his head. "Man, if you've got some sort of plan to get her back, I'm sure they'd join in. You know they would, even just to stop things from getting worse."

Gods, Ker had not expected to finish his day getting emotional about Evlo Fucking Lindin. He *cared*. Nothing he'd done before now had convinced Ker of that fact. Evlo cared, and he cared about something beyond killing dragons, making fun of his teammates, and being the best at killing dragons.

"Like I said," Evlo went on, Ker's stare apparently prompting him. "If anyone doesn't deserve this, it's your sister."

Was he in love with Kella? Evlo had always enjoyed flirting

with her, sure, but Ker suspected that Evlo would enjoy flirting with a rupricaprin if he thought that he would get a reaction out of it.

"Honestly, I've known you guys for a while now, and Kella's awesome, okay? I know you heard me back there. I didn't exactly grow up in a place that cared a whole lot about freedom. But you people all just have it, and most of you don't even seem to know or care what you've got. She was the first person I met when I got here who seemed to know exactly how lucky she was, exactly how free she was. She was happy to have it, and she'd kill to keep it. I'd never met someone like that before, like someone in a story."

Ker stared for a long, hard moment, trying to decide how he should play this and wondering if Evlo usually avoided speaking much to avoid drawing attention to his strange accent. Useful as he might be, there was no question of him coming with Ker. But after a speech like that, Ker was a lot less willing to simply turn him down flat.

"Have I ever seen you this drunk?" he asked eventually.

Evlo shrugged. "Maybe not. You've not known me that long. What, a year? Year and a half?"

"Something like that."

"Look, I know the odds aren't exactly on our side, but I came here to learn how to stop dragons from hurting anyone else I care about."

The dragons were the gods.

"I've got as much a stake in this as you, I want to help get her back, and I can help best by killing anything that gets in our way. You know it would be my *pleasure*, Kerali."

It was easily the longest conversation they had ever exchanged that wasn't laced with sarcasm or peppered with insults. Evlo genuinely wanted to help him, and that was…still inconvenient. "Look," Ker started, "I do have a plan." He shifted uncomfortably and pointed somewhere behind Evlo's head. "You see that mountain?"

"What?"

As Evlo turned, Ker took a deep breath and tried to focus on what it was that Findan had talked him through on their last session together, only days before he and Kella had been arrested:

"Why do people sleep?"
"To recharge, to dream, to—"
"No. That is why we say we sleep after we have done so. Why do babies fall asleep?"

"Because their parents—"

"But if there are no parents?"

Ker hated when Findan put him up to riddles like these. Or that wasn't exactly true. He hated not immediately knowing the answer to them. "Because they're tired, I guess."

Findan snapped her fingers smartly, only her eyes betraying any pride. "Exactly. We sleep because we are exhausted. So if you were intending to force someone into falling asleep against their will?"

"I would make them exhausted?"

Findan smiled. "Exactly."

It took a lot of concentration to pull energy from a person without killing them, and Ker didn't have any time. Evlo was a much better and quicker fighter that he was, even after a few drinks. Ker had watched him in bar fights, and he was as scrappy as Kella and twice as mean, and Ker couldn't risk him realising what he was doing and calling for help.

Putting a hand solidly on Evlo's shoulder and continuing to point toward the darkened horizon, Ker started to *pull*, wishing he'd had more time to practise this.

"All magic is a mixture of pushing and pulling. Decide which you need and do that. But it's not like a door which might be both or will give you the chance to try again. You could seriously harm someone by getting that wrong."

Ker breathed deeply, closing his eyes as he grasped for what he wanted to find—energy, whatever force it was that was keeping Evlo awake—and he *pulled*. It came to him slowly, frighteningly slow at first, but it started speeding up so that Ker could feel sparks of energy dance into his fingers, though he was probably imagining things. Magic wasn't something physical or visible, as Findan had always been forced to remind him, but the human mind would always try to fill in the details. Ker knew this was working, so his mind supplied him that information in a way he could understand. That was probably all it was.

The other thing Findan was always telling him was that he should never use magic on people for anything other than to save his own life. This was what they'd once lopped off the heads and hands of witches for.

He didn't want to lose his head. Or his hands, although without his head, it was unlikely the latter was going to bother him.

He didn't want to do this.

But he was, and it was working.

When Evlo fell with nothing more than a sigh, Ker stopped his head from hitting the rocks and stood, feeling like a murderer.

Because his own thoughts were frightening him, he knelt to check his friend was still breathing.

What happened? What have you done?

Straightening Evlo's legs, Ker tried for a smile at the panic he could feel from Ellonya. *I had to use magic. It was to stop them coming after us. I had to.*

I understand that. What I can't understand is why you feel so much shame over it.

What?

In using magic, you feel worse about yourself, more ashamed than you did when you first considered bonding with me.

Ker breathed out slowly and started walking away, wishing he'd managed to find some food. *I guess I didn't notice. That's just magic. It's not something you're supposed to feel good about using.*

Why?

I don't know, it just isn't. You ask a lot of questions.

How else should I be learning?

Litz was glad that it had gotten darker, and she could no longer see the expression of pity Kella had been wearing ever since they'd joined the main encampment and seen that dragon. Looking at her like she was worried Litz was about to break.

Almost out of spite, Litz didn't feel broken yet.

"It's not like dragons don't ever suffer illness," Litz said carefully, reminding herself as much as she was informing Kella. "It's not common, but they're not immune to physical or mental afflictions." But this felt different. And to be so apparently widespread, it was like a mental illness that had become endemic before morphing into something completely new.

The chained and bloodied purple dragon didn't even act like a dragon. There was something not quite there behind its eyes, and the way it occasionally thrashed implied that it wasn't aware that none of its actions would help get it out. Litz had met elders who no longer seemed to remember who they were, but this went beyond that. This dragon didn't even seem to know what it was. Pride, the inherent ingredient in even the youngest dragon's personality, simply wasn't in this one.

It was difficult to see Kella's expression in the low light, but she gave a slow, companionable nod.

Loren would have found this new truce amusing. They'd started as strangers, moved on to being prisoner and captor, and now they were on exactly the same level. Convicts together. How strangely the world turned.

"But this is different, isn't it?" Kella ventured.

"Yes. It seems so in pain, just so lost."

"Capture might give you that vibe."

"Not to a dragon. They have much stronger sense of self than we do. Usually." Litz sighed.

Kella made a noise that sounded like a strained chuckle. "You're homesick too?"

Fairly sure that Kella couldn't see her clearly, Litz hugged her knees a little tighter. "I haven't seen a tree in a week. There are places I don't think I will ever be able to get sand out of. I can't feel Loren. I'm supposed to be extraditing you for something I'm not even certain I can blame you for now." Litz shook her head. "Do you have any stories, any knowledge of real, thinking dragons? Do dragons really eat people here?"

Kella took a few moments before answering. "Not usually. About as often as a shark would. Usually, only if they're hungry, and someone's looking like an easy target. More often, it'll be by accident."

"That seems so bizarre to me." It didn't help that she couldn't reach Loren. It made her feel like she might have imagined her entire life.

"Imagine how I felt when Loren started talking to me."

For some reason, Litz found this the funniest thing she had ever heard and couldn't help but laugh so long and hard that soon, she was gasping for air. She could only laugh harder when Kella started to join in. Soon, they were both helpless on the floor of their cage, their limbs tangling like vines.

But it was wrong to be laughing when Loren was trapped.

Seeming to sense the downward change in Litz's mood, Kella sat up. "We do have some stories about dragons that think. But, y'know, stories."

"Tell me."

"You didn't like my story the other day," Kella pointed out suspiciously.

"I didn't, no. But you told it well. And if we have to play another game of 'sky is blue,' I think I'll go mad. Especially with you. You got too morbid too fast."

"Heh. You admit it's a terrible game."

"I didn't say that, I just said—"

"Okay, okay. Right. When the Earth had retreated into herself but the world was still new, there lived an old couple far north of the desert who had little money but had managed to raise two fine sons. One day, when they were both reaching manhood and longed for adventures of their own, they bid their parents good-bye and ventured into the desert."

"Ah, I think I know this story."

"I don't care, I'm telling it, so you can shut up. Anyway, the boys ventured into the desert, and on their way, they found a maze of jagged rocks where a great and terrible noise was coming from the centre. The older brother was wary and wanted to steer clear, but the younger brother was naive and sweet-hearted and wanted to see if there was an animal in need of help. Reluctantly, the elder brother followed him, and in the centre of the maze, they found a dragon who'd been speared and barred by the rocks that had fallen on its wings when it landed badly.

"Remembering their mother's warning never to trust dragons, the older brother wanted to continue on their way, but the younger brother was mesmerised by the creature and could not help feeling pity as he listened to its cries.

"'I will help you,' the younger brother declared, and reluctantly, his older brother helped in tugging the dragon's wings free. When they had finished, the dragon sighed in relief.

"'Thank you,' he told them. 'I owe you both a great debt. Tell me what it is you seek out here in these wastelands, and I shall help you find it.'

"'We are looking for a new home,' the younger brother said. 'Somewhere better than where we came from, that we will never have to leave again.'

"The dragon smiled toothily. 'I know where you can find that. Some ways east from here, little one, you will find a forest filled with all the food and shade and water you could ever ask for. You will never go hungry there, and droughts will never touch you.'

"The younger thought this sounded like paradise and demanded to leave at once, but his older brother was still suspicious. He shook his head. 'Dragon, I am grateful for your advice, but I left my old home to find a new one I would build for myself. It is for that I will keep searching.'

"Unable to agree, the two brothers parted ways. The younger went east and found his paradise, an oasis with no end, with trees larger than the great whales and serpents of the sea and still growing. But his paradise wasn't all it first appeared. Farming for any longer than a season was impossible. The ground would wither and die with overuse. Everywhere, there were insects and plants and animals which sought to kill him. The paradise soon became a torment, and daily was it that the younger brother thought how well it would have been had he followed his brother west.

"The older brother had travelled west until he found the sea, which he had never seen before and was glad to now. He learned that the sea could be both danger and boon to him, and he learnt how to respect that. He learnt how to farm in places where rain was scarce and built himself a home from the strong cliffside rocks. Though he often wondered how his brother had fared, he never regretted carving his own way. Why are you shaking your head?"

"Because your story is wrong."

"How could it be wrong? It's *my* story."

"In the version they told back home, that wasn't how the ending went at all."

Kella shook her head and scowled, but Litz suspected she was enjoying the debate. "Okay, then, Princess, how would you tell it?"

"Oh, I'm not really any kind of storyteller."

"You should be if you're going to criticise me."

"Oh, fine. In the version I know, the boys reach the desert, and the suspicious brother is still suspicious of everything, and the younger brother still wants to see the best in everything."

"So…they saw other things?"

Sighing, Litz waved a hand. "Oh, they saw, I don't know, they saw some food that the younger brother thought would be worth eating but the older brother thought would be poisonous, and there was a trickster gremlin who tried to spin them a tale about good jobs nearby for strong young men, something like that."

"You're right, you really are bad at storytelling. For all the flowery language Aelshians use, they still—"

"Okay, but the point is that when they reach the dragon, the younger brother wants to trust him, and the elder goes on a tirade of how typical this is of him, and obviously, it won't turn out well because when does it ever? But the younger brother follows his heart, and he finds the home he was looking for, and it was everything the dragon had promised. The stubborn elder brother found nothing, only dust and harsh, hot winds, but he would not leave. He was too proud to ever accept help or advice."

"He won because he followed his heart? That's way less cool."

"But it's sweet."

"Is that really the way your mother told it to you?"

Litz snorted. Again, it was something she knew that Loren would have found amusement in had she been able to hear it, and the silence gaped loud in her mind. "I have heard the story many times from different people. But never from my mother. She's not exactly the storytelling kind."

"And that's coming from…"

"Yes. That's coming from me."

"Neither of you tell it true," said a voice from beside their cage.

"What?" Litz said as Kella, who had seemingly forgotten that their cage was currently being guarded, let out a small squeal.

"I said neither of you tell the story true," said the man again in broken Jeenobian.

"I thought none of you guys spoke anything but Narani," Kella said suspiciously.

The man tilted his head from side to side. "Not many of us."

"Fine, let's hear your version, since it can't be worse than hers."

"*Hey.*"

"To begin, there were not two brothers. There were three."

"Okay."

"And when they left home to search the sand sea for a better one, it was not a dragon in distress but a woman that they found, the most beautiful woman any of them had ever seen."

"Of course she was," Kella said, sounding fond.

"She was tall and shapely, with skin as dark and warm as their mother's cooking pots and eyes that shone as brightly as the stars."

He's a good storyteller, Litz allowed, forgetting for a moment that Loren wouldn't be able to hear. And she certainly wouldn't be able to hear the story for herself. He spoke so softly, it almost sounded as though he was trying to caress this woman with his words.

"She had been the dragon's captive for a long time, the crown of his jewelled hoard, since he recognised her as the most wonderful treasure mankind could ever hope to possess. They did not know this when they first laid eyes on her. They only knew that they would do all within their power to see her safe again. So the brothers made a plan to rescue her. While the middle brother distracted the dragon with his beautiful singing, the youngest brother helped the woman run and hide, making sure she was safe as the oldest brother, who was skilled with weaponry and the strongest of the three, plunged his sword into the weakest point of the dragon's flank, the join at his wing."

As Litz shifted uncomfortably, Kella said, "Wait, but how—"

She made a mutinous noise of complaint when their storytelling guard held up a hand but fell silent to allow him to finish his tale. "When the dragon was slain, his captive was so grateful to the brothers that she offered each a wish. She was favoured by the moon, you see, and had the power to do so.

"'Ma'am, we all possess the same wish,' the eldest brother told her. 'We all wish for a new home, a better home than that which we have left behind.'

"'Very well,' said the lady. 'What is it you want in this better home? Is it the same for all of you?'

"'Oh, Lady,' said the eldest, 'more than anything, I dream of the sea. I wish to see it, to sail on it, and live by it and feel its breeze cool me through my day. I would also desire somewhere I could easily defend, so that if I am lucky enough to have a family of my own, I will never worry that I cannot protect them.'

"'I can give you that,' the lady said. 'Walk as far west as you are able, and you will find a rocky cliffside by the sea. The sand and sea will be harsh but nothing a person with sense cannot learn to respect and tame.' Then she turned to the second brother. 'What is it you desire most in your home?' she asked him.

"'Oh, Lady,' he answered. 'I do not dream of the cruel sea. I dream of a warm forest where I will never need to pray for food or rain.'

"'I can give you that also,' the Moon Lady told him. 'Walk as far east as you are able. And you shall find a forest larger, taller, and wider than you could ever dream. There will be many dangers but choices of food aplenty, and you will never want for rain or shade.'

"Then she turned to the third brother. 'What is it you desire in your home?'

"'Oh, Lady,' the boy sighed. 'I fear that all I wish for in a home—something to love and care for, to return to each day—already stands in front of me. Never have I met or shall I meet your equal in all my days. I care nothing for where and how I am to live if I am permitted to do it by your side.'

"To his shock, the Lady smiled at him. 'Ah, but a person cannot be a home, only a piece of it.'

"'Then tell me, Lady, what I might do to have both you and a home?'

"'Boy, I have no home. I wander this desert as it pleases the moon who favours me. I live my life waiting to be returned to her lands in the sky, as all people should.'

"'Then, Lady, could I not join you?'

"'Three conditions you must promise me first,' she said. 'If you are to consider me a home, I cannot stop you, but you must never consider me any less a person for being so. Second, like me, you must wait for our return to our moon and the stars and learn well the songs that will guide us back there. And three, we must never stay long wherever we go. No home lasting longer than a season will we create, no lands will we farm. For this world does not belong to us. It is the domain of dragons. Like them, it is magnificent to gaze on, untrustworthy in character, and sometimes too fiery to bear.'

"'All this, I swear to you,' the youngest brother promised, only hope and awe filling his heart. And so he walked by her side until the end of his days, feeling always in love and always at home."

"He's a better storyteller than you," Kella said in the ensuing hush.

"He's a better storyteller than *you*," Litz said icily, to a dismissive hiss from Kella. "Is that how your people started wandering?"

Another shrug. "It is how some tell it." He smiled, and the brightness of it was visible even in the darkness. "I like you two," he said. "Good listeners."

"We're a, uh, a *captive audience*, you might say," Kella put in.

The joke did not seem to pass through the language barrier, and their storyteller did not laugh, which Litz suspected bothered Kella.

"Are you a magic-user as well as a linguist?" Litz asked, a little giddy with her own daring. At home, such a question would be ridiculous, dangerous for both persons involved in the conversation.

At her uncle's urging, the first time she'd practised using, she had gone home to her bed and had told no one what she'd learned. No one she loved would have had a sympathetic reaction to her new stories, so though she'd been barely more than a child, she'd buried them all. Here, Litz had witnessed near twenty magic-users trap a dragon and her rider in one smooth, rehearsed motion that would bring the entire Aelshian Empire to its knees. If they ever tried to teach that to someone in Aelshia, the money that could be worth…

And Litz thought that perhaps it was no coincidence that magic use was banned and demonised back home. It had the power to threaten dragons. And her mind went involuntarily back to Kella's challenge before, about how their alliance with the dragons' Circle from its earliest days had seemed like "cheating."

"I'm not sure I understand," their guard said eventually.

Litz found this unlikely following such a well-narrated story, but she let it slide. It was becoming easier, but there were still a lot of times when she had to ask Kella to repeat herself or deal with the fact that she couldn't make out a word she was saying.

"If you were me, how would you try to escape?" Kella started, scratching thoughtfully up into her hair.

Litz slapped the palm of her hand into her forehead. "*Kella.*"

"What? If you don't *ask*…"

But their guard no longer seemed to be paying any attention. He'd turned to face a small figure coming toward them with a light and started yelling in rapid Narani.

"What's he saying?" Litz hissed.

"Too slow, I think. Yeah. This kid was too slow with the…*food.*" Kella sat up and clung to the bars. "He's bringing over food."

Litz wanted badly to mock Kella for her sudden earnestness, but the rumbling in her own belly cut her short. She had been given a meal since waking in the cage, but that felt like a very long time ago now. "How much?" she asked, joining Kella at the bars as they watched a child carrying the bowls reach their guard. After some huffing from the guard, he passed them two bowls.

Litz had no idea what was in the bowls, other than something mushy that had a pleasantly spicy flavour. By the time she realised that their guard was gone, she was already halfway through her bowl, and Kella was holding a stilted conversation with the child.

"I think," Kella explained, "that our storyteller heard that there was alcohol and is feeling insulted that no one gave him any. He is also upset that his bowl is the same size as ours, so he's left Darsin here in charge while he runs off and bashes some heads."

"How do you know all that?" Litz said, looking pointedly at the child. "He's barely said a word." Her food might have consumed most of her attention, but it hadn't robbed her of her senses. And Kella had not exactly proven herself an expert in Narani.

Kella shook her head. "No, no. I only spoke enough Narani to get his name and say hi. Darsin's signing this to me. At least, I'm pretty sure we're using the same language. It's dark." Kella grinned. "It's funny how they speak different but sign the same, don't you think? I think it's weirdly comforting."

"When did you learn sign language?"

Kella shrugged. "Rall, the guy who used to hunt with us? He was deaf. Issue is, I think this kid's both deaf and either mute or he's still learning to speak."

"And that's an issue because?"

"Think about the culture for a minute." Kella had that voice that seemed to indicate she wanted to be angry, but she was holding it back until Litz had thought.

"Oh. They sing their way home. Their moon stories."

"You got it."

"Oh." Litz felt real pain for the child still staring like a bush baby from outside their bars. He couldn't be any older than twelve. "How awful," she said. "You mean they all think that he's—"

"Broken. Cursed. A sad case."

"Like a cheetah who can't run."

Kella nodded and signed to the boy, who nodded and started walking away. "Or a dragonrider in Jeenobi," she said quietly.

"From what I've now seen of your dragons, that would be strange."

"Mmm. Litz?"

"Yes?"

"Would you tell me another story?"

"Why, so you can insult me some more for my lack of skill?"

"No, because it's dark, and I'm homesick, and the kid I'm hoping I can convince into helping us won't be back until morning. Please?"

Litz wasn't optimistic that Kella had charmed the boy enough for him to come back, and she didn't really feel like telling stories. She felt like freeing her dragon and finally being able to speak with her, to breathe again. But they had no way for her to do that. And even if she couldn't make herself feel any better, that didn't mean she couldn't help

Kella. "There's one story I heard from a sergeant I did basic training with."

"That sounds like a good one."

"Only, I'll leave out the part where they have to seduce a man because I couldn't possibly look at you again when it's morning."

"You wilting jungle flower. I wanna hear the version the sergeant told you."

"Well, you're not going to. This is the story of the parrot, the orangutan, and the emu who decided to make themselves into a man by standing one on top of the other."

"Oh, I *definitely* want you to tell me the sergeant's version."

CHAPTER EIGHTEEN

The cage had been left uncovered in the night, with nothing given to them other than a single blanket, so Litz again got to wake up with sand in her mouth and a wicked crick in her neck.

Had Kella not been the worst audience for any complaints, Litz would have had several to say aloud. Because any complaints she had would *have* to be spoken aloud: the place inside where Loren should be was still missing.

Accepting that the new day had not handed her any reason to welcome it, Litz sat up and looked at Kella, who was staring intently at the camp, the sunrise gently mapping her face.

She seemed so still, like a guard dog at its post. Until she turned. "What are you smiling about?"

"I can't smile for no reason?"

Kella narrowed her eyes suspiciously but eventually shrugged and returned to her post.

"What are they doing?" Litz asked, nodding at the group Kella was watching. They stood in a circle, facing each other with their hands open. It was by no means the entire camp, but it included everyone who'd been involved in their capture, and there were all ages, some of the children looking no older than seven.

Kella frowned. "Oh yeah, this is familiar. Something to do with their religion or something."

"I thought their religion was about singing and stars."

"Maybe it's about…" Kella squinted and sat up straighter. "Wait, I recognise some of that."

Among the group, the magic-user who Litz had tripped up held her stare.

"*Burd-nasor*, that's like, 'and I'll say it again.' I get that a lot when they don't like whatever I'm offering but not so bad that they'd act offended. I think it's like *reaffirmation* here."

"Reaffirmation of what?" Litz watched, fascinated as Kella continued to listen.

Kella seemed to spend so much time being certain or pretending to be. Seeing her concentrate on learning something was an education. She looked as though she belonged in a library listening to lectures about philosophy, not out in the desert in bloody clothes. "Living. Living free. Living without any shame."

"Shame of what?

"Themselves. Their own power." Understanding dawned on Kella's face. "Their magic. Interesting."

"Interesting?" Litz moved her eyes over the group. There was a strange, hard-won pride glowing from their faces. It reminded her of the look Kella had worn when Litz had forced her to get back in the cage after her first escape attempt. Defeated but utterly thrilled by the transgressive continuation of her own life.

"They do think that magic is wrong, but they do it anyway. Why?"

Kella's nose wrinkled, but she kept her eyes facing the circle. "I dunno. Why, do you?"

❖

"What's this place they want back so badly?" Kella asked a few hours after they'd started moving that morning.

Litz sighed, continuing to stare at the horses moving around them. Kella wondered again what they were doing to keep those horses so healthy. Drugs? Magic? At this point, there were very few options that would surprise her. Spending this amount of time in a moving Narani camp had revealed far more about them than years of arguing with their merchants in markets had, and she still found them strange.

"It's where they believe we first arrived on Earth, I think."

"And? Why do you guys have a problem with that?"

"The king doesn't want anyone having visitation rights to our land who may be dangerous or may be spies and are under no obligation to obey our laws."

"Right."

"But it's not an issue I take much interest in."

As Kella leaned on the rattling bars, a smile twitched at her mouth. "What political issues do you take interest in?"

"In the interesting ones. But Loren has a better head for it than me. Why do you ask?"

"Because if we can't start figuring out an escape plan, I'm hoping you're politically significant to your people back home."

Litz still didn't look away from the horses, but she did squirm a little. "I'd rather take escape ideas."

"That bad?"

"That complicated."

Kella winced. "Gods, that sounds even worse. Okay. They've kept your powers bound."

"Yes."

"You can't do *anything* magical?"

"No."

"Do you think that's just while you're in this cage, or?"

Litz had started rubbing her forehead. "Let's just assume for now that my abilities are gone."

"Could you teach me? They wouldn't expect that, right?" Kella wasn't sure how much she liked her own idea, but it did feel like a sensible thing to suggest.

After going quiet for a few moments, Litz shook her head again, "It would take weeks to teach you. And even then, we'd be working under the assumption that you'd have the, well, the knack."

Kella shrugged, trying to hide her relief. Having the knack was Ker's thing. If she did have it, he'd have already done it first, which would sting. And if she didn't, well, he would be the special one. By choosing never to find out, both scenarios could be neatly avoided.

Gods, she was petty.

"I'm a fast learner," was what she said. "Under pressure."

"I think we need other ideas." Litz gave her a smile so false, it looked as though her mouth was held up by strings. "You've escaped from military personnel twice in almost as many days. So?"

"Okay, but these escapes weren't successful," Kella said. "I mean—" She gestured as far as the cage would allow her arms to spread. "What about you? You've had experience with, like, military tactics or whatever they teach you in *officer training*, right? What would you tell your people to do in this situation?"

"Be prepared to kill themselves to prevent further war?"

Kella stared, aghast, and Litz sighed, her whole body seeming to deflate.

"Okay. Assess their surroundings, the people holding them. These people's main advantage is their magic use, but that must be tiring for them to be keeping this up for both me and Loren. Especially if they're also using it to sustain their horses."

"That's what I was wondering."

"It would mean that their strongest users are going to be distracted and exhausted."

Kella nodded, privately enjoying Litz's tone switch as she began laying into her military planning.

"Their priorities are us and their captive dragon, which they're probably selling parts from. It's worth a lot to them but likely not as much as it once was. Now, their families are travelling with them too. They've been working hard to keep them out of sight, but there are children here. So our captors' objectives are protecting their people and successfully reaching Aelshia to trade us for rights to their land. This won't work, or at least, it won't go as smoothly as they're hoping, and they're probably aware of that. They should also be aware that any sign of dragon mistreatment as they cross into Aelshia will only win them enemies, or they're hoping it *will*, which would be a new problem."

As Kella cocked her head, Litz ignored her and continued.

"Our objective is escape. For ourselves, Loren, and the other dragon before we get too close to Aelshia and someone discovers everything that's happened."

Litz had Kella nodding along solemnly with everything until about midway through her sentence. "Wait. What? You want to free the other dragon?"

"It's trapped, and it's in pain." Litz snarled. "And it's going to cause chaos," she added, a little shame creeping into her voice. "Enough chaos to allow us to escape."

Kella choked out a laugh. "Yeah, chaos. You realise it might end up killing all those kids you just mentioned? Don't tell me you didn't consider that with your officer brain working full speed. That beast isn't going to be anything but…oh."

"Oh?"

"What if that's where they're drawing all this power from?"

Litz narrowed her eyes. "What do you mean?"

"Y'know, isn't magic all about pushing and pulling? What if they're pulling magic—or strength, energy, whatever—from the dragon? Didn't you say they're unbelievably strong?"

Litz's lips parted slightly. Watching her nod, Kella wondered if Litz realised she was mouthing her thoughts. Maybe the separation from her dragon was already driving her mad.

And this had scarcely been more than a day.

"Maybe."

"I'm a genius."

"You're definitely something," Litz admitted, granting Kella a slight but real smile.

"But genius was what you wanted to say, I could tell."

"Now that we might have the facts assembled, can you assemble us a plan, genius?"

"I can't do all the work around here," Kella put in as she stuffed the last piece of the orange they'd been given for breakfast into her mouth. "Hey, guard-lady, how would you escape?"

The woman walking by their cage gave no reaction.

"Hey, all your singing will bring only the pain of labour once more to your mother," she said. When this still received no response. "She definitely doesn't understand us."

"How can you tell?"

"Any Narani would have reacted to that. Especially coming from a barbarian like me."

"If you say so."

"Anyway. She's not our first choice of ally. I want to talk more to the kid."

Litz seemed visibly underwhelmed by this idea. "The kid who hasn't come back all morning?"

"He might be doing chores. Or have misunderstood what I was saying. It was dark."

"True. But it's probably smarter not to rely on allies at all. It's an unreliable—"

"And I mean, I will start looking pretty ridiculous if I befriend *everyone* who captures me."

Litz raised her eyebrows in what was probably the closest expression to irony Kella had ever seen her face adopt. "You'd call us friends?"

"I'm a friendly sort of person, Princess. Don't let it go to your head."

❖

Litz's hopes were briefly raised when their guards walked away from the cage the next time they stopped. Until she remembered that they still didn't have a plan. In fact, they had so little of anything like a plan that it was turning into a game.

"We could convince them that we're beloved by the gods and that they have to set us free."

Litz frowned. "I don't think the Narani even believe in gods."

"What if we could make them start believing?"

"Hmm. What was it you used to get Loren's attention, to distract her while you attacked?"

"I wouldn't say I attacked."

"What was it?"

Smiling sheepishly, Kella produced a small wooden whistle which had been crudely formed in the shape of a dragon. "My friend Zebenn makes cool inventions. Since it wasn't a weapon, nobody bothered to take it off me."

"No hidden knife this time?"

"I actually didn't have it hidden. I was worried it might fall out and stab Janx."

"Janx?"

"The camel."

Litz glared at the whistle, not sure if she was impressed by the achievement of the invention or unimpressed by its appearance.

"You want a demonstration? *Hey*, maybe we could get the other dragon to start panicking over it. Even if it can't move, it might distract them enough to…still not get us out of here."

"No."

Kella flopped to the floor of the cage, causing a loud clanging noise that worried Litz. "Then we've still got nothing."

"Nothing." Litz frowned. "It didn't look like a Janx."

"Yes, he does. What did you call your one?"

"I didn't name mine."

"Killjoy."

Litz stared at the world continuing outside the cage, as always surprised at how normal it seemed. Happy. Children were playing with a ball and getting in their elders' way. The camels and horses were being fed, a prized group that Janx the camel had been adopted into because Litz could no longer tell it apart from the rest. It had been adorned with the same type of Narani saddle worn by the other camels.

"This seems like a good way to grow up," Litz said, the longing in her own voice surprising her.

"I dunno. Life in the desert, avoiding sand terrors, sandstorms. No privacy living out of a tent, either. Trust me on that."

"I know. But..."

"They look happy?"

"Yeah."

When Litz turned, Kella was looking at her strangely with an expression Litz had no idea how to place. For a moment, she found it so paralysing that she barely noticed their cage being approached.

"Hello again, Ambassador," said the man in front. Litz recognised him as the man who had done all the translating on the night of their capture.

"Hi, could you please fuck off? We're trying to work on an escape plan, and you're interrupting," Kella said as Litz cleared her throat loudly.

"What can we help you with?"

"Not we. Just you. We're going to open this door, Ambassador, and we would like you to come with us without being any trouble."

Kella caught Litz's gaze again with a slow, deliberate glance. Without needing the kind of bond she should still have with Loren, Litz was certain Kella was thinking something like *Oh, we'll cause more than just* any *trouble.*

Kella would probably listen to her. If she gave a quiet shake of her head advising against attack, Kella would hold off. But maybe she *had* been separated from Loren for too long, and she was losing her sense of judgement. Or maybe she was just curious as to what Kella would do this time.

So she shrugged as they opened the cage and shifted to the side as much as she was able. Somehow, Kella understood that Litz was giving her the space to make an entrance and rolled forward out of the cage, legs first to kick at the figures still stood at the door with surprising force.

Litz followed, jumping on the back of the one Kella had not kicked down, biting and scratching and screeching. And having the most fun she'd had since they'd danced in the oasis together. More, probably. This was far less awkward.

It only took minutes before they'd been pinned down and recaptured. The attempt had been a tactical disaster, a futile waste of energy, but for some reason, it felt worth it. Litz wondered if that had been what Kella's first escape attempt had been all about: reminding herself and her captors that she was still a force to be reckoned with.

But now that force of nature was back in her cage, and Litz had both her arms roughly pulled behind her.

"Would you like to explain what that accomplished?"

Litz shrugged at the panting translator and glanced back at Kella, who grinned wide, obscenely stretching her now split lip. "I get to die having watched Princess Litz of Aelshia have a good try at biting your ear off. So I'm feeling better," Kella told them, beaming.

But as they took Litz away, rather less gently than she suspected they might have before, she looked back at Kella, wondering if she just hadn't been able to let Litz pass into their hands without convincing herself that she'd tried to stop them.

Had Kella been under Litz's command in battle, she would have either given her a thorough lecture or been forced to send her home. That kind of heroism either got people killed or it didn't survive a battlefield.

And far worse, it was proving infectious.

Thoughts and feelings didn't need to keep up with each other, Kella knew that. But over the past few days, she'd been forced to reevaluate both so often that she barely felt capable of understanding either. The only thing she was currently certain of was that if anything happened to Litz now, it would be Kella's fault.

The pain of a beating helped. It was grounding enough to inspire urgency. These people might make nicer guards than the Jeenobi ones, but they'd taken Litz, Kella had let them, and she still had no escape plan.

Findan would have had a plan. *Ker* would have had a plan.

And he'd probably gone and planned something stupid without her there. She wanted to believe that if Findan hadn't allowed for a rescue mission, Ker would have reluctantly stayed with the team, but she remembered the sight of him stubbornly there at her side, insisting that Kella hadn't killed the dead dragon without help. People tended to assume that Ker was the smart one, the sensible one, but Kella knew that was only in comparison to her.

She was so caught up in her own spiralling thoughts that when a small hand reached through the bars and lay softly on hers, she winced before taking a second and recognising the boy from the night before. She narrowed her eyes and clumsily signed out, "What took you so long?"

Darsin shrugged and gave a little smile before signing, "Chores. The worst."

Kella smiled, grateful for, if nothing else, having someone to talk to. "Do you know where they took my friend?"

❖

She'd spent three years commanding troops on the battlefield, yet Litz had been lucky enough to be forced into interrogation duty only once. Though she had flatteringly and not-so-flatteringly been described as "intimidating," "cold," and once, "scary," Litz had never felt qualified for the task of making others talk when they didn't want to. That seemed to require being adept at speaking to people, which wasn't something she'd ever considered herself to be.

Obviously, the school of acquiring information through torture still thrived, but in Litz's experience, the method wasn't effective enough to warrant its cruelty. Litz just hoped they were too civilised to resort to trying. If she'd had Loren to link to, she wouldn't have been afraid. She could have retreated from her own body, could have had someone with her to urge her to stay strong.

Without that to fall back on, she had no idea how strong she might be.

Maybe she wasn't, she thought, feeling fear clutch her as they led her toward a large empty tent. Maybe she believed herself to be strong, witty on occasion, brave, reasonable because she'd had Loren. The last time she hadn't had Loren, she'd been eight years old. She definitely wouldn't have been able to stand up to any kind of torture then.

Oh gods, but she had to be strong.

By the time they sat her in the only chair in the room and tied her hands behind her back, she had never been so afraid in her life, but she was determined not to let it show. She had some sort of reputation to hold on to. Which she was sure would be exactly what Kella would be telling herself if she was sitting in Litz's position, and for some reason, that thought helped.

Someone had laid a brightly coloured rug down. Surely, it was too pretty for anything too bloody. "Now, Ambassador, we have no intention of harming you," the translator told her with an impressively warm smile considering the fresh scratch marks down his face.

Litz's heart dropped to her stomach. *Oh no.* "But you don't sound as though you've ruled it out, either," Litz said evenly, trying to finish with her best impression of Kella's smile. She wasn't certain it had worked, but the translator's solemn expression did waver a little.

"Obviously, we hope to draw on your experience as a diplomat for getting through successful negotiations with your people. We want things to go well for everyone, and we would appreciate your cooperation in working toward that goal."

Joke's on you. I've been playing ambassador for all of two weeks, and all it's done is land me here, thought Litz and was only momentarily dismayed when she received no answer. She had to handle this alone, and she would.

Experience as a diplomat. Right. "What kind of cooperation did you have in mind…I'm sorry, what do I call you?"

Always ask questions, always seem in control, always put the weapon back in their hand. It will make them nervous. That was what her father would say. They might not have always understood each other very well, but Litz had always managed to bond with her father through their shared lack of ease in the Aelshian court. He had never been considered an appropriate match for Litz's mother, which had made him deeply self-conscious, but if he hadn't told her that, Litz might never have known. His background might have been military, but he had a showman's ability for flamboyantly masking his insecurities, even if the comparison would have deeply offended him.

"You may call me Fieranon, Ambassador." He was very careful to always address her with respect but never with enough to use her full title. "And as to the matter of your cooperation, we simply wish to ask you several questions."

"You know, your Aelshian really is excellent," Litz offered in her best regal tone. And although the translator did not seem visibly rattled by her attempt to demean him, the man and woman circling her seemed rather confused and frustrated that the conversation was not progressing as they'd hoped. Litz still seemed too calm for their liking? Good.

"Now, Ambassador. You will answer these questions for me, or—"

"Or what?" Litz smiled wider than felt natural to her. "You'll harm me? Let me explain something to you, Fieranon. I do have some ambassadorial knowledge to share. You currently hold three hostages you intend to barter back to my king, correct?"

A flicker of a smile. "Crude but correct."

"Do you know who your most valuable hostage is?"

"Yourself?"

"Incorrect. It is Loren. My dragon," she clarified when they looked nonplussed. "The dragon you did not bother learning the name of before binding her so cruelly. She is the hostage you have the most to gain from and the most likely of us to be successfully released. Now," Litz continued before the translator could cut her off, "do you really want to release a highly regarded dragon whom you have forced to endure the pain their rider went through? How do you think said dragon is likely to respond to this violence? They are not known as forgiving creatures, if you know much about them at all, Fieranon."

Fieranon held her gaze a moment before speaking rapidly in Narani to the people with him. "I assure you, Your Highness, we never had any intention of harming you," he told her eventually with a tight smile.

Satisfaction warmed Litz like a campfire. *Liar. Because now I'm Your Highness.*

"Wonderful," she said and left it at that.

"I confess, much of what we wish to ask concerns our ignorance on Aelshian current affairs."

"I would not wish for anyone to approach such a delicate situation unprepared." Crossing her legs, Litz tried to pretend she felt comfortable here, as in charge as she would feel back in her home barracks. In five minutes of feeling intimidated, she felt more empathy for Kella's bizarre behaviour than ever.

"Mmm, indeed." Fieranon stared at her, his head to one side.

He's trying to make me squirm, Litz realised and narrowed her eyes slightly.

"Your use of magic, for instance. We find that very strange. I had assumed most Aelshians were in acceptance of *Venarquin*."

Litz blinked as she watched one of the nonspeakers circling her smirk at the switch in language. "Forgive me, my Narani is poor. I don't recognise this word."

"Forgive *me*, I would have translated had there been an option for it in your language. It means the Great Shame. It is what we name the negative feelings surrounding magic use or of the reluctance to use magic. The shame in our abilities."

Litz worked hard to keep her face from betraying her too much. "Yesterday, I saw you. You were…"

He nodded. "Our morning affirmations, yes. I wonder how you survive without it. Or does your dragon help feed on your shame?"

Everyone wanted Loren to be feeding on her somehow. No one was happy with hearing that Loren only wanted her company. "Fieranon, I am a soldier. Sometimes, that means doing things you're not proud of."

"Yes, where would the Aelshian Empire be if it let any kind of shame keep it from its intent, hmm?"

Litz stiffened reflexively. "Magic is not something commonly encouraged in my home country, as I'm sure you're aware."

"I am. Dragons do not like magic, and I'm sure you can understand why after watching us work. We have long suspected that dragons have encouraged, if not been the very root of, the shame associated with magic use."

"I'm sorry, what *shame*?"

Fieranon smiled slightly, as if she had just asked him if he knew where she could find some sand. "Surely, even a princess does not feel pride when they push and pull at the fabric of the world?"

"Of course not," Litz said, trying not to snap. "There's a reason it isn't legal in any civilised land, no more than murder. It's wrong."

"And there is the shame speaking."

Litz frowned, unconvinced as Fieranon gave a long, elegant sigh and turned to his leader to translate the situation in rapid Narani. When he'd finished, they shook their head as well. Litz looked between them, trying not to seem lost. "Are you saying that the cultures of the world are biased against magic?"

"On much of this continent, yes. But it goes deeper than the cultures. They knew that we were dangerous. All those kings and queens and dragons, they infected us with shame in what we were and what we could do so that we would keep ourselves controlled, and they would never have to lift a finger."

"And they all managed this by working together?" Litz said, unimpressed. "All these kings and queens and dragons?" Litz might use magic, but she'd never tried to delude herself into thinking that she was somehow doing the world a favour by doing so. Maybe it wasn't as terrible as murder, but saying it was a good thing was almost as ridiculous as alcoholics insisting their habit was medicinal.

Fieranon leaned down, watching her. "But you *are* one of those kings and queens. Maybe you never thought of the way things are as being a disadvantage because it isn't, not for you. No. Daughter of

Aelshia, you'd never had any power forbidden to you before this one, had you?"

Litz wanted to press him about this, all of this; her uncle would be thrilled to hear the stories when she finally returned home, but she was afraid of sounding either ignorant or belligerent. She wanted to negotiate, which meant keeping her tone reasonable. "You did not ask me into this tent to discuss the ethics of magic use."

"No, we did not," he agreed, straightening his back once more. "Concerning rumours have reached us recently. Is it true that your king is dying?"

For a moment, Litz was too shocked to answer. King Narin had famously taken on a new consort only the year before. She appeared at every public event she was required to attend, and if that involved dancing, she would dance. In recent years, she'd remained active and opinionated in both political and military decisions while also putting more effort into mothering her young son than she ever had either of her daughters. If there were any truth at all to these rumours, then this had to be so recent she wouldn't have heard—

Oh.

Unless the king had sought to hide her vulnerability. Which she would, of course she would. She was the king, and she'd always been a suspicious and canny one, which was what had kept her on the throne so long and so comfortably.

In her last meeting with Litz, she hadn't seemed fragile or weak, but all her consorts had been watchful, and she hadn't exactly been her brisk and energetic self. The oddest part of the meeting had been the calling of it in the first place. Litz had assumed it would be about her undertaking the first ambassadorial mission to Jeenobi since the war had ended. But since it was the first time King Narin had summoned Litz since she'd received word that Litz intended to become a dragonrider, Litz had been confused when all the king did was speak vaguely about her gladness that Litz would ensure peace with the dragons and Jeenobi while prioritising Eisha's safety, her beloved, absent daughter.

Ah.

The king had summoned her for deathbed words.

But she'd looked fine.

And Litz had assured Eisha that "Everything at home is going as it always does." Eisha, who had always done her best to ensure Litz picked up some basics in the study of human behaviour.

"I'm very sorry to hear this if it's true," Litz said dryly, relieved to see that Fieranon's only reaction was irritable disappointment. Perhaps her expressions were not so transparent as Kella insisted.

Fieranon recovered his nonchalance quickly. "I apologise, perhaps you are not the best person to ask, but unfortunately, you are currently the only source of information I have access to. Though I will confess, I find it odd that you trust your dragon to defend and protect you more than your own family."

"Family can take many forms," Litz said primly. "And my king has more important matters than family to consider in the decisions she makes."

"To us, such a statement seems cruel."

Litz privately agreed but did her best to smile. "Ah, but Fieranon, you ask for my opinion as a diplomat, and politics is cruel. However, whether for familial or political reasons, nowhere on the Aelshian border would be safe if you were to harm me," Litz added, feeling this fact warranted reiteration.

"Of course," he said, but he sounded distracted and was no longer looking at her when he spoke. None of them were. All three Narani were now staring out the crack in the tent's opening to where a lot of noise seemed to be coming from the camp.

And from the looks on their faces, they hadn't been expecting this. This had to be of Kella's making. "Is something the matter?" Litz asked politely.

"Of course not, Your Highness," Fieranon said, still obviously distracted and even a little shaken. "Nothing will harm you in here."

❖

Kella had gotten very, very lucky. She had been lucky that when she'd convinced Darsin to find the key for the cage, no one had been around to hear or guard her. She had been lucky that it took nothing more to convince the boy to help her than a promise she would take him with her. Help that included stealing a scimitar that she was very lucky no one saw him running around with.

Maybe it was more accurate to say that she was lucky no one seemed to pay much attention to the kid at all.

And she was very lucky that she already knew how to kill a dragon quickly and quietly.

But the fact that she had gotten this lucky was making her feel a whole fuckload worse now that she was trying to climb its basically immobile neck, scimitar feeling uncomfortably light in her hand.

It didn't seem all that concerned that she was there. They. They didn't seem all that concerned that she was there. She couldn't pretend she still believed in the righteousness of dragon killing, especially not after feeling that thought-blast from Loren, even if this one definitely wasn't quite right.

She was almost certain that the Narani's primary source of power was this dragon. That meant that this dragon had to die if they were going to have any chance of escaping. And that however she might feel, she was going to have to kill it.

After her first couple of battles, Kella had never attempted to keep score of how many creatures she had killed. She knew that it was a lot. She'd never been one to walk around wearing trophies made of dragon teeth. If what she did couldn't speak for itself, it wasn't worth doing. And though many fights had found her terrified, none had ever made her hesitate.

It would be a mercy, she reminded herself. Both its body and its mind were severely damaged, probably irreparably. Some of the places they'd ripped its scales off were bleeding. Even if it got away without hurting itself or anyone else, it was going to be a beacon for predators for miles off. Vultures might just peck it to death one day, thinking it was already dead.

And that was assuming it got out of the camp without more tragedy. If it really was in as much pain as it looked, it would be a danger to everyone in the immediate area if it was let go. If it had any power left, it would only need a few moments to send the whole encampment up in flames.

Kella could not let that happen. She protected people, *that* was her job.

When she slid her sword hard and deep through the dragon's eye, the creature died slowly and loudly, but the effects of its death were instantaneous. The moment it stopped moving, Loren began to roar in triumph, and Kella's whole body relaxed in relief.

She'd done the Right Thing.

Sort of.

Maybe.

Gods, she missed being sure.

❖

Litz wasn't sure how to feel when she realised the power pushing down on her. There was sadness and a simmering anger as soon as she understood what Kella had to have done. But more overwhelmingly, there was relief, joy, release. She was *free*. Free to be all of herself and have no reason to keep that hidden. The tension headache that she'd been nursing for days had finally gone.

It was a bonus to see the looks on her captors' faces as they realised the loss of their own power reserves.

"Thank you for the talk," Litz said, quietly *pulling* apart the ropes which bound her. "I think I am going to leave now." She got to her feet and allowed herself a smile. Because oh *gods*, she could feel Loren again, and she knew that everything was going to be all right, that it could be again.

It's going to be fine, Loren told her, and Litz wanted to weep. *Just get to me and I'll get us away. No one will ever hold me like that again.*

I missed you. You were gone—

I know, Loren said, mentally nudging Litz forward. *But now I'm not. Now come back to me before I start setting people on fire.*

Grinning, Litz walked forward, using the surprise of the magic-users around her against them, and *pulled* with all the strength she had until each of them fell to their knees in exhaustion.

She walked from the tent feeling like a king.

Almost immediately, Kella called her name, which, Litz somehow heard over everything, even the screams and shouts of the entire encampment. Too many leaders had been in the tent with her, Litz realised, and no magic-user was at full strength.

Reliance on anything other than yourself for strength will make you weaker when it has gone, her uncle had always taught her. *Like splinting an arm that is no longer broken.*

Adding to their vulnerability was Loren in the middle of it all, triumphantly coughing pillars of fire into the sky. No one seemed to know what to do about this or be inclined to learn. There were children to calm, none of whom had probably ever seen a dragon not within their elders' control. They were terrified.

Litz had known from a childhood spent poring over old tomes on warfare that the ideal plan in a battle in which you are outnumbered is to cause panic and confusion amongst your enemy, so she was smiling as she started running through the encampment toward where Kella was releasing Loren from the last of her chains. But although Kella was still on the ground, someone was already seated comfortably on Loren's back, eyes lit with anticipation.

"No," Litz said in horror. "We are not kidnapping a child."

Kella growled without looking up from her task. "He asked to come with us in fair payment for letting me out."

After a nervous glance at the Narani beginning to organise themselves again, Litz shook her head and *wrenched* at what was left of the chain with her mind, breaking it instantly.

Flinching as though stung, Kella muttered, "Way to show me up in front of our son."

"We are not adopting any children, we are escaping."

"Actually," Kella took a few steps back from Loren as she stretched her wings wide in triumph, "you guys are escaping."

Litz blinked. "What are you talking about?"

Kella gulped before giving an uncharacteristically high laugh. "Yeah, no. I'm still not flying anywhere. But don't worry. All this chaos? I'm bound to get away quick."

"And get captured again almost as quickly if you're lucky and they don't simply leave you to die in the desert."

You're angry.

Of course I'm angry, she's being impossible.

Not exactly. She's just not saying what you want to hear. She has proven herself capable of surviving much, and neither of you owe each other anything now. But if we do not move quickly, we will all be recaptured.

Litz looked back at the camp. They had a minute, maybe. "No," she said aloud. "No, I am not leaving you behind."

"Unless you want to get captured again, you're gonna."

Sneers did not come naturally to Litz, but she did her best at summoning one. "I can't believe that the legendary dragon-slaying heir of Jeenobi is this much of a coward."

"Nope," Kella said, folding her arms and taking another step backward. "Not baiting me like that. Farewell, Princess, it's been swell. Now get on your fucking dragon."

Litz took a deep breath. "Won't you trust me?" she asked.

Had Kella had a dragon she was bonded to, Litz would have believed her to be in the middle of a very strongly worded debate with them in that moment. Eventually, someone seemed to win.

"Fine," Kella forced out through her teeth. "I'll—"

Litz wasn't willing to wait for her to change her mind. When Loren crouched, allowing Litz to clamber on, she hoped Kella would follow her example. But when Litz got seated behind the boy, thanking the gods their captors had at least left Loren's reins on, Kella still hadn't moved. She was staring up at Loren, eyes darting like a child watching their worst nightmare come to life in front of them.

"I…I can't," she muttered, shaking her head, and Litz realised that Kella was doing her best not to cry.

Litz was tired from taking out her guards but not that tired. She *pulled* Kella's hands up high enough to grab them and pull her on behind herself and the boy.

"Fuck," Kella screamed and continued to scream this and a few other choice words like a litany until Loren took off, and the roar of the wind meant that Litz could no longer make out if Kella was still using any words at all.

CHAPTER NINETEEN

K er had never visited an entrance of the Heaven Mines before, though Findan had spent so much time talking about them that he felt like he had. The mines, though worked with all the good intentions in the world, Ker was sure, could not practically exist for the sake of the digging alone. Often at the entrances to the mines, whole towns had been built upon the rubble and the money from precious metals dug up almost carelessly by the religious miners. Almost half the homes in Malya had been built with stone from the Heaven Mines.

Ker was visiting, with Sallvayn nestled in his bag, for two purposes. If Kella had escaped, this would have likely been her first stop. And following his disastrous encounter with Evlo the night before, Ker still hadn't succeeded in finding any food, and he was starting to feel that bite at him. Civilisation might be risky, but it was too tempting to avoid entirely.

Not that this hill town was exactly civilisation. It was barely more than a village built around the mining business and had no perimeter walls nor tall buildings, so it didn't feel ideal for sneaking about in. It had promised none of Malya's anonymity; a person walked in and announced themselves. The buildings were similar in colour to the poorer sections of the Jeenobian capital, but Malya always seemed to blaze with a life and colour that this place lacked the energy for. It looked as though it was trying its hardest to fade into the mountain. Which it really was doing, Ker realised as he passed the long stairways leading into the ground. People here used the mountain caves, both natural and created, to keep themselves and important goods cool during the day. It also offered natural protection from dragon attacks.

Sallvayn had expressed curiosity to see how humans had been living. But from the few times Ker had taken off his bag to talk to them, they did not seem terribly impressed.

But since they'd gotten close enough to the marketplace to smell it, Sallvayn had grown quieter. Ker suspected they were, despite their insistence, as hungry as he was, and the sight of all this food was making their mouth water. Though Ker did not have much coin with him, he did have some of Ellonya's toenails Sallvayn had been working on trimming and hoped that someone would take an interest in them.

"How am I supposed to know these are auth-en-tic," the first trader with a stall filled with food said, pronouncing every syllable very deliberately.

This is insulting.

Yes. But shh, I'm concentrating.

"What else could they possibly be?"

"Rocks?"

"Rocks? *That's* insulting. These are legitimate, and they're worth far more than what I'd be taking, and you know it."

The trader crossed her arms and leaned over her stall to get closer to what Ker was holding out, which gleamed a little in the sun. "Can't get all that much for toenails." She sniffed. "But there have been dragon sightings lately. And I hear that some of the Mabaki slayers were nearby. Could be there's truth in what you're telling. I suppose I can accept these."

She started reaching for them when Ker closed his fingers over them. "I want another dannia cake to go with it."

"You cheeky piece of—"

Ker smiled, trying to master that elusive attitude between confidence and charm that Kella had always worn so well.

"Boy means to beggar me," she muttered, but she handed it over, prompting Ker to pass over his own goods. "Well, may the sun strike you. I hear that dragon goods might be flooding this place soon, so I'll have to be selling these fast."

"Oh yeah?" Ker asked, his heart starting to race.

I'm safe, Ellonya reminded him, warmed by his concern. But it didn't make Ker feel any better. They'd taken down countless dragons before, most of whom hadn't thought themselves in danger.

"Mmm," the trader said, nodding knowingly. "Bunch of tattered king's soldiers just clambered their way out of the desert. Say the king sent them out to escort a dragonrider from the jungle, heh? But the dragon turned on them all, and they barely kept their lives. And not all of them managed that much."

Ker stared.

"Least that's how I heard it told. Can't see why a dragon needs an escort in the first place." She nodded to herself, seeming to forget that Ker was still there. "Maybe the king needed to send 'em along as like, tribute, snacks for the journey. Yeah. Not sure about the king these days, if I'm being honest as I can be. Married to a chit like—hey! Is that all you were wanting?"

❖

Shortly after landing, Kella became aware that the noises she could hear were coming from her own mouth, but it took her a little longer to wonder if it was the laughing or crying that was almost choking her. Both. Neither. Some weird hybrid of the two, maybe.

She'd flown. On a dragon. And she wasn't dead. She wasn't even hurt. She was, fuck, she was alive, thank all the fucking gods above and below, she was *alive*. And that thought was so big, so important, that it left little room for her to register that Litz was saying her name.

"Kella, you can get down now. Kella, we've stopped."

Her hands were gripping something. Litz's shirt. Right. She hadn't been able to reach the reins or maybe had been too stubborn and frightened to try. But they hadn't had any kind of saddle. They'd just ridden a fucking dragon bareback. Gods, the insides of her legs felt like they'd been flayed off her.

But she was alive. "The kid," she mumbled after coughing.

"Is safe and on the ground. Look, he's down there." As Litz nodded at the ground—they seemed to be away from the dunes, thank the gods—Darsin waved up at them. Because they'd just kidnapped a little Narani boy. Right. "We're all safe. We can get down. Breathe, c'mon, you can do this."

"Don't. Stop patronising me. Gods, not a, I'm not a fucking baby."

"When you stop acting like one, I will stop treating you like one, okay?" Litz said, her tone continuing to sound sweet and even. And despite sounding unnatural, it wasn't *not* comforting to hear. She was trying, gods bless her.

Kella could manage the same. Trying, right. Because she still wasn't dead, and life always demanded effort. She swung her leg off the dragon. The dragon. She was *sitting* on a *dragon*, and they weren't trying to attack each other. Because that might be normal now.

Kella scrambled down so quickly, she almost fell flat on her face, her legs as wobbly as a newborn calf's. They couldn't even have been flying for that long. All Kella knew was that her throat felt as though she'd tried to eat an entire barrel of sand. She hoped she hadn't screamed for the entire flight. That would be embarrassing. Ruinous, as Litz had tried to taunt her with earlier, to her reputation.

But what was that even supposed to be now?

She'd killed a dragon today, but it hadn't felt noble, it hadn't felt heroic. It was making her sad to even think about it. Not like she'd done a good job that day, like she didn't have a job anymore, didn't have a role at all.

She stared at her hands, a little grazed from breaking her fall. Breathing. Right. That was how you started moving forward. It was how you started to do anything. Her mother had always said that.

In a way, it was her mother's memory saving her from breaking down in existential horror. Kella might have been doing a lot of reevaluating lately, but that didn't mean she was ready to admit that her mother had ever been wrong about anything. She wondered if that thought was self-aware enough for Litz to find attractive.

"You know," Kella said when she trusted that her breathing was steady enough. "Between that cage, the camels, and now bareback dragon riding, I have some very tender parts that I do not see recovering any time soon."

Litz awarded her a small smile, and Kella did her best to focus on that.

Breathing in, breathing out, awesome. Kella got to her feet and tried to return Litz's smile, though she had a feeling it wasn't an expression her face was handling with any elegance. "What now?"

Litz shrugged, looking as lost as Kella felt. Which was as lost as they actually were. Kella certainly had no idea what direction they'd been flying in, but then again, maybe the dragon knew where they were going. Which was another weird thought. Because dragons thought about directions. Why not?

When Litz still said nothing, Kella risked a glance at the dragon. The desert had obviously started to take its toll on her. She was dusty and obviously weary from their flight, but she was also—and Kella wasn't sure how she understood this—happy. Content, even.

"No, the boy helped us escape…Well, *I* wasn't doing the negoti-ating," Litz was saying to the dragon, speaking aloud, assumedly for Kella's benefit. Which was kinda nice. Litz looked at Darsin, who was staring at the ground he sat on with his legs splayed. He looked at the darkening sky like he'd never seen it before and then promptly…started crying. Gods. Kella really had kidnapped a child.

But he had asked.

And kids had the right to choose this sort of shit. She wasn't going to waver on that.

But he was crying.

Though no one would ever accuse Kella of being maternal, she was an older sister to all her bones. As she went and sat next to him, she instantly felt herself calm. She had someone to look after now. She was going to be okay because she had to be, because someone else needed her to be.

"Hey," she signed, "that was something, right?"

He nodded vigorously, starting to smile even as his eyes continued leaking.

"Thank you," she signed before saying it aloud in Narani, which hurt her head a little to think about. "I don't know how to say that enough."

"You got me away," he signed back.

"You got us away. It was really that bad?"

He shrugged. "Not all bad. But I won't have anything after. And they thought that meant I shouldn't have anything now. But I thought, why not, if I'm doomed anyway."

Kella grinned but felt like crying herself. "Seems…smart to me. Sorry. My…words are not good."

"You're trying," he signed back, looking more cheerful now.

"Who taught you signing?"

"My mother. She died."

"I'm sorry. So did mine."

He looked at her hard and nodded in solidarity. "What happens now?" he asked.

Kella breathed in deeply. "We're working on that. Did you bring any food in that bag?"

"Some."

"Okay. Then we're going to make food. That's what happens." For now, that was all Kella had to go on, so it would have to do. She'd been told she had a bright enough smile to sell fish to fishermen, so she smiled. And it took a few moments, but eventually, he gave her a smile in return.

❖

The soldiers weren't difficult to find. This seemed to be a place where very little happened, so the sight of half a dozen of the king's guard, desert parched and wearing bloody clothes, was causing quite the stir. Well-meaning townspeople surrounded them, attempting to lead the group to medical or residential centres, clearly in the hope that the soldiers had something valuable to trade. Ker doubted that, but he stayed quiet as he tagged along behind the group that split as they reached the main town, some going in search of medical attention, and others going straight inside the nearest inn.

But one soldier remained outside and seemed to be taking a few moments to breathe and collect herself.

Certain that this was as good an opportunity as he was likely to get, Ker moved toward her. "Hey," he said, lifting himself up to sit on the inn wall and feeling Sallvayn cling to the insides of his bag as he did so. "Are we under attack?"

She blinked and turned, slowly realising that he was speaking to her. "What?"

He smiled. "I mean, usually if anyone sees the king's best all the way out here…"

"Oh." She shook her head, curls bouncing free from the knot she'd kept them scraped back in. "No. That was us. We were under attack."

"Aelshians?"

"We could have taken Aelshians," she snipped. "No. Sand Terrors."

Ker nearly slipped off his perch. Kella hated those things. Everyone hated those things. It was even rumoured that dragons had few defences against them. It was rare to hear of them leaving the deeper regions of the desert. On the rare occasions they did, they'd been known to decimate entire villages.

Ker had once spent most of a full job helping defend a small group of merchants against them. Though they'd only lost one of their charges, Ker had been left certain that he never wanted to be in the same vicinity as one ever again. "I'm sorry," he managed to get out without choking. "How many of you were there?"

She sighed. "Not including who we were guarding?" She narrowed her eyes at him. "Wait." She marched the few steps between them in seconds and gripped his jaw. "You're the brother, aren't you?"

He quickly weighed up his options. She had a sword on her belt and, unlike him, was probably more than proficient in using one.

Are you okay?

I'm…negotiating. "Yes. Yes, I am, okay? I just want to know if she's all right," Ker said as clearly as he was able without spitting on her, switching seamlessly to his secondary plan of acting like a kid. Few people knew how old he was supposed to be, except younger than Kella, because they all knew that part, and he was lucky enough to possess what Zebenn called a "dimple-pocked face."

The soldier let him go but remained wary.

"Please," Ker said when she continued to say nothing. "What happened out there?"

Loren was, by human standards, old. She'd experienced a great deal in her long years of life but had never suffered such a feeling of powerlessness as she had over the last day, and as such, a short flight with additional passengers had exhausted her beyond measure. These weren't feelings she was used to experiencing at all outside of the secondhand channelling from one of her charges, and she didn't care for it.

Dragons had many Echoes, many shared feelings, about the nature and history of the world but had no real belief, no real creation myths. It simply wasn't something they'd ever seen the need for. They could understand the natural order of life without needing the intricacies and meaning of it explained to them. And the natural order was ultimately that dragons were in control of it.

Humans in high numbers had always been more than capable adversaries if any of them so chose or learned how, but most of them did neither. Dragons were naturally enchanting to humans, just as humans were charming and amusing to dragons. Most of the time. Loren's feelings toward the human race at large were significantly less fond today, and she was happy to be left alone by her little group.

So at first, she did her best to regally ignore the boy creeping toward her. Were she feeling more charitable, she might have thought of him as sweet. Whether he'd chosen it or not, leaving home and family was a big event for humans, and this little one was not making much of a fuss and had capably built a pyre with few resources for Loren to set aflame for the group.

Litz should have left the boy with more than this one task while she argued with her former captive over what they could afford to spare to cook for dinner. He needed more to focus on than simply staring at Loren.

Awe was the most common reaction, especially with young ones, and this one had assumedly only seen dragons grown rabid and insane. When he'd brought food to her the night before, it was probably his first encounter with a real dragon.

Though she was beginning to get slightly insulted that he hadn't attempted to speak to her yet. That was usually…

Ah. The boy couldn't speak in the human way, could he?

Loren didn't *have* to say anything to him. She'd suffered through listening to enough inner voices of humans who were not her rider to last her for decades. She shouldn't have to subject herself to one more trauma after a week of indignities.

Hello.

The boy started and looked around before eventually staring up in awe at Loren, his mouth agape.

You may speak back. She pushed her wings out before settling more comfortably. Though she was certainly changing things now, she did not normally allow this, especially with children. Their minds were usually so eager, so loud.

You…you're speaking to me.

Yes. Yes, I am, Loren agreed, amused.

The boy gulped. He was scrawnier than most children Loren had been acquainted with. He was certainly no chubby-cheeked palace child. *Hello*, he said.

Shouldn't you have said that first? Loren pointed out, hoping he was aware that she was teasing.

Dragons talk? Like this?

Where I'm from.

It sounds wonderful, he said, sitting again. *Where you're from, I mean. I wish I could talk like this all the time.*

Technically, I don't 'speak' either.

Oh. Right. This thought seemed to warm the boy, so Loren continued:

Maybe you're less of a broken human and more of an odd dragon.

As soon as she thought it, she regretted it. Humans were sensitive creatures and their offspring even more so. It was probably in very bad taste to call a child "broken," even if she'd lifted the term from his mind, and her statement was intended as a compliment.

But to her relief, the boy smiled. *I'm Darsin*, he offered.

And I am called Loren, she said gravely, adding, *it is nice to meet you*, because she knew that was something humans often told each other, and she wanted this boy to feel at ease.

What's going on with them? he asked, nodding toward where Litz and her former prisoner were still bickering over provisions. *Are they joined?*

Joined? Loren understood only when she scanned his surface mind for flashes of meaning. Among his people, marriage was uncommon. Instead, there was a "joining," the use of rope or hair or fabric to briefly tie hands together or if such materials were unavailable, by holding hands for what was deemed a suitable length of time. It meant that the people, mostly two, though not always, were bonded, whether for a night or their whole lifetimes. To unjoin, partners only needed to commence a backward ceremony that Darsin was hazy on the details of.

It was strange, maybe, but Loren had grown to appreciate Kella. There was such a dragonish pride and sense of self ingrained in the girl that, had they met under almost any other circumstances, Loren might have urged Litz to grow closer to her. Because against what Loren knew to be the common misconception of dragons and their riders, she enjoyed watching her charges grow and start families. Her first rider's family had moved into its fourth generation now, and Loren knew all their names and faces, though it was rare she could remember much else. The youngest of them had dreams of dragon riding one day, Loren knew. But it would not be with her. She had decided a long time ago that Litz would be her last partner.

She was becoming too old for heartbreak and far too old for situations like this.

Ah. No, Loren said but did not choose to elaborate. Whatever happened next was going to hurt her rider, and she wished it wouldn't have to. *But I understand. Dragons where I am from have a similar tradition.*

Did you ever have a...a mate?

A long time ago, yes, Loren told him.

What happened?

What happened is that my mate died. Since then, I have only had riders, not mates.

Right. Darsin was thinking, but due to Loren's unfamiliarity with the pattern of his thoughts, it was difficult to understand. *When my aunt's partner died, she started breeding horses.*

Loren snorted. *You know that's not so inaccurate a comparison. How do people become dragonriders?*

Loren mentally shrugged. *It's a little like romance. It's usually expected to happen organically.* She felt disappointment there. Ah. Of course. Most children where she was from dreamed of dragon riding, but she could recognise an extra level of longing there too. Darsin finally had a taste of someone understanding him with complete ease.

Litz had been thrilled at the thought of having someone in her life who would never lie to her.

Sometimes, things are organised differently. If a dragon is seeking a rider, they may ask for all young and willing prospective riders to come forward and meet them on a given date.

He perked up a little at this. *Do you think I could?*

Why not? This seemed to cheer him so much that Loren continued with *Any Aelshian dragon should be honoured to have such an independent mind as yours linked to their own.*

He liked that too. *Independent mind.* A giant grin lit up his whole face, transforming it. *How did you pick her?*

I met Litz when I was working in the palace where she grew up. She always wanted to talk to me, to be around me, but she never wanted to ask. Loren looked over at her, still bickering but looking happier than Loren could remember her looking in far too long.

Yes, Litz had never been good at asking for what she wanted.

"But if we go locust hunting while we still have some light left and while I can still hear them—"

"I still haven't heard any," Kella said firmly, crossing her arms. "And I don't think I trust you to know what a locust sounds like."

"Where there's noise, there is life. That's a—"

"Okay, *okay,* but right now, we've got life that wants food already, so will you please let me start cooking? You can go chasing your phantom crickets if you want to." And with that, Kella sat by the one small cooking pot Darsin had brought with him.

Litz sighed and sat next to her, gazing toward the flat expanse of the desert. She couldn't see any traces of green yet, especially not in the growing darkness, but she felt like they were nearing the edge of the grasslands, that they were closing in on home. The fact was, though she still thought it a good plan, she hadn't the faintest idea of how to catch locusts, but she wasn't about to admit that. Kella already had a knife and a small vegetable in her hands.

"How are your legs doing?"

"Heh?"

"Are they bleeding? From the flight?"

Kella shook her head and rubbed sand off the back of her neck. "Don't think so."

"And what are those?"

"What?"

"On the back of your neck. *There*," Litz added, pointing and growing concerned as Kella flinched away. "What happened there?"

Kella smiled a little sheepishly. "Didn't you wonder where the knife from my first escape came from?"

"You were keeping that in your *hair*?"

"You didn't find it, did you? So I say that it worked."

"You're not doing that again."

"Like you're the boss of me."

Litz sighed. "Yes, anyone showing any concern for your welfare must be trying to boss you around."

Kella kept her eyes on her hands as her mouth was wrangled in a smile. "Look, thank you," she muttered so quickly that Litz wondered if she'd imagined it.

"What was that?"

"*Thank you*," Kella repeated, sulky as a dog with no dinner and still not looking up from her knife. "You might be bossy, but I wouldn't have made it out without you, so thanks."

"You're welcome."

Kella smiled a little. "Yeah, well. Anyway, how bad were they back in that tent?"

"What? Oh. They didn't really..."

"You smooth-talked them?" Kella waggled her eyebrows.

"Not exactly," Litz said, allowing herself a small smile. "They just wanted to talk, and we didn't get far into that before they got distracted. But they..." Litz shook her head.

"What?"

"They wanted to know the news back home. They asked if my king is dying."

Kella blinked and sat up. Then she hit at the back of her ear twice, which Litz was pretty sure meant she wanted Litz to know she was paying full attention. "Is she?"

"I don't know. I've been trying to think, but…" She shrugged, at a loss.

"What will that mean if she is?"

"I really don't know." She furrowed her brows. "My cousin will become king."

"The bitch?"

Litz gave Kella a look but decided that further comment was unnecessary.

"And how's she feel about…" Kella screwed up her face.

"The war? Jeenobi?" Litz shrugged. "Like I said, we're not close. But she and her consort weren't happy about the war ending, I don't think. Her consort comes from a long line of dragonriders. He's"—she paused, annoyed—"what some would call dragon-bent."

Kella looked up, the unidentifiable peeled vegetable still cupped in her hand. "Do explain."

"Some people can get a little odd if they spend a lot of time around dragons." Litz gritted her teeth, the words sticking awkwardly in her throat. "They acquire something like an inferiority complex."

"Let me guess. People have flung this one at you before, am I right?"

Litz sighed heavily. "Mostly just my mother."

"Sounds like we might not have gotten on so badly before this time last week."

"Oh, believe me, you're very wrong about that."

Kella's eyes sparkled with glee. "Wouldn't she approve of me?"

"There isn't much I've seen her approve of in my entire life. You're not special in this instance."

"Okay, so sometimes, I'm special, thanks very much. I like to think so too."

"No, I…" Litz stopped, dazzled by the smile lighting Kella's face. "Fine. But in any case, what do you want to do now?"

"I want to make more food, and then I want to eat the food. We've been over this already."

"No, I mean, tomorrow. Are you coming with me to Aelshia? Because I would advise—"

"I'm sorry, were my previous escape attempts so forgettable?"

"Not to hand you in. I gave you my word I wouldn't do that."

"Yeah, but you also gave Jev your word that you would, so either way, your word is worth—"

"Technically, I told King Jevlyn that I would take you to Aelshia and keep you safe on our way there," Litz said quietly.

Gaping, Kella looked up. "You *lawyer*."

"Really, I just—"

"You want me to run away to the jungle with you and our son."

"Again, he is not even slightly our child, and all I am trying to say is that there is water and transport and *food* in the direction I am travelling in. For—"

"For warmth, for companionship?" Kella batted her eyelashes melodramatically. "For protection?"

"No, because you're clearly not taking your own survival seriously enough, Miss Knife Hair."

"I don't see that sticking."

"So that means someone else should. And I gave my word that until we reach Aelshia, that person would be me."

Kella shook her head, but Litz was almost sure that she was pleased. "You might have some points. Pass the jerky, lawyer."

❖

Jev looked at the faces around the stuffy council chamber and hoped he looked like he knew what he was doing. He had a roomful of people to juggle, and none of them were expected to agree on anything.

And his Aelshian wife hadn't even arrived yet.

Gods, this was going to be interesting.

He'd actually been looking forward to this. Dreading it in almost equal measure but ultimately looking forward to it. This was what it was all supposed to come down to, what all of it was supposed to be for. And it was, so far, underwhelming. It was almost an identical committee to any his mother would have assembled for any major issue.

It was past time for him to make real changes. He'd stopped the war, yes, and that might have been his goal, but that had only created more problems to solve. It had also won him no friends and had definitely lost him a few.

But he needed to deal with the consequences of the peace he'd bought first. Kella had been right. They were all right. He knew what dragons were, and he'd agreed to a deal that guaranteed his people no real protection from them. No danger from war, currently, but every danger from dragons, who would likely only grow bolder and move nearer the city again with no adequate deterrents to stop them. Technically, Jev had vowed that anyone under attack from a dragon could expect protection from the state, but he hadn't exactly administered that promise into practice yet.

The situation with Aelshia had never been so delicate, and the fact was that his troops were all terrified of dragons and had barely received any formal training in how to face them. Jev could give them that training. He'd even entertained a mad notion that he'd be able to get Findan or Kella's help in that, perhaps in some cooperation with the Aelshians, if they were willing to share some of their secrets. Surely, if they could live without the need of constant violence between the species, there shouldn't be any reason Jeenobi couldn't. He hoped he wasn't putting too much pressure on Eisha to provide some additional insight as an Aelshian who'd lived in Jeenobi for months now.

Somehow, they were going to have to work out *how*. All—Jev did a head count, mentally adding and then subtracting Eisha—eight of them.

General Valsso was the oldest person around the table. Her career had spanned double his lifetime. Jev had no idea what her opinions on dragons would be, but he knew that no one fought on that number of battlefields without having a good idea of the carnage dragons could cause.

Gharif Chastingle sat beside her, opposite Jev. He was the Gharif of Malya and as such, held powerful political sway locally. He wasn't a man Jev was able to like, partly because it was difficult to feel strongly in either direction about someone who rarely expressed their opinion on anything, dragons included. As was usual for him when away from his public, the Gharif looked bored and was staring at the hand of the sollon next to him as though trying to read something on it.

Sollon Astchin caught Jev's eye and smiled. Jev had a lot of fondness for the royal sollon. Despite his mother's general disinterest in religion or spirituality, the sollon had nevertheless been a close confidante to the royal family. To attain the utmost closeness with the Earth Mother, sollons vowed to give up all family and possessions and even claims to any name, gender, or sexuality they might have had before joining the order. They owned nothing but the simple green robes the order provided. As a result, Jev usually found sollons difficult to talk to. But Sollon Astchin was more likely to tease him for any of his wrongdoings than treat him to a sermon. Jev was interested to hear their opinions on an issue like this. He was hoping they would add something refreshing to the conversation.

He had none of the same hopes for his great-uncle Tashno, whose viewpoints were consistently embittered and outdated on the occasion he remained at events long enough to express them. He was already casting sidelong glances at the gilded door, which the royal treasurer Binjik was observing, unimpressed. Though she was usually busy stressing about things Jev still barely understood, and her sense of humour could be drier than the desert wind, she was a friend, and other than Jev, she was the youngest around the table. But that was discounting the newcomers, and now that Jev was giving the more academic of the two a second look, he realised that she couldn't be much older than he was, if at all.

Jev didn't know her personally, but Nevsha Drallnock had come highly recommended from the university as their only expert on the history of Jeenobian relations with dragons. She looked nervous, shuffling her papers every few moments and avoiding the eyes of those around her, made easier by the impressively colourful headscarf she was hiding in, but from the way her shoulders were set, Jev didn't worry that he would have to coax her into speaking.

The last figure at the table had also been invited for their unique expertise on the subject. Jev knew him by reputation but not personally, and the reputation of Hallen Trailfeet was chequered, to put it delicately. The most famous living dragon slayer who didn't bear the Mabaki name, the first thing that was noticeable about Trailfeet was the burned flesh all down the entirety of his left side. Many said that his youth had been spent with Kira Mabaki, and by some accounts, they'd been lovers. Some said the burns should have killed him, but that when he'd killed the dragon who'd inflicted them upon him, its blood had restored him.

The people who told that story were usually selling what they claimed to be dragon blood.

Jev knew little about him, but he did know that he'd been most recently working as a trail-finder and protector for merchants taking the dangerous mountain routes between Jeenobi and Nayona, and he was very good at that. And he knew that Trailfeet did not look the slightest bit intimidated by the company he was currently keeping and had made no effort to smarten his appearance.

Jev glanced again at the empty chair next to him. He was very curious as to what Eisha would think of this man. If his opinions on dragons didn't succeed in offending her, his outerwear would.

More, Jev was terrified of what she was going to think of *him* after this meeting. Perhaps that was why she was running late. Things had been going unexpectedly well between them the last few days. It could be she did not want to spoil that.

But Jev couldn't afford to put his own happiness, or the happiness of someone he had come to care about, above the realm he'd been chosen to serve. At best, that would be recklessly irresponsible. Not to mention hypocritical, following his decision to extradite Kella.

And Eisha wanted to be here; she'd helped him plan this. This meeting represented their first plan together, made in the unfortunate circumstances of the bad news she'd received from home: her mother was dying. She knew she would likely never see her again and that her sister taking on leadership could mean a return to war, and to Jev's shock, she'd sought his comfort.

When she'd finished explaining herself through tears which shockingly weren't pretty, he'd wordlessly slipped his hand around one of her trembling hands. She left it there while using the other to wipe viciously at her streaming eyes. "I...I thought you ought to know immediately. To help you prepare. Politically."

"Thank you," he'd said eventually. "But I am far happier to know this because it will upset my wife. Not, not happy *because* it makes you upset but—"

She curled her fingers back around his. "I think I understand. Thank you."

They'd sat there in silence for several minutes. And he knew that, just as she said, this could spell the beginning of a newly disastrous time to navigate his country through. But it was so difficult to focus on that when Eisha had chosen to sit next to him, to lean gently into him enough for him to smell the floral fragrance in her hair. It was difficult to muster stress when he had never been so hopeful about his marriage and what it might become.

They'd sat there until a few soft knocks had come from the door.

"Your Majesty?" It was the handmaiden he'd assigned to Eisha, Beyta. "Is the queen with you?"

Eisha had looked up, her eyes still bright from tears, and met his eyes with a smile. "It's fine, Beyta. I'm in here."

The footsteps had receded, and Eisha had started to giggle. "I still can't get used to how informal everything is here."

"You miss your little courtesies?"

She'd smoothed her dress, slipping her hand from his, and moved to stand. "No. I miss my family. I miss the rain. I even miss dragons." She'd raised her hand and ran the back of it softly down his cheek. "But the little courtesies…"

He'd caught her hand and held it against his face. Maybe, if he held still enough, she would run a hand through his hair.

"I think I can learn to live without those."

He'd held her stare. He'd been married for months. He should know how to kiss his wife or to ask if she wanted to be kissed. But instead, he asked, "How do you tame dragons?"

She'd laughed again, though with much hesitance. "You don't. We just talk with them. Doesn't anyone ever try that here?"

"I don't think we're confident of receiving an answer."

She'd smiled faintly, her eyes searching his face for the joke. "Your country needs a little optimism."

"Will you help give us that?"

Eisha had held her smile, standing still only a little above his eye level. "I'm here to help, Jev."

Back in the meeting Eisha still hadn't arrived for, Sollon Astchin was now looking at Jev with considerable concern. "Your Majesty?" they said quietly, but the room was so quiet that the remark seemed loud. "Would you like us to wait for our queen's arrival before we begin?"

He cleared his throat, aware now of all the eyes in the room on him. But then, they were always turning to him, even if he couldn't see it. "No. I will enquire after her welfare once our meeting is concluded. We have delayed too long already." He mustered his best kingly smile and pulled his chair closer to the table. "So," he started, "dragons."

That got a few nervous laughs, but Jev doubted that anyone, whatever their opinions, had found it particularly funny.

CHAPTER TWENTY

Because of his connection to Ellonya and her joy at being on the trail of another dragon and the searing hopes she held inside her, it was hard for Ker to stop smiling as they flew over the desert, even while none of his own emotions matched up. Mainly, Ker was terrified for Kella, though there was some anger and pride mixed in there too. Because risking her life, condemning herself all over again just to do the right thing? Gods, it was so, so like her. And now she was stuck in the desert, probably dying of hunger and thirst or maybe already dead and unburied. The best scenario was that she was physically fine but stuck with a dragon-riding witch as her only company, and that was hardly comforting.

You know, you are also a dragon-riding witch.

Not like that. Ker sighed. *I only ever learned a little, okay? And I'm not very good at it.*

But you are a dragonrider.

Well, yeah.

That is the part you're worrying about. Her finding that out.

Ker gulped and stared out at the clear sky. *I'm mostly worrying about not finding her or finding her dead.*

That's a lie, Ellonya said, not unkindly. *You fear she will reject you because of me. You don't really believe she's dead, though you do fear that too.*

Shaking his head, Ker attempted to shift the focus from himself. *What about you?*

What about me?

You're worried about what will happen if she rejects me when she sees you. Don't worry, by the way, I don't regret this, and I wouldn't change it.

It took some getting used to, knowing that he wasn't lying about that. He did not have a lot of people he cared about that he hadn't known for all his life. The fact that there was a dragon he'd only known for days who he felt like he could never be parted from should have frightened him. He remembered the terror he'd felt from the dragon, from Loren, of losing her rider.

I know, Ellonya said, sounding mollified regardless.

But you also worry, I think, about meeting this dragon. Right?

My feelings about meeting this Aelshian dragon are complicated.

You're telling me.

She thought this amusing. *It's just...I've never had another dragon to learn from.*

He nodded encouragingly. Dragons were probably reptiles, as far as anyone understood. Ker had always thought they were most like crocodiles. Maybe not in looks, but he'd heard of them carrying hatchlings in their mouths in the same way, and they were quickly capable of living on their own and were as a species predisposed to solitude. He wondered what had happened to Ellonya's parents.

We've spoken of the sickness making us different to the Aelshian dragons, to how we were. But I think I might not be sick at all, she said carefully.

What do you mean?

I think perhaps my parents were and all the dragons around me. And so, I never learned.

That would make sense. You're not like the others you've met, that I've met. You're something new.

Yes. But I can't restore the old.

Ker's heart broke for her, but he could think of nothing further comforting to say, so offered nothing.

That dragon the other night, the clarity of her thoughts in my head. I think the idea of meeting an Aelshian dragon fills me with nerves because I desperately want them to be everything I long for them to be for me, but there is no way I can control that. I may even have to fight them. I don't want that. But...

Finding them could be interesting for both of us, then, Ker said as he looked at the ground far beneath them. They seemed to be passing out of the dunes now, having flown southwest from the mountain edges of the kingdom. They were still a long way from Aelshia, but maybe not such a long way from the natural straight road through the desert from Malya. If Kella had progressed like he hoped she had, or if she had been the girl in the strange dragon's memories that had escaped, they could be close, but they could still be far, far off. She could have been taken away on the dragon to Aelshia already or could have convinced them to take her home, and this was all a colossal waste of time.

Interesting.

Should we stop? Even Sallvayn's fallen asleep, I think.

Are you trying to delay the interesting?

I'm mostly hungry. Ker huffed out a laugh. *You're right. I don't really think she's dead. Or logically, I guess I know she might be, but I can't believe it yet. And if she is, getting there faster won't change anything. They probably won't move again until the morning, and that's probably a smart idea for us too. My hands are getting cold.*

Then let us descend, my poor warm-blooded friend, she teased and began to take them lower. *But I really can smell dragons. They're so close to us, but...*

Dragons? Dragons, plural? Kella was only supposed to be travelling with one, Ker pointed out, feeling uncertainty gnaw at him as Ellonya smoothly landed in the sand. *Are you sure?*

Almost sure. Or perhaps Aelshian dragons smell more than the ones I am used to.

Ker snorted and, trying to shake his sense of unease, slid off Ellonya's back. As he hit the ground, he heard Sallvayn's "Ow! We were sleeping."

"Sorry." Ker peered into the bag to see them rubbing their neck. "But since you're awake, I was going to make food."

"And since we're awake, we suppose you want us to clean your grubby pot for you again?" they grumbled, lifting their head out of the bag. "And why can we smell dragons?"

Ker's eyes darted around. It was getting darker now, but he could make out nothing. "Maybe some dragons passed through here earlier," he said, struggling to think of something logical to soothe Ellonya's fears. But what if this *was* Kella? What if—

"Or maybe they're flying above and waiting for us to look up," Sallvayn said grimly, pointing a gnarled finger toward the sky.

Ker slowly raised his head. Above them, flapping their wings in a unison that tricked the ear into thinking it heard the wind, were four dragons, circling.

There's one human up there with them, Ellonya told him. *I don't suppose that's your sister?*

Smoothly, as though they shared one mind, the dragons in the air began to spiral toward them.

Get on my back, Ellonya ordered.

As Ker hurried to obey, eyes fixed on the smooth, hypnotic descent of the dragons, Sallvayn spoke again. "Don't, it's too late," they said before hiding back in the bag.

Sure enough, Ker did not even have the chance to make it to on Ellonya's back before the dragons began releasing steady streams of fire, trapping them on the sand. The largest one, almost on the ground, managed to turn the sand to glass.

I think, let's stay here for now.

If you say so. Maybe they're friendly.

Unsurprisingly, the council meeting that night did not become the source of any groundbreaking changes in policy. There had been arguments, there had been kofi, and there had been slim areas of agreement. For instance, all agreed that they would simply never have the resources to imprison a dragon. Either they left them alone and stayed out of the way, viewing them as uncontrollable forces of nature, or they put precautions in place so that when they attacked, the state would be able to bring them down.

The most interesting speaker of the night had been Professor Drallnock. Though she might have had no practical suggestions for present-day interactions with dragons, she'd explained that the state of those interactions was something of a modern phenomenon.

"All sources dating back more than three hundred years consistently imply the same thing," she had told them. "Structurally, we did not live in a society resembling modern-day Aelshia, and yet, dragons did not attack us. Look at Malya, our oldest settlement, and none of it built underground. Though it may have been seen as heroic to stand against them, it was never expected that there would be any reason to stand against them. Like in Trehnon today. They have no history of dragon riding or love of dragons but nothing close to our fear of them. I believe something…that something happened to our dragons. That something changed them. Made them wild."

The Gharif of Malya had raised his exquisitely threaded eyebrows. "Imply? Believe?"

But the scholar had stood her ground. "Yes. Imply because it was not something anyone would have thought to waste the time writing down. It was simply how things were. It did not need explaining. And believe because all I can do with the scant information I have is provide theories."

"Miss, in the king's council, we do not work with theories but with facts," the gharif had said, sitting back with the comfort of his victory.

But the general had spoiled it for him. "I believe this woman," she'd said with her characteristic disinterest in learning anyone's names. "The Aelshian dragons I have witnessed on the field of battle are not like ours. They are cunning. They think. I would be interested to learn if, with training, we could raise dragons here to become battle-ready in the same manner."

Trailfeet had dropped the knife he'd been spinning on the table, scoffing aloud as the sollon had looked alarmed. "Are we so hopeful to see more war?"

"It's possible that our dislike of dragons and of witches are linked. They do date back to the same time," Drallnock had said as if doing her best to continue despite the interruptions. "Again, in Trehnon, they do not criminalise magic use."

The general had seemed to consider this and, smiling, laid her hands on the table as though she planned to rise. "An interesting note to take on board, is it not, Your Highness? We could train dragons and witches for war."

Jev had smiled, confident that few people would notice how uncomfortable he was.

"And we return to preparation for war," the sollon had pointed out with a sigh.

And around and around they had gone. And no matter how many times Jev had looked over at the door, Eisha did not walk through it.

It was a terrible thing, but he almost hoped that when he arrived at their chambers, he would learn that she'd fallen badly or that she had received another letter from home that had upset her, that something other than her wanting to avoid the evening had stopped her from attending. But Jev knew he shouldn't be hoping that, and he doubted that any of the scenarios he could envision were true.

He'd seen her vulnerable the other night. That did not mean she was ready for a change or a strengthening in their relationship, either personally or politically. Taking advantage of that, or assuming it meant more than it did, would be foolish and selfish of him. Perhaps she was even ashamed of the way she had broken down with him and now regretted it.

But it had meant something to him. When she'd started crying again later that night, he had stroked her hair, and for the first time in months, had felt like he was helping and not hurting someone.

He was hurrying back toward that now.

Jev was rarely aware of his uncommon height, but stalking the corridors with someone doing their best to keep pace with him brought it starkly to his attention. It felt like an unspoken rule that to diminish his stride to suit another would be un-kingly somehow, so he continued at the same speed, hoping that the general was capable of catching up. As a result, Vallso sounded a little out of breath as she began her inevitable entreaty.

"Should the queen continue not to arrive to these meetings, it may be we should look at more forceful methods of wrangling dragons, if that is something we indeed plan to pursue."

There seemed little point in feigning stupidity. The general was not known for her subtlety, which was why Jev had often found it difficult to understand why his mother had been so certain in promoting her to a position that demanded a familiarity with secrecy. But delaying her from getting to the point seemed appropriate. They were, after all, in a public corridor, even if they no longer had dangerous civilians like Trailfeet looking at them. "Forceful methods?"

Still fighting to keep up, the general still delivered her next line as though she had forced him to stop and look her in the eye. "Our friend in the maze."

Jev forced his expression to remain neutral. "Our friend is not a weapon," he said wearily. "And I would hesitate to call her friend. Why should she want to help us?"

"She hates them. That's always been enough in the past."

"Yes, and in the past, we were only trying to kill them. Controlling them? I'm sure she wouldn't want to even if she was able."

"Well, you have your professors, and I have my spies. And what the southern river clans of the Aelshian forest have to say about witches and dragons is fascinating. If anyone had the power to make these beasts do what they don't want to—"

"But the Aelshians don't *make* them do anything, by their own reports," Jev pointed out mildly, relieved to be back on less confidential grounds.

"But they're insane religious freaks. I hope we don't consider ourselves on that level. Who knows how their connection with the dragons works? It's nothing any civilised people want to know anything about."

"Whatever the Aelshian Empire might be, their children don't grow up fearing being burned alive. I'd consider that civilised." As he nodded gratefully at the guards stationed at his door, Jev said good night to the general and his two personal guards, hoping to finally see Eisha.

His shoulders slumped a moment after closing the door behind him. Except for his servant, Salin, the room was empty. He really thought they'd been starting to build a real relationship, that when she'd told him she'd be there, he could trust in that.

"Salin," he managed after recovering his voice. "When was the queen last in her chambers?"

"She and Beyta left the rooms earlier this afternoon."

He relaxed a little. Beyta had been the youngest of his mother's servant guards, and her family had been in his family's service for generations. He could trust that if Eisha was with her, then she was safe.

But where were they?

"Your Majesty."

Jev turned to his guards, who had been quietly leaving the room but now stood at the door that they'd left ajar.

"There's someone here to see you. Permission to bring them in?"

Jev looked at their cautious expressions and nodded. A moment later, the door was flung open, and two guards were wheeling in Beyta on one of the palace wheelchairs. Her face was bloody and looked as though it had taken a long beating, and when she sat up straighter and looked him in the eye, Jev saw that her right eye was badly swollen.

And Eisha was still nowhere to be seen.

"Where is the queen?" Jev asked he crouched to take her hand, doing his best to avoid her raw knuckles.

"I'm sorry," she croaked.

"Just tell me what happened, Beyta," he ordered.

"We...the queen received a message. She wanted to go out and meet the writer. They said they wanted to meet outside the city."

"I see," he said, fighting to keep his face impassive. They'd received no mail that morning when he'd left the room. "And you got her out without telling me?"

Lip trembling, Beyta nodded. "I'm so sorry, Your Highness, I thought—"

Jev's mind was racing. They'd left in the afternoon. Eisha could have been gone for hours.

"It was the Aelshians, I think. They wore no uniforms, but there was a dragon. I did my best to fight—"

"And Eisha?"

"They were all gone when I came to. I think they took her. They didn't seem to want to harm her."

Jev nodded slowly and carefully withdrew his hands. "Beyta," he said, "you would not have taken her out of town without telling me and certainly not without taking any extra protection."

Her eyes filled with tears. "I can't say enough how sorry—"

"No, you can't." Slowly, he stood. "This note she received?"

"Yes?"

He crossed his arms. "Beyta, did you write it?"

Her face froze. Behind her, Jev was aware of his guards putting hands on their weapons.

"Someone paid you to lure her out of town, outside of the walls, without me knowing, didn't they?"

She shook her head, tears falling faster through the blood still clinging to her cheeks. "No, no."

"No, what?"

"It wasn't for money," she said quietly, the horror slipping from her face. Salin gasped. They were relations of some kind, Jev remembered distantly.

And suddenly, he felt very alone.

"The king…the *real* king would have never allowed any of this," she said, her words not sounding malicious but very certain. "An Aelshian sleeping in her quarters every night."

"You did not do this for the approval of a dead woman," Jev said and looked at the guards who had wheeled her there. "Take her to the physician and stay with her. I will be there soon."

Salin and the guards quickly faded away after that, leaving Jev alone to reach his bedroom and close the door behind him. He could have questioned Beyta; it wasn't sympathy for her wounds that had encouraged him to send her away. He just needed a few moments to process what was going on. To deal with his anger that was, more than anywhere else, directed inward.

He had known it wasn't like Eisha to shirk her duties, but instead of finding out why, he'd made them start the meeting. He had assumed he could trust the staff to guard her, had been certain that their loyalty to him would naturally extend to his wife.

And now someone had taken her away. Or Beyta had lied, and Eisha was already dead. Dead because he'd failed to protect her.

He wanted to pull back time like a witch in an old story. Almost as badly as he wanted his mother alive, he wanted Kella standing beside him, hands casually on her hips as she declared that this wasn't a big deal, that there would be an easy way of dealing with the situation if Jev only stopped panicking long enough to realise it.

But there was no Kella either because he'd sent her away.

He would have to find a way to stop panicking on his own.

❖

"You see?" Ker's captor told him once he had finished tying him up. "The funny thing is. we were actually looking for someone else when we happened upon you."

"That's hilarious," Ker said evenly, again flitting his mind through Ellonya's, who was still surrounded by the other older, larger dragons. The man speaking to Ker seemed to be the only human with them. *Are you okay?*

They won't speak to me, she told him, and he could feel how that stung her, *but they're not trying to harm me.*

For now, that's good.

"Mmm. We certainly didn't expect you, whatever it is you might be." The man tilted his head to one side as though Ker was so perplexing, he needed to concentrate from several angles before he could figure him out.

"Who do you think we are?" Ker asked, striving to get a reaction beyond cold amusement. He was a dragonrider, a real one, he had to be, but so far, that was most of what Ker had been able to work out. He was in his thirties, maybe. He walked with a slight limp, but that didn't seem to affect his aggressive style of fighting. And he liked to think that he knew everything.

"Well, I know that your companion must be one of the unfortunate ones. And Jeenobi doesn't have dragonriders because its dragons don't keep them. I think that something must have made you desperate enough to become the first because you haven't been doing this long." He smiled, not looking away from Ker's face. "How am I doing so far?"

Ker tried to keep his face blank but suspected he was failing. "We're just trying to cross the desert and go south."

The man nodded as though Ker had put forward a new philosophy. "Interesting. Especially since you looked to be flying east. Were you lost?"

"Who are you?"

"My name is Ebsin. I am the rider of Calino behind me." There were four dragons behind him, but Ker did not point this out. He thought he could guess which one the man was referring to. A large red dragon kept looking their way while the others appeared considerably less interested in humans and their conversation. "And we are looking for someone."

"Yeah, you said."

"Actually," the man chuckled and looked at his boots, "several someones. We think they might know some things it wouldn't be convenient for the general population of Aelshia to be aware of." He looked back to Ker, eyes wide and childishly lit up. "Hey, wouldn't it be even more of a coincidence if we were looking for the same people?"

Ker pressed his lips together tightly, heart racing. That thought-blast from the unknown dragon they'd been following must have reached far more people at a much shorter range. These people would know that Kella, a dragon-slaying Jeenobian, was being escorted to Aelshia with the knowledge that those dragons weren't anything like she was used to. Say someone found out she knew, guessed from that strange message. And they didn't want the people in Aelshia to know because…why?

What was it Sallvayn had said before, about some people not being happy that the war was over? And why hadn't Sallvayn said anything, done anything, since they'd been surrounded?

"I can see you're thinking about it," Ebsin said encouragingly. "Now, I'm just going to be over there for a few minutes, but I'll be bringing you some food along, okay, buddy?"

"Okay, buddy."

As Ker watched Ebsin walk away, he reached out for Ellonya. *They're looking for Kella. They must be.*

I don't suppose they're interested in cooperation. I still haven't received any response. Except for one that called me an abomination.

That's not hopeful. Have you seen Sallvayn?

No. Aren't they still in your bag?

I think so. He eyed the bag that Ebsin had left facing him. That might be a Sallvayn-shaped lump in there, but again, it might not be. *I hope. Maybe we can still make it out of this.*

He still might not know all that much about gremlins, but he was starting to know Sallvayn. He doubted they'd let this be the end of the story, even if they wouldn't put it that way.

❖

The stars were looking down on Kella when her dream woke her. She didn't usually fall asleep on her back, but there those stars were, regarding her sternly. Wiping at a brow lined with sweat despite the cold, she rolled over and found only empty space. Uneasy, she sat up, rubbing viciously at her eyes and cricking her neck out of the position that sleeping on her bag had forced it into. Dawn had to be hours away, but for now, she was awake and cold, and Litz's absence worried her more than she'd like to admit.

There was Darsin, curled up tightly by the dragon for warmth, the two of them snoring, but where…

Squinting in the darkness, Kella found a figure silhouetted by the moonlight. Ah. Shoulders falling in relief, she walked quietly over to Litz. "Looking for locusts?"

Litz glanced up, momentarily startled, before smiling that stupidly sweet smile that *did things* to Kella's insides. Like make them perform acrobatics the rest of her didn't even want to think about attempting. "No. I couldn't sleep. The blankets Darsin stole for us are nice, but—"

"Stifling, yeah." Kella sat. "I kicked mine off a few hours ago, I think. You know I don't sleep easy. What's up with you?"

Litz splayed her hands and shrugged. "What's not up?"

"I'm not sure that's how you—"

"You know what I mean. I'm not sure I'm ready to go home yet."

"Yeah? Me neither."

"There're so many responsibilities waiting back home. Probably. And I should probably do something about, about—"

"The dragons?"

"Yeah."

"Me too. Or, y'know, I should not do what I usually do."

They sat in silence for a moment, and Kella was surprised to find that she didn't feel the need to fill it. "And maybe it isn't just…I mean, maybe that's not the only thing I was doing wrong before," Kella said quietly, almost forgetting she was talking to someone for a moment.

"Hmm?"

"Litz?"

"Yes?"

"You've never lied to me."

"No." Litz's turned to her curiously. "I tend not to."

Kella smiled, bracing herself for the words she hadn't found yet. She knew this would hurt, but this might be her last chance to ask. And strange as it might be, she did trust Litz. "Hypothetically," she started, drawing out every syllable carefully, "if a Jeenobian dragon, like, imprinted or whatever on a person, what would that look like?"

"It would help if I knew something more about them," Litz said. "The only dragon I've ever seen here died soon after."

"Okay, hey, we agreed I didn't have a choice if I wanted to get you out."

Litz looked down, and Kella couldn't make out her expression clearly. "No," she said quietly. "I suppose you didn't. You didn't even consider leaving me there, did you?"

"That's not what we're supposed to be discussing. Swing back to the point please, Princess."

Litz sighed, but that tiny smile remained stuck to her lips. "I'm still not sure I know what you consider a 'Jeenobian dragon' to be. But from what Loren observed back at the Narani camp..." She let out a long breath. "Creating a bond between dragons and riders isn't a small thing. It's a meeting and joining of souls. However tangled or faded the mind might be, the human would understand it all and vice versa. Oh, it might just be instinct for them to attempt to improve their own mind by connecting it to something. Like how a drowning person will hold on to anything." She shook her head. "I still don't understand what could possibly cause such a sickness to spread so far if it has, as you claim, affected all the dragons of your region. Perhaps even reaching farther than that. It's horrible."

"And if," Kella pressed, "one of those sick dragons died after making that kind of connection with a human?"

Litz narrowed her eyes. "You saw what I was like for even two days without Loren, and that was knowing she was alive and not far. And if that dragon didn't know what it was doing, then the joining itself might have been even worse."

"Worse how?"

"It's a delicate ceremony. I don't even fully understand it myself. But I know that giving too much of yourself to anything can become dangerous, unhealthy. Especially if you don't have the wits and discipline to help you to stop."

"It could change you."

"Yes. There is a long history of riders being unable to live without their dragons, and there is a reason for that. It's the subject of a lot of long, sad poems."

Teeth gritting now, Kella nodded. "Right."

"This isn't simple intellectual curiosity, is it?"

"No," Kella admitted, and let out a long breath.

"This is about your brother?"

Picking up a stone and weighing it in her hand, Kella threw it away and listened to the thudding of it hitting the ground. "What gave it away?"

"What you said before about seeing him 'attacked' by a dragon."

"Yeah, yeah, I get it." Kella got that her mami was dead because of her, killed over something that hadn't even been life-threatening.

Probably.

"But wouldn't he be…" Kella paused, and saw Litz watch her neck move as she gulped. "Like, more messed up? Diseased?"

"Maybe it was so old, it wasn't infectious anymore. Or maybe it's not something that can transfer between dragons and humans."

"Maybe. But what do you think that even does to a kid? If I'm right, he was chained to something that was mad and then dead, and he could never talk to any of us. Not even to me."

A hand rested on Kella's leg. "But you were a child too. And your whole world had just been taken from you."

"But I was supposed to—"

"Shh." Litz's face was suddenly very close to hers.

"Are you shushing me?"

"Yes," Litz said softly and turned her own chin to close Kella's mouth with her own, tugging at Kella's bottom lip with unbearable slowness.

And the thing was, Kella didn't get kissed very often. If there was ever a first move to be made, she was the one making it. But here she was, being shushed. And being kissed breathless.

Fighting the odd urge to whine, Kella gently started pushing Litz back into the dirt, putting herself at a better angle to kiss back, to—

They weren't alone in the camp, Kella remembered, trying to ignore the almost painful softness she could make out on Litz's face now that she'd opened her eyes again. And they weren't really away from the sand yet. And…

She'd never hesitated before to move straight into sex. Why not?

It was a fun way of drawing a line under a situation, a flirtation like this. But maybe, for once, she was less interested in drawing lines. Maybe this time, it wouldn't be a line drawn but a springboard set up, one neither of them was ready to leap off.

"What?" Litz asked, so sweet, so accepting, it made Kella want to weep.

"Just…" Kella gave her a lopsided grin and lay on her belly beside her on the sand. "You're pretty amazing, you know that?"

Litz rolled on her side slightly, seeming amused. And maybe a little disappointed. "Yeah?"

"Yeah. That's why I stopped in the marketplace."

"What?"

"Y'know. Back in Malya." Kella grinned, unable to help herself. "You just looked so lost, but like, if anyone tried to tell you that or touch you, you were going to knock them down for daring. I think you were trying to blend in, but you really don't do that very well."

"No, I'm not exactly well-suited as a spy." She made a face. "Or a diplomat."

"I'm sure when I get to Aelshia, all I'll be hearing is how lucky they are to have you."

"When?" Litz's mouth split into a slow grin. "You're coming with me?"

"Oh gods, don't look so pleased with yourself. Like you said, how else am I supposed to get home?"

"Well, I'm pleased."

"Yeah?"

Litz's gaze focused on Kella's, making her fight the urge to squirm. "I don't think I'm ready to say good-bye to you yet."

Kella didn't know how to answer, so instead, she reached out and closed her hand over Litz's. They held on like that, saying nothing. When they curled up together under Litz's blanket, Kella slept without a single dream haunting her.

CHAPTER TWENTY-ONE

"Hey. Hey."
　　　Blearily, Ker started opening his eyes to try to focus on what was shaking his shoulders. "Sallvayn?"

"Shh!"

If Ker's arms hadn't been tied behind his back, he would have rubbed at his eyes. It hadn't exactly been a restful night's sleep. "Good to see you," he said in a quieter voice. From what he could see behind them, the dragons weren't awake yet, and Ebsin was nowhere to be seen. Yet.

"Don't take that tone with us. What were we supposed to do before this?"

"Do that freeze magic?" Again, if his hands were free, Ker would have waved around.

Sallvayn made a noise emphasising how ridiculous they thought that idea. "We could no more do that on him than we could on you now. You're both under the protection of dragons, and they're a lot more powerful than gremlins, even if it's rare they make use of that."

Ker nodded, filing that note away for later as he wriggled his hands in their bonds. "Okay, but you can get me outta here, right?"

"Out of those bonds? Yes. But to get out of here, you'll need Ellonya, and though the dragons watching her all *look* asleep…"

Slumping, Ker sighed. "Okay, I get it. No way out."

"That's not what we said," Sallvayn said sternly. "No. We might have a plan that might work. But it definitely involves you keeping yourself alive until then. Being persuasive, being nice."

"I'm nice all the time."

"*Shh.*"

"Guess we found you some real dragons after all, heh?"

Sallvayn looked hurt as they started untangling the ropes binding Ker. "We were never looking for 'real dragons.' We were looking for hope for the ones they abandoned here."

"Abandoned?"

"Boy, no one can become so forsaken without someone to forsake them, even if that is not done on purpose."

"Ah, you're awake," Ebsin said from behind them. Ker was about to look at Sallvayn to remind them to leave, but with a drop in his stomach, he realised that Sallvayn was gone again. They really were fast.

What did Sallvayn tell you?

They might have a plan. But until they go for it, we have to sit tight.

Though Ker knew she was irritated by this, he felt Ellonya's worry ease. She trusted Sallvayn deeply, on an instinctual level, and that gave Ker a little more courage. "Barely," he said. Nice, he reminded himself as Ebsin came around to face him and crouched.

"How was your sleep?"

"Patchy."

Ebsin gave a hearty laugh. There was a musical lilt to Aelshian voices, and even though Ker hated this man, the sound of his laughter was strangely cheering. "Desert travel is never kind in that way. But now, it is morning, and I'm afraid we must decide what is to be done with you and your companion." He smiled, and frustratingly, it was still a pleasant smile, as though he was discussing what sort of meal he wished to have for breakfast. "You see, it is of the utmost importance that we find the people we are looking for soon. But I have my insatiable human curiosity to satisfy, and I would dearly like to know where it is you've come from and why."

Ker met his gaze, asking himself what Kella would do. She probably wouldn't be nice. "I'm afraid our tale might take some time to tell."

"You seem like a smart boy. I'm sure you can find a way of shortening it."

Ker sucked in a quick breath. One day soon, people were going to stop calling him a boy. "True," he said carefully. "But forgive me. Why should I trust your intentions after I have finished? I don't think it likely you're planning to let us go. But," he added quickly before Ebsin could cut in, "take me with you, cumbersome as we may be, and you may find that we can be the leverage you need in dealing with those you seek. Perhaps." He paused, unsure if he wanted to risk throwing out this bait. "Perhaps we are looking for the same people, and this has all been a, a terrible misunderstanding."

Ebsin sat on the ground and laughed again, though the sound was not as pleasant this time. "Amusing indeed, boy. But I would much prefer to know something about you first, and I would prefer if I did not have to become *creative* to do so. I know very well the unique bond between dragon and rider. You feel one another's pain. Such an interesting relationship to explore and test."

I'm sorry for dragging you into this.

Never apologise for that which is not your fault.

If it was Findan in his position, she would attempt to consolidate what she knew and maybe even use magic if forced to it. Ker hadn't eaten properly today, and his hands were tied, which left him feeling less than confident he could do anything more than trip this man up. And even if that was enough to be effective, he'd be dead before he could run for it. So he was left with having to outthink him.

Ebsin was a dragonrider who enjoyed the sound of his own voice so much, it was slowing down his operation. He was the only human there. Was he the only one the dragons trusted to bring with them? Surely, he was bonded to one of them. And while Ebsin wanted to know where Ker came from, he suspected the dragons were not so interested. They had not spoken to Ellonya, had barely glanced at him, and Ebsin had referred to his need to know more as his "human curiosity."

Before Ker was able to think of something he could do with this information, he began to detect a whirring noise, and as he looked around the small camp, he saw that they'd become surrounded by a wall of sand. It was like a sandstorm had trapped them in its eye with no warning. Or like—

"Sand terrors," Ker shouted, genuinely afraid even as he tried to bury his one small hope.

To his relief, he saw answering fear in Ebsin's eyes. "The dragons," he murmured and stood to run toward his dragon as Ker called to his. *Now, while they're distracted!*

With a roar, Ellonya flapped her wings and ran to him. Even with the full awareness he had of her intentions, it was still hard for Ker not to flinch. A dragon running full pace in his direction with their wings spreading out remained a terrifying sight. After wriggling out of the rest of his bonds, Ker clambered up her back and found Sallvayn already sat there, nestled in the feathers crowning her neck and looking so pleased with themselves, they might burst.

"How?" Ker yelled as Ellonya took off, unchallenged for now.

"I told you we run fast," Sallvayn said smugly. "Fast enough to create a sand cloud. And then we froze the sand to make it stay where it was in the air."

Throwing his arms around Sallvayn's spindly body, Ker planted a kiss on their head and whooped at the sky.

"*Hey.*"

"You do a nice thing, you get affection."

"Then we are never doing anything nice for you again," they said, wiping at their head and not looking as upset as they sounded.

They'd been flying for about half the day when Litz finally spotted it.

"Grass," she breathed.

It was patchy and brown, and she hadn't noticed any water yet. But there it was.

"You sound excited about seeing grass," Kella put in, not letting her grip on Litz's back loosen even slightly.

"Where there's grass, there's water," Litz reminded her, yelling over the wind. But more than that, she'd almost forgotten the world was full of more colours than yellow and brown. Her eyes were feasting on the richest fare they'd enjoyed in weeks.

They landed the moment they spotted water. It was shallow, but it was there, and it looked drinkable. They had reached the kinder, disputed savannah of western Aelshia and northern Trahlin, depending on who you asked. When Kella asked where they were, Litz told her the name of the nearest town she knew of.

After Loren scared off the animals crowding the lake, the rest of them rushed to fill their water sacks. A crocodile eyed them from the water, no doubt frustrated they'd frightened away all the prey, but it too gave them a wide berth.

"I'm thinking we can rest here for a little while," Litz said, water dribbling down her chin.

"Good plan," Kella managed before drenching her face again. "Now I'm going to be doing some real fishing. And not have to rely on chasing bugs."

A smile twitched Litz's lips. "Sounds good to me."

"We could always go crocodile hunting. Get your dragon to bag one for us."

Litz gave another glance at the crocodiles. "No," she said eventually. "That feels unlucky."

"Yeah, we don't need any more bad luck." Kella gave a long exhale. "But if one of them comes for me, I'll take that as a sign we're all right. Eat or be eaten and all that."

"Have you ever eaten dragon?"

Kella's expression became more guarded, and the way she curled in on herself was confirmation enough. Litz nodded. "In an emergency. It didn't taste good enough to try again," she said eventually, relaxing as she seemed to understand that Litz would not continue her questioning.

She was about to explain to Darsin that they would be stopping for a while before remembering he wouldn't be able to lip read if he was only vaguely familiar with the language. "Could you tell him what's going on? I don't want him to feel like we're ignoring him."

Kella smiled, then crouched and started signing rapidly to the boy. After a few moments, she started laughing and looked over at Litz. "He wants to know," she said pointedly, "if we're going to need some privacy."

"You're just saying that."

"No, I swear!" Kella said, still laughing. Beside her, Darsin shook his head, smiling widely.

Loren was surprised when Kella left Litz and the child to their fishing attempts and moved toward her with the excuse of needing to find something in her bag. And it definitely was only an excuse because she sat next to Loren without even glancing at the bags.

"Hey," she said, "just thought I'd come over and see how you were doing."

Accepting this as human preamble that was unnecessary to any ensuing conversation, Loren remained silent.

"Actually, that's a lie. I'm over here because I've got a few things to say to you before this is over, and I don't really want an audience for it."

Loren idly wondered if she was there to try to kill her but quickly dismissed the idea. Her thoughts weren't loudly spiking with anything, and they would be. Kella was not one for calculation but for basing her actions on momentary impulse and feeling.

"Okay," she said, still not looking at Loren, "I'm just gonna go for it, and you don't need to say anything. I know that'd only disgust you or whatever, and I guess I'm still not a big fan of it either, but it would be cool…Okay. Here goes. So. Thank you for saving my life. I know it probably wasn't something you did, like, on purpose, but you did it, and I never thought I'd be saying this to a dragon, or talking to a dragon at all, but thank you."

Loren was beginning to feel some interest in where this odd little speech was going.

"And I guess the other thing I never thought I'd be saying is sorry. I'm sorry for pushing that shit up your nose. I'm sorry for consistently being a bitch toward you because of what you are. And I'm really sorry that you've had to be around me considering what I am."

And what is that?

Kella started at the words, and her hands started shaking, but she still didn't look round. "A killer. A dragon killer."

No, that's something you've done. And it's not something you should be apologising to me for.

"Yeah?"

You should apologise to those you have wronged. You did not wrong me. You wronged those you killed, and you cannot beg their forgiveness because they are dead. But perhaps you can learn to forgive yourself. But that too is none of my concern. After all, you did save me too. I do not forget.

Kella chuckled, but it wasn't a happy sound. "Heh. I guess we really managed to turn this whole thing about dragons into a human thing."

You people turn everything into a human thing. It's how you process the world. But don't worry. It will be a dragon thing soon, if it is not already.

Wrinkling her whole face up, Kella finally turned to look at her. "What do you mean?"

I mean that there is no possibility that dragons know nothing of the state of dragons in your region. Yet it is not common knowledge. Loren stopped and turned her head. She could sense at least one dragon flying fast toward them. They'd be upon them in moments. *Litz!*

What?

Attack. Maybe. Get under me, the others too.

Obediently, Litz grabbed the little one's hand and started running toward her.

Another dragon is approaching now, was what she told Kella. She wasn't sure why. Litz was there and about to tell her the same. The words were entirely unnecessary.

It had been a long time since Loren had fought another dragon. She *was* still in her prime, she reminded herself as she watched the very young dragon above her stretch their wings wide and begin descending. Or maybe not her prime, but…

And as the dragon came close enough, she saw that their rider looked a little young for a solo enterprise this far from Aelshia.

"Ker?" asked a voice from under her.

The boy on the other slid off clumsily—somehow, he was new at this, very new—and landed in front of Kella. "Hey," he said.

For a moment, all they did was stare at one another while Kella looked as though she wanted to be violently sick, but she seemed to force it down and even managed a smile. But though she licked her lips like she planned to say something, she remained silent, and Loren could feel Litz's anxiety over the situation rapidly turning to frustration as the boy named Ker mirrored Kella's awkwardness, raking a hand over his hair and looking like he wanted to be anywhere else in the world.

Finally, Kella's feelings seemingly became too loud to allow her to stay quiet. "What took you so long?"

He blinked but recovered quickly. "Do you even realise what a bitch you've been to track down? Do you?"

I'm very confused, Loren admitted to Litz, breaking eye contact with the obviously nervous young dragon facing her. *I think I've had enough of humans on this trip to last me for years. You talk too much to have such terrible communication.*

They ran forward, embracing one another as if they hoped to never let go, and they were thumping each other on their backs and crying and laughing at the same time and it was all so messy.

And Litz was feeling left out.

Oh dear.

I'm fine. I'm just curious.

You thought you'd have longer before you had to say good-bye.

CHAPTER TWENTY-TWO

Nobody voiced it, but everyone seemed to agree that no one would move until later that afternoon. It had taken Ker some time to tell even a slim version of his journey, and by the time he reached his explanation of the dragons chasing him, the urgency had been somewhat pulled from his tale.

He could tell that his story worried the dragonrider, though. Kella had introduced her as Litz, though he had a feeling she warranted some titles in front of her name. Not that she seemed concerned by Kella's casual attitude, but that tended to be Kella's effect on people. They forgot themselves all the time around her.

And Ker had found her. He'd done what he'd set out to do, and better, she was not only alive, but she didn't seem to hate him. She hadn't attacked him with too many questions, and she only seemed a little nervous around the dragons.

But Ker knew her too well to be fooled. This was quiet for her, so he didn't feel settled. Besides, he'd been running on too much adrenaline and fear to be expected to relax and exchange polite hellos and good-byes.

"The people chasing us are different types of dragons and dragonriders than you guys?" he said, struggling to drag them all back to the point.

Litz shared a look with her dragon, Loren, and gave a sort of shrug. "The same, I assume. There is only one kind of dragonrider in Aelshia, but dragons have their hierarchies just like humans do. And those within the dragons' High Circle make decisions others follow. If anyone would have the authority to hurt you—"

An image blasted into Ker's mind, and it was almost familiar to have Loren contact him once more through images. And with that communication, that passing on of themselves, if one dragon became sick in the brain, all dragons who had its echoes passed to them would become sick in the same way. As a virus, it would have quickly been everywhere, the very act of asking for help would have doomed both dragons involved.

Ker blinked and realised that the other humans in the group—Kella, Litz and the small boy they claimed to have rescued—were all clutching their heads in the same way.

"I think Loren is right," Litz said in a croak.

So this is how a dragon communicates with multiple people.

Nothing like that blast she got to us before, though.

No, this was more subtle.

"If you wish to discover what is the cause of the Jeenobian dragons' decline, we are the best to question," Sallvayn asserted, finally stepping out of Ker's bag and garnering a reaction from Loren that was almost sweet. From his few days with Ellonya, Ker guessed from Loren's shudder that she was delighted by Sallvayn's reveal.

Kella had shuffled back, looking like she wanted to spring. She'd never seen a gremlin, never mind a talking…ah. Sallvayn had said before that it was only the dragon in Ker allowing him to understand.

Litz smiled and turned to the rest of them. "Loren heard that the gremlins outside of the forest had almost died out."

"Without the dragons to sustain us, that has sadly been true," Sallvayn said, placing a small scaled hand on Loren's foot. "But those of us left, we remember." They sighed, and though there was real and deep emotion there, Ker could tell that they were enjoying their centre stage moment. "We believed someone or something spelled a dragon who had started losing parts of themselves."

Ker nodded and spared a glance at Kella, who amazingly still hadn't said anything but was starting to look left out. And like she was waiting for someone to explain the joke.

"That one dragon had been spelled to spread their illness, degenerating the brains of those around them. The infected had few eggs, but those that hatched were not infected. The young dragons simply had no one to teach them about themselves." Sallvayn stumbled to Ellonya and placed a comforting little hand on one of her front feet.

"But why would the Aelshian dragons want to keep that a secret? Why wouldn't they help?" Ker asked.

"They probably tried, at first," Litz said. "But this would have grown wearying, especially if it affected those they sent. Think of how humans quarantine each other, and we have much stronger pack instincts. So it became something they didn't talk about, were maybe even ashamed of, but it seems they kept that knowledge within the Circle." Litz bit her lip. "And then the war happened. It didn't start over dragons—Aelshia always sought expansion that Jeenobi opposed—but real enmity grew because of the monstrous way we saw each other. And maybe it suited the Circle to be secured in the position they'd found themselves in. We needed them when war came, and now they have almost equal political power in the Empire as the king herself."

Litz looked up at Loren as if lost. She'd been a soldier, Ker remembered. Learning that the war she'd fought might have been encouraged by lies had to sting. "I'm going to get some water," she announced shakily as she got to her feet.

"Me too," Ker said. He wasn't all that thirsty, but for some reason, he felt reluctant to be left alone with Kella. When they'd both filled their skins and taken long drinks, Ker grinned at Litz, pushing down the nerves he'd felt about meeting her. "Any tips on dragon riding for me?"

She smiled. "You're going to want a better saddle than a few vines."

"And how would you suggest getting a hold of those in Jeenobi?"

To his shock, Litz raised a hand to her mouth and started to giggle. "A Jeenobian dragonrider."

"That's me."

She turned a harder look on him now. "You know, there's supposed to be all sorts of ceremonies going into bonding with a dragon. It's a delicate process that should take years."

"Heh. Well, see, I don't actually remember how it ended up happening."

She looked stricken. "That's not a good sign."

He mustered up a weak smile as they started walking back to the group. "Still standing, right?"

She shook her head. "You certainly share your sister's lack of basic self-preservation instincts," she said, staring at Kella, an expression on her face that was oddly familiar.

"You're the girl in the market," Ker shouted, eyes widening.

"I—"

"You *are*." He started to laugh, and gods, that felt good. He had found Kella, and not only was she alive, but she was still doing exactly whatever it was she always did to make everyone fall in love with her. "Do you know that she mooned after you that entire afternoon?"

The look of comical horror on Litz's face started softening into amusement. "Really? Wait, mooned?"

Ker screwed up his face. "It means that she longed for you as the moon longs for the earth."

Litz blinked and slowly started to smile. "Oh *really*?"

Kella sat up, seemingly informed by some additional sense that she was being discussed. "What are you saying? Ker, *what are you telling her?*"

They both burst out laughing, and for a moment, Ker didn't feel like he needed to worry.

❖

Kella decided to let Ker have his time with Litz—take up Litz's time, she thought before squashing that—talking over dragonrider things like basic designs for saddles he could commission. Apparently, it was more like a horse's than a camel's, but "Really, you wanted to have the thing made-to-fit," or whatever.

Her brother, the dragonrider. Possibly the first dragonrider, and twice over, who'd spent his entire life assisting in the killing of dragons. And now he got to have his redemption just handed to him.

But Kella squashed that thought too and remembered what she was doing. She was cooking, and she was teaching Darsin the best way to do that. Because if she wasn't a dragon slayer, what was she? Well, she was a half-decent cook, and that was about all she could come up with right now. So for now, she was going to cook something. She was with a kid who was even more afraid of the future than she was; for his sake she could be tough a little longer. And that was maybe half the reason she'd brought him along, a traitorous voice suggested, but she squashed that too. She was getting good at burying all these inner voices.

"You'll like my home," she told him, trying to speak aloud while signing in tandem, but after remembering how difficult that was, she stopped and simply signed it out again, more clearly this time. She figured Jeenobi would be useful for him to learn eventually, but she wasn't going to be the person to work out how to teach it to him. "It's in a big city. And our da loves teaching things and taking care of people."

He raised his hands cautiously, sceptically even. "I can come home with you?"

"Of course." It wasn't like Ballian didn't have the space in his home or heart. He signed just fine too and knew a lot more Narani than Kella, so that should work out okay. With Darsin, at least. Ballian wasn't going to know what to do with his actual children anymore.

Darsin smiled, but it hadn't been as big a smile as she'd been hoping for. Kella nodded and concentrated on deboning the fish before dropping it and signing, "Let me guess. You want to go east and be a dragonrider."

He nodded, at first looking guilty, then with shy enthusiasm.

She sighed. "You and everyone else today, kid," she said aloud. Then she nodded at Ker. "I guess if you come with us, it doesn't mean you can't ride dragons."

"Do you think he would teach me?" Darsin asked shyly.

"He likes teaching too," Kella assured him. Gods, but she felt like Ker was slipping away. Her whole adult life, there'd been this terror hanging over her that he'd become somehow linked to the dragons they hunted, that they'd hurt him in ways she couldn't see, couldn't protect him from. She knew everything about him, but she'd never dared ask him about the day their mami had died. And now he was everything she'd ever feared he'd turn out to be, but that was supposed to be a good thing now. Or at least, a neutral thing. And she was proud of him, she was.

But.

Feelings and thoughts, can't expect them to keep pace. Right, right.

She was cooking fish. That was something safe to think about. As she continued stirring, she felt an aching attack of homesickness. Not for any physical place but more specifically and unhelpfully for a time. For when home had meant something more, something safe. And even when she hadn't had someone there to look after her, she'd trusted herself enough to be that for someone else. But Ker had done fine without her. Better than fine, since it turned out that she'd only ever been hurting him his whole life. She was never going to get that fantasy back; he was never not going to be a dragonrider again.

He was never going to need her again.

"He's really cool," Darsin signed, his face betraying how much he was gushing.

"Yeah. He is."

"Dragon…" And by that and the look of frustration on his face, she guessed that he meant Loren. "She told me that the dragons where you are got sick, that they need rescuing. Are you going to go home and rescue them?"

Kella blinked. It helped somehow that someone still thought she was a person to turn to for help. "You know," she told him with a light elbow in his ribs, "that might be a good idea. Somebody should. You gonna help me, big guy?"

❖

Loren regarded the young dragon next to her who was pretending to sleep. She must have truly spent little time around other dragons if she believed that would work. Loren felt another wave of Litz's sadness at the thought of flying away from the others. Just the two of them had never seemed a lonely thing to her before, but apparently, things had changed. Loren looked at the other dragon again and remembered that a whole world had changed. *He calls you Ellonya.*

The other dragon froze a little. *Yes.*

Is that the name your mother gave you?

No, she said shyly, *I remember little of her.*

There is no shame in that. There may be some shame in your bonding, but I can understand your hunger for it.

Ellonya bristled. *Ker is not a killer any longer.*

Not for that, though that too is odd. For many reasons you would know if you only…No. It was reckless to take on a rider who had already been claimed by another.

But he wanted—

Children want many things their parents deny them, and humans never grow past the ages of our children. But you have never known dragons as you should. In knowing him, you substitute the adult dragon figures who should have already been in your life. But, child, he will die long before you are old. He is not—

I know this much, Ellonya said and gave a growl for emphasis.

Loren was pleased. Finally, some fire.

We are both new to this, and I am sure we are doing none of it right. But we are learning together. Surely, that is not wrong?

No, Loren agreed eventually, looking at the fire that the humans sat around together, seeming for all the world as though they had known each other all their lives and travelled into this patch of nowhere for no better reason than leisure. Pack bonding really was humanity's most fascinating and successful survival technique. And though Loren complained about it, she never got tired of watching it work. *Perhaps you are something new. And perhaps that does not need to be a bad thing.* She thought a moment longer. *And you have a gremlin accompanying you. That counts for much. Tell me, was the gremlin alone when they found you?*

Sallvayn was with Ker.

That was interesting. Gremlins weren't supposed to be solitary, and they certainly weren't natural companions to humans, and Loren wondered briefly why this one had imposed either situation on themselves.

But if she still had this much to learn about her own kind, perhaps she should not assume she knew any other species as well as she thought she did. Today, she was not even certain of how well she understood Litz. She had been quiet when Ker and Ellonya had arrived, and Loren had put it down to her reluctance for Kella to leave. As it continued, she began to understand it as something more.

He doesn't remember, Litz eventually sighed back after hours of Loren nudging her. *Isn't that convenient?*

I'm not sure what you're implying, Loren said, not sure why she was attempting to lie. She knew exactly what Litz was implying, and her tone stung more than Loren had thought it would.

I don't know why you're lying.

Loren went silent. *I'm not,* she tried again. *I'm not trying to conceal anything. It's more that it's difficult to explain, to make a human understand, I mean. It's not—*

What wouldn't I understand? What wouldn't I understand now?

None of my other riders did. None of the others ever asked. And we don't speak about it amongst ourselves. It's more like how some of you can become private about sex or religious beliefs. This isn't some Circle conspiracy to keep us all quiet, it's just not...not what we do.

You know I would never keep something like this from you. The hurt in her voice was difficult to hear.

I know. I promise to...I will try to find a way of helping you understand.

I will hold you to that.

❖

Loren left for one last hunting trip, expressing a hope of finding an elephant, but Ellonya stayed behind. She claimed she had eaten too recently, but Ker knew that she could not bear to leave him unguarded so soon after their narrow escape. And he could also feel her anxiety as she waited to be properly introduced to Kella.

Ker was nervous about that too, which was likely where her fears were mostly coming from. He still didn't quite understand the difference between the mind-skimming dragons were able to carry out and the deeper, ever-present bond he and Ellonya shared. But he was starting to feel the difference more clearly.

"C'mon," he said to Kella after trying to tease a smile from her by mocking her food's lack of seasoning. "I want you to meet Ellonya."

He watched as her face ran through a flurry of emotions, none of which lingered long enough to be read, before she eventually landed on a smile. "I mean, I've said hi."

Beside her, Litz was smiling. Ker pulled at Kella's wrists to get her on her feet. "So," he said as they started walking away from the fire, "tell me true, did you sleep with her?"

Kella clapped a hand over her mouth in exaggerated horror. "Why, the cheek."

"So did you?"

"No." Then she tilted her head thoughtfully. "Not that I haven't thought about it."

"Heh. Knew it."

"No, you didn't, or you wouldn't have asked," she said primly, but that smile on her face was a gift. They knew what they were doing in a conversation like this because this, at least, was normal, was familiar.

Ellonya wasn't. *Would you like me to greet her?*

Would you like to greet her?

Ellonya seemed to decide and bent her neck to regard Kella with consideration. *Hello*, she said, stretching her voice to them both.

Kella swallowed, rattled but not badly. "Hello. Thanks for keeping my brother safe. I know it must have been a challenge."

You're welcome.

"And I'm sorry that if this had been last week, I would probably be attacking you right now."

And I you. Do you intend to continue hunting others of my kind?

"No. No more than I do my own kind, which is to say, I'm not gonna rule out self-defence."

Ker looked up, startled. He'd seen that she felt differently, but he hadn't expected that she'd be ready to say such a thing just yet and certainly not without any doubt clinging to her voice as she said it.

Ellonya nodded as gravely as though they'd just agreed upon a contract. *We travelled far to find you. I am glad you are worth it.*

"Gonna try to be." Cautiously but not fearfully, she raised a hand and patted Ellonya's snout, still looking her in the eye. Then she smiled at Ker, and without needing to say anything, they started walking back.

"You happy leaving soon?" Ker said, his voice a little hoarse.

She nodded, seeming distracted. "Yeah. But where are we going?"

"What?" He stopped and faced her, aware that they'd barely looked each other in the eye since he'd found her.

"We're outcasts now, right? I'm supposed to be exiled, and our criminal friends probably aren't that interested in hanging out anymore, are they?"

His shoulders slumped. He'd avoided talking about the others, and he'd known Kella would notice. "Kel—"

"They didn't want to come after me, and now they are not going to like your new friend. Jev might be fucking delighted with you for solving all his problems, but I'll just make things worse for him. Who are 'we' going home to?"

He swallowed. "Da. And the shop."

"You're going to fit a full-grown dragon in the shop? And what do you think your da's gonna think of that, gonna think of *her*? He's going to think we're possessed, 'dragon-bent.'"

"We'll figure it out." Gently, he clutched her arms and realised that she was shaking. "I told him I would bring you home with me, whatever it took, so that's what I'm going to do."

She wiped the back of her hand furiously over her eyes, wiping away the tears that threatened to fall and smiled. "Yeah, okay. Sure."

He smiled but he badly wanted to bury his face in his hands. He couldn't remember ever feeling so awkward around his own sister.

"Sure," she repeated and shrugged. They started walking again, and she threw an arm up and almost managed to reach around his shoulder. "Gods, have you gotten taller again?"

He ignored this. "Y'know, they really did want to come after you."

"But Findan said no."

"Yeah. How did you—"

"I've had a long time to do nothing but think. And there was no way Findan was ever going to risk the rest of you on something so stupid. Not even for me." She clapped a hand on his back and smiled. "Thanks for coming anyway."

He thought he could feel her heartbreak, and he thought that he might understand better what the dragon echoing was all about, now. "I'm sorry," he said, knowing it wasn't enough.

"Not your fault. Besides, I probably deserved some punishment."

He stopped them again. "What?"

"I'm supposed to look out for you."

"Yeah, and you always have."

"But this isn't the first time that you've been dragon-bonded, is it?"

He went very still. "No."

Her hair beads loudly clacking against each other, Kella shook her head as though trying to shake the tears away. "Gods, Ker, you were a kid. You were scared, and we must have, *I* must have made you feel like shit your whole life and—"

More roughly than he'd meant to, he pulled her into a hug. "No," he said shakily. This was one of the first times he'd seen her cry sober since that day. And actually, no, not even then. He had. She'd been strong. "No, you didn't. Give yourself a break, heh? And gods, you gotta get over this self-importance. You were only a kid too. And you probably thought I'd just got our mami killed."

"No, I knew I did that," she said, sniffing as she pulled back.

"How could it possibly be—"

"I saw you. I saw you, and I went and told her. I told no one else. And I told her it was attacking you. Because what else would it be doing?"

For a moment, all he could do was stare, before remembering about breathing and how important that was. "So we both killed her. Gods, we're fucked-up."

She nodded, looking considerably cheered as she rubbed her eyes with the back of her hand. "Least you came and got me. Now we can be fucked-up together again. It's like drinking, I think."

"Yeah?"

"Alone, it's sad," she explained as they kept walking. "And together, it's still kinda, but at least it's sociable."

He nodded, pouting. "I get that," he said as her shoulder knocked against his arm.

"Hey," she said, "wanna know what I saw on the way here?"

"A talking dragon?"

She ignored him as she continued to beam bright as the sun. "A *chimera*."

"*No.*"

"Oh yes, I did. It liked me."

"It *liked* you?"

"I sang it a song, and it came over and licked me right on the face like a big puppy. And they've got really scratchy tongues, so if my face still looks a little red, then—"

He turned his face up to the sky, smiling in despair. "You are a lying piece of shit."

"You know," Litz said as she came upon Kella stretching, preparing for another long bareback dragon ride, "I know a few breathing exercises that might help keep you calm while you're flying."

Kella let her arms fall limp at her side. "Not sure breathing's really gonna help me much, Princess. But don't worry. I'm adaptable as a cat. I'll get there."

She was at that, Litz agreed. A day ago, Kella had been unable to get on a dragon of her own will, and now, she was considering it with nothing more than mild nerves.

"I'm going to miss your cooking," Litz said because she could see Ker looking up at Ellonya, and she knew that she was running out of time to say something nice. But she'd never really had to do anything like this before. Now it was almost sundown once more, and they would part, and if nightmares woke Kella again in the night, Litz would not be there to soothe her back to sleep. No more chances to kiss her and for Kella to actually want to keep kissing her back.

Because Kella had stopped kissing her before, and Litz had been trying not to think about that fact ever since.

Kella smirked, her eyes sparkling. "Yeah? Reconsidering letting me go?"

Yes, Litz wanted to say, stay with me. But instead, she smiled and said, "Of course not. I made you a promise."

Kella raised her eyebrows. "Thank you for the reminder, Ambassador."

She started to turn away, and for a moment, Litz felt panic clutch her. Kella was slipping away, and Litz wasn't even functional enough at holding a conversation to let her know that it bothered her. "I would still like to show you my home," she blurted out. "One day."

"If I'm ever in the neighbourhood?" Kella smiled. "You're way more likely to be in my area again. So look me up." So quick that Litz almost wasn't ready for it, Kella placed her lips softly on Litz's cheek before she withdrew, but her eyes didn't.

"I don't want to go home," they'd both said the night before. But they had to, and soon, there would be an entire desert between them again.

And moments later, Kella made the first steps to put it there as she and the others took off, clinging to Ellonya. As Litz watched them go, she felt more tired than she ever had leaving a battlefield.

I'm sorry, Loren said. It was one of the only times Litz could ever recall Loren indulging in that strangest of human impulses: apologising for that which was not her fault.

CHAPTER TWENTY-THREE

Flying was getting easier, but it was still something Kella would be avoiding for the rest of her life, she decided again as she clutched at Ker's back. If nothing else, the torture of flight helped her to ignore how bad it felt to leave Litz behind.

It only got briefly worse when Ellonya stopped and started flapping her wings in one spot like she was treading water in the air.

"What the *fuck*?" Kella screamed because for some reason, this was definitely worse.

"She's trying to tell if..." Ker nodded, and it was creepy seeing that look that Litz always worn now on Ker's face, but she was glad she'd gotten used to seeing and spotting it. "She thinks there's other dragons coming."

"So let's fly faster than them."

And they did, to Kella's immediate regret. Faster was even worse than not moving. Until they stopped moving again, and that was bad too.

"What now?"

"They're not chasing us."

"Awesome! We got away, let's keep doing that."

Neither of them spoke for a moment as Ellonya continued to hover.

"Fuck. They went after the other two, didn't they?"

Ker's silence was all the answer she didn't want to hear.

Litz hadn't even had the chance to get on Loren's back when they found themselves surrounded from the air.

It was a classic Circle-taught move that Loren knew well: using the advantage of being a group against your enemy and surrounding them from the air, giving them nowhere to run. If dragons had a weakness to exploit, it was that looking up took effort for them.

Having the trick turned on herself was eerie, and Loren hated it. She hated more that she must have brought them here, whoever they were. She'd shown weakness, sent out a violent cry for help as far as she could push it, stretching herself unnaturally thin out of desperation, and here were the consequences. Someone had heard.

Your magic use, she asked, *how tired is it?*

I am tired, but it's nothing like after the sand creatures. I could likely hold them all still for a few minutes, but only while drawing on your strength. And that would mean you couldn't move to take them out, so we could only make it through that plan by bluffing.

Loren had a moment's frustration that Litz's soft human heart was taking time to be glad that the others had gotten away safely. It was sweet, but in this moment, a waste of thoughts. Loren was wasting thoughts too but only to be glad that dragons did not tend to gloat for long.

Loren.

Llevint. You wish us dead?

Wish? No. But must we make you so? Yes.

We would tell no one of the little we understand.

You lie. The Aelshian people must not be made aware of the abominations of which you are veering far too close to becoming. You are too fond of humans. It makes you less dragon than you should be.

Careful, Llevint, you betray human tendencies yourself by creating excuses for what you do as you do it.

True. Thank you for catching that. It is that human storytelling tradition we now rely on, however. Your disappearance will be assumed to be the work of Jeenobians because that is what fits their story.

The one human with them said nothing, just as Litz did not. As long-term dragonriders, they knew not to interrupt their dragons when they were discussing important matters. They knew their place, and for the first time, that was not a source of pride for Loren. It made her uneasy. She was very fond of humans, that was true. It didn't mean she'd much questioned the fact that they were lesser than her.

She was questioning a lot of things now.

I'm just going to try keeping them all back. It's as much as I can manage for now, I think, even with your strength.

Loren could feel the energy seeping out of her, could see the dragons hang oddly in the air, like they were bumping themselves into invisible glass, and watched their human's face contort with rage. "Witch," he spat.

Yes, my rider is proficient in the use of magic, Loren said smoothly, hating having to speak to this human who meant them harm but knowing she needed to drive the threat home. *Would you like to find out what she can do if you continue to test her?* Loren asked, pushing her fear far beneath the surface of her thoughts and asking her own human, *What now? If they leave knowing of this, you can never go home. Between them and the Narani, there is no possible—*

I know, Litz said, her frustration and exhaustion seeping through sharply. *But what choice do we have? I don't want us to die.*

Neither did Loren, but… *Aha. Pack bonding instincts.*

What?

Look up, but don't make it obvious.

She was still only a spec on the horizon, but that was Ellonya flying back to them, her passengers all still with her. And the attackers had not noticed her yet because they were too focused on Litz's wall of pushing magic.

Which meant Loren really was about to help destroy at least one dragon of the Circle, she registered with a mixture of emotions as Ellonya crashed rather clumsily into one of the dragons above, her jaws sinking into their neck as she twisted.

Abomination, one of the others thought with so much disgust that Loren could hear it from the ground as her strength drained away through Litz's hands. She'd never liked the idea of Litz being involved with something so reviled. But now it seemed to be saving their lives. The dragons in the air could just about move, but the one now falling to the ground had proved little better than a sitting duck against Ellonya's jaws.

The sound of their body thudding to the ground had Loren flinching. She didn't know this dragon, she reminded herself, and in any case, she hadn't been the one to snap their neck.

Rising again, her belly charred, it was clear that Ellonya was exhausted, and Loren felt her hopes fail. But it became clear that the humans on Ellonya's back did not share in her despair for their lives, though there seemed to be nothing preventing them being fired on by the flames of the remaining dragons.

They looked tiny but resolved, even the little boy. And Loren realised again what a thing it was, those little humans spending their short lives running around fighting dragons. How absurd, how admirable.

Especially now. Kella stood, shaking yet bold, on Ellonya's head, and Litz's breath hitched at the sight.

And then Kella *lunged*, a knife in each hand and a grinning snarl taking up her face.

❖

A lot had frightened and confused Kella over the last few days. By comparison, this was simple. She couldn't let Ker and Darsin watch her die, so she wasn't going to die here. There were bad guys to fight, and they were even familiar-shaped bad guys that she knew how to fight.

She leapt onto one of the two remaining riderless dragons, and the moment she did so, it hit her with images just like Loren had earlier, but these were angry, they cut and told her she was about to fall off, that the dragon had started to descend when it hadn't, that behind her, Ker had been set on fire, and that was the part where she turned and nearly lost her grip on her knives, only one of which she'd successfully rammed through the scales of the tail to reach flesh.

She'd never killed one in the air. She'd never done anything in the air except scream. But here she was—*not* screaming—painstakingly climbing the dragon's spines, sometimes with the help of her knives. And she was going to kill it.

Not because it was a beast, a demonic force of nature to knock down to her level and defeat. Because it was a thinking person, and it was trying to hurt her friends. And that might not feel so righteous a fight as it had before, but she had one thing she'd spent her life getting good at, and it wasn't cooking.

The dragon kept moving, kept trying to shake her off mentally too, but though it made her arms ache from the strain, and her legs felt sliced to ribbons by its scales, she managed to make her way to its neck.

She wanted to stop at the wings. It would be vulnerable at the join, but it wouldn't be smart to make her move there. She might make it without rolling off, and it might go down, but its jaws would still be able to reach her. If she didn't just fall.

The best hope she had of killing it and making it off alive was getting it in the eyes.

She gripped the neck between her thighs as if it was her lover's back on their last night on Earth, and she plunged the knives into the eyes.

A dual bull's-eye. She'd barely ever managed that before. "The things you pull off under pressure," she muttered as she leaned right back to avoid the tower of flame the dragon sent hurtling into the sky. As it tipped its head upward, the blood from its pierced eyes dripped onto her legs.

But she had no time for self-congratulation. The dragon was falling. Right. Because that was what happened when a dragon died. "Little help over here," she screamed, ripping her knives out of the dragon's bleeding skull as Ellonya came flying up beside her.

"Jump," Ker shouted as they all continued plummeting toward the ground. And gods, she could not look down.

Jumping was about the worst thing she could imagine doing. But she loosened the iron grip on the dragon's neck and jumped anyway, and the press of Ker's magic *pushed* her up while his hands pulled on her arms as she threatened to slide off Ellonya's back.

"Thanks," she said, heaving in a breath as she sat herself firmly down. "Did I look cool?"

He gave her a look of amused disappointment that made him resemble his father so painfully, but before he could say anything, he had to stop her from falling again because one of the two dragons still in the sky sent fire flying their way. Right. Because they were only halfway through these fuckers.

As Litz watched, the entire situation seemed to slow as her concentration narrowed on the power flowing out of them, the power keeping the other dragons from moving any closer.

Litz, Loren was saying to her now, *we'd be of better help in the air.*

Yeah? She was losing too much energy to even think. But it didn't really matter because all she was supposed to be focusing on was—

You are giving too much of yourself and too much of me. We would be better off in the air.

Litz groggily registered what was going on around her as if witnessing a dream come to life. Or a nightmare. That man up there was Ebsin Jeash, one of the most highly praised dragonriders of the war. He had once invited her to join a drinking game when he had seen her looking lost at a party.

He was trying to kill her.

Or his dragon was. Which meant that he was too, and wouldn't Litz do the same for Loren?

Litz, get on my back, Loren commanded, *but don't drop your shield. Keep it up as long as you can.*

It's not exactly a shield.

Litz.

Moving carefully to maintain her concentration, Litz clambered up. She dropped the shield as Loren took off, a killer headache attacking her as she did so.

Kella had found a way onto the last riderless dragon's back, while Ker seemed to be doing his best to *push* at the dragon so it wouldn't be able to spin as much as it wanted to. Oh, that was why Kella was so comfortable with the concept of magic.

Which left the dragon with the rider, Calino, whom Litz recognised as a fast-rising dragon of the Circle, and as Ebsin's dragon. Ebsin, her friend. The two of them were now circling Ellonya, neither sparing a glance down. Though dragon scales kept them almost impervious to fire, another dragon's teeth or claws could manage serious damage, and no matter how Ellonya was trying, those claws were starting to leave marks, and her riders weren't fireproof.

But odd as all this was, Litz had to be a soldier about this. She probably couldn't do anything about the other dragon, but the rider…

Her uncle had never wanted to teach her this trick. This was one of the reasons people feared magic-users so greatly. But Litz had insisted. She'd been a soldier too long to not come up with a hundred what-ifs.

And now the what-if day had arrived. She had just enough strength, just enough wits and more than enough rage left in her. It only took a moment and most of her remaining strength to pull his neck toward her, effectively snapping it and allowing Loren the space to attack his dragon as he roared with pain and rage and grief. In the ensuing fight, Ebsin's corpse plummeted headfirst toward the ground.

Instead of watching him fall, Litz turned wearily to see how the others were faring. And that was another dragon going down, but Kella had only gotten one eye this time, and it was angry and still fighting as it began to fall. Ker was not able to hold it, and Ellonya was not going to be able to reach her in time.

Loren, we must.

Loren snarled as she took another snap at her opponent's leg. *If I let him go now, he will live.*

Let him! Don't let her die, we can't.
And Loren let go and swooped down with no further questions.

❖

Kella had hit her with a shaking thud. Ker's last-second attempt to hold her up in the air had managed to prevent the impact from being too damaging and didn't seem to have broken her. She did not smell dead, so Loren was not worried. Not that she likely would have anyway. Litz was worrying enough for them both, and Loren could still feel it gnawing away at the back of her head even as she moved away from the little party crowding around the fallen dragon killer.

Kella wasn't the only living thing who hadn't gotten back up after the fight.

He was faking it well. That breathing was very carefully shallow, but his fire had not yet dimmed.

Let me die in peace, Llevint said when her approach proved inexorable, and she finally stood above his broken body. Kella had stuck her blade into his eye well, but although Llevint was blinded now and certainly in some pain, it hadn't proved a fatal blow, at least not yet.

No, Loren said. Litz, she knew, might have allowed in an *I wish I could* or some other excuse designed to protect the sheen of her own conscience. But Loren was a dragon and had no time or use for such things. She could feel that Llevint respected her a little for that. *I need to know more,* she said simply.

You bound yourself to a witch. I don't want your mind touching mine, not even in these last moments.

And that's what it's all about, isn't it? Loren said, pushing at his wounded side. *Witches.* He did not answer, but she felt how right she was. He had made a mistake in opening his mind to her as much as he had, now and before. *I've felt what they can do to us when properly trained and organized. But I was never made aware of the danger they posed because witches of such power, they hide. Humans hate them too, on either side of the desert.*

She was careful to keep her emotions flat, whatever conclusions her mind might be reaching. She did not want to make Litz aware of this conversation if she could help it. *And I wondered at that,* she said, pressing a claw into his wounded eyeball. *I wondered at how convenient it is for us that the only humans capable of truly challenging us have been hunted and shunned wherever they go.*

It did not start as a precaution but vengeance, Llevint said, growling. *Perhaps the witch did not intend to infect the whole region, but her actions had consequences, and those consequences might have been the end of us all had we not responded to them.*

She only meant to curse one. But the echoes... Loren could imagine it easily enough. Dragons did not often feel the need to reach out to their own kind. But the pain, the confusion of losing their own minds, just as that dragon in the Narani camp had, that would have been enough to force even the proudest soul to beg for help.

Selfishly, she was pleased that Kella had killed it before she could have touched its mind. She doubted it still had the power to infect, but she did not feel ready to experience even the ghost of that pain.

It might have spread farther if—

If we hadn't cut off communications. And the witches? You blasted the humans, didn't you? All the Circle did, as far as the fear could be spread, the knowledge in every human head from the Aelshian forest to the Western Sea. You made them know *that witches were something evil, something to be feared. You taught them that lie, embedded it deep. And now they all feel it, even if they don't think about it, even if they use it themselves.* And it was something these newer generations had started to break free from just a little, Loren realised. Because although magic was a thing that on some level made her feel ashamed, Litz did not share in the belief of so many of her kind that it was somehow evil, wrong. That deep-set cultural disgust had not affected her, had not stopped her from continuing her studies.

You dare place blame on us when you've so long benefitted from our actions? We could have perished.

And to save ourselves, we doomed our humans? Halted their development? Loren found it was becoming more difficult to prevent her feelings from spiking. It might rarely have affected her personally, but she had flown in that war, many, many times, with many different riders and had never interrogated her reasons for it overmuch, just as she'd never thought much on why the magic-using clans of the forest had been so thoroughly beaten down by the Aelshians, by the dragons who'd so conveniently stood by them.

Lies. Everywhere her mind went now, it found new lies in the past she thought she'd been certain of.

Everything they did, they did to themselves.

Loren shook her head, which wasn't something she'd have done to express her disagreement fifty years ago, perhaps, but it was something that she'd slowly picked up. Humanity could be infectious that way. *I don't think that can satisfy me anymore.*

The Circle will not let you just fly back home.

If they dare stop me, I will send a blast out to every dragon in the forest who cares to hear me. I wonder how righteous they'll feel about the decisions they've been making once everyone knows about them. Hundreds will know what I know, will feel what I feel as I die. But they won't with you, Loren went on with some certainty. *Because you, Llevint, are a dragon with manners, and you would not stoop to such vulgarity. And because none but me are alive here to feel it.*

And with that, because they had finished with their conversation and she could see the pain in his eye, she bent and carefully, forcefully, clamped his neck between her jaws and snapped it.

❖

Kella hadn't realised she'd blacked out until she opened her eyes. And there were definitely worse sights to wake up to. "Earth Goddess?" she quipped weakly, earning herself a laugh from Litz, who was beaten and bloody and clearly exhausted but alive.

"I want you to know, I'm embarrassed for you," Ker said, looking in.

"Why would you be embarrassed? Didn't you see me up there? I looked so..." She paused and narrowed her eyes at Litz. "I did look cool, right?"

Litz nodded gravely. "Very."

Darsin snorted, which for a moment, made them all laugh.

"What happened next?"

"We caught you," Litz told her. "But you hit your head against Loren's skull, so please be careful sitting up."

Kella rubbed at her head. "Fuck. Loren's got a hard head."

"I've always said so."

Kella managed a shaky grin, hearing Loren make a noise of disapproval as she moved closer. And that sight wasn't as frightening as it might have been before. "Did we get all the bad guys?"

Litz and Ker exchanged a Look.

"One very pissed-off dragon got away?"

"Pretty much."

"Shit. Gonna be a lot harder for you to go home, heh?"

"Maybe."

"Is it cool if we stay where we are one more night? No one's after us anymore, right? And I mean, I probably shouldn't be moved and could, like, use some water." She added a dry cough for effect.

Ker smiled and tapped Darsin's shoulder, indicating they should go to the pool. Ker could sign his way through a few phrases, Kella remembered, but he'd never been as quick to pick it up as her.

Maybe she was good for things other than dragon killing after all. "I thought you were going to die," Kella said, meeting Litz's eyes, making her smile.

"You came closer to it."

"Yeah, but I mean, I don't want us to just leave this behind now." Kella's lower lip trembled, and she wished she had the resolve to stop it or, better, to stop herself from speaking.

"What do you want to do?" Litz's voice was softer than Kella had ever heard it, and it made her want to melt.

Gods, one concussion and she turned into a romantic. "I want to go back home, but I want to go back so we can…" She didn't have any of the right words for what she wanted, but that had never stopped her from keeping on talking anyway. "So we can make the world kinder. I don't want to say good-bye to you again."

Litz looked like she wanted to melt too, but she managed to keep her physical form intact and took hold of Kella's hands. And for the first time, Kella realised that both of their hands were rough from old blisters, an occupational hazard of a life spent touching hot dragon scales at the wrong moments.

At least there was one thing they shared.

"I like the sound of that," Litz told her.

CHAPTER TWENTY-FOUR

His dragon wasn't there to do the honours, but Litz made sure Ebsin burned. He might have been trying to kill her, but he'd been a friend once, and she'd snapped his neck with magic.

Mostly, though, Litz had dealt with his body because the moment that Kella was back on her feet, she'd asked Litz what she wanted done with all of them. His remains were still on fire when Ellonya took off for the second time in as many hours, taking her passengers with her. This time, Kella had waved.

They'd been forced to leave the dragons where they'd fallen. There was little that could be done about something so large with only hard earth beneath them, two very exhausted magic-users, and nothing to burn them. The sun had set by the time they took off themselves, but getting away from the tiny battlefield had seemed important. Litz had seen many horrors in real war, but she could feel those stabbed eyes watch her no matter how far from the scene they flew.

And on cue, she could feel Loren struggling to come up with something that would distract her from that. *You wanted to know more about the bonding.*

I thought you didn't have the words for it, Litz put in, sitting up straighter. She could see the forest now, and the homes and settlements that started to pass beneath them were full of people who cheered and waved when they noticed them. The land was starting to look like something Litz recognised.

I might now. Why do you think we never take on gremlins as riders?

With effort, Litz stopped herself from asking why a dragon would *want* a gremlin as a rider?

They've been great friends to dragons for a very long time. You must have wondered.

Ashamed, Litz realised that she hadn't, not really.

That's okay. They like not being thought of much, I think. They are very different to humans in that way and in many ways besides that.

Litz tried to focus on the beat of Loren's wings, a rhythm which could always calm her down. And she was calm; she hadn't really needed to hear what Loren had to say. She'd only needed to know that she wasn't being shut out of something.

I really wasn't trying to shut you out. Loren sighed. *Humans do so much with words, and it's hard to find words you've never used before. You see,* she continued, stalling a little, *gremlins are different to humans, who are different to dragons. But humans and dragons are more similar. We have something like a soul, as you would call it. Gremlins don't have those.*

That's an awful thing to think.

I don't think it. I know it. That's not a bad thing, however. Gremlins are a little like hyenas.

Now, that's really a terrible thing to say.

No, it's not. They scavenge things, they grow. They are better than us in some ways, perhaps. They don't start off with something in the same way we do. They have to develop it very personally, very actively, over a long time. Which is probably why they think about selfhood in such a fascinating way.

I always thought that was strange.

And it is. To us.

Oh. So it's not that you don't bond with gremlins because you don't want to, it's because—

We can't. Not in the same way.

Because it involves souls.

Yes. Even this small admission seemed like a struggle for Loren to get out. *We are not the sociable creatures humans are, but we still hunger for deep connections. You know this. Bonding with another soul is something many dragons choose not to do. But most who do pity those who do not. It's a widening, an emptying of the mind unlike anything else. By echoing back through another's. Sort of like...*

The horrible connotations in Loren's mind reached Litz before she had time to think it. *A parasite. You're not, though.*

No, but dragons don't share much of our souls in our lifetimes. But to our riders, we bare them completely. In doing so, we take pieces back for ourselves. That's why some dragons who haven't experienced it think of us as less dragon, especially dragons like me, who've taken on multiple riders, multiple minds.

I don't think you're a parasite, if that's what you were worried about. You have some of my soul, but... Litz smiled gently. *I guess I knew that already, in a way.*

So the idea of that boy worries me, Loren said heavily, as if grateful for Litz's words, but moving swiftly past them. *Dragons often take more riders. But a human bonding to more than one dragon? Forgive me, but I did not think your souls were...*

Strong enough?

Durable. Have you ever heard of a rider who survived their dragon?

Litz shook her head. *A few stories. But they weren't happy ones.*

It's not appropriate to comment on another dragon's choice, Loren mused. *But they worry me. That young dragon...so many dragons have failed her.*

Litz had the sudden unfamiliar feeling that Loren was letting guilt creep into her thoughts. *You didn't know.*

I know now. And mostly, I plan to keep what I know to myself. I do not want to make myself, or you, into larger targets of the Circle than we already are. Though truly, I think they would not dare to attack us, not now we are so close, so visible.

Litz frowned. *But with the king dying, much could look different on our return.* More for Eisha's love for her than her own, Litz wanted to believe Xoia would make a good First Mourner to the Empire, a good king. Xoia had spent her whole life following her mother into every meeting, every ball, every event. She didn't have anything of her mother's charisma, but she could imitate it well enough. Litz just had no idea what she'd want to use it for.

But despite the danger of change awaiting them, Litz had assumed she'd feel happier by the time she reached her homeland. Home, where the air caressed instead of burned, where everywhere, she was surrounded by water, noise, life from the moment they burst through one of the famous "Dragon Doors" at the southeastern edge of the forest. Here, the trees had been grown apart from each other in their highest branches to create a natural opening for even an old dragon with a large wingspan.

But all Litz could do, despite Loren's best efforts, was return to wondering if the others had made it away safely and whether she owed Ebsin's family an explanation. She'd never had to worry over that before. She'd never killed anyone she'd known personally. She'd never killed anyone with magic either. For some reason, that made it feel more like murder. Up there with their dragons, they'd been equally matched, but she'd given herself an unfair advantage.

Nothing is unfair when your life is on the line, Loren reminded her. She, at least, was happy to be home.

I know, I know.

But news of another death soon pushed that one almost entirely out of her head. Their first stop in a river clan's port brought Litz overheard gossip before she could refill her water skins. She was back to being one more face in an unfamiliar market street. And since they weren't people who would call themselves Aelshian, she heard "The Aelshian king is dead" and not "*Our* king," and for a moment, Litz didn't feel like she'd made it home at all.

It was slower travelling through the forest. Litz had almost forgotten that. Still mostly shocked that no one appeared to be trying to stop them, she and Loren took the waterways home. It was simpler and a luxury to be surrounded by water after their desert trek, when the very sight of water had made her dizzy.

They made it home to Verassez to the most rushed of ceremonies, but after witnessing the spartan greeting customs of Jeenobi, this still felt like too much.

You became a diplomat after all, Loren told her fondly as they parted, and she flew to her own quarters.

Though Litz was uneasy about separating, she could do nothing about it, so she allowed herself to be led to her rooms. But after her bath had been poured, she requested no attendants. She hadn't spent any time alone in over a week and needed a little space before greeting her cousin. Her king. King Xoia.

The bitch, she couldn't help hearing Kella saying as she walked through the tree's main entrance and made her way up the steps. Though Litz considered herself able-bodied and fit enough to be up to the challenge of them, she longed for the finished installation of the lift that would allow for quicker access to the throne room. It was carved into the tree where its trunk began to branch off in earnest, stretching out in welcome to all granted the right to enter.

She bowed low before getting a chance to see her cousin's new appearance. Litz had never been close to her aunt, but she was more reluctant than she'd expected to see another sitting in the place of the only king Litz had ever known. And when she eventually looked up, she had to blink hard to remind herself that she was.

Both Eisha and Xoia took after their mother more than they did their respective fathers, but on neither had it ever seemed a striking similarity until now. Though this was an illusion of a kind. Litz suspected that King Narin's illness had failed to be so widely perceived because she always wore such thick makeup. That same distinctive colourful face, the painted red eyelids particularly, was one her eldest daughter now wore. In combination with her mother's bright robes, the effect was eerie. As was her consort, Agsdon, sitting at her side. That felt particularly dissonant, wrong. King Narin would have never allowed any of her consorts to take a chair beside her throne. But Agsdon had never been just a consort to Xoia, had he?

"Your Majesty," Litz said, recovering quickly, remembering that the ruler should never be expected to open a conversation here. "To hear of your mother's death filled me with sorrow. I offer you all the condolences on the good Earth. She was a great ruler and will be missed. But I know you will be as loved and successful a king as your mother before you."

"Thank you, dearest cousin. Please, rise," she urged as she stood from her throne and moved toward Litz to pull her in for a hug.

Litz could *never* remember receiving an embrace from Xoia before. Litz had always been too awkward, the crown princess too aloof and important, and again, they had never been close. "Does Eisha know?"

"Eisha?" The king bit her lip. "Why, Eisha has…" Her face crumpled.

Litz was worried but not for Xoia, who would never publicly let herself cry like this, not without some purpose.

"Oh, Litz, she's been…" More of the lip trembling that felt rehearsed. "We've tried not to let the news out yet. We obviously can't consider war before we have more facts."

"War? Your Majesty—"

"I know it was him," Xoia insisted. "I never wanted her going near that kingdom, and now they've killed her, like the dragons they continue to slaughter there without mercy, whatever they might pretend."

Litz had stopped listening at "killed." "No. He—"

"He may have put on a good face for you, just as he did in his negotiations with my mother, may the sky keep her soul." She took a deep breath, and Litz began processing that she really might be watching Xoia be affected by an unplanned emotion in public. "But Eisha's *disappeared*, disappeared from his palace, and they expect us to believe she simply wandered off on her own?"

Litz swallowed, gathered herself. "We don't know she's dead."

"No. We know almost nothing. But I know it in my gut, Litz."

Disappeared, not dead. Which meant Litz could not believe it. "We will find her. I fear I may have seen relations sour further on my journey home," Litz started automatically, for hadn't she expected her own drama to be the only one awaiting her at home? She'd made an agreement with King Jevlyn she'd been unable to keep, with many of his soldiers knowing her to be a magic-user. A group of Narani travellers had attempted to trade her back to her family. The Circle had just tried to kill her.

Xoia dismissed her with a wave, removing Litz's need to come up with an excuse, a story. "For now, my only priority is finding my sister. And if the Jeenobians cannot provide her?" She heaved in a kingly sigh before looking Litz cold in the eye. "Then, yes. War."

❖

Eisha had been alone for hours when her sister slipped back into the room.

It really wasn't a prison cell they were keeping her in, she could concede that much. So long as the iron bolt across the door was ignored. It was only a little smaller than her childhood bedroom, and she suspected only a few floors beneath it. It was plain; arranged almost decoratively through the room was a shelf of books, a jug of water regularly refilled, and a bowl of fruit. And of course, she'd had regular family visits.

Xoia had changed her earrings. It looked like she'd taken their mother's. Which wasn't exactly *bad*, but Eisha didn't like it. Somehow, that stung, even in their current context. Xoia could have been kind enough to ask her permission to wear them, even if she had not been allowed to observe their mother's funeral. That, at least, had been sensible. This just seemed thoughtless, cruel. Which wasn't usually her sister's style. The sister she'd thought she'd known, that she'd always yearned to be closer to, was thoughtful to the point of aggravation.

"You spoke to Litz?" Eisha asked, looking at her lap.

"I did. She's suspicious, but she loves you." Xoia sat on the bed and smiled thinly. "She has always been the grunt of the family, so I expect she'll fall into line soon."

"And bring you the support from the army you need?"

"Mmm." Xoia nodded. "I could have killed the Circle for almost ruining that for me," she continued as though she'd forgotten Eisha was there. Or that Eisha *was* there, but that she'd finally become the adoring, obedient little companion Xoia had always wanted and not a force at court in her own right.

"You know that my husband will not let it come to war," Eisha said calmly, wondering what would happen if she lunged and squeezed Xoia's neck until she stopped breathing. Since their brother was still only a child, Eisha was still technically her First Mourner, her heir and arranger of funeral, unless Xoia had already fixed something to change that. Which she probably had.

"He will if we start setting fire to his kingdom. And husband, really? You don't carry his child. My sources suggest that he never even touched you, Eisha. Which shows an interesting amount of honour for a former criminal. But obviously, I could never have left you there with him. With a dragon killer who hates our people. I had to get you out."

And she really did believe it, Eisha realised numbly as she stared at that grim, fond smile. Xoia really had decided that this would be what was best for Eisha. The fact that it would conveniently deliver her own ends was almost irrelevant.

"And if, by some bizarre happenstance, he does consider you his wife, well, he'll assume I've stolen you. Which won't sound terribly convincing."

As Xoia smiled that bright, beautiful smile under the layers of their mother's makeup, Eisha couldn't think of a single thing that might get a reaction from her.

"In any case, you won't be in here long. We can miraculously 'find' you in a few weeks, and you can tell everyone how horrible it was over there." Xoia reached for Eisha's hands. She let them hang limp, remembering how Jev had held them the night she'd broken down. "And then, I want you to find someone who makes you happy."

Eisha snatched her hands back. "I *was* happy, knowing I was doing something with my life and position that might help people. We were preventing war."

Xoia rubbed circles into her temples, looking like she wanted to drill into her skull as she stood. "This sacrificial attitude is very unhealthy for you. You need to start valuing your own life and what you want."

"My life isn't supposed to be valuable. Not to me. Not weighted against the people I'm doing this for. If war breaks out again—"

"*When* war breaks out again, people will go for you. Because they love you." With the pointed nail of her index finger, Xoia tilted Eisha's chin up, a slight look of puzzlement crossing her features. "You've always been so good at making them do that."

And she always thought she was smart, Eisha thought, and now she thinks she's won.

But she'd also always underestimated Litz. Grunt? Never.

As Eisha watched Xoia walk from the room, she thought of watching Loren fly Litz away home from her balcony in Jeenobi. Litz, who was home already. Because as Eisha had confidently assured her husband that night, Litz's honour was a fixed point to depend on. If she said she would get something done, it would happen.

And if Eisha knew her at all, Litz would have already sworn to find her and punish any responsible for hiding her. She'd sworn it, and so it would happen now.

Xoia dismissed Litz for her skill in fighting and lack of interest in politics, not even realising what a dangerous combination that could be if turned against her. She might have gotten her war, but she had no idea what she'd brought on herself.

As Eisha listened to the bolt to her room slide shut, she managed to feel a little sorry for her sister.

About the Author

Jenna Jarvis wrote her first book at the age of five—a nonfiction work about dogs. Since then, she has continued to seek attention through writing and has branched out into fiction. Her degree in literature and history has never helped her find a job, but just like the eclectic mix of jobs she has held, it's definitely given her writing inspiration. *Digging for Heaven* is her first published novel. She is happiest in mismatched socks and earrings, enjoys watching horror films with her dog, and thinks karaoke is healing for the soul. She grew up in Edinburgh, Scotland, and now lives in Glasgow with her partner.

Books Available From Bold Strokes Books

Digging for Heaven by Jenna Jarvis. Litz lives for dragons. Kella lives to kill them. The last thing they expect is to find each other attractive. (978-1-63679-453-2)

Forever's Promise by Missouri Vaun. Wesley Holden migrated west disguised as a man for the hope of a better life and with no designs to take a wife, but Charlotte Rose has other ideas. (978-1-63679-221-7)

Here For You by D. Jackson Leigh. A horse trainer must make a difficult business decision that could save her father's ranch from foreclosure but destroy her chance to win the heart of a feisty barrel racer vying for a spot in the National Rodeo Finals. (978-1-63679-299-6)

I Do, I Don't by Joy Argento. Creator of the romance algorithm, Nicole Hart doesn't expect to be starring in her own reality TV dating show, and falling for the show's executive producer Annie Jackson could ruin everything. (978-1-63679-420-4)

It's All in the Details by Dena Blake. Makeup artist Lane Donnelly and wedding planner Helen Trent can't stand each other, but they must set aside their differences to ensure Darcy gets the wedding of her dreams, and make a few of their own dreams come true. (978-1-63679-430-3)

Marigold by Melissa Brayden. Marigold Lavender vows to take down Alexis Wakefield, the harsh food critic who blasts her younger sister's restaurant. If only she wasn't as sexy as she is mean. (978-1-63679-436-5)

A Second Chance at Life by Genevieve McCluer. Vampires Dinah and Rachel reconnect, but a string of vampire killings begin and evidence seems to be pointing at Dinah. They must prove her innocence while finding out if the two of them are still compatible after all these years. (978-1-63679-459-4)

The Town That Built Us by Jesse J. Thoma. When her father dies, Grace Cook returns to her hometown and tries to avoid Bonnie Whitlock, the woman who pulverized her heart, only to discover her father's estate has been left to them jointly. (978-1-63679-439-6)

A Degree to Die For by Karis Walsh. A murder at the University of Washington's Classics Department brings Professor Antigone Weston and Sergeant Adriana Kent together—first as opposing forces and then as allies as they fight together to protect their campus from a killer. (978-1-63679-365-8)

Finders Keepers by Radclyffe. Roman Ashcroft's past, it seems, is not so easily forgotten when fate brings her and Tally Dewilde together—along with an attraction neither welcomes. (978-1-63679-428-0)

Homeland by Kristin Keppler and Allisa Bahney. Dani and Kate have finally found themselves on the same side of the war, but a new threat from the inside jeopardizes the future of the wasteland. (978-1-63679-405-1)

Just One Dance by Jenny Frame. Will Taylor Sparks and her new business to make dating special—the Regency Romance Club—bring sparkle back to Jaq Bailey's lonely world? (978-1-63679-457-0)

On My Way There by Jaycie Morrison. As Max traverses the open road, her journey of impossible love, loss, and courage mirrors her voyage of self-discovery leading to the ultimate question: If she can't have the woman of her dreams, will the woman of real life be enough? (978-1-63679-392-4)

A Talent Within by Suzanne Lenoir. Evelyne, born into nobility, and Annika, a peasant girl with a deadly secret, struggle to change their destinies in Valmora, a medieval world controlled by religion, magic, and men. (978-1-63679-423-5)

Transitioning Home by Heather K O'Malley. An injured soldier realizes they need to transition to really heal. (978-1-63679-424-2)

Truly Enough by J.J. Hale. Chasing the spark of creativity may ignite a burning romance or send a friendship up in flames. (978-1-63679-442-6)

Vintage and Vogue by Kelly and Tana Fireside. When tech whiz Sena Abrigo marches into small-town Owen Station, she turns librarian Hazel Butler's life upside down in the most wonderful of ways, setting off an explosive series of events, threatening their chance at love…and their very lives. (978-1-63679-448-8)